BLOOD MARRIAGE

CAMELLIA CARROLL

Blood Marriage by Camellia Carroll

Published by Camellia Carroll
CAMELLIACARROLL.COM
Copyright © 2024 Camellia Carroll

THIS IS A WORK OF FICTION. This book is set in an alternate earth. Though names of real,
existing locations or historical figures may be used, the depictions of these places and all characters in
the story are entirely fictionalized. Any similarities to real people are entirely coincidental.

Cover and title illustration by Camellia Carroll
Chapter graphics by Camellia Carroll using Canva assets

ISBN: 978-1-971243-02-3 (print)
ISBN: 978-1-971243-03-0 (ebook)

Printed in USA
Second Edition

Blood
Marriage
CAMELLIA CARROLL

ALSO BY CAMELLIA CARROLL

◆

APPALACHIAN MAGIC SERIES

Blood Bargain
Blood Marriage
Blood Memories (Coming Soon)

STANDALONES

Weaver
A Touch of Death
Ambrosia Rising (Coming Soon)

VISIT CAMELLIACARROLL.COM
FOR THE MOST CURRENT LIST OF WORKS

FOR ALL OF THOSE IN THE APPALACHIANS
AFFECTED BY HURRICANE HELENE. MY HEART IS
WITH ALL OF YOU.

#APPALACHIANSTRONG

1   IN WHICH ALICE WANDERS

Alice carefully adjusted her dress in the mirror, smoothing over the green calico fabric and unable to keep a bright smile off her face. Not one hair was out of place, her vibrantly red curls tucked into a set of braids neatly pinned over the top of her head like a crown. She'd even tied a ribbon around her throat that matched her dress, bringing out the bright green of her eyes.

Perfect. It was perfect.

The only thing that wasn't perfect was the strange pattern of scars that marred the inside of her left wrist, an oddly artistic marking of loops and swirls that she'd had since birth. It looked less like a cut and more like a burn or a brand, but it could be easily covered by long sleeves.

"What do you think?" she asked the two birds perched on her windowsill.

"Very pretty," one chirped back.

"Yes, yes!" said the other.

Though Alice's magic wasn't considered particularly strong by the witches she'd grown up with, she had the innate ability to speak to animals. All animals, not just Other animals like hellhounds or shifters. Though her mother and sisters largely considered her a magical failure, the joy of little animals realizing she could understand them was enough to keep her spirits up.

Especially now that she no longer lived with her mother and sisters.

Growing up in a small village of witches just outside the town of Boone, North Carolina, Alice Little had only been trained for one thing: bear powerful children. From an early age, her mother determined that her gifts weren't strong enough to bother nurturing, especially when there were five other sisters that all exhibited stronger magic. Instead, Alice was trained solely as an almost-human housewife, as someone feminine and sweet and whose use was to bear more witch children, to keep their line strong. It was always seen as her duty to the family.

Ever since the Appearances began nearly half a century ago, bringing with them the return of true magic, the duty of witches was to keep their line strong. Their numbers were few compared to humans and Others alike, and they needed to keep their kind from becoming entirely extinct. The best way to do that was to birth a child with a strong magical parent. Most preferable would be a full-blooded Other— one of the many demons, vampires, fae, shifters, or other non-human beings who began to show themselves on the earth in the 1880s, much to the shock of the fully human population.

Witches gained magic from their Other lineage. It was said that some Others, very powerful ones, had been able to take a physical form long before the Appearances, and their relationships with humans resulted in modern witches. When the Appearances started, that ghost of magic running through the blood of their descendants had veritably exploded into something more tangible, identifiable, and *powerful*. Alice's line wasn't as old as some others, like the Sader family, but it was old enough that some of that pre-Appearance magic was in her blood. Once, her primary goal had been to nurture that magic, to give birth to children stronger than she was, to keep their kind alive...

All of that changed a year ago, in spring of 1928.

It started when her mother smacked her across the face, leaving a bruise on her jaw and deep scratches across her cheek.

It ended when Ellie Sader had the previous lead witch of their little village arrested for murder.

Since then, the North American Council had made the decision to dissolve the community, dispersing any members who hadn't already

moved away to larger witch settlements in Virginia and Tennessee. The buildings were mostly abandoned now, except for the mice and the birds roosting in the rafters.

Now, in May of 1929, Alice had happily joined a small group of friends in a large house on Howard's Knob. She had a room all her own on the second floor and worked with their small community to maintain the land, the houses, and the gardens. Over the last year, they'd focused on putting together several gardens, mapping out the land, and setting protections over the area. There were three whole houses now!

Alice still lived in the first house, the main one that belonged to Ellie and Kaz— *technically* it belonged to Ellie, but she'd heard him gently prodding at her about marriage. It wouldn't be *too* far in the future if things kept going as well as they were. In any case, she had a]whole bedroom to herself, and that was more personal space than she'd ever been allotted. Alice spent her childhood and teenage years crowded into a small home with five sisters and her mother. An entire room to herself was practically a castle.

The second building was home to Miriam Blake and her family, a practical house painted a cheery yellow with dark green shutters. With a husband and two children arriving with her, it was a general consensus that the next house they built should be for the Blakes. The kids were cute, but they needed their own space, and there was only so much room in one house.

'Mornin' Miriam!" Alice called, waving wildly to the woman harvesting herbs from the garden in front of the second house in their tiny village.

"Hey, sweetie!" she called back.

Miriam was a tall woman with medium brown skin, her African descent obvious in her magical practice and the herbs she chose to grow. Her husband and children had even darker skin than she did. The children, one boy and one girl, ran barefoot through the yard just like young mountain children should, gathering yellow dandelion flowers for their mother as they chased each other back and forth through the spring grass.

Miriam, her husband, and her two children had moved southward from Virginia when Ellie and Kaz acquired the chunk of land

on top of Howard's Knob. It was safer here, at least by a little. The Blake family had a whole group of protectors now in case anyone decided to take issue with the color of their skin. They didn't have to live on their own anymore, and Alice thought the kids brought a lot of sunshine to the place.

"You need any help?" Alice asked, smiling as the children squealed.

"Not right now, but later would be good. You still wanna learn that salve recipe?"

"Yes!" she clapped her hands together excitedly. "Thank you!"

"I'll see ya later, honey," Miriam said with a smile, reaching down to accept a dandelion bouquet from her little girl.

Alice turned away from the garden, steering towards the third house on their property. This one only had one occupant, but he'd been able to afford to have it built without community financial help after selling the home he already owned in Boone proper.

Said occupant was outside already, sitting on the covered porch with a book in his hand. His long, dark hair was tucked into a neat braid that draped past his shoulder blades. The sunlight caught the metallic reflection of the strange pendant he always wore around his neck, but Alice much preferred the way it caught on the golden blonde streak in his hair, peeking in and out of the braid thrown over his shoulder.

He looked up briefly from the book to adjust his glasses and wave hello as she approached, nodding towards her in greeting. Alice's heart soared, a grin pulling at the corners of her mouth as she increased her pace and made her way to the porch.

"Mornin, Hart," Alice said brightly.

"Good morning," he replied, looking up from his still open book. His glasses were ever so slightly askew, his blue button-down shirt just a little more rumpled than normal. Perhaps he was tired? Maybe going out would be good for him.

"I'm goin' out to pick berries down the path. You feel like comin' along?" she asked carefully, batting her eyelashes. "Can't sit here readin' all day."

Hartley paused for a long moment, green-gold eyes flitting between her face and her basket. He carefully closed the book, placing a

bookmark to keep his spot, and Alice had to stop herself from giggling. If he was ready to come along for a walk, that was all she needed.

He was *beautiful*, she thought. They both had strong green eyes and good skin, and he had money to support a family like she'd always wanted. He was kind to everyone he met. He would make an excellent husband, and he was an Other, too. Not only would it be a peaceful marriage, it would be a *powerful* one.

"Alice," Hartley said gently. "I'm afraid I must decline."

Her stomach dropped, a wave of sudden cold passing through her chest.

What?

"It's... it's just a walk," she said softly, wringing her hands.

"It isn't," Hartley insisted, shaking his head. There was no malice in his tone, but it hurt all the same. "I'm old. I'm not blind."

Alice blinked, brow furrowing. "You're not old."

On the contrary— anyone with eyes could quite easily tell he was in his prime.

Hartley outright laughed at this, shaking his head, but he sobered quickly.

"I am thousands of years old, Alice. Have you thought about that?" he prodded, eyebrows raised. "Have you thought about what that means? What I've seen? What I've *done*? Have you considered that it is entirely impossible for anyone who has lived as long as I have to be a good man?"

She hadn't. She hadn't considered any of that.

Hartley was a gentle man with a stable job as a professor at the Appalachian Teacher's College. He was kind to animals, kind to people, but secretive about his personal history. Besides Kaz and Ellie, he had few close friends, though he got along well with everyone in their small community. Alice had been trying diligently to crack his walls open for months, and she finally thought she'd been making progress. He returned her smiles, he spoke when she passed by, and now she'd been hoping to get some further information from him.

She hadn't expected *this*, though.

What... what *had* he done, she wondered? What was his past? Could she live with whatever it was? Would he even tell her?

"W—well, I don't care," Alice said stubbornly, placing her hands on her hips. "It doesn't bother me."

That was a lie.

It was a lie, and by the way his expression shifted ever so slightly, Alice knew he could hear it in her voice.

Thousands of years old... Did he see her as nothing more than a child even though she was a grown woman in her own right? It shouldn't matter if he was on a different path. It shouldn't matter how old he was. As long as he loved her, she would be safe.

It didn't matter if the knowledge rattled her. It didn't matter what he'd done in the past. Hartley was her hope for salvation at the moment. She would stick to her plan. She would make him love her. She had the skills to seduce him, the wherewithal to run a household, and they would both be safe for years to come.

Alice opened her mouth to protest once more, but Hartley held up his hand to silence her.

"I didn't want it to come to this," he sighed. "I'm sorry, but I can't reciprocate what you're feeling."

"You... but you... I thought you *liked* me," Alice said, voice growing softer with every word. "I thought you'd want to give things a shot and... Well..."

"I like you perfectly well as a person, but the reality is that I can't give you what you want..." He paused, tone growing softer and gentler. "And... I'm looking for something that I don't know that you're ready for."

"What is *that* supposed to mean?" Alice scoffed, bristling. The heat in her cheeks flared anew, a wash of shame obscuring her shock and sorrow for a moment.

"You want someone to love you, and you think I'd be a good candidate," Hartley said softly. "I assure you that you are wrong."

"Wha—" Alice stuttered, cheeks flushing red. "N— no, I just... I thought..." she trailed off, eyes glued to the floor.

"Let me assure you that loving another person and wanting to be loved are two very, very different things," he said slowly. "I think you want

to be loved. I do not, for one moment, believe you really love *me* as you think you do.”

His tone was gentle. She was lucid enough to recognize that, even though the words felt like a knife in her heart.

“You... you don’t know anything,” she snapped, voice cracking as tears sprung to her eyes. “You don’t know *anything* about what I feel!”

Hartley was silent, and somehow that hurt more than if he’d tried to argue with her.

Hot tears sprang to Alice’s eyes, clogging her throat and weighing heavily in her chest. She took a step away from Hartley almost without thinking about it, without thinking anything at all.

And then she turned away entirely and started towards the woods.

Following the path away from the little group of houses, Alice started off towards the tree line at a brisk walk. The walk didn’t feel like enough, though. Her blood screamed with something that needed to be let out, something wild and warm and untamed.

The thought occurred that if anyone was watching, she’d have to explain herself later, but she didn’t care. Something inside her cried out for more, for something else, to be anywhere or anyone else. Maybe it was shame, maybe it was heartbreak, but she didn’t make it far before the emotions in her chest crashed down in a thundering wave.

Alice answered the scream building inside her by taking off at a run.

Fighting not to trip over roots or underbrush or her own shaking feet, she dashed through the trees as fast as she could. Her lungs burned and her heart pounded, and the stitch in her side felt cathartic instead of truly painful. She kept going until she could go no farther, until her legs felt like soup and she collapsed to the ground at the base of a large buckeye tree, tucking herself amongst the roots and leaning against the trunk as she gasped for air.

As her breaths calmed, the cries finally came. Alice let herself scream then, let herself wail as she collapsed against the tree and hot, salty tears ran down her cheeks. Her basket fell to the side, and she ripped the ribbon away from her throat. Rather than a pretty decoration, it now felt like it was choking her.

A possum crawled into her lap as she cried, curling up there as it tried to comfort her.

Alice sniffed, looking down at the little creature. Normally the noise would drive off most animals, but sometimes they treated her like one of their own. Maybe this possum saw her as one of its young, crying out in distress or pain.

"Thanks," she mumbled.

The possum chittered at her and snuggled up more closely, but Alice's mind was too scrambled to be able to translate what it said, if anything. Sometimes animals just chittered for the sake of chittering, just like people sang for the sake of singing... or cried for the sake of crying, she assumed.

Leaning her head against the rough bark of the buckeye, Alice took a long, slow breath to try and steady herself, but it failed miserably. Her tears still continued to fall. Her heart felt like it was cracking into pieces.

Hartley was the best marriage hope she'd ever met. He was kind, handsome, gentle, financially secure, and had all the hallmarks of an excellent husband and a good father. He passed every standard and more, he knew the witch world, and yet...

And yet he didn't want her.

What had she done wrong?

✦

After she'd cried herself out, Alice sat at the base of the buckeye tree for a long while. She found herself gently petting the scraggly possum, watching a few squirrels leap through high tree branches, and looking around for summer mountain herbs growing wild among the underbrush.

The familiar routine of identifying bloodroot and sprigs of goldenseal was enough to calm her down, distract her, and finally the possum on her lap adjusted itself, cocking its head to look up at her with dark eyes.

"You okay, little one?" the possum asked.

"You seem like the little one to me," Alice whispered, gently patting her new animal friend.

"Little is a matter of heart," the possum said proudly. "I have a big one. You look like you need some extra heart."

"Smart critter," she mumbled, giving the creature a gentle scratch behind the ears.

Possums were some of the smartest animals she'd ever interacted with. Alice couldn't say she was fond of speaking to wild turkeys or toads, mostly because they didn't usually have much to say. Possums, on the other hand, were often better conversationalists than most dogs.

That said... the intelligence of her new companion was the least of her problems. Looking around, Alice realized she was in an unfamiliar part of the woods.

She knew the direction she came from, but she didn't recognize the area itself. In her distress, she'd gone so far into the trees that she'd gone outside Ellie's land, outside even the farthest ring of protective spells placed on the acres of land around Howard's Knob.

Logically, that was a bad thing. Scrubbing her tears from her face, the possum still in her arms, Alice scrambled to her feet and took a look around. She could see signs of where she'd crashed through the underbrush that would help her retrace her steps, and in general, if she kept walking East she should see something she recognized. At the least, if she could make it back inside the wards, Ellie would be able to track her down come nightfall.

The possum showed no signs of moving, its tail curling around her forearm and little claws firmly holding onto the fabric of her dress.

"You wanna ride, lil missy?" Alice asked, voice scratchy from crying as she gestured to her basket.

The possum sniffed at the woven basket experimentally, and then decided it must be good enough to rest in. It skittered down Alice's arm and plopped down on top of the checked cotton cloth inside.

"*Comfy,*" it squeaked, wrapping its tail around the handle.

Possum friend settled in place, Alice scrambled to her feet and looped her arm through the basket handle. She checked left, checked right, and then went back down the path through the underbrush she had crushed on her way through the woods the first time.

As she walked, Alice took note of the different visual markers, trying to remember what she'd passed while running towards the buckeye tree. She followed the underbrush trail and worked her way vaguely East, eventually running into the edge of the familiar path through this part of the woods. She sighed with relief when she saw the narrow footpath, knowing it would take her back towards Ellie's land. This was still a ways out from any protections, but taking the path would expedite her return significantly since she wouldn't have to pick her way around the crushed underbrush.

Alice hurried down the path, dabbing at her eyes with her sleeve and hoping she'd be able to sneak inside the house and up to her room without anyone seeing her. Especially Granny. Alice loved Ellie's grandmother like her own blood family, maybe more than her own blood family, but the older woman wouldn't stop pressing if she thought something was wrong, and Alice was not in the mood to discuss her love life.

Still, something called her forward. She felt like she needed to go back, maybe not all the way to the house, but she needed to go *somewhere*.

Alice's steps slowed and stopped as she realized that something had taken hold of her, as if it was pulling her through the woods. Something squirmed under her skin, goading her to move down the path in front of her. It didn't feel like instinct, though. It was something *else*.

It felt... it felt almost like a drawing spell, like something meant specifically to entrance her. Normally Alice would turn the other way upon that realization, but the draw was... different. Stronger.

Young witches were routinely exposed to spells like this to help them recognize simple manipulations. Truth spells, attraction spells of any sort, and spells that lowered inhibitions better than the strongest moonshine were all things that Alice learned to recognize as a child. However, something was different about this magic.

Drawing spells were subtle, meant to work on the subconscious mind, but this... This felt like an itch she couldn't scratch. It felt like a voice just barely out of an earshot saying something she had to hear, like a shadow she couldn't quite see clearly. It pulled to her. It called to her. It *sang* to her.

Even more so, it seemed to call her down the path in the direction she was already moving. She walked faster, keeping an eye on her surroundings. That was when she noticed that it seemed like something was off.

She and her possum friend were moving one direction, but it seemed like every other animal in the forest was moving the opposite way.

The animals were... running towards her? Or... past her?

Alice paused, watching as they scattered, suddenly realizing that they were not running towards her, but away from the shadowy clearing just ahead and off the path.

That... was not good. Animals had incredible senses. If they ran, there was a good chance that you should run in that same direction for the sake of your own safety.

Still, that force called at her to keep moving, to look ahead, to see what the animals were running from. The logical part of her brain was long buried beneath some feral instinct to *chase* and *find*, and Alice felt almost frantic in wanting to follow that pull.

"Is this a good idea?" the possum asked. "We should go around."

"... I know," Alice admitted, even as she took another step in the direction of that strange, magnetic force.

She stepped off the path and towards the clearing, weaving through the trees and towards whatever otherworldly force called to her. The shadows seemed to surround Alice and the possum despite the fact that it was almost midday. It seemed like a false knight was falling in the woods, and among the trees, something *glowed*.

And as she grew closer, the glowing thing began to move.

It looked like the silhouette of... a deer? Alice had never seen a glowing stag before, antlers glinting like stars in the night sky among the shadows, but she had seen plenty of stranger things. The deer rested on the ground, but she couldn't tell if it was reclined or injured.

"You okay, fella?" she asked, sniffling a little. Her voice cracked as she spoke and her nose was still dripping from crying, but she tried to make her tone gentle.

11

A lone stag normally wouldn't be enough to alarm any of the local animals. This one was special. Alice approached cautiously, eyes adjusting to the darkness around the animal. When she was within only a few feet of the deer, it turned to stare at her, and she realized exactly why this animal was so special.

It was glass, but... not glass. It was clear but not clear all at once, and when she put her hand on the deer's flank, it was warm in a way that glass should not be. It expanded with the deer's breath in a way that glass should not expand. It glowed from within in a way that glass should not glow, giving off a soft light almost like a beautiful lantern, but the light was so cold that it seemed to be tinted blue.

Most interesting of all, there seemed to be a design carved into its left front leg. It was a little hard to make out among the swirls of reflected light inside its not-glass body, but... it was...

Alice looked at her own left arm, gaze landing on the pattern of swirling scars. She might need to get a little closer to examine the pattern on the deer's flank, but it was clear that they were similar in shape, size, and design. Leaning a little closer, Alice held her arm up to the deer and looked at the designs side by side.

That was the moment she realized that they weren't similar designs. They were the *same* design.

Why was her lifelong scar etched into the flank of a deer made of living glass?

The stag looked at her with wide, dark eyes for a long moment. Then, unmistakably, she heard it speak. It wasn't a voice in her ears so much as in her mind, ringing through so clearly that it couldn't be mistaken for anything else.

"Run."

2 IN WHICH ALICE RUNS

Alice did not hesitate to follow instructions. Hitching up her skirts, she took off down the path the way that she'd entered the woods. The basket bounced wildly, but the possum hunkered down rather than jumping out, wrapping its long tail around her wrist for stability as they ran.

"Go, go, go!" the possum encouraged her. "It's following!"

She could hear the sound of pounding hoof beats behind her, but she didn't dare look back. Looking back meant a chance to trip over something, and that was not a chance she was willing to take.

Alice didn't know why a stag made of living glass would encourage her to run only to chase her down. She didn't know why there was a stag made of living glass in the mountains at all! It was clearly something Other, but she didn't know what kind. Angels were so rare that she'd never seen one, and she'd never heard of an angel shifter. Kaz could surely sniff out another demon. Perhaps it was some other kind of shifter, maybe a fae, maybe a—

Alice nearly tripped over a root and her thoughts left her. She needed to concentrate on her footing right now.

Her bones seemed to vibrate as she passed the first ring of protections, but it wasn't enough to stop the animal chasing her. The

best hope now was to break through the tree line and get to the heaviest layer of wards and traps, the ones that circled the main house.

"*Ellie!*" she shrieked, skirts up past her knees as she ran at breakneck speed towards the main house. Her hat flew off her head, but she didn't care, just trying not to tangle herself in her own boots as she sprinted towards the property line. If she could make it there, she'd be safe. From what, she didn't know, but they'd spent the better part of a year fortifying their protections. This was her best chance.

"Alice?" Ellie called, poking her head out the back door. "What's goin— *holy shit!*" She ran out of the house with Kaz only a moment behind her, hunting rifle in hand.

Ellie made a wide, sweeping gesture with her hand. Alice couldn't see what was happening behind her, but she felt the ground tremble. Casting a quick glance over her shoulder, she saw the injured glass stag following towards her, but there was a barrier of tall, thorny brambles quickly growing between Alice and her pursuer.

The stag skidded to a halt just before the barrier, right on the border of the heaviest protections. It seemed to sniff at the plants a little, to examine the air around them, before it carefully took a few steps away. It didn't want to cross that barrier, didn't want to become entangled in their protections, and Alice wasn't sure if that was good or bad.

"Who are you?" Ellie snapped, one hand in midair as she directed the growth of the thorny underbrush. "And why the hell are you chasin' one of mine?"

"Interesting," the stag's telepathic voice said. "Your magic is aligned with the mountains."

"Yeah, ain't that fun. Want to tell me 'bout yours?" she snapped.

Ellie could hear the stag, Alice realized. Ellie did not possess animal speak, which meant it was more than just an ordinary stag. Granted, that much was obvious, but it was quite likely that this creature was either a shifter or a familiar, possibly with a witch or Other speaking through it rather than being present.

"*Not particularly, no,*" the stag said, tilting its head. "I would much prefer it if you let me inside."

Alice's legs began to shake, either from fear or exertion or both, but her friend stood firm.

"You ain't steppin' one foot inside my property without my permission, I'll tell ya that right now," Ellie said firmly, crossing her arms over her chest. She stepped protectively in front of Alice, staring down the ethereal Other across the borders like she was a hawk and he was her prey.

Ellie radiated utter fearlessness. It was something Alice had always envied. In fact, Ellie didn't even flinch when the living glass animal made one final attempt to cross the wards.

The stag took two steps back, and then *charged*, barely prepping at all before taking a flying leap through the air. He was trying to clear the thorn barrier, obviously, but there were plenty of invisible protections he would need to cross even if he managed to get past the vines.

Ellie flicked her wrist once. That was all that was needed.

The vines caught him in midair, pulling him back down to the grassy ground outside the wards. More vines grew over the deer's shimmering body, effectively tying him to the ground. Though he thrashed against the greenery and tried to cut it with his antlers, the thorny vines did not move. They also did not seem to draw blood from the stag's glass body, no matter how tightly they twined around him, but he was clearly stuck in place, leashed to the ground.

"What did I tell ya 'bout steppin' foot on my land? Don't think ya heard it the first time," Ellie said, frowning. The stag struggled, but the vines only tightened around him every time he moved even the slightest bit.

Alice watched with wide eyes, only turning when she heard the distinct sound of a rifle cocking behind her. Kaz was just as prepared as Ellie, in his own way.

"Try that again, and we'll see if your glass body cracks like other glass does," Kaz said, shouldering the firearm. "I think a diamond-tipped bullet is strong enough to pierce the skin of most Others. Feel like gambling?"

Diamond-tipped? Alice wasn't surprised that Kaz, of all people, was able to get his hands on something like that, but she certainly hadn't

known about it before now. Living out in the woods meant protecting yourself from anything you might come across, be it natural or supernatural.

"Impressive," the stag grunted, clearly straining against the plants. After another moment of struggling, he finally went still, the shallow rise and fall of his chest as he breathed the only motion that Alice could see. "Fine. If you would kindly release me from these vines, I would happily speak to you in my human form."

Ellie loosened the thorns with a small nod, but didn't entirely remove them. Instead, they stayed in place in something like a thorny cage that moved as the stag shifted.

At first, the glass seemed to shine brighter, to glow from within, moving in a way that made it look molten as it seemed to melt into another shape. It was indistinguishable for a moment, but soon Alice could make out the ghost of arms, legs, and a humanoid head. As the glasslike figure stood, his skin seemed to cool and darken, taking on a softer texture as it formed into muscles and sinew, bones and blood.

It lasted less than thirty seconds, but the process was entirely mesmerizing. Alice had a thousand questions! How did animal organs shift to human ones? How did it feel having your entire being rearranged? Did it hurt? Did it feel cathartic? What were animal bodies like to control?

But then the shift finished, and those questions faded in the presence of the stranger who chased her through the mountain woods.

He was... *big*. Alice stared up at a mountain of a man, body rife with functional muscle. His skin was a warm, dark brown, and he retained the same glasslike antlers from his stag form. Black hair fell past his shoulders in neatly styled braids, the smallest hint of stubble on his jaw. His eyes were the most dazzling, though. His irises were eerily white, rimmed with long lashes.

Incredible, she couldn't help but think.

Kaz did not lower the gun, not even as the stranger bowed to them from the other side of the vine barrier.

"My name is Xavier," he said, bowing. "I am king of the Shadow Fae."

"Why did you run me down in the woods?" Alice asked, the words out of her mouth before she even thought about them.

"I am here for *you*, seventh daughter of a seventh daughter," he said simply, inclining his head towards Alice.

"I... shit," she whispered, knees shaking.

She *was* the seventh. Alice had five living sisters, but she was the second born of a pair of identical twins. The first didn't make it, barely breathing five minutes before she passed away quietly. That much she'd known, and she was well aware that was part of why her lack of magical power was such a disappointment. But... seventh *of* a seventh?

"M— my momma only had two sisters," she protested.

"She did not. It's easy enough to sense not only their lives, but their deaths," he said with a shrug. "They cling to you. It's a sheen over your own energy."

"You can... sense death? Or spirits?"

"We are fae creatures, born of nature and magic, but you could consider us death-aligned, if you like. If it makes it easier for you to comprehend."

Alice thought she was simply a seventh daughter. She didn't know her mother was *also* a seventh.

That made a world of difference.

Outsiders to witch traditions likely wouldn't understand the importance, but everyone watching the scene knew well enough to understand the gravity of the situation. A seventh of a seventh showed up in folktales for a reason. A seventh son might be especially strong or skilled, primed to be a hero from birth. A seventh daughter was a brimming well of overflowing magical power, like a bubbling volcano looking for a moment to explode. A seventh of a seventh? Nearly unprecedented, unquestionably volatile, and potentially very, very dangerous.

How could that possibly be *her*?

"I'm certain you recognized this," Xavier said, holding up his arm. "I know you saw it before you ran. You have been promised to me since birth."

"Promised by who?" Alice asked instinctively.

"Your mother made a bargain with me when you were no more than a babe," he explained, pale eyes trained on Alice. "She secured an advantageous marriage for you."

"She cut ties with the woman who birthed her last year," Ellie said carefully.

"The bargain stands, as my part has been fulfilled," he said nonchalantly. "Even if it had not, these scars indicate a connection far deeper than any bargain could ever run."

Alice ran her fingers over the slightly raised scars on her arm without thinking, surprised to see Xavier smile when she did so. There was an eerie feeling of static to it, a strange pull that she couldn't deny, like an itch she couldn't reach.

"What the hell are you implying?" Hartley's voice came from behind, his footsteps swishing through the tall grass as he came closer.

"Nothing that need concern you," Xavier shot back as though the other man was a fly. "In any case, if I cannot go to her, I will simply wait outside your lines until my bride comes to me," continued calmly. He took two steps backwards, just enough to put him outside the range of activating the wards, and took a seat on the grassy ground with his legs crossed.

"It's up to you, Alice," Ellie said, blue eyes cold as steel as she glared. "You didn't make the bargain. You don't need to do a damn thing you don't want to."

"What do you think?" Alice whispered.

"I think you're safer on this land than anywhere with somebody who's known ya two seconds."

"I've known her for her entire life," Xavier insisted. "I have been watching. Waiting. Looking for the right time. She disappeared from my sight a year ago, and I was never able to find out why until now. Your protections are strong, mountain witch." He inclined his head towards Ellie in a gesture that almost seemed deferential, but the silver-haired witch's defensive posture did not change.

"Alice," Ellie said suddenly, placing a hand on her shoulder, voice low. Her eyes were wide, the sunlight flashing off her long, silver hair. "You asked me my opinion. This is a bad plan, *trust me*. You don't wanna be involved in bargains you didn't make for yourself."

"I have to second," Kaz said under his breath, looking back and forth between Alice and the massive man waiting patiently just outside Ellie's wards. "It would be safer to stay in the wards until you find a way to break or wiggle out of the bargain."

"Alice," Hartley asked, "would you allow me to look at your scar?"

Alice looked over at him briefly, pulling down the sleeve of her dress to cover the scar before she turned away. Hopefully that would be enough of an answer to him. After that morning, she wasn't fond of the idea of letting him anywhere near her, even if he was trying to help. The last thing Alice wanted was pity from anyone, anyone at all... but especially Hartley.

Instead, she took two steps towards where Xavier sat, ready to question him herself.

"Why did you tell me to run earlier?" she asked, hands on her hips. In the basket she had yet to sit down, the possum squeaked in agreement.

Xavier's eyes narrowed and he shook his head. "I never said such a thing, I assure you."

He sounded incredibly assured, but... Alice wasn't convinced. She lacked confidence in herself in some ways, but animal speak was not one of them. She knew what she heard. He'd told her to run, and then... chased her down?

Xavier stood slowly, and Alice was once again struck by his towering figure.

"I swear to you that you will be cherished at my court. You will be my bride— Queen of the Shadow Fae," he said, bowing to her. "You will have a home with me in the palace, and you will want for nothing."

"Palace?" Alice asked, nose wrinkling. "Never heard'a anything like that way out here."

"It's well-hidden, but still part of the mountains you call home. I have no intention of taking you away from the land you are obviously tied to."

Interesting.

As much as this offer seemed a little suspicious, the plan was more and more appealing by the minute. She wouldn't have to leave her

mountains, but she would still be free. Separate, to some degree. Able to make her own way and choose her own life.

"I don't like it," Ellie hissed under her breath.

Some part of Alice agreed. Her mother had always said to be suspicious of things that seemed too good to be true... but her mother wasn't here now, and her mother was a bitch anyway. As she thought, Alice's hand crept to her jaw, fingers tracing over the place where long healed slashes from her mother's nails across her cheek once were.

She had the opportunity to be loved. Choice or no choice in the original bargain, Xavier was here chasing her down. He wanted to make her a queen— more powerful and pampered and adored than she ever dreamed she could be. It didn't matter how well her sisters married. It didn't matter that all those years she'd been pressured to marry a full Other, to have powerful children, and it didn't matter that those years of conditioning still rang out somewhere in the back of her mind. This opportunity was her *victory*.

She'd always wanted to leave, Alice told herself. Some small part of her mind whispered that she'd already left the witch village, but she could justify that. This way she could leave Boone entirely, see a new world and get a fresh start.

You have a fresh start here, her mind whispered.

A fresh start where you'll still be all alone, her heart shot back.

As much as she liked the people she lived with, Alice wanted more. She wanted love. She wanted someone all her own. Xavier was offering her the connection she'd been craving so desperately her entire life, and the prospect was beyond intoxicating.

"I..." Alice paused, lips parted slightly, hand half reaching towards the man with sparkling, glass-like antlers. She bit her lip, shoulders tensing for a moment, and dared to look back over her shoulder.

Hartley's expression was somber, and she could see the barest movement as he shook his head. He didn't think this was a good idea.

... but he also didn't want her.

Alice turned back to the fae standing on the other side of the wards, reaching out to fully place her hand in his. She was surprised to find that his dark skin was cool to the touch, harder than she thought it would be. It was almost like taking the hand of a living statue.

"I'll go," she said firmly, green eyes fixed on the face of her future husband.

He smiled, though she couldn't tell if it reached his eyes or not. It was a little difficult to read his expression, and knowing he was fae, Alice wasn't sure if he would even show emotion in the same way humans did. But... it was enough for her. It was enough to know that he wanted her enough to come for her, to wait all this time for her.

It was intoxicating, in a way.

"Excellent," Xavier said.

"Alice..." Ellie hissed in warning, brow furrowed, but it was too late. She'd made her decision.

When she stepped up to the wall of thorns, they parted to let her through. The magic around here knew her, knew to let her out, and even if Ellie disapproved of her choice, Alice didn't think she would forcibly stop anything.

She was twenty-five years old, more than old enough to make her own decisions. Obviously, the town and their little village didn't have anything left for her now, but here... here he was. Xavier came for her.

Alice gently placed her basket on the ground, surprised that her possum friend was still there, but she didn't have time to think about it long. Xavier pulled her forward, wrapping her in his arms and holding her against his chest with a speed that made her gasp. He was much taller than her, and much stronger, too. It seemed like nothing at all to scoop her up in his arms like a princess and press his mouth to hers.

A dizzy rush ran through Alice at the feeling of her first kiss. She felt like she could melt or collapse right there, but Xavier's strong arms kept her in place.

"My bride," he murmured against her lips.

His skin was as cold as ice, but his hold on her was gentle. His mouth on hers was soft.

And, most importantly, he *wanted* her. He *loved* her.

Everything else would work out from there. Alice was absolutely certain of it.

3 — IN WHICH THERE IS A FAMILY MEETING

"It's time to go," Xavier said as soon as he broke the kiss.

She risked a glance back at the crowd standing behind her, at her friends and neighbors, and tried to ignore the fact that they looked like they were sending her to her grave. Ellie, especially, looked like she was watching a ghost, and that was saying something considering that Ellie had spirit sight.

It was fine, though. It had to be fine.

When she looked back at Xavier, the tall fae was already halfway through his shift into the living glass stag, reversing the process she'd previously seen until his human bones shifted to animal form. It was fascinating in an almost morbid way, and she planned to ask *many* questions about it later.

Alice's dream, up until roughly twenty minutes ago, had been to finish school and learn to be a veterinarian. She'd taken a few biology courses at the Appalachian Teacher's College over the last year, and though she'd been afraid learning about the bloodier parts of animal care might turn her stomach, she found herself utterly enthralled by all of it. She wanted to know the ins and outs of the way things worked, of how bones and sinews worked together to bring life and movement

to a form, how the body converted food to energy, why some things were poisonous and others were not—

She stopped herself from thinking about that too much as Xavier completed his shift into the stag, taking a few small steps towards her. Alice didn't need to worry about biology studies any longer. After all, she was going to be a *queen*.

This was the ideal outcome, after all. She'd be taken care of for the rest of her life, have everything she'd ever wanted or needed, and she'd never have to worry about hearing how useless and weak she was again. She would *never* be weak again, not as Queen of the Shadow Fae.

Beside her, the possum shuffled in her basket, and Alice jolted back to reality, watching as her adventurous new friend finally scuttled out. . It seemed time to part ways, even if she did find the little gray creature endearingly scruffy. It was just part of animal speech— eventually everyone had to go their own ways.

... Humans, too, she thought. Eventually they all left you behind, too. They got married, or they turned bitter, or they decided they didn't have a use for you. It was better to take care of yourself first and foremost, better to make sure you were loved and valued and treasured, utterly indispensable to the world around you. It was the only way to ensure your survival.

Ellie and Kaz are okay, a little voice in her head reminded her.

For now, her cautious conscious mind replied.

"Thanks for the company, lil missy," Alice murmured, patting the possum's head as it clambered out of the basket.

However, instead of running away into the woods, the possum gave a sharp squeak and scrambled up Alice's arm, settling itself on her shoulders. It was a little surprising, but not uncomfortable. The possum was a warm weight against her skin, and she found that she liked the determined nature of her new companion, even if their companionship was temporary.

"You comin' along?" she asked softly.

The little creature unmistakably nodded, holding on tight with its paws. Alice wasn't about to turn down a friend if she wanted to come, so she simply nodded back and approached the glass deer. As she drew

closer, the deer knelt, lowering itself so that its broad back was closer to Alice's hips than her shoulders.

"Get on my back," Xavier said in Alice's mind. The deer's mouth did not move as he spoke. *"Straddle. You'll need to hold on tight."*

If she'd been riding a horse, it might not have been a problem for Alice to hitch up her skirts and swing one leg over the side of the animal, planting herself firmly on its back. As it was, though, knowing that this was a humanoid shifter— and one she would soon be married to— Alice keenly felt the heat in her cheeks as her bare thighs touched the deer's body, melding against the animal like she was always meant to be there.

As Xavier the stag stood, Alice suddenly felt exposed and out of control, her feet dangling in midair as she tightened her legs around the deer's body, scrambling to balance herself. The possum on her shoulder seemed unperturbed, but Alice needed a moment to adjust.

The glass still felt like *glass*, if she didn't think about it much. It had a little give to it beneath her thighs, as something alive should, but it was *cold*. When she first touched the deer in the woods, the glass was warm, but now all the warmth seemed to have drained away. The possum scrambled from her shoulder to her lap, where she could be a little better shielded from the wind and still hold on tight.

"Hands on my antlers," the stag said. "Whatever you do, do not let go."

"Can you run with me holdin' on like that?" Alice asked, nose scrunched.

"Don't worry about me. Hold tight."

She risked one glance back at the group of witches and Others on the opposite side of the wards, safe behind Ellie's protections, and wished that she hadn't. Their expressions were almost unreadable, but she could see the clear overarching tendency between all of them: fear.

Alice didn't have time to be afraid, though. This was her chance, perhaps the only chance she would ever have. At this point, she couldn't afford not to take it. She wouldn't waste her shot at a better life, at a life where she was loved and adored, based on a little fear.

... Or even a *lot* of fear.

She couldn't stop the scream that ripped from her throat as the stag *leaped*, taking off without warning, but she certainly did hold on tight.

The not-glass stag was supernaturally fast, moving through the woods at a blinding pace. Alice was forced to keep her gaze far in the distance and focus on keeping down her breakfast as they traveled west. She tried to close her eyes, but that only made the nausea worse from the jolting, jarring, and unexpected jumps of their ride. Trees flew by in a blur of brown and green, waves upon waves of foliage moving at a rate that was sickening, but she held her stomach from willpower alone.

The possum scrambled from Alice's shoulders to her lap, shielding itself from the worst of the wind and the cold, but Alice was not so lucky. Her cheeks burned from the blasts of wind as they ran through the trees, stung where small branches that were impossible to entirely avoid whipped at her skin.

She'd thought the deer was cold at first, but she was wrong. It was *frigid*. It was like riding a block of ice, and her thighs screamed and her hands ached from it within minutes. The glass material was magically alive, yes, but it was also nothing like the touch she remembered in the woods. Her thighs ached from the sheer width of the deer's back, and the cold only made it worse. She wondered if eventually everything would grow numb, but it never did.

Time and distance were strange on the back of the stag. By the time his pace began to slow, Alice wasn't sure how long they ran, if they ever changed directions during the journey, or even where they were at all. By the time they stopped, Alice tried to pry her fingers from Xavier's stag antlers, but found that she simply couldn't move.

Her vision swam, then blurred. The possum chittered in her ear, and she could faintly hear voices coming from humanoid figures in the distance, but couldn't quite make out what they were saying before she felt herself lose consciousness.

***

Things in Ellie and Kaz's living area hadn't been this tense since the day an albino raccoon snuck inside through the open back door, managing to overturn Granny's soup, break three jars of Ellie's medicines,

and make a nest out of Kaz's shredded manuscript papers before anyone could catch it.

That was six months back, and still no one had admitted to leaving the door open.

Hartley almost chuckled at the memory, but then he remembered that it was Alice who managed to get the little creature out in the end, and the guilt gnawing at his chest came back with a vengeance. He couldn't help but feel responsible for everything that had happened that morning, at least in some capacity.

"This is my fault," Hartley sighed, taking a seat on the sofa in the living area of Ellie and Kaz's home.

Their little group had gathered for something of a family meeting, at least those of them who were around. Ellie paced restlessly around the room while Kaz leaned against the far wall, playing with the ends of his white hair as he stared into space. Miriam was the only one who seemed relatively calm, sipping on a mug of tea from one of the armchairs while she waited on her husband to return from checking the wards.

"This is damn well not your fault," Ellie snapped as she suddenly stopped pacing, hands on her hips. "You didn't make the bargain and you didn't make her leave."

"I rejected her this morning when..." he trailed off, cursing a muffled blue streak under his breath in a language too old for anyone else in the room to know. He should have known better. He should have been able to do something different, to tell her things in a gentler way.

Alice had always been sensitive and volatile, but he never thought she'd do something like this. He'd only been tired of trying to gently break the news to her for months! She simply hadn't understood any of his subtle attempts to distance himself.

"Hartley," Miriam said softly, placing a hand on his shoulder. "We want Alice safe, but we also want you happy. You shouldn't have to fake your feelings. Honesty was the right call."

"I was too harsh," he huffed.

"She was too impulsive, though," Ellie mumbled, crossing her arms over her chest. "I wish Harper were here— might'a been our only chance to talk sense into her."

"When she and Simon get back from town, we can talk to her," Kaz said, patting Ellie's shoulder. "For now, let's go wake up Granny."

"You know we're gonna have to keep her from chasin' Alice down with a switch," Ellie grumbled, rubbing at her temples.

"Let me do it, then," Hartley suggested. "She might listen to me."

"She just thinks your face is too pretty for your own good," Ellie said, laughing.

"If it helps keep Granny from running off, I'm all for weaponizing Hart's freakishly well-structured cheekbones and sparkly skin," Kaz snorted, wrapping his arm around Ellie's shoulder.

"I do not *sparkle*," Hartley grumbled, crossing his arms over his chest. He knew exactly why they were saying that, but it wasn't accurate. Not technically.

Not only that, it was *embarrassing*. And, if anyone happened to run across another member of his species, a dead giveaway. However, it didn't seem that anyone had drawn those connections yet. Hartley kept his exact Other origins to himself for his own reasons, and he wasn't ready to unpack those reasons yet.

"You do, a little," Miriam said hesitantly, looking to Ellie for help. "Just a shimmer."

"In the right light," Ellie agreed, wincing.

Hartley just sighed. There was no point in arguing— they all had bigger problems to deal with at the moment.

"Does anyone have any ideas where he might have taken her?" Hart asked, glancing around the room.

"'Fraid not," Ellie admitted. "I could ask some of the land spirits if they've seen anything, but—"

The front door creaked open, and everyone in the room simultaneously twitched. However, a familiar face peeked through the doorway, and they all relaxed. It was only Samson, Miriam's husband, walking inside with a toolbox in tow. He wiped a sheen of sweat from his dark skin with a blue handkerchief and ambled inside, closing the door behind him.

"Any progress?" he asked, putting down the toolbox with a clunk and a metallic rattle.

"Not much," Ellie admitted. "How's it look out there?" She moved towards the kitchen as she spoke, reaching for a glass and working the hand pump on the sink to pour out some water for Sam.

"The wards seem to be holdin' up just fine, based on what ya taught me to look for, but it can't hurt if you wanna boost 'em later. Fences look alright, too, just physically," he said, brushing his hands together. "Then again, I'm a better trapper than a woodworker, so maybe Simon should give 'em a look when he gets back."

"Thank you, baby," Miriam said, standing to hug her husband. Sam held her close for a moment and kissed her forehead before they both took a seat.

"It's a huge help, Sam," Ellie said, handing him the glass of water as she spoke. "Alice is still technically cleared to get through the wards, so if she wants to come back..."

"What if she doesn't?" Sam asked, voicing the question they were all too scared to speak. He took a long drink from his glass, just waiting to see if anyone had ideas.

There was a long, horrible silence in the room. No one wanted to admit that they might have just seen Alice for the last time, and Hartley knew he probably wasn't the only person in the room who felt like they had failed her in some way.

"Then she doesn't," Kaz finally said, sighing as he scratched at the snow-white stubble on his jaw. "I hate to say it, but... she may have made her choice. I don't know if it's even *possible* to track her."

"I could try," Miriam offered. "She's a sweet girl. I'd hate to lose my favorite babysitter," she said with a small smile, clearly trying to lighten the mood.

"If you could, that might be helpful. Even if we can't get to her, just knowing where she is might bring... some sense of peace," Hartley said helplessly, resting his head in his hands.

Miriam was one of the best trackers he'd ever seen, magical or otherwise. She was incredibly perceptive, and capable of picking up even the faintest traces of trails left behind by people or animals. If another person with strong senses could help her, there was very little they couldn't pick up together.

Unfortunately, that extra person was usually Alice. Her knowledge of animals and ability to speak with them was an incredible complement to Miriam's tracking ability. If either of them lost the trail, chances were that nearby animals could help re-establish it.

"I'll see if Harper might be able to smell her when she gets back," Miriam said, nodding slowly. "Before the trail goes cold. It'll help get me a start."

"Well, I think you're in luck, hon," Sam said, nodding towards the front of the house. "Looks like they're comin' this way."

Hartley glanced out the large windows at the front of the house that gave a clear view of the mountain path leading up to their tiny village from the town of Boone. Sure enough, two humanoid figures were very deliberately making their way up the path, followed by a whole host of canines.

Harper, a blond vampire with a particularly strong sun sensitivity, walked along with a black parasol in hand to help shade her from the midday glare. It wasn't necessary to look at her feet to know that she was wearing heels— she always wore heels, in fact. She said it made her feel powerful, though Hartley was convinced she didn't need special shoes for that. The daughter of Kaz's close friends, Harper was the demon's adopted niece, and an incredibly powerful vampire in her own right.

Simon strolled along beside her, occasionally bending down to redirect one of the smaller dogs padding along behind them away from sniffing the wrong plant... or batting at the wrong bug. A witch who grew up in the same community as Ellie, Simon had turned twenty years old earlier that spring. Ellie was like a sister to him, as Simon's last remaining family passed away when he was very young, so he'd chosen to come along and stay with their little group. Though Simon didn't do much in the way of magic, besides working on basic wards, Hartley was consistently impressed with his architectural and woodworking skills.

"Hell-ooooo!" Harper sing-songed as she pushed the door open, striding inside and shutting her parasol. "We're back! We brought some bakery goodies from Emmaline, too."

Simon and the hounds piled into the house only a moment after Harper, and not for the first time, Harlet thought it was a very, very good

thing that Kaz decided they needed a large living area in the house to host guests.

Ellie's adopted pup immediately bolted towards her, practically knocking Simon to the floor in the process. Rosemary wasn't even two years old yet, and she was a ball of boundless, fluffy energy. She also loved Ellie fiercely, having developed more of a bond with her than any of the other pups in the litter that Harper's hellhound friends, Charlie and Luna, brought with them to Boone.

"Hi, baby girl!" Ellie said, dropping to her knees to pick up Rosemary in her arms. "How was your walk?"

"*It was good. I tried to catch a squirrel, but it didn't work,*" the pup said with a little snort. Voices of Other canines weren't physical so much as mental, an echo in the minds of those close enough to hear it. Though it could be a little strange at first, they were all very much used to their canine companions by now.

"You'll get em' next time," Ellie said firmly, giving Rosemary a little scratch behind the ears.

"She's going to be too big for that one day," Kaz said pointedly.

"Well, if she's too big for me, you'll just have to hold her," she said nonchalantly, flashing Kaz an innocent smile. Hartley had to hold back a snort, but he sobered quickly.

"Perfect timing," he said somberly. "We've got news."

"As always," Harper said, smiling brightly, but her smile fell as she took in the atmosphere of the room. "... Who died? Did somebody die? Oh, god, what happened?"

Slowly, and with the help of Ellie and Kaz, Hartley related the events of the day to Harper and Simon. He hadn't seen quite everything, but Ellie could fill in most of the details he'd missed.

Unfortunately, what they weren't sure about was how Alice ran into the Shadow Fae in the first place. She'd been distressed, and perhaps had wandered outside the wards. But... why was there a matching mark on their arms?

Something about the situation nagged at the back of his mind, turning gears that just couldn't seem to catch on any solid ideas. Things weren't lining up well, even from the little he'd seen. As much as he'd wanted to tell Alice to stay behind, to give them a few days to investigate

31

the bond between them, Hartley knew that plea might have the opposite effect if it came from him. He couldn't blame her, not really. She could take the time to be upset with him, and that wasn't an issue. It was more concerning that she'd chosen to compromise her own long-term safety over a whirlwind of short-term emotions.

That was just how Alice was, though, he supposed. She was young, volatile, and hadn't been given the chance to know herself yet. He wondered, on some level, if he should have acquiesced to her request and simply tried to court her... but no. Alice was fiery and starry-eyed, and it was endearing on some levels, but he was simply too old to balance that anymore. He needed...

Well, it didn't matter what he needed, did it? It mattered what was happening to Alice.

"I leave for *one day*!" Harper cried, flopping down on the sofa with a huff. "One! One day! All the good stuff happens when I'm gone!"

"Right, because assisting in a murder investigation last year wasn't enough entertainment for you. Got it," Kaz huffed, rolling his eyes.

"That was a whole year back! I need something new, an' I missed it by the skin'a my teeth," she grumbled, crossing her arms over her chest as she tossed her blonde hair.

"I'm concerned about the bond he mentioned," Hartley said, ignoring Harper's dramatics. "The scars. I can check through some of the Other journals and notes I've collected in my personal library, but something seems... off."

"You'd know better than any of us," Kaz said with a sigh. "You've seen more."

"And I have rarely, if ever, seen a physical mark of a soul bond that wasn't forced into existence. Considering my age, that's significant."

"How old *are* you?"

"... Older than twenty thousand," Hartley finally sighed.

Kaz gave a low whistle.

"Damn," Ellie whispered.

"And that's why I don't mention it often," he sighed. "It upsets people."

"Sooooo... can I call you Grandpa Hart now?" Harper asked, raising her eyebrows as a catlike grin spread across her face. Kaz tried and failed to hold back a snort.

Hartley just glared.

4

IN WHICH ALICE TAKES VOWS

Alice was shivering when she woke.

Her body was no longer entirely numb, but everywhere felt painfully stiff and a little swollen, like when she was a child and went outside in the snow without proper clothing. It was like she could feel the blood returning to her extremities with every heartbeat, and it *hurt*. Her fingers and toes protested as she wiggled them, eyes still squeezed shut.

And, she noticed, her head was on someone's lap. Gentle hands ran through her hair, nearly soothing her back to sleep, but Alice wrenched her eyes open and forced herself to look up at the person above her.

She wasn't sure what room they were in. It looked something like a parlor, or perhaps a study. There were bookshelves built into the gray stone walls, and the room was large enough that even the roaring fire in the marble fireplace didn't do much to warm the space. She was lying on a plush sofa, looking up at a pair of ghostly pale eyes.

"Welcome back to the waking world, my treasure," Xavier murmured, still running his fingers through her hair. "You gave us a scare."

"W—why is it so cold?" she asked through chattering teeth. Though she tried to sit up properly, it felt like her body was slow to respond, and Xavier had to help support her.

35

"We're higher in the mountains than you were before, and a little farther north. We'll need to get you warmer clothes before we can proceed with the ceremony," he said, bringing her hand to his lips to kiss her knuckles. "Come. We'll get you warm."

"C—ceremony?" Alice managed, giving a slight squeak as Xavier picked her up in his arms. She wished there was a blanket close by, or an extra coat. Something, *anything* for a little insulation.

Xavier wasted no time marching her down the hall. She looked for any other castle inhabitants as they moved swiftly through the building, but there was no one. They seemed to be alone, despite the lit torches in the hallways and the few doors that appeared to be open.

"Where is everyone?"

"Gathering for the celebration, I imagine," Xavier explained, adjusting her weight in his arms. "We are to be married, and then we will join the rest of our court for a wedding feast."

"Now?!" Alice asked. "As in... *now*, now?"

"As soon as you acquire proper clothing, yes. Within the hour, surely." As he spoke, Xavier paused in front of an ornate wooden door. Instead of putting Alice down to open it or shifting her weight, though, he simply raised his leg and kicked it open. The door swung wildly on its hinges, revealing a plush, dimly lit bedroom.

Alice wasn't sure if the door was unlocked before, broken now, or why he'd chosen that manner of entrance, but watching him casually kick the door open lit some kind of fire inside her that she couldn't describe. If she'd felt cold before, she certainly didn't as Xavier sat her own on the plush bed that was the room's centerpiece.

Alice took in the room as her husband-to-be lit a fire, fanning the flames until she could feel a little of the warmth seeping into her bones. The furniture was entirely in dark wood and black fabric, the firelight glinting off it as the sun set outside the westward windows. Besides the bed, there were two large wardrobes, two nightstands, and a desk on which papers were stacked in front of a high-backed chair. On the wall to the right of the entrance, another door presumably led to some kind of bathroom.

"Here," Xavier said, handing Alice a pile of fabric. She assumed he'd found them in the wardrobe while she was busy looking around the room, and was a little surprised to find they were not human clothes.

The first item was a pair of leggings lined with soft fur, which Alice gratefully slipped on underneath her dress. They weren't quite like what humans of this century wore, but they weren't bad.

The stranger piece was the dress. Shirt. Shirt dress? Alice stared at it for a long moment before she had an idea of how it was supposed to work. It was a long-sleeved garment with a wide neckline, and at first glance the dress appeared to be floor length. However, long slits on either side went all the way up to Alice's waist, ending near the top of her leggings. She would be entirely covered, but it certainly felt a little strange. She slipped the dress over her head anyways, though, keeping her back turned towards Xavier as she did. Finally, Alice wrapped a braided belt around her waist, smoothing out the dress before she turned around.

"Fae clothes suit you," Xavier said approvingly. "You'll need shoes as well, of course, but your old ones will do for now."

It was at that moment that Alice realized— she did need fae style shoes, and he couldn't have prepared them in advance because he didn't know her shoe size. The clothing, however, fit *perfectly*. Perhaps it fit a little too perfectly.

How did he know her size?

How long had he been watching her?

Alice pushed away the cold dread tickling at the back of her mind. Xavier watched her because he *loved* her. He knew they were fated to be together, and he'd taken care of everything to make this transition easier for her.

"Now, let us begin the ceremony," Xavier said calmly. He walked to the writing desk and opened the drawer, pulling a silver dagger with a jeweled hilt from the desk. The blade was slightly curved and looked wickedly sharp, and it made the hair on the back of Alice's neck stand on end just looking at it.

"Don't we need— I don't know, maybe not a priest, but at least some *witnesses*?" she stuttered, eyes locked on the dagger, but Xavier seemed entirely nonplussed.

"No witnesses are necessary. It's a blood marriage ceremony," Xavier explained, drawing the blade across his palm. A thin line of blood welled up across his dark skin, and where the light from the window streaked across it, the blood glinted a deep blue. "We bind ourselves together in the old fae way, by sharing our blood three times. The first has already been taken care of."

"Wha—" Alice wanted to ask for clarification, wondering how she'd managed to share blood with him when they'd never met before, but Xavier drew her in close and kissed her, cutting her off before she had the chance.

"We will be bound together, my beautiful bride, in body and soul. One heartbeat. One will," he murmured, smiling gently down at her. "It won't take much blood, if that's what worries you. One drop would be enough, given willingly."

He pressed the handle of the knife into her hand, willing her to take it. Alice's fingers automatically closed around the wood of the guard, and she let him position the blade over the outer part of her arm. He rolled up the sleeve of her tunic, baring her skin for the cut.

"You must make the cut, but it will hurt less here," he said gently, taking his hands away.

She paused, the blade in her hand poised over her arm, and looked up at Xavier.

"Why me?" she asked, locking her gaze with his. "Out of everybody else in the world, why do ya want *me*?"

Xavier looked at her with his pale, piercing eyes, and smiled softly, reaching towards her with his free hand to stroke her cheek. However, what came out of his mouth was not what she expected.

"Have you ever wondered why your mother hated you?" he asked, still smiling softly.

Alice flinched. This didn't seem like the time for that question in any way. However, Xavier had answered her questions so far, and she decided to give him a chance to make his point. Alice was silent for a long moment, but she finally nodded.

"It is because you have all the power that she never inherited herself. You have the potential to be more than she could ever dream of

becoming," he said, smiling down at her. "You, Alice, are the perfect magical balance to my power and might, and that is why I want you."

A tiny thrill shot through her chest at those words. No one, in all of her life, had ever called her powerful.

"But... but how do I...?" She trailed off, hands waving in the air a little helplessly. She could be as powerful as a landslide crashing down the mountain, but that was useless if she didn't know how to use that power. Alice had no idea how to access any of this supposed well of magic inside her.

"I will teach you, of course," he said, waving his hand as if it was nothing. "You are a queen. You will be treated as such. You will learn magic and court etiquette, and we will spend the rest of our days together in... bliss."

Something about that felt strange to her, though.

"But you... you don't love me," she said softly, hating the way her voice cracked.

"Alice, my treasure," Xavier sighed, taking her hands in his. "Loving you is an inevitability that I cannot avoid. As birds fly and fish swim, so it is in my nature to love you. We have been divinely matched by the universe itself."

Alice had never been entirely sure what it meant when a lady swooned in books, but just now she thought that she understood. Her cheeks burned as a dizzy rush came over her. Xavier gently trailed his fingers across her cheek, over her jaw, and down along her skin until he reached the pulse point at her neck. He smiled at her as he tracked the tempo of her pounding heart, leaning in to press a kiss against her forehead.

"Drink," he said, holding up his bleeding hand.

Alice blanched, staring at the shining trickle of wet blood running down his dark skin. She had not considered that literally ingesting blood would be on the wedding menu.

"Remember: just a drop will do," he said reassuringly. "It must be done to cement our bond."

"This is normal?" she asked hesitantly, trying to keep her expression neutral.

"Normal? Yes, it's been practiced for centuries."

"O—okay," she said, steeling herself.

Alice half expected the drop of blood that landed on her tongue from Xavier's palm to be cold, just as the rest of him was. It wasn't exactly warm, but it wasn't frigid, either. It didn't taste of iron like human blood did— instead, an almost cloying floral taste spread across her tongue. She couldn't identify any particular flower, but it was enough to make her sneeze from the strength of it. Xavier didn't seem to mind the sneezing, in any case, patiently waiting as she recovered..

"My turn," he said softly.

Alice gritted her teeth, gripped the knife, and drew it across the back of her left arm. Blood welled almost instantly, even though she hadn't cut deep enough for much to trickle out.

"Do you give this blood willingly?" Xavier asked, bending over her arm.

"I do," Alice breathed, nodding.

Xavier cleaned the trail of blood from her skin with one long, slow lick that sent a shudder down her spine. It didn't feel like something her body normally did. It felt like cold and lightning, like something alive crawling under her skin and settling there.

"What was that?" she gasped, eyes wide. Xavier just pulled her in close and held her against his chest, her ear pressed against his heartbeat.

"The bond is growing," he crooned. "That's our magic responding to the blood ceremony, twining together inside our bodies."

Something about that probably should have made her uncomfortable— something about it *did* make her uncomfortable, but it was vastly overshadowed by a feeling of being wanted. Being claimed. Xavier wanted her enough to merge their magic together, their very beings together.

She'd never felt something that visceral in her life, and it was intoxicating to think it was directed at her. Alice would do anything to keep it this way, to make sure he continued to want her like this. Now that she'd come across this feeling, she couldn't bear to let it go.

She wouldn't go the rest of her life feeling unwanted. Never, never again.

"Of course, we still haven't completed the ceremony," Xavier said softly, his breath tickling her ear. "The bond will be truly complete when we consummate it. That will be our third sharing of blood..."

His hands slipped down her back, fingertips tracing down her spine until he found the curve of her ass, lifting her up so she was flush against him, forced to wrap her arms around his neck and legs around his waist for balance.

"Just... here," he breathed, his teeth scraping along her neck. "Just one bite, taken while we are joined."

"T— thought you were a fae, not a vampire," Alice gasped, leaning into his touch on instinct. Xavier laughed softly, lips brushing her skin as he spoke.

"Oh, treasure, all creatures can bite."

Another shiver, followed by building heat, seared through her bones and blood. Alice wanted to touch, to reach out to him, but she wasn't... sure... *how.*

She knew how animals had babies, and she wasn't completely naïve to human sexuality. However, her mother kept a close eye on her the entire time she'd grown up, and there was never much of a chance to do anything at all. Even stolen kisses had felt like an impossible dream, much less anything more intimate.

Nervous flutters built in her stomach. Alice wanted to do this right. She wanted to do what she was *supposed* to do, to be a good wife and a good partner, to be...

She didn't even know how to articulate what to be.

"W—wait," Alice stuttered, cheeks flaming. "I dunno if I'm... um..."

"No matter. We can wait," he said with a shrug, stepping away. "We have all the time in the world, and we have a celebration to get to."

"Sorry," she muttered, looking down as she fisted her hands in the skirt of her dress.

"Follow me. We'll go downstairs," Xavier said, holding out his hand

He didn't seem angry, and that was the only small comfort that she had. As cool and calm as ever, Xavier betrayed no emotions. It was

clear that he would be hard to read, but she hoped that one day she would be able to see even the smallest show of emotion.

Alice took his hand, her smaller palm practically engulfed by his, and let him lead her down the hallway. As they walked, she noticed that one of the hallway windows was open, perhaps from cleaning, and that a little bird was sitting on the sill.

Offering the little gray bird a smile, Alice waved her free hand to wave, and the creature tilted its head.

"Stay alert," the bird said, but before Alice could ask what it meant, it flew away into the orange-tinted sunset.

When they walked down the last flight of stairs to the main floor, Alice was overjoyed to see a little ball of gray fur running towards them. Without thinking, she dropped Xavier's hand and surged forward, dropping to her knees in the hallway.

"There you are!" Alice cried, holding her arms out. The possum jumped up towards her, happily settling itself around Alice's shoulders.

"That took long enough. I was worried," the possum said, nudging its furry head against Alice's cheek.

Xavier's nose wrinkled as he frowned, eyeing the creature warily.

"Must you bring that... *beast*... along?" he asked hesitantly.

"He's not a beast—" Alice said quickly, shaking her head.

"She," the possum corrected, nudging Alice with her nose.

"*She's*, um..." Alice paused, fumbling for a moment. "Missy. Her name's Missy."

"Missy?" Xavier's eyebrow quirked, but he didn't immediately dismiss it.

"She's a friend," she said with a firm nod. "She goes where I go."

"Oh, special adventures," Missy said, chittering happily.

"If she must," Xavier said, nodding. He was no longer frowning, but he still looked a little suspicious of Alice's animal friend.

"Never seen a possum before?"

"They are... interesting creatures, I must say," he said carefully, still looking warily at the possum.

"Not from your world, I guess," Alice said with a soft laugh.

"My... world?" Xavier frowned, his step hitching just slightly, but Alice attributed it to the rough stone floors they were walking on.

Others came from Other worlds. That much was common knowledge, though some of what Alice knew came directly from Kaz. When the Appearances began, when Others started to show up in the human world, it was because they'd somehow been stuck here, forced into physical forms on Earth. They didn't have a choice in the matter.

Alice assumed Xavier's world was quite different from hers, but he seemed confused by her commentary. Kaz and Hartley had always been very forthcoming with the fact that they came from other worlds, so it was a bit surprising to see Xaiver's hesitance. She opened her mouth to ask about his home, but never had the chance to do so. Instead, her jaw dropped and stayed open as they approached a grand pair of doors.

The doors themselves seemed to be made of carved crystal, something like cloudy quartz. Lights danced on the other side, flickering and floating and refracting in the stone.

"Welcome to our wedding reception," Xavier said, the corner of his mouth quirking in a small smile. Without further explanation, he pushed open the doors.

Alice didn't know what to expect from a fae ballroom, but she couldn't have imagined anything even close to reality.

Crystal pillars that matched the doors lined the large, rectangular hall. Inexplicably floating candles lit the room, their yellow flames contrasting with sparkling, floating white lights that looked like stars caught and brought to earth. Vines crawled up the wall, blooming with strange, white flowers like none that Alice had ever seen. A sweet fragrance filled the air, but it was unclear if the aroma came from the flowers or the incredible plethora of food on banquet tables placed around the large, white-tiled dance floor.

"You built all this since the Appearances?" Alice whispered.

"It took us time, of course, but yes," Xavier said, a hint of pride in his voice. "Fae are quite resourceful, if I may say."

If he said anything else, Alice couldn't hear it over a round of absolutely raucous applause. She wasn't sure how many fae had crowded into the room for the celebration, but she imagined it must be every member of the Shadow Court present on Earth. There were at least a hundred people in the ballroom— perhaps *two* hundred? She couldn't tell. The shifting shadows cast from the candlelight obscured their numbers well, and as Xavier guided her into the room with a hand at the small of her back, Alice found herself swept away by the atmosphere. She gave up entirely on trying to count the people present in favor of watching her step, letting her husband lead her up to a grand crystal dais upon which sat two silver thrones.

Husband.

Her husband.

A rush of giddy enthusiasm swept through her at the thought. She was married! She was married to a full-blooded Other, *finally*! This was what she'd wanted her whole life, what she'd been prepared for since before she could remember. Everything had finally fallen into place.

Though... Alice realized she did not have any idea what she wanted for herself now that this matter was settled.

Ah, well. She was a queen now. She didn't need to want anything.

Xavier guided her forward until they reached the crystal dais, but rather than letting her follow him up the steps, he picked Alice up by the waist and twirled her in front of the crowd, pulling her up to the raised silver thrones. The volume of applause only increased, and a few scattered whoops and whistles floated through the air as Xavier kissed her in front of the crowd, then sat her down on one of the two matched thrones.

Both thrones were delicate, built of unidentifiable silver metal twined into the shape of interlocking branches that formed the base and backs of the chairs. Sparkling green gems winked in the light near the top of the thrones, where the silver branches flared outwards slightly to create limbs and leaves.

Alice had no more than a few seconds to settle in place before Xavier walked towards her, placing a delicate silver crown on her head. It was inset with green gems that matched the thrones, and somehow he had seemingly pulled a matching one from thin air.

"A crown for a queen," he said, nodding approvingly.

Sure her cheeks were flushed red, Alice had to fight not to fidget as Xavier took a seat beside her, making a dismissive motion with one hand.

The rest of the room returned to their own individual celebrations. The festivities mostly seemed to include dancing, but there was also plenty of food on display, and there was a pile of wedding gifts near the back of the hall. Nothing seemed amiss, though Alice wasn't quite sure what to do. She was about to ask what their evening duties were when a short, blonde courtier approached the dais. Xavier signaled the man to come forward, and he stepped onto the crystal. He was dressed in the fae style, and his frame was lean and willowy, like many in the room.

"Congratulations, my queen," the short man said, giving a deep bow. "It is a blessing indeed to find one's mirror soul."

Her list of questions was only growing as the night went on.

"Mirror?" Alice's brow furrowed. "What's th—"

"Our new queen is a little stressed from her journey. I'm sure you understand." Xavier placed one large hand on Alice's shoulder as he spoke, drawing her closer to his side.

"O—of course," the courtier said, blanching a little as he glanced at Xavier.

The king looked utterly unphased at first glance, but there was something in the set of his jaw that made Alice glad she was not on the receiving end of that look. The courtier's expression seemed strained as he bowed to them both once more.

"May the shadows shelter you, Your Majesties," he said quickly, taking a few steps back.

If Alice didn't know better, she'd say he fled into the crowd. However, as happy and celebratory as the rest of the court seemed on the dance floor, she thought it must certainly be a trick of the light...

But what if it wasn't?

"What's that mean?" Alice whispered, learning over towards Xavier. "And why'd he bolt outta here like a cat on a hot tin roof?"

Xavier sighed, leaning in close to kiss her cheek. Even his breath on her skin felt cooler than it should. He pulled away slightly, taking her chin in one hand so she would look at him, her green eyes meeting his glassy, pale ones.

"While you are here, you will speak like a queen," he said so only they could hear. His tone was gentle, but firm.

"Is... the way I talk a problem?" Alice blinked, suddenly self-conscious.

"You need to gain the respect of your subjects. Manner of speech is an important part of presenting yourself as a queen," he said simply, and though he had a point...

Alice had heard plenty of ridicule about the way Southern folk spoke. The students in her biology classes at the Appalachian Teacher's College looked at her a little strangely when she spoke, too, as her accent was stronger than most of theirs, even if they grew up in the South.

It was a point of semi-spiteful pride to keep her accent, something that made her feel like she retained a part of herself, no matter what the world thought of her.

"I can't be a queen in my own voice?"

Rather than answering, Xavier did something that Alice realized he was very good at: he changed the subject. Again.

"Why don't you go take a look at the wedding gifts? I'm certain there have to be a few things over there you'd like for yourself, hmm?" He patted her shoulder gently, nodding towards a table laden with gifts on the far side of the hall.

The subject change disappointed her, but Alice told herself that she should be grateful for her new husband's generosity. She had never thought a life in the lap of luxury was within reach, but now it was a reality. She was a *queen*.

As Alice rose from her silver throne, she felt the crown on her head shift slightly. The wrong size, she thought. Perhaps it could be adjusted later.

"Come on, friend. Let's go look," she said to the possum on her shoulder. The creature sniffed, nodding as best she could.

The crowd of dancing courtiers parted for her as she swept through the room, letting her pass smoothly through the masses of fae to reach the back of the room. Alice tried to smile as she passed, tried to conduct herself with decorum and dignity, but she was too worried about tripping over her own long skirts to put on much of a performance.

Thankfully, no one seemed to want to do anything to contradict Xavier, and that included questioning her place as queen.

Maybe, in the future, she would have a chance to cement her place in the role on her own. For now, she was glad for the shelter that Xavier's affection provided.

The gift tables at the back of the hall were even more imposing up close. What had seemed like a vague, shimmering mass from a distance was instead hundreds— possibly *thousands*— of objects piled high on tables, on the floor, on errant chairs that seemed to be placed there just to hold gifts. There were gems of all shapes, sizes, cuts, and colors. Silver and gold chalices, plates, and other dishware gleamed in the candlelight. Rolls of luxurious, iridescent fabric were piled higher than Alice was tall, waiting to be made into beautiful clothing.

There was not, she noticed, even a scrap of iron.

Fae were sensitive to iron. At least, some of them were. Some witches descended from fae were also sensitive to it, but that was less common the farther removed they were from fae ancestors. Alice could understand erring on the side of caution among a court full of fae with varying sensitivities to the metal, and assumed that's why she couldn't see any common iron nearby.

Except...

Alice squinted at the pile, moving forward hesitantly. Leaning closer, she examined what looked to be a pocket watch lying near the edge of the table. It was silver in color, studded with green gems like her crown, and she wondered how the inner workings of a watch might be made without any iron at all. Maybe the sensitivity was different if the iron didn't touch fae skin?

She reached out to examine the watch.

"Ah, ah, ah, I wouldn't touch that," a voice said.

"Wha—" Alice turned, pulling her hand away suddenly.

Alice thought she might be looking at the most beautiful woman in existence.

Her skin was the same dark shade as Xavier's, but dotted with stark white freckles that looked like stars against a dark background. Her eyes were bright green and vivid, like spring itself, and her long, curling hair matched her eyes. She sported the same crystal antlers as Xavier and

a scant few others in the room, but instead of humanoid feet, her legs ended in matching crystalline hooves that peeked out below long, wispy skirts.

"It's a soul trap," the woman said. "Very convenient for the more ruthless bargainer, though I admit it's an unusual wedding gift. Dangerous, too."

Managing to tear her gaze from the deer woman, Alice glanced back to the table full of gifts.

"I thought it was a pocket watch," she breathed, eyes wide as she took a step back.

"Just don't open it with the face towards you, and you'll be fine," she said with a shrug. "Technically, you need to open it and recite someone's true name to trap them inside, but it's better to be safe than sorry."

"Yeah... yeah," Alice said slowly, taking another very purposeful step away from the table. If that watch was only *one* of the gifts, who knew what other dangerous items were sitting here within reach.

"So... I hear you're the seventh of a seventh. Impressive." The woman shoved the not-watch to the side, quickly changing the subject. Alice wasn't oblivious to the awkward transition, but she chose to let it be. It was better to *not* talk about objects that slowly destroyed souls, probably.

"Can't be that impressive if I ain't earned it," Alice grumbled, slipping back into her natural accent without thinking. She clapped a hand over her mouth, embarrassed that she'd slipped back into her normal voice without thinking.

The woman laughed, showing wickedly pointed incisors not unlike a vampire's fangs.

"Oh, I like you. We'll get along just fine," she said, nodding approvingly. "I'm Willow. I'm the king's cousin."

"What do you think of him?" Alice asked slowly, careful to enunciate her words.

"Don't worry about hiding your accent around me. I don't give a damn," Willow said with a snort. "It doesn't change who you are."

"Yeah, I know," Alice said bitterly. "Plenty'a people come through town just to call us dumb hillbillies and leave."

"That isn't what I meant." Willow placed her hand gently on Alice's shoulder. "But anyways, what do I think of the king?"

"Yeah. I mean, he's..." Alice trailed off.

She didn't know what he was. She didn't know him. She knew her heart beat faster around him, she knew that he wanted to keep her safe, and she knew that they were soulmates on a level that seemed almost impossible to comprehend.

However, she wasn't sure she knew Xavier as a person.

That was probably silly, though. They'd only known each other a day, and that wasn't enough time to brush him off entirely. Surely things would work out. They were soulmates, after all.

"He's okay, I guess," Willow said, nose scrunching as she shook her head. "Sorry... got a little lightheaded, there. I've known him since we were kids, but it's like my memories are all scrambled."

"Are you okay?"

"I'm fine," she said, waving Alice off. "My father says it's from the fall off the horse I took when we first got here, but that was so long ago that I think he's grasping at straws."

"I know more about animal biology than humans," Alice admitted. "Sorry."

"You like animals?"

"I'm an animal speaker," she said with a shy smile, reaching up to pet the possum still clinging to her. Her shoulder was getting a little sore from the weight, but she wasn't about to give up the company of a friend. The possum hissed in a way that sounded a little like a laugh.

"Really?!" The way that Willow's eyes lit up made Alice smile even brighter. "I've always wanted to be able to do that! It feels so silly being a half-shifter and not able to talk to animals like full shifters can in their nonhuman forms."

"Half-shifter?" Alice squinted, shaking her head. "I didn't know there were half-shifters."

"It's a colloquial term for anyone who can't quite shift to a full animal or full human form. I'm luckier than most, if I'm honest. I can make it to a centaur form," Willow said sheepishly. "I have a fox friend who keeps her ears, tail, and claws even in the most human form she can get to."

"That's..." Alice trailed off for a minute, mouth hanging open.

"I know, it's weird. It used to be rare, but with more humans marrying in, it's becoming more common."

"It's so *amazing*, though!" Alice practically squealed.

"It's... what?" Willow blinked owlishly, bright green eyes wide.

"Just think about how your bones an' muscles have to shift to make that happen!" she said excitedly, clasping her hands together. "Not to mention heightened animal senses, a whole new center of balance, extra limbs, and you just change back and forth like it's *easy!*"

"I've... never really thought of it that way, honestly," she said slowly, one hand coming up to gently touch her crystalline antlers. "Thanks."

"I'm just glad it didn't freak ya out," Alice muttered, wrapping her arms around her torso a little self-consciously.

Out of the corner of her eye, Alice caught a glimpse of Xavier standing from his throne. He was tall to begin with, but on top of the dais, he towered over everything and everyone in the room. She turned towards her new husband, flashing him a bright smile. He returned it with a small grin, a nod of the head, and a beckoning motion.

He wanted her to come to him. That was enough time apart for the evening, apparently.

"Looks like somebody's calling for you," Willow said, nodding towards the pair of thrones at the far end of the room. "And that's my cue to go. It was good to meet you."

"You, too," Alice said, flashing a tiny smile. Maybe there was a chance for her to find friends here, after all, if there were more people like Willow.

5

IN WHICH ALICE MEETS A PRINCE

Sleeping next to Xavier was a little like sleeping next to a statue.

It wasn't just the cold. It was also that his entire body seemed to be made of rock-hard muscle. Even the parts where a normal person should have fat deposits of some kind were just... solid. It was a little unnatural, the polar opposite of everything that Alice knew about human and animal forms alike.

She thought for a moment that she should ask Ellie if this was an Other trait that went across the board. Ellie would at least know from her own experiences.

... And then she wondered if she'd ever see Ellie again.

Alice didn't sleep much that night, and not just because she was in an unfamiliar place sleeping next to someone who felt rather stiff. Xavier tried once more to entice her into sex after their return to their room, but Alice felt... almost a little nauseated thinking about it. She couldn't figure out exactly what was wrong or why she felt so uneasy around a man who was clearly affectionate towards her, but...

Stay alert, the bird had said. Alice didn't know the fae, but she knew animals. Birds didn't like to lie.

It might be best to do a little more investigating before she lost herself in married life... no matter how badly she wanted to embrace the idea of a royal marriage.

At least she wasn't entirely alone. Xavier was cold, but Missy's warm, furry little form stayed firmly tucked next to her all night. Possums were largely nocturnal creatures, but Missy hadn't moved, staying by Alice's side while she slept. It was possible that the little animal had decided to adjust her schedule to match a more human one, but she had yet to confirm.

"Does that animal really need to accompany you everywhere?"

"Like I said, Missy goes where I go," Alice said, shrugging. The possum let out a huff of agreement from where she sat on Alice's bare shoulder.

She was wearing fae style clothing again, this time with shoes that matched. Instead of her old, short, leather boots, she wore knee-height, soft-soled shoes of smooth suede. They laced up her leg and fit like a glove, leaving her feeling like she was almost walking barefoot through the gardens.

Her dress was blue today, long and flowing, designed with a halter neckline and an open back that made her feel incredibly exposed. The fabric was beautiful and soft, and the sun was warm on her back, but she thought it might still take a while to get used to the looser style of fae clothing. As she walked through the gardens, Alice jumped every time leaves brushed the freckled skin of her upper arms, used to looking for poison ivy, spider webs, or other hanging hazards in the woods.

The palace gardens were very much not the woods, though, and could hardly be described as hazardous.. Rather than familiar pine and birch trees, the walled space just outside the palace had a few large oaks and crepe myrtle trees, bushes growing six feet tall and laden with out of season flowers, and green ivy vines snaking up the outer walls, the coverage so thick that Alice couldn't see the stone at some places. There were even fruit-bearing plants dotted here and there, though Alice didn't recognize the fruits. They looked a little like mountain blackberries, but perhaps the magic around had changed them.

It was a beautiful space, but... she couldn't help but notice that the few animals in sight seemed to veer away from them. Just when she'd catch sight of a bird or a squirrel, it seemed to look at her, look at Xavier, and immediately bolt in the opposite direction. A garden so laden with

fruit and flowers would normally be an incredible attraction for animals. Instead, they seemed to be giving Alice and Xavier a wide berth.

"You are welcome to enjoy the gardens a little longer, if you'd like, but do not leave the walls," Xavier said as they rounded a corner taking them back towards the place. "I shall see you for our midday meal."

"Why can't I leave?" Alice asked, nose wrinkling. "And where are you goin'?"

"You know as well as I do that there are dangers in the woods. Between here and your home, plenty of Others, spirits, and creatures make their residence. Best to stay where it's safe," Xavier said, gently patting her head.

"Where ya off to?" she pressed. "I could come with you."

"I assure you that it will be very boring business," Xavier said with a chuckle. "I will return soon, my treasure."

"But—"

"Soon. Just enjoy your rest," he insisted, bending down to kiss her forehead.

And then he was off without giving Alice another chance to protest. If he was going to do political business, shouldn't she go with him? Even in the human world, queens went to political meetings, but maybe it was different for the fae?

Oh, well. At least she had a lush, entirely out of season and out of habitat garden to enjoy. Mountain flowers that bloomed in spring and ones that bloomed in late summer were right beside each other, and though it fascinated her to a degree, she missed the presence of chirping birds and rustling mice. The silence made her feel lonely.

Sighing, Alice plopped down on a patch of soft grass under one of the large oak trees. If she was stuck here for a while, she might as well find a shady place to sit and observe the garden. None of the animals had come out from hiding, even now that Xavier was gone. There wasn't a bird or rabbit in sight, and that was highly disappointing.

There was a possum, though, and she looked around curiously from Alice's shoulder.

"Should'a asked if you were okay with me callin' ya Missy," Alice said, embarrassed. "Sorry 'bout that."

"I like it. I've never had a name in a human language before."

"What's your possum name?"

Missy made a noise that sounded something like a hiss, a scream, and a sneeze all together.

"Not sure I can pronounce that one too well," Alice said, smiling as she reached up to pet Missy.

"It's okay. Even some possums struggle with it."

"Where are all the other animals?" Alice asked as she gently ran her hands through Missy's fur.

"Oh, they'll come back in a few minutes. They'll make sure he's gone first, though."

Alice jumped at the sound of a voice in the garden. It was coming from the far side of the space, away from the palace doors, and it sounded... strangely familiar.

Turning towards the sound, she saw a tall figure languidly walking towards them, his posture relaxed and motions as fluid as water. He had crystal stag antlers, dark skin, and pale, pale eyes, and Alice had to look again to make sure of what she was seeing.

It was... Xavier?

"You..." Alice blinked, looking back towards the palace doors, in the direction the king had gone not long ago.

The man in front of her smiled softly.

There was no way Xavier could have gotten all the way to the other side of the gardens without her noticing. It was physically impossible, unless he'd somehow gained an ability to shadow travel that she hadn't been aware of before. Also, this man was... softer. She couldn't exactly put her finger on it, but his posture wasn't quite as stiff as usual, and the smile on his face crinkled the corners of his eyes in a way that she'd never quite seen it do for Xavier.

What was more, the animals that bolted from the garden when Xavier walked through now peeked out from their hidey holes, sniffing and gradually approaching the tall man in front of her.

"You must be Lady Alice," he said with a slight bow. "I've heard a great deal about you."

"Are you... Xavier's twin...?" Alice asked slowly, squinting. They looked so alike it was uncanny.

The man in front of her shrugged.

"Most find it difficult to tell us apart," he said.

Alice tilted her head slightly as she looked the man up and down. Yes, they had the same glass-and-crystal antlers that seemed to catch the sunlight and hold it in shape. They had the same dark skin, the same eerie white irises, the same muscular build, but...

"It ain't all that hard," Alice murmured. "You're..." she trailed off, unsure how to articulate it.

He was softer. Where Xavier was all hard edges and cool calm, this man looked a little flustered, had a slight sheepish slump to his stance. He seemed more alive, more fluid, less like a statue than Xavier did. And, rather than scattering to their hidey holes, the animals slowly came out of their hiding places to sniff at him. Even Missy looked curious, shifting slightly around Alice's shoulders so she could get a better look.

A daring squirrel was the first to come close, tilting its head to sniff at him in a way that Alice had only ever seen animals act around herself. The squirrel calmed down, chittering at his feet, while a couple of raccoons came out from the trees to join him, moving slowly and looking a bit bleary-eyed. It investigated for a moment, seemed to deem him acceptable, and then moved back towards the shade, looking very much like it wanted to sleep after a night of activity.

"They like you better'n him," she mumbled, reaching out to pat one of the raccoons on the head as it settled in. The animal snuffled at her for a moment, then took a deep breath and yawned.

"Florian," he said softly. "I'm Florian."

The thought occurred to her that he must be a prince. If his brother was king, he was also royalty. However, every bit that his brother was cool and composed, calculating and distant, he seemed... something else.

"Nice to meet'cha," Alice said, giving a small wave. She trusted the animals, trusted their instincts even more than her own, and if they felt comfortable around Florian, she assumed it was safe enough for her to relax just a little.

"Where... are you from? I've never seen you here, and you look..." he trailed off, as though trying to figure out if it would be offensive to tell her.

"Human?" Alice offered.

"Indeed," he said, nodding. The sun caught his crystalline antlers as he did, and they flashed in the morning light.

"Other side'a the mountains," she said, but then frowned. "Why? You think I talk like I'm stupid, too?"

"Did someone say that?"

"Not... in so many words," she mumbled, unable to keep the bitterness out of her tone.

"It's like him to judge someone by an accent," Florian scoffed.

"'S'okay," Alice said with a shrug. "Ya get used to it." Missy crawled from her shoulder into her lap and turned over for belly rubs, chittering pleasantly.

"*Well? Introduce me!*" Missy insisted, nudging at Alice with her nose.

"This is Missy," Alice said, smiling. "She wanted to be introduced."

"It's very nice to meet you, Missy," Florian said with a small smile, holding out his hand so the possum could sniff it.

"*He passes,*" she said, giving a hissing sound that did not seem like approval at all to anyone who didn't know possums. "*He's pretty, too. Prettier than sour face back there, even if they have the same face.*"

"She says you pass," Alice said, laughing. She tried her best to ignore the rest of Missy's commentary, but it was a little difficult... especially when the possum was very, very right.

"You like animals, then?" Florian asked, walking a little closer. He took a seat beside her on the soft grass, letting Missy tentatively sniff at his fingertips. She didn't move to rub her head against his hand for pets, but she seemed to find nothing wrong with the smell, remaining calm and relaxed in Alice's lap.

"They're better'n a lotta people," Alice said with a smile. "Some people are okay, too, though."

"They are certainly worthy of respect," Florian said, nodding politely at the raccoon she'd previously petted. If Alice didn't know better, she could have sworn the raccoon bowed back. "They know this world well, and they live in harmony with it."

"Yeah," Alice agreed, smiling. "They're smart little boogers."

Florian gave a laugh that was half a snort. "That's one way of putting it for sure."

Alice glared, tensing and on the defensive. "You makin' fun of me?"

"Never," Florian insisted, shaking his head. "I find your speech refreshing."

"... I'm choosin' to believe you for now," she mumbled, still skeptical, and crossed her arms over her chest.

As she moved, the skin around the shallow cut on her forearm pulled painfully, and she winced. The wound didn't reopen, but it was enough to draw Florian's attention. Leaning in a little closer, he peered at Alice's arm, frowning.

"You're hurt?"

"Oh, it's okay. It's just from the weddin' yesterday. It'll heal soon," she fumbled, brushing him off. He was close enough that she could really get a good look at his face now, and... it was confusing how he could be so different from his twin. Even small changes in posture and expression made Alice's entire impression of him change.

And... she liked the impression. So far, at least.

"Why did you cut yourself for—" and then he paused, eyes going wide. "Xavier made you take *blood vows*?" he whispered, voice laced with abject horror.

"He... he didn't *make* me—" Alice stuttered, half defensive and half embarrassed.

"But he didn't tell you the truth of them."

"The truth?" she frowned, opening her mouth to ask for more information, but a call from across the garden cut her off.

"My Lady? Are you here?" A feminine voice echoed off the stone walls. Alice cursed under her breath, recognizing the voice of the speech tutor Xavier had assigned to her.

"Alice," Florian said slowly, "I know that you do not know me, and that you have no reason to trust me. Please, I'm begging you: do not consummate your marriage. Not under blood vows."

"Why?!" she hissed, reaching out for his hand, but Florian pulled away at the last second.

"Lady Alice?" the voice called again.

"I'm comin'!" she yelled back, turning towards the palace momentarily. She needed to get more information from Florian before—

But when Alice turned back to where he had been sitting, he was gone. It was almost like he'd disappeared entirely, if it wasn't for the crushed grass where he'd been sitting beside her.

An eerie chill ran down her spine, and Alice carefully traced her fingers across the cut from her wedding vows. Florian might not know everything. He might not be able to be trusted. Xavier loved her, he wanted her, he wouldn't do anything to hurt her...

Though, it couldn't be a bad idea to look for more information when she had the chance.

———— ✦ ————

Xavier paced in circles around his bedroom, muttering to himself.

Three days, and she still wouldn't sleep with him.

Why, he wondered? This body wasn't unattractive by human standards. It was certainly attractive by fae standards, based on reactions of the other fae around him. Surely Alice found him lovely to look on.

Perhaps he needed to show her more attention? But he was a little afraid of stifling her. Humans didn't seem to like that, and Alice was just human enough to apply that logic.

He could try showering her with gifts, he supposed. That always seemed to work when he was trying to seduce someone in the past. Alice was... different, though. She was a bit of an enigma, and he wasn't certain that his usual strategies would work on her as they had worked on others.

Xavier knew, above all, that Alice wanted to be wanted. More than that, she wanted to be needed. However, he couldn't risk giving her too many responsibilities. It might compromise his hold on the Shadow Court, and that was the last thing he wanted.

The gaps in his memory were becoming more frequent. He was still able to maintain control, but there was more of a chance than ever that he might slip, and there was no telling what would happen if—

Xavier groaned in pain, raising his hand to his chest as it felt like a wave of fire burned through his blood. His natural affinity was for the cold and dark, which typically fit the Shadow Fae well, but some of them had magic that *balanced* shadows rather than controlled them. Light casters were uncommon among Shadow Fae, but not at all unheard of.

A pity he had to deal with this one. It was a particularly painful nuisance to have to shove away magic so different than his own. Not only did the moment steal his breath away when the pain came, it made it very obvious that something was wrong. The last thing that Xavier needed was for anyone to learn what he was struggling against.

Especially Alice.

"You get back in your place," he said through gritted teeth, mentally pushing away the overwhelming wave of fire and scorching sunlight.

The fire pressed back, but Xavier's magic crashed into it in a cold wave, smothering the flames and clouding the bright sun. He breathed slowly, carefully, waiting for the burning sensation in his chest to recede.

He wasn't sure how much longer he could hold his control. At this rate, it might be a couple of days at most before there was an *incident*. It would be best to cement the bond before then, and then he could finally be done with all this business, in full control of himself and his court.

He *needed* her. The power she possessed was a lifeline, even if she seemed dense. No matter, though. Alice wanted someone to love her so badly that it should be a simple matter to get her to willingly come to his bed and complete the ceremony. He'd spent centuries perfecting the art of speech, the ins and outs of bargaining, the subtle ways of working his way into a person's heart and mind.

Alice wasn't even thirty years old, and the few interactions they'd had made it clear that she was desperate for attention, desperate to matter to someone. A little more wining and dining, and she would be putty in his hands. Xavier was sure of it.

This would be *easy*.

IN WHICH ALICE QUESTIONS HERSELF

Ellie Sader was at her wit's end.

She wasn't keen on anyone leaving the wards at this moment, but they had no other choice when it came to tracking down Alice. Though Ellie knew better than most that there was no blanket good or evil description for all Others, that fae who rode off with Alice left her with an awful feeling in the pit of her stomach.

At first, rather than anyone leaving their protected area, Ellie had asked the forest spirits if they'd seen anything. There were a few that responded, but all they had was a general direction. Unfortunately, that wasn't enough to make any . After almost a week without any progress locating Alice, Ellie thought it was time for a change in course.

Sitting at the kitchen table, pencil in hand and map unfurled in front of her, Ellie marked a dotted line from her home on Howard's Knob up to the last place any spirit had indicated they saw Alice. She could trace them just past the state line, up into Virginia, but not any farther. After that, any trace of them just seemed to *vanish*.

Ellie was no stranger to magic. Having grown up in a witch community, she knew a laundry list of tricks and traps that any magic user, witch or Other alike, could use to disguise their presence, but the search area was just too broad. Ellie fiddled with her long,

silver, braided hair nervously, pouring over the map for the thousandth time.

As she puzzled over possible solutions, a few other members of their community entered the house. Kaz, her partner, and Miriam were first.

Kaz stopped to bend down and place a soft kiss on Ellie's lips, and she managed a small smile for him. She was stressed, but he always helped to keep her as levelheaded as possible, even in terrible situations. They'd met last year while conducting a murder investigation, and had been inseparable ever since.

"How's it going?" Kaz asked, peeking at the map.

"Not good," she groaned.

Kaz took a seat beside her at the table, scooting his chair close to hers so he could put his arm around her. Ellie leaned her head on his shoulder as Hartley walked through the front door, looking frazzled. Rosemary, Ellie's young hellhound companion, sniffed at him long enough to say hello before she ran over to Ellie, jumping up on her lap. A little over a year old now, she was getting a bit big to be a lapdog, but Ellie didn't mind.

"Well, looks like we're in... high spirits?" Hartley sighed, shutting the door behind them.

"Okay, folks, this kitchen is officially a war room," Ellie said, sitting up straight and smacking her hands on the table.

"A war room with... lemonade?" Kaz asked, staring at the cups and pitcher on the kitchen counter, where Miriam was serving herself a glass.

"War rooms might get more done if they had more lemonade," Miriam said with a shrug. "It can't hurt."

"Who are we goin' to war with, exactly?" Harper asked, yawning so widely that her fangs showed as she stumbled down the stairs to the living area. Her house hadn't been finished, so she had a bedroom on the second floor of Ellie and Kaz's house. Though it was well past 2PM, she still had on a nightgown with a robe tied over it, sleep mask pushed up to her forehead.

"Slept late, I take it?" Kaz asked, raising an eyebrow.

"On the contrary. It's past my bedtime," she mumbled, making a beeline for the lemonade. "I wouldn't even be up if Granny hadn't enchanted the windows to filter the sun for me. Too bright out here."

"Where *is* Granny?" Ellie asked, nose wrinkling. "Ain't seen her all morning."

"I think she's stress gardening," Miriam sighed. "Can't say I blame her."

Rosemary whimpered from her place on Ellie's lap. Older hellhounds and Other canines could speak human languages through something like telepathy, but Rosemary was young and still getting used to telepathic speech. Most of her communication still came in barks and sniffs.

"I managed to get a little information on the Shadow Fae," Hartley said. "One of my contacts was familiar with them, and thankfully answered his phone. Arthur can be difficult to reach."

"What did he say?" Kaz asked, taking a seat and wrapping his arm around Ellie's shoulders.

"And did it involve kidnapping brides?" Ellie grumbled.

"He's never heard of anyone named Xavier," he said, sighing. "According to Arthur, the last king he knew of was named Graithen, and his son was named Florian."

"Any chance he decided to abdicate?" Miriam asked.

"There's no way to say for sure, unfortunately," Hartley mumbled. "Florian was apparently known for being a little rowdy, more interested in the outdoors and combat training than politics, but he wasn't a bad candidate for the throne."

"So where is he now, then?" Kaz mused, running a hand through his snowy hair.

"And where did Xavier come from?" Miriam continued. She took a long drink of her lemonade, and then sighed. "All good questions, but somehow I doubt we'll get answers any time soon."

"So you're sayin' we got no choice but to wait?" Ellie asked, resting her head in her hands.

She felt like crying. In the last year, Alice had gone from an absolute nuisance to something like a younger sister, someone she felt responsible for protecting and mentoring. She'd always been a little naïve

and girlish, but never quite this reckless. Ellie wasn't one to tell another person how to live their life, but in this case, she wondered if she should have.

"I could have stopped her," she mumbled, squeezing her eyes shut for a moment. Kaz placed a warm, reassuring hand on her shoulder.

"We all could have. Maybe we should have," he admitted. "It's her life, though. If she wanted to go, holding her back would have just made things worse."

"She's always been stubborn," Ellie groused. "Probably would have just gone outta spite if we told her not to."

"At least she knows she can come back," Miriam said gently. "We didn't kick her out. She knows."

Ellie wasn't convinced, but it was the only bright spot they had right now, and there weren't many other options besides grabbing onto it with both hands.

"I hope she does," she finally said. "God, I hope so."

On the fifth day in the Shadow Court, Alice was finally starting to get bored.

She probably shouldn't have been bored. She certainly wouldn't have been bored if she had been allowed to do much more than go to the library or the palace gardens, constantly escorted by Xavier. If he couldn't be around, someone would supervise her in those areas until he returned, or she could spend time in their shared bedroom.

Alone.

It was *awful*.

Growing up with five older sisters meant that there was always noise in the Little house. There was always cooking, always someone walking around upstairs, always someone looking for the hairbrush or the sewing scissors. Even after moving to Howard's Knob, it was normal to wake up to the sounds of Granny cooking, Ellie making herbal brews, or Kaz stomping around. She was used to that. She *wasn't* used to this kind of silence. It unnerved her.

She supposed someone like Hartley could manage in this place just fine. Anyone content to bury themselves in books probably wouldn't mind being confined to three spaces. Alice, on the other hand, was not much of a reader. She preferred to be outside, learning from animals and the land rather than books.

The thought briefly crossed her mind that this was a fundamental personality difference between herself and Hartley, but she pushed that thought to the side. She was married now, and married to...

Well...

Alice tried to conjure up an image of Xavier in her mind, but she found that every time she tried, it wasn't *really* Xavier. It was, instead, Xavier how she wanted him to be. He was softer, smiled more, looked at her more like...

Florian, she realized.

Cheeks going red despite the fact that she and Missy were alone in the bedroom, Alice stared at the dark floorboards in front of her, thoughts wandering towards the prince once more. She sat in the chair in front of the large wooden desk, having spent most of the morning staring out the window, noting the both mundane and infrequent comings and goings of castle staff.

She hadn't seen Florian in the last two days, despite checking the garden multiple times, and she'd been too shy to ask Xavier about him. Though it was a little odd they hadn't been introduced right away, Alice didn't mind so much. Xavier probably had an explanation for that... as he always did.

Was it terrible that she felt she knew more about Florian in those twenty minutes they spent together than she knew about Xavier across several days?

Alice snapped out of her thoughts as the door opened. Missy huffed from her position on Alice's lap, clearly in no mood to move. Xavier entered the room only a moment later, a small smile on his face that still didn't quite seem to reach his eyes.

"Hello, treasure," he said quietly, crossing the room to place a kiss on her forehead. "How have you been?"

"Okay," Alice lied, forcing a smile. She didn't want him to think she was unhappy. It might just be an excuse to get rid of her, and she did

not want to end up tossed out into the mountains alone, especially not knowing where she was.

"I have a treat for you tomorrow," he said, taking a seat on the edge of the bed. Missy perked up a little at that, pink nose twitching.

"Really?" Alice's spirits lifted just a little at that. He'd been thinking of her!

"You'll begin etiquette, speech, and diplomacy lessons tomorrow morning in the library," Xavier said. "I've found a tutor."

Alice's spirits immediately dropped again.

"... Oh," she said carefully. Xavier chuckled, reaching over to take her hand in his chilly, larger one.

"I know it isn't the most thrilling, but it will certainly help your transition into life as a queen," he said gently, reaching up with his free hand to brush a bright red curl out of her face.

"Okay," Alice conceded. "Yeah. I mean, yes. It should help."

Xavier smiled at that. "I apologize that I can't teach you myself, but I find that my days have been much busier of late."

"It's alright. I can guess you and your brother have a lot to do," Alice said, shrugging it off.

Xavier, on the other hand, froze in place. He blinked owlishly, a strange expression for him, and there was a long, awkward pause before he finally spoke.

"Brother...?" Xavier asked, brow furrowing as he pulled his hands away. "I have no brother."

Alice blinked.

For a moment, she entirely second guessed herself. Maybe she'd dreamed up that meeting in the garden. Maybe she just remembered it wrong. Maybe it was Xavier there the whole time.

"But... he was... he looked just like you," she said, shaking her head.

"Alice, my treasure, are you certain you didn't imagine it? Or dream it? The stress of acclimating to a new home can take its toll on the mind, especially in a place with so much wild magic afoot."

That was true. There was enough magic running rampant around the Shadow Court that it could have been anything, even a trick of the

light. He seemed so *real*, though. And she knew she hadn't imagined the animals reacting to his presence.

... Right?

"I... Maybe," she mumbled. "I thought I talked to him."

"There is no one like that in this palace, I can promise you. Perhaps we need to make sure you're drinking enough water if you're wandering the grounds all day. The heat could be getting to you."

They were high in the mountains, even higher than Alice was used to. It wasn't hot, and the heat wasn't getting to her, even in the height of summer. If anything, the constant chill was driving her insane.

Maybe that's why she'd imagined someone with such a warm presence...

But, obviously, asking about Florian was going absolutely nowhere.

"What's a mirror?" Alice asked suddenly, changing the subject.

"As... as in a looking glass? One that you use while dressing every morning?" Xavier raised an eyebrow, gesturing towards the large reflective panel on the wall by the wardrobe.

Alice huffed, shaking her head. She was starting to wonder if he really, genuinely thought she was stupid, and had to force herself to stomp out the angry fire rising in her chest.

"One'a the guests said somethin' about a mirror *soul*. Back at the wedding?"

"Ah, I see," he said, nodding. "I thought you were aware."

She was not. Obviously.

... And, in theory, he should have known that from the wedding, when she expressed confusion in front of one of the courtiers. Had he forgotten?

"You and I have a special bond, Alice," Xavier said slowly. As he spoke, he turned his arm over to show the looping, ornate scar pattern that matched the one on her forearm. "These marks are a reflection of our souls on our skin. It's a rarity to find someone with a mark matching yours— a rarity to have a mark at all. We are unique. *Lucky*."

"I... thought it was just a scar," she mumbled, glancing down at her forearm.

"It's far more than that. It's an indication that you and I were made for each other. We fit perfectly together, on every imaginable level of compatibility."

She looked back and forth between their scar-like marks, searching for any differences, but she couldn't find any. They were exactly the same, down to the smallest detail, but... something didn't sit right in the back of Alice's mind. Something felt a little strange, a little off. If they were already destined to be together, a perfect match in every way, then why...

"Why the blood vows?" she asked, looking straight into his ghostly eyes. "If we're already matched or fated or mirrored, why do we need those?"

"The blood vows double our power, treasure. They give us a special bond that goes beyond our verbal promises and down to our very minds, our bones, our souls," he crooned, running his fingers gently through her hair.

"So it's for power," Alice said distastefully, trying not to frown.

"It's for deepening our connection," Xavier countered, bending to kiss her lips. "We can talk through all the elements of it later, but it will allow us to have an understanding on a soul-deep level that isn't possible through any other combination of bonds. Mirrors and blood bonded *together*."

"... Okay," she whispered, nodding.

"We'll need to complete the blood vows soon, though," Xavier said, standing. He pulled her up from the chair and drew her towards him, pressing their bodies together. Missy jumped off her lap in the process, moving to settle on the bed instead.

"I— is there a time limit?" Alice stuttered. She wasn't quite sure what to do with her hands, so she wound up placing them on Xavier's shoulders, looking up into his eyes.

"Well, no," he admitted, "but is it very wrong for me to want to hold my wife?"

Something in her chest jumped at that, at the smirk on his face as he spoke. Heat rushed to her cheeks and a wave of lightheadedness washed over her as Xavier bent his head, moving in for a kiss. Even though she still felt a little conflicted over the strange progression of events

since arriving at the Shadow Court, Alice didn't have it in her to deny him the kiss.

He made her feel wanted, and that had been her greatest desire for a long, long time.

But as Xavier's lips met hers, as she felt the strange wash of heat and cold run through her, Alice wondered if it was still her desire. She wondered what she would do once that desire was fulfilled. Was having Xavier enough? Was his cold touch the thing that made her heart race?

Was he really the person she wanted to spend her forever with?

"I'll see you later, treasure," Xavier murmured as he broke the kiss. Only a moment later, he was on his way out the door, leaving Alice alone with Missy once more.

"Do you think he knows I can understand everything he says and does?" Missy asked.

"Probably not." Alice sighed, sitting down on the bed beside her friend. "I think he assumes you're stupid... like me," she muttered bitterly.

Missy hissed angrily.

"You are not!" she snapped. "Neither am I."

"Thanks," Alice said, a small laugh escaping her.

She flopped over on the bed and curled up into a little ball. Missy paced in circles around the mattress as the silence seemed to grow more and more stifling around them.

There was something wrong. It had only been a few days, but it was getting harder and harder to deny it. Alice wanted love. She wanted this for herself, a life away from people who made her feel worthless and small...

But the more she thought about it, the more she realized she felt more worthless here than she ever had in the witch village. And for the last year, when she'd moved away to Howard's Knob... no one had ever made her feel worthless once. She'd simply wanted more than she had, and she let that blind her to so many of the good things.

What she wouldn't do for Granny's cooking... but now she didn't know of a way to get back. Instead, for the first time, she'd have to deal with her problems all by herself.

"Missy," Alice whispered. "Am I crazy? Am I seeing things that ain't there?"

"No, not crazy," the possum squeaked, "But I think he's hiding something."

"... What do we do?" she asked, hugging Missy close. The possum nuzzled her cheek comfortingly, thinking for a long moment.

"We gotta find Florian again," she finally said. "And then... we go from there."

IN WHICH MISSY LOCATES A FRIEND

Etiquette lessons were exactly as boring and torturous as they sounded, it turned out.

The instructor was named Lila, a Shadow Fae with dark purple hair and ghostly pale skin. She was fine. A little strict, perhaps, but no one had threatened to go and get a switch from the tree out back yet, so as far as Alice was concerned, things were going well. Missy wasn't with her, having been shooed off early in the lesson, but she was close by. Every now and then, Alice could hear her friend skittering around the back shelves.

She'd never enjoyed school as a child, and she'd been a mediocre student when it came to book learning. In fact, she'd snuck away from the local schoolhouse more often than not, spending her time outdoors, learning from the animals that wanted to speak to her. It took her longer than an average child to learn to read and write, and her mother insisted she was slow.

Alice had other skills as a child, though. She could pick out a bear's trail through the woods without a second thought, knew which berries were tasty or poisonous before any of the other children, and knew how to walk the woods and stay safe... Which was more than some adults could say.

"Thank you for having me," Alice said slowly, careful to articulate her words as clearly as possible, to

show as little of her accent as possible. She glanced at Lila, hoping for approval, and she gave a small nod towards her.

"Much better. Remember to put space between your words. Don't let them slide together."

Lila had not taken kindly to the idea of *fixinto* as a part of Alice's vocabulary, among other things. However, now that they'd made some progress, perhaps it was an opportune moment to ask about her other project.

"Lila," Alice began hesitantly, "do you know of anyone named Florian in the palace?"

"Florian?" Lila paused, frowning. She blinked rapidly, her mouth opening and closing like a fish for a moment, before she finally squeezed her eyes shut and shook her head.

"Lila?" Alice put a hand on the woman's shoulder, trying to see what was wrong, but she just couldn't tell. Maybe Ellie could have done something, if she were here, but Alice was resigned to simply waiting.

Only a moment later, Lila took a deep breath and opened her eyes, standing up straight.

"Forgive me, I was seized by a terrible headache," she muttered, blinking. "No, I can't say I know... what was it?"

"Don't worry 'bout it," Alice said, brushing her off.

Lila's eyes narrowed. "Proper pronunciation, please. We will not end our lesson on... whatever *that* was."

"No need to worry," Alice said through gritted teeth. She was almost positive she looked like someone about to go on a warpath.

"Now smile," Lila pressed.

Alice grimaced. Apparently, that was enough to count.

"Excellent. You may go," Lila said with a nod. "I release you from lessons for today."

Alice stood from the study table in the library so quickly that she almost knocked the chair over. Lila glared, but she didn't verbally complain.

The Shadow Court library could possibly be described as peaceful. Stone and crystal walls stretched three stories high, with railings around the upper two floors full of bookshelves. Long, dark, sheer drapes covered high windows, muffling some of the sunlight trying to sneak

through. The bookshelves seemed to be made of the same dark wood as the furniture in Alice's bedroom, and they were packed to the brim.

The Shadow Court library could also be described as very, very creepy. In order to find any of the tomes, you had to carry a lantern down the rows between the stacks so you could see the titles. Only one librarian worked in the room, sitting at a desk by the main doors, silent as the shadows playing along the cold stone walls. Somewhere in the darkness, Missy was skittering around, but Alice found chasing the shuffling noises very unpleasant. She didn't have vision suited for darkness like her possum friend, and instead she found herself whispering into corners as she searched for Missy.

There was no response anywhere she looked, and after about fifteen minutes, Alice was getting a little flustered.

"Missy?" she hissed, leaning around the end of the bookshelf. "Where are ya?"

"Are you alright?" A masculine voice echoed through the empty library.

Alice practically jumped out of her skin, yelping as she turned around to see a familiar figure. At first, she thought it was her husband, but it only took a moment for her to realize that it was not.

"Florian!" Alice cried, slumping in relief. "What in the world are ya doin' here?"

"I enjoy reading?" he offered, raising an eyebrow.

He was wearing the same thing Xavier had been, which was a little odd, but perhaps it was something twins did even when they grew older. Either that, or it was just a common way to dress, though... it did seem a little strange that they'd both choose to wear a dark blue shirt with silver embroidery on the same day.

"*I found him!*" a little voice squeaked in her mind, and a fluffy body suddenly emerged from the shadows beyond the bookshelves.

"Missy!" Alice sighed in relief, holding out her arms so her friend could jump up and perch on her shoulders. At this rate, there would be little possum claw holes in the shoulders of all her dresses, and she couldn't say she minded one bit. "You scared me."

"Sorry, but I was on a mission."

"Oh, you were?" she teased, gently tapping Missy's pink nose. "How did that go?"

"Good. I found him," Missy said proudly.

"It's good to see you," Alice said, smiling as she turned to Florian. "Was startin' to think ya disappeared."

"No need to worry," he said with a shrug, but his words brought back memories of the horrifying etiquette lesson, and Alice frowned without thinking about it.

"What's wrong?" Florian asked, stepping a little closer.

"Nothin'," Alice mumbled. "Just... never mind."

"Maybe... I can cheer you up," Florian said, reaching out towards Alice. He didn't grab for her, but he offered his hand, and after only a moment of hesitation, she accepted.

His touch was like pure sunshine.

There was something about being near Florian that made her less wary of the shadows around her. Even in the Shadow Court, he felt like a bright spot. It was strange how similar he was to Xavier in appearance, considering how incredibly different they were in personality.

He guided her through the shelves, barely missing hitting the corners of them with his crystalline stag antlers. Alice had to jog to keep up, but she felt a smile come to her face even as she gasped for breath. After three more turns, he slid to a stop in front of one of the backmost bookshelves, hand hovering over the spines of the books for a moment before he pulled a green one from the shelf.

"Try this," he said, handing it to Alice.

It was heavier than she expected, and she nearly dropped it, but steadied herself quickly. The title was written on the cover in flaking, gilded letters: Tales of the Woods.

"Is this... a kid's book?" Alice asked as she opened the book, looking down the table of contents. It did, in fact, look to be some kind of fairy tale book, though she didn't recognize the names of any of the stories.

"If you think fairy tales are only for children, you might want to look at them again," Florian said gently. Somehow he managed to make his point without ruffling Alice's feathers, which she had to give him credit for.

"Well, let's find a place to read, then," Alice said, tucking the book under her arm.

Florian and Alice sat on the floor at the very back of the library, shoulder to shoulder with their backs resting against the wall. Missy had moved from her usual perch on Alice's shoulder to sit by Florian instead, and the prince absentmindedly patted her scruffy fur as they thumbed through the fairy tale book.

They'd managed to find a spot near one of the high windows, tucking aside the dark, sheer curtain enough to let a ray of light come through. It was much easier to see the text when they weren't squinting through the shadows, and Alice wondered momentarily if all the Shadow Court members had the same nocturnal vision that Missy did.

Since Alice couldn't read the old fae language, they'd transitioned from flipping through the book together to Florian reading aloud, whispering old Shadow Court tales into her ear, and some from outside the Shadow Court, too. It was interesting how some of them seemed to parallel human fairy tales. The symbolism was different, but many of the moral lessons seemed to be the same.

A wave of sleepiness washed over her, and Alice had the urge to lean her head against Florian's shoulder. He made her feel safe, even though she'd only known him a short time.

Was this how it was supposed to feel when you were falling for someone, she wondered? Was this the kind of head rush she wanted, the kind that didn't make her want to scream and fight back, but fall into his arms?

"The seer cut her arm, allowing three drops of blood to fall into the silver cup, and told the man to drink."

That made her wake up.

"Blood vows?" Alice asked, leaning forward and suddenly very awake. "Is this... real?"

"It's a storybook, but the concept is real, yes," Florian said. "It says that the first of three vows leaves a mark on the skin, making sure the

man never forgot his promise to the seer, or the consequences if it was not fulfilled."

"What happens in the end?" she asked, looking back and forth from the indecipherable text to Florian's face.

"It... she... The man breaks his promise," Florian said, stumbling. "So she takes her revenge by using the vow to transfer all his remaining years to herself."

Shit.

Alice's chest went tight, her heart rate quickening. Beside Florian, Missy made a distressed squeaking noise and scrambled back over to her usual shoulder perch. Xavier said their wedding vows would tie them together... but those were very different from the promise in the fairy tale. The protagonist failed to fulfill his promise, so there were consequences. The only promise they'd made was...

To each other?

Alice glanced at Florian nervously. What would happen, she wondered, if her tiny, niggling infatuation became any stronger? What would happen if she failed Xavier in that way?

She didn't want to think about it. There were too many other things to worry about at the moment, too many layers to this awful situation, and she had no one to blame but herself.

"The beginning of the blood vow leaves a mark..." she murmured, hugging her knees to her chest. "I thought he said that mark was because we're mirrors."

"Alice..." Florian said softly. "I..." but he trailed off helplessly.

"What?"

"If... If you ever want to leave here," he said slowly, keeping his voice low, "I will help you. I cannot break the blood vows, but I can get you away from the Shadow Court."

"Can *you* leave?"

"I'm afraid not." Florian shook his head sadly. "It would be a little pointless for me to do so."

"Then I guess you're stuck with me a little longer," she muttered, closing the book in her lap. "I think you're the closest thing to a friend I've got here, and I'm not leavin' ya high and dry and... forgotten."

Florian opened his mouth, but he promptly shut it again, gaze fixed on the floor. He wanted to say something. It was easy enough to see that in his eyes. He just... *couldn't* for some reason. Not wouldn't, but couldn't.

"Why doesn't anybody remember you?" Alice asked softly, reaching for his hand and twining their fingers together. He didn't pull away, but he didn't immediately speak, either.

"I... wish I could tell you more," Florian sighed. "The best I can do is point you in the right direction."

"You can tell me about blood vows... but not about you?" Alice raised an eyebrow, leaning in a little closer.

"I have a... specific set of restrictions," he muttered.

"What—"

"Alice," Florian said, placing his hands on her shoulders. "I have to go now, but remember what I said to you before. If you want to leave, I'll help you."

"Why are you runnin' off—" she tried again, but Florian just stood up, already starting to walk away from the spot they'd been sitting for the last hour or more. Everything had been fine only a moment earlier, but now there was a sudden sense of urgency in his tone, a sense of panic in his gaze.

"The magical history section is that way," Florian said, pointing. "Make sure you put them back right where you found them when you're finished."

"Why? And how am I supposed to read those?"

It was a fair question, but apparently not one he had time to answer.

"It... would be best to be discreet," he mumbled. "I'm sorry- I have to go now, but I'll see you soon."

Florian practically ran from the room, disappearing around the corner with all haste. A moment later, she heard the doors to the library close in the distance, signaling his exit.

That settled it.

Firstly: Florian was real. She hadn't been imagining it, and it wasn't a trick of the light.

Secondly: something was very, very wrong.

8 IN WHICH MISSY FINDS A LATCH

Rather than wait on Xavier to pick her up after her lesson, Alice snuck past the silent librarian and out the doors, deciding to find her own way back to their room. She took a few wrong turns, but did manage to make it back to the room.

The palace seemed oddly empty. Despite the fact that there had been a crowd at their wedding, no one was around now. She wondered if there was a town outside the castle walls where the courtiers and other Shadow Fae lived, but if such a thing existed, she wasn't certain she'd ever get to see it.

At least... not if she kept listening to Xavier.

Once in the bedroom, she decided to search for anything that might give her more information, anything that might tell her something about Florian. Alice didn't know if there was a separate office that Xavier kept for palace work, but there had to be a desk in the room for a reason. It was probably best to start there, and then she could move to searching the wardrobes, under the bed, and looking around the walls for hidden compartments.

That last one might have been a stretch, she thought, but it couldn't hurt to check every possibility.

The secretary-style desk was practically empty, with only a blank notebook, some pens, and a few documents in the fae language.

Alice traced her fingers over the top of the desk, pulled out all the drawers, and found nothing.

"Look under the bottom. I see a latch," Missy said, staring up at the underside of the desk from her position on the floor.

Alice reached under the bottom of the desk, moving her hand until she found a small indention in the wood. When she pulled the right way, something clicked under the desk, and a small compartment opened.

Perhaps checking for hidden drawers wasn't a stretch, after all.

Leaning forward, she hesitantly reached inside until her fingers found two objects. The first was a leatherbound book with deckled edge pages, the cover water-stained and worn from use. Alice flipped it open to look inside, but almost immediately cursed under her breath.

Whatever it was, it wasn't written in English. There were markings at the top of each entry that looked like numbers, possibly indicating days and years, so she assumed it was a journal. However, that was all she could intuit. Even the characters looked strange and otherworldly, like the fae writing had in the library earlier. Alice wasn't one to learn languages quickly, and she wasn't sure how it might translate, so she simply shut the book for the time being. It had to be important if it was hidden... she just didn't know why.

The second object in the drawer was, at least, something she'd seen before. As she reached into the back of the compartment, Alice's fingers touched something cool, round, and metal. She wrapped her hand around the palm-sized object and pulled it towards her, surprised to see the silver pocket watch from the wedding gift table.

"Soul trap watch...?" she muttered, glancing at Missy.

"Looks the same to me," the possum confirmed. "Let's not open it to find out, please."

"Good plan," Alice said, staring down at the silver watch.

Why would Xavier choose to store this in his desk? And why hide it? If it had been a wedding gift, wasn't it something that should be in the treasury?

... Did the Shadow Court *have* a treasury, she wondered?

In any case, this watch had been specifically picked out from the rest of the gifts. Xavier had chosen to keep it close, within easy reach, but hidden. He hadn't once mentioned it to her, either, and Alice did not like

the pressing feeling in the pit of her stomach when she thought about that. She didn't understand why it was here, but this was *dangerous*. Shouldn't he at least have told her about it if he was keeping it in their shared room?

That was when the doorknob started to turn.

Acting on instinct and adrenaline, Alice shoved the journal back into the compartment under the desk exactly as she found it, slamming the hidden drawer shut. As the door started to open, she realized that the silver watch was still sitting on her lap, not quite in plain view, but it was too late to put it back into the drawer. Instead, she shoved it into her dress pocket.

"Looking for something?" Xavier asked as he stepped through the threshold. It was all Alice could do not to flinch, though she felt her heart rate increase.

"I can't read most'a the books in the library. Thought there might be somethin' to help translate in here," she said with a smile. It was the best excuse she could come up with on short notice.

"You can always bring it to me, and I'll translate for you," Xavier offered.

"Aw, that'll take a whole lotta time, though," Alice said, pouting. "I know you're busy."

"Not too busy for you," he said, moving closer to her. He bent down to place a chilly kiss on her forehead, slipping his hand under her chin so she was forced to look up at him. "What has my lovely wife been up to? Did your lessons go well?"

"They went fine," Alice mumbled, glancing away.

"What's on your mind, treasure?"

"Nothing," she sighed, shaking her head. It wasn't like she could ask him why he had a death watch hidden in his desk.

"Now, now," Xavier said. "Talk to me."

Alice gasped as he scooped her up from the chair, moving them both over to the bed. He sat with his back against the headboard, settling her on his lap. It was comfortable, but also not comfortable. She'd wanted someone to hold her like this for far too long, and a part of her just wanted to relax and enjoy the embrace. It didn't matter if he was cold. It didn't matter what he did.

Just as long as someone loved her, she would be okay.

For a moment, Alice let her head relax against his chest, wondering what it would be like if she stopped questioning quite as much and let him take control. They could have a chance at a good life together, she thought. They'd be bound forever, able to know each other more fully and deeply than anyone ever imagined possible.

... But was that what she really wanted?

The longer she stayed in the Shadow Court, the more Alice wasn't sure she really understood what love was at all. She didn't know what she wanted, didn't know how to give what someone else wanted, didn't know what to do except what was expected of her. And, more than anything, she wondered if she'd ever see the people she left behind again.

"Why did you bargain with my momma for me?" Alice asked hesitantly. "If we're already mirrors or soulmates or somethin', why bother with more?"

"I've told you the reason for the blood vows already. Was that explanation insufficient?" he asked, brow furrowing.

Alice did not think of herself as stupid. However, she wondered if playing dumb might be an advantage in this situation. Xavier clearly thought, at the very least, that she couldn't speak correctly. She wondered if she might be able to get some useful information out of him if she leaned into that.

"I don't know..." Alice said softly, reaching out to hold Missy as the possum jumped up into her lap. "I just don't get it, I guess."

Adjusting her weight on his lap, Xavier sighed and seemed to think for a long moment before he spoke.

"She wanted someone to take her pain away," he said, brow furrowing. "She lost your sister, lost your father, and lost *herself* in grief so dark and deep that she couldn't care for you. I saw the opportunity to help her and secure my connection to you, so I took it."

Alice narrowed her eyes.

Help might have been a strong word. Based on what her older sisters remembered, their mother had entirely changed after the birth of Alice and her stillborn twin. She'd been softer, more forgiving. Everyone assumed that coming out of that deep well of grief had changed her, but...

What if that wasn't the entire story?

"Trust me, my treasure– I only made that bargain to ensure an easy road towards what was already destined to happen," Xavier insisted. His tone was even and calm, but Alice was starting to realize that it was *always* like that.

"An easy road?" She raised an eyebrow, hoping for more information.

"I did not want to fight another man for you if it could be avoided," he said simply.

"F–for *me*?" Alice stuttered, heat rising to her cheeks despite her reservations.

"I was not about to let the other half of my very soul slip away," Xavier murmured, picking up Alice's left hand in his own. He placed a soft kiss over her wedding ring and pulled her closer. Missy squeaked in protest, jumping out from between them as Xavier shifted his hold.

He gently pressed his lips against hers, kissing her slowly, his hands tracing along her waist. Alice sighed into the kiss without thinking about it, leaning into the touch. It was strange being this close to someone, and it felt nice, but it also felt like something was missing. Something was underwhelming where it shouldn't be.

His tongue slipped into her mouth, and Alice pulled away, embarrassed. Not deterred, Xavier shifted to pressing kisses against her neck, down her collarbone, over the swell of her small breasts. His grip shifted to her hips, pulling her towards him.

"I– I don't know if–" Alice stuttered, hovering somewhere between responsive and pulling away.

"Relax, treasure," he murmured against her skin. "This will feel good."

It... did feel good. Maybe.

Did it feel good?

His lips were soft, but they were also cold. His hands running down her arms sent chills down her spine, heat building low in her belly and breasts growing heavy and tight as he stroked them over her nightgown.

Something felt *wrong*, though. Alice was well aware of what happened between husbands and wives, even aware enough to know that

her body wanted him like she thought a body should. The sight of his muscular frame nearly made her swoon. He was objectively handsome, devastatingly so, but...

But he wasn't...

"N—no," she croaked, voice barely audible.

This wasn't right. This wasn't supposed to be happening, not with him. It didn't matter how her body reacted. Her mind and her heart were terrified.

"No, stop. *Stop*!" Alice cried, pushing Xavier back with all her strength. He fell back against the headboard, eyes going wide as she scrambled away from him, shocked and panting. She stood on shaking legs and stared, unsure what to think.

No, she was only thinking one thing: He wasn't Florian.

She didn't want Xavier. She wanted... Florian.

Missy hissed from her position on the floor, backing towards Alice as Xavier looked on, mouth opening and closing like a codfish.

She scooped up the possum and bolted for the door before she consciously made the decision to do so, sprinting into the hallway and away from the bedroom as quickly as she could.

All she had wanted was to be loved, to be wanted, to have the life that she'd envied all this time. Now, she was married to a man that she didn't want to touch her, trapped in a Fae Court she couldn't get away from, and running to nowhere in particular just to gather her thoughts. Not to mention, she was very quickly developing an overwhelming attraction to her new husband's twin brother, who no one seemed to remember existed.

This was an incredible disaster.

———————— ◆ ————————

Xavier stared at the open doorway, wondering where the *fuck* his bride had decided to run.

No matter. He controlled every inch of this court, every inch of these grounds. There was no way Alice would be able to leave without him knowing, and as long as she didn't leave the grounds, he would find her. She would come wandering back to him, eventually.

She was absorbing the magic from the land and the Shadow Fae nicely. He could feel it building inside her, a well of power deeper than anything he'd ever hoped to tap into, but until their blood vows were consummated, he wouldn't be able to access it. Alice was too slow and dense to be able to utilize that power herself, he'd realized. She wouldn't know how to channel raw magical energy into the shape it needed to be, and thus he needed to be able to access it for himself.

He was so, so close. One more step and their magics would combine, one more step and he could take what he needed from her.

Icy rage bloomed in his chest as Xavier pulled himself to his feet. He hadn't counted on her being quite as afraid as she was. Yes, she was starry-eyed and desperate for love, but she clearly required more *coddling* than he'd expected. It wasn't as though he lacked time, but he had aimed to perform his spell on the eve of the full moon, when the muted silver glow signaled completion.

It would signal the completion of a decades old bargain that still trapped him halfway between one form and the next. It would signal the completion of centuries of planning. And, ultimately, it would signal the completion of his rise to power.

He had three weeks left before the full moon. She'd damn well better submit before then.

9 IN WHICH VINES CLIMB WALLS

Alice didn't really know where she was running. She passed only one person in the hallway, a maid carrying a stack of linens who seemed a little surprised when she ran past, but otherwise there was no one. She held Missy close to her chest, only slowing her pace when she was forced to lean against a wall and catch her breath.

"*Let me down,*" Missy chirped, wiggling a little in Alice's arms. "*That was a nice ride, but I can run.*"

"Sorry," Alice gasped, loosening her grip so her friend could jump down. "I didn't wanna leave ya back there."

"*Good. You're stuck with me,*" Missy said firmly, even as she trotted a little farther down the hallway. "*Did you mean to run to the gardens?*"

She certainly had *not* meant to run anywhere specific.

Squinting into the shadows down the hallway, Alice could see a familiar wooden door. A large tree had been painted in silver on the wood, and though there was no window, she knew it led outside. Xavier had led her through that door several times in the last week since she arrived.

Hell, had it only been a week?

She counted the days on her fingers as she followed Missy down to the garden door, but she kept

coming up with a total of seven. It seemed so much longer than that, and so much shorter at the same time. How had she managed to run from everything she'd ever known, marry a king, and develop a strange emotional attachment to his possibly nonexistent twin brother *in a week*?

Ellie always said she was too reckless. Now, Alice was starting to believe her friend was right. As a child, her mother had always controlled what she did, where she went, and who she associated with. She could barely get away with trying to play with other children from their witch community without questioning. Every step had to have a purpose, every movement had to be justified, or else she was wasting valuable time and resources that could be better used on her sisters.

The freedom that came with moving to Howard's Knob was glorious, but it was also unprecedented. Over the last year, Alice had become bolder, wilder, letting herself wander the woods and make decisions that she never could have made under her mother's roof. She'd gone to school, met new people, even allowed herself to flirt with some of the human boys in town... even if none of it had gone anywhere.

And, finally, she'd allowed herself to really fall for someone... or so she thought.

The longer she was at the Shadow Court, the more she realized that falling for Hartley had been less of a true emotional journey and more of a calculated decision. A careful decision. She'd picked someone who was kind and boring and safe, all the things she knew would help her survive.

Alice wasn't happy with just surviving any more. If anything, the rejection from Hartley had made her want to live, to truly experience the world... but what had gotten herself into because of that split second decision? She'd let her anger get the better of her, let herself be seduced by the promise of someone offering her more, just like Granny and Ellie warned her about, and now she was stuck in deep, deep trouble.

In any case, it was too late to back out now. She was stuck in the Shadow Court... but maybe not forever.

"Missy," she whispered. "I think it's time to try escaping."

"What did you have in mind?" Missy asked, skittering back over.

"Let's go outside," she said, pushing against the garden door.

The gardens might be one of the most obvious places to look for her, but there were also many places to hide among the foliage. Even better, right outside the high stone walls were the Appalachian woods that Alice knew well. If she could find a spot sheltered enough from view to climb her way over, she could make a run for it.

She crept towards the back of the garden, trying to stay out of view of the main palace windows. It wasn't hard to make her way to the back wall, but it took a minute or two to find a spot that looked like it was feasible to climb. The walls were perhaps fifteen feet high and made of stone, with very few cracks or indents that could be used as climbing holds. The massive oak trees might make a good starting spot, but they seemed almost strategically placed *just* too far from the walls to be useful.

Luckily, there were a few places where thick, strong vines seemed to crawl up the wall, their very roots latching onto the stone. Alice thought the vines might be their best bet at a climbing aid. They seemed healthy and green, decently sturdy, and pale blue flowers bloomed at intervals among the large, teardrop shaped leaves.

It was worth a shot.

"Up and over," Alice said, glancing towards Missy. "Can you do the climb, or do you want me to carry you?"

"I can make it. Let me go first," Missy said. She took off towards the wall without another word, jumping onto the vines and using them to scramble up the stone. Possums were natural climbers, not to mention quite agile, and Missy made the climb seem easy.

Once she reached the top, Missy perched at the edge for a moment, surveying the other side.

"I can see the woods out here. It's a drop, but we can make it."

Good enough.

Alice was glad that fae clothing involved wearing leggings under long skirts with slits for mobility. It meant she could still climb.

Hands at the top of the wall, Alice raised her leg to swing over the side—

And crashed against what felt like an invisible rubber barrier.

It was all she could do not to scream as the impact pushed her backwards, making her lose her hold on the wall. She grabbed for more of the vines, but they broke off in her hands as she slid down the wall,

scrabbling at the uneven stone. All sense of balance abandoned her as Alice spiraled to the ground, dropping almost fifteen feet in a free fall.

The last thing she consciously remembered thinking was that someone had put very, very strong wards around the garden walls, and presumably around the whole castle. Wards were usually meant to keep intruders out, but in this case, they were keeping Alice in.

Her back hit the ground, her head followed, and her vision faded to black.

Alice didn't know how long it took to wake up from her fall— it could have been seconds or hours— but she certainly knew she didn't want to try that stunt again.

"Ow," Alice groaned, not bothering to move or open her eyes.

"Alice? Thank god— what happened to you?! Did you put your nose in a Sibella flower?"

Wrenching her eyes open, she found herself looking up at a figure who first made her gasp and flinch away. Dark skin swam in front of her eyes, and she automatically tried to move away. Her body wouldn't quite comply, the world spinning and shaking around her as she tried to get up and failed.

"Alice! Calm down, it's *me*," he said, brow furrowing.

That was when she finally managed to register that the man standing above her wasn't Xavier. It was Florian.

Taking deep breaths, Alice allowed herself to collapse to the ground again, all the fight draining out of her. She wasn't interested in running from Florian right now, though she didn't truly feel like talking to anyone, either. All she really wanted was to sleep... but judging by the state of her head and everything Ellie said about concussions, sleeping was a bad idea right now.

It had been afternoon when she ran from Xavier, and it wasn't night just yet. The sun was starting to set, but the sky wasn't entirely dark, the lights and shadows playing off the garden foliage in a way that might have been beautiful... if she wasn't incredibly sick to her stomach.

"A... what now?" Alice asked, voice dry and cracking. Her throat hurt. Everything hurt. With great difficulty, she managed to push herself into a sitting position, the world still spinning around her. She experimentally flexed her fingers and toes, glad to find that all her limbs moved as they were meant to, but when she pressed her hand to the throbbing spot on her head, her fingers came away stained with blood.

"Those," he said, gesturing to the flowering vines she'd been using to scale the wall. "That's a Sibella blossom. Breathing the pollen will put you to sleep almost instantly."

"Great," Alice deadpanned, coughing. Her chest felt like it wanted to collapse in on itself after that fall. "Could use a nap... Where's Missy?"

"*Here*," came a squeak, just as a wet nose nudged her cheek. She sighed in relief, glad her friend was okay. Apparently, whatever enchantment was on the walls hadn't affected her, but it had certainly stopped Alice from climbing over.

"If you didn't fall asleep from a Sibella flower, what *were* you doing?" Florian asked, kneeling to get a better look at her.

"Tryin' to get out," she mumbled. "Wasn't exactly asleep."

"I told you I'd help with that— you're *bleeding*!" he cried. "What happened to you?"

"Keep your voice down!" she hissed. "I don't want people to *know* I'm tryin' to escape. Somethin' weird knocked me off the wall when I was at the top."

"I'm more concerned about your head wound than my volume," Florian scoffed, his hands hovering awkwardly around her, like he wasn't quite sure where to put them or what to do next. "I didn't know he'd enchanted the walls, but I can't say I'm surprised."

"It was sort of a last-minute decision," Alice muttered, rubbing her back where she'd hit the ground. The impact certainly would have left bruises.

"You seem to make those rather often," Florian said, tilting his head as he looked between Alice and the garden wall.

Unfortunately, he had a point.

Last-minute decisions got her into this place. Last-minute decisions were probably not going to be the solution to getting out.

"Shit," she whispered, resting her head in her hands. "Shit, shit, *fuck*."

"Alice," Florian said gently.

"I don't know what to do," she admitted, voice breaking as hot tears sprang to her eyes. Nausea roiled in her stomach and bile rose faster than she could control it. Barely managing to move in time, Alice turned and retched over the back of the bench, upturning her last meal on the garden grass.

Florian paced anxiously back and forth as she fetched, taking a step towards her, then a step back, then moving in a circle. When she had finally emptied her stomach, she spit onto the grass and drew in a shuddering breath, shoulders slumping. She was in too much pain and too dizzy to even be embarrassed at the moment.

"You need to go back inside," Florian said with a sigh. "You might have a concussion from that fall, and you need treatment."

"What? No! I'm not spendin' the night in that room," Alice snapped, looking up so quickly that the garden started to spin again. "Ain't no way, no how."

"What happened?" he asked, biting his lip as he gazed into her eyes. "You can talk to me."

Slowly, haltingly, Alice managed to stumble through the barest explanation of what had happened. She did not tell him the conflict she felt between her heart and her body. She certainly did not mention that she'd been wondering what it would be like to be with him instead, to have him hold her, to hear what he had to say about marriage...

Instead, she stuck to the basics. Xavier kissed her. She was afraid. She panicked. She ran.

"I'm sorry," Florian whispered. "I'm so sorry."

"What if he tries again?" Alice murmured.

"I... think that may be unlikely," he said slowly. "The consummation of the blood vows has to be willing for it to take, and he wants you to complete those vows. He won't hurt you."

"But *you* don't want me to finish the blood vows," she said carefully, eyes narrowing.

"I don't," Florian agreed. "I'm not entirely sure what he's planning, but I don't think it's good. I don't know if you understand how much power you have, and the blood vows—"

"What good is it if I can't use it?!" Alice snapped. "All y'all creeping around here like you know things I don't, so why won't anybody just tell me the truth for a change, huh?"

Florian was silent for a long moment.

That might have been a harsh judgement, but Alice was tired of being lied to. She was tired of feeling as though her life wasn't her own. There were things that Florian couldn't talk about, and she knew that, but this was a breaking point.

"Will you let me go find someone to treat you, at least?" Florian finally asked.

At that moment, it dawned on her what felt so strange about this interaction with Florian. He wasn't the same as he had been in the library— kind and concerned, yes, but he was distant. He kept reaching towards her and stopped just short, his hands hanging in midair, and now he wouldn't even reach out to check her head wound.

"You won't touch me," she observed, looking at the short space between them.

"Do you want me to?" Florian asked, brow furrowing.

Alice thought for a long moment.

She wanted to know if his skin was still warmer than Xavier's was. She wanted to hold his hand and give it a squeeze as if they were two children hiding from their parents in the tall grass, not adults seeking comfort in the night. She wanted to lean her head on his shoulder just enough to feel his voice reverberate through his chest when he spoke.

But right now, all she could think about was Xavier's hands. All she could think about was how that touch felt, wonder if it was how it was supposed to feel, wonder if Florian would feel different—

That wasn't the point here, though. The point was that Florian was acting strange, and she needed to find out why. However, in that moment, Alice couldn't separate her emotions from the logic of wanting to know what was happening. She just wanted to rest. She wanted her head to stop pounding.

"... No," she finally whispered, gaze dropping to the ground. "Not right now. I can't... I can't *think* right now."

"So you just... decided it was time to go climbing over walls?" Florian asked, eyebrows raised.

Not exactly, but she wasn't sure who to trust. Every instinct cried that she should tell him the truth, but Alice wasn't ready for that. She didn't want to talk about what had just happened to her, and she certainly didn't want to tell anyone that she regretted her marriage. What kind of person made decisions like that?

A wash of shame crept over her.

Someone unwise made those decisions, someone immature, someone who wanted love and freedom so badly that it burned and bubbled underneath her skin. She had only herself to blame for this circumstance, and now that her escape plan had utterly failed, she didn't know what to do.

"I just... had to do something. I couldn't stay there," Alice lied.

"I can understand," he said with a sigh. "Now, I'll ask again: Will you let me find a healer for you?"

"Yes," she said quietly, brushing her wild tangle of red-orange hair out of her face. There wasn't really another option at this point, considering he seemed to have an aversion to touching her. On another day, she might have been offended by that.

"Good," Florian said, reaching out towards her again, as if by instinct, but he stopped just short and sighed, backing away.

He *wanted* to touch her, Alice realized.

Why wouldn't he?

"Hey... before ya go," Alice began, speaking slowly so her words wouldn't slide together like the green leafy garden surroundings blurred in her vision. "If you're twins, then... how did ya pick who's king?"

"You choose *now* to ask?"

"Yeah," she said, shrugging. "Nothin' better to do." In truth, she'd been wondering for a while how Xavier was chosen as a ruler over his brother, how Florian had been forgotten... but she wasn't sure what he could speak about.

Florian laughed, but there was a bitter undertone to it. "It was my role, originally."

"And now ya hide in libraries and gardens?"

"I... gave it up," he admitted. "Foolishly. Irresponsibly."

Well, at least she wasn't the only one with a history of unwise decisions.

"There's a compartment behind the bench over there," Florian said, gesturing to a bench against one of the main walls of the castle. "It'll have a cloak that should keep you warm. Use that until I come back."

"How do you know that?" Alice muttered, looking over at the stone. She wasn't sure if it was the head trauma, the shadows, or the craftsmanship of the hidden door, but the wall looked like plain stone to her from this distance.

"It's mine," he said, smirking. "I made the compartment to hold a few things for when I'd climb out the window and sneak out of the grounds in the first days of the Appearances. I wanted to explore the world."

"Ah-ha, so you can't say a word about me wantin' to stay out here," she said, pouting.

"They are very different reasons, little rabbit, and I didn't have a head wound when I went exploring," he said with a soft, humorless laugh. "I'll be back soon. Try to stay awake for me?"

"Don't bring Xavier," Alice said, pushing herself to her feet. She had to hold a low-hanging tree branch for balance, but she managed to stay standing.

"I wouldn't," Florian said gravely. "Stay awake. I'll get help soon."

10 IN WHICH WILLOW RETURNS

Alice really, truly tried not to fall asleep. However, the tree roots seemed more and more comfortable the longer she lay there. Missy did her best to help, chattering in her possum squeaks and hisses to help keep her awake.

Her head *throbbed*. It didn't seem to be actively bleeding anymore, but it certainly didn't feel good. The only head injury she'd ever had in her life was from fallin]]]g out of a tree as a child, and it hadn't felt like this. This felt like there was something reverberating inside her skull that wouldn't stop, like it rattled her very thoughts the longer it sat.

Despite Missy's best efforts, Alice's eyes had already fluttered closed by the time she heard footsteps. It felt like a battle just to turn her head and look, and she sincerely hoped it wasn't Xavier there to retrieve her. It could have also been the palace guards, she supposed, but there weren't too many of them, and she'd hoped it might take them a while to get around to searching the grounds. The inside of the place was enough to scout through.

Luckily, it wasn't either of those.

A delicate woman with dark skin and white freckles like stars softly padded towards her, footsteps rustling in the tall garden grass. She was dressed in a long, dark brown robe that helped her blend into the shadows, but it was easy to recognize those freckles, as well as the beautiful, crystalline antlers extending from her head.

"Willow?" Alice murmured, squinting.

"There you are!" she cried, rushing over with wide eyes. "Have you been out here all alone?"

"Uh... yeah," Alice said drowsily. Missy squeaked indignantly. "Okay, not quite alone," she amended.

"We have to go *now*. If the guards drag you back, it'll be trouble. You have to make it look like you came back on your own," Willow insisted. "Come on, get up."

Alice groaned sleepily, tripping a little as she pulled herself to her feet. Willow immediately slipped an arm around her, giving Alice something to lean on. That was quite fortunate, considering that she absolutely would have fallen without support. It felt like Willow had taken most of her weight.

"We're taking the servants' passages. Come on, let's go," she said, gently urging Alice forward.

"Where are we goin'?" she slurred, taking careful steps along the stone garden path.

"To bandage your head," she said flatly. "That's first priority."

"Wait. *You're* the help he got?"

"Florian found me, yes," Willow said. "I... I haven't seen him in so long. It was like when we were children, and we used to play hide and seek in our Shadow forms."

"Shadow..." she murmured, but almost immediately tripped on the edge of a large stone.

"Fuck," Willow muttered, shifting her hold. "Here, get on my back and hold tight. It'll be faster this way."

Alice somewhat fell forward against Willow's body, letting the taller woman carry her piggyback out of the gardens and down the hall. For someone who looked so dainty and graceful upon first glance, Willow clearly had hidden muscle. She crept through the palace hallways, checking around corners and ducking into strange, narrow passages that ran in confusing directions to avoid being seen. Missy trailed along behind them like a silent guard, keeping pace and sticking to the shadows. Alice didn't see a single soul along the way, and that was good, but she also had no idea where they were when Willow finally opened the door to what looked like some sort of medical wing.

It was a long, narrow room with a row of narrow beds on one side. The other wall was lined with shelves packed with herbs, countertop spaces with tools for brewing potions, glass bottles filled with assorted liquids, plants that seemed to glitter strangely and had long outgrown their pots, and even a stack of— were those *bones*?

There wasn't time to ask about it. Willow gently sat Alice down on the bed, and it suddenly became obvious that everything in the room was covered in a thick layer of gray-white dust. Wherever they were, this room hadn't been used in a long while. There was one spot on the countertop that looked like it had been freshly cleaned, though, and a few herbs and bottles set out. Among them was a small, dark glass bottle with a cork. Willow snatched it up and hustled back over to the bed, uncorking it as she walked.

"Drink. Now," she urged, pressing the bottle against Alice's lips.

Alice swallowed without complaint. The concoction was bitter and chalky in a way that made her cough, but it wasn't the worst she'd ever had. There was only enough in the bottle for two small swallows, but Willow looked satisfied as Alice handed the empty vial back to her.

Almost immediately, the pounding in her head lessened. The places where her body was bruised from the fall felt a little warmer, a little less sensitive, and the nausea in her stomach eased. She took a slow, careful breath, and was delighted to see that the room didn't spin in circles from the oxygen rush, that her hands weren't shaking as badly as before.

She felt a drop at the corner of her mouth and reached up to wipe it away, surprised to see a sparkling, green-tinted liquid residue on the back of her hand.

While the medicine took effect, Willow was already on her feet again, heating water in a cast iron kettle over a small gas burner that looked a bit out of place in the Shadow Fae palace— a bit too human, a bit too modern. However, when she dipped a cloth in the warm water and used it to dab at the crusty, clotted blood sticking to Alice's hair and skin, Alice thought that gas burner was in the perfect place after all.

"What was in that?" Alice asked, already feeling like the world had started to stabilize around her. She flexed her fingers slowly, blinking

as she looked around the room. In less than a minute, things had stopped spinning. It was like—

No, it was not *like* magic. It *was* magic.

Alice had plenty of magical experience, but she'd never known something this effective. It felt like her shattered thoughts had dropped back into place, like she could think properly again, and all just from one little bottle.

"Something special my mother taught me to brew up for emergencies," Willow explained, gently dabbing at Alice's wound with the cloth.

"It... sparkled?" Alice blinked, looking at the spot where the drop had spilled on her hand. A small smile crossed Willow's face as she gently tapped at her own antlers.

"Dust," she said. "You don't want to take pieces from your antlers often, obviously, but if you can get your hands on sheds, it's like a concentrated shot of magic. That's why it took me so long to get to you— I had to brew it."

Alice wasn't sure if she should be nauseated by the idea that she'd just downed powdered fae antlers, but in the end, she didn't care. The biology of magic growing like crystals fascinated her beyond belief, but right now wasn't the time to ask. Instead, she reached over and threw her arms around Willow's neck.

"Thank you," she murmured.

Willow stiffened for a moment, but then returned the hug. "That doesn't mean you're totally healed, you know. I still need to bandage you," she said with a sigh.

"I already feel twenty times better than before. That's some miracle dust," she said as she let go. The nausea was entirely gone by then, and she felt truly lucid for the first time since waking up from her fall.

"Don't mention it," Willow said, continuing to gently clean away the blood with her warm, damp cloth. "I mean it, too. It's a family secret, and we only shed about every fifty years. I keep a little with me from my own sheds for emergencies, but... not enough to go around, if you know what I mean."

Alice nodded gravely. She could only imagine the chaos if anyone found out about it, especially humans or witches. Others might leave them alone in solidarity, but witches and Other hunters wouldn't stop until Willow's line was extinct. Humans were greedy like that, and this... this was extraordinary.

"I won't tell," she promised, drawing an X over her heart with her finger.

"I know," Willow said with a small smile.

"*I won't tell, either,*" Missy piped up, jumping up on the bed beside them. Willow smiled and patted the possum gently on her head.

"But you... you just met me," Alice muttered, brow furrowing.

"And I think I can trust you with this," she said firmly, patting Alice's shoulder. "Florian doesn't form an attachment to just anyone."

She finished her work with the cloth and stood from the bed, dumping the water down a clay sink on the far side of the countertop space. Alice felt like her cheeks were burning, and she wasn't quite sure how to stop it.

She liked Florian. More than that, she... she was very attracted to Florian. It was almost embarrassing how happy it made her feel that he'd formed an attachment to her, though they'd only met a few times. It would be nice, she thought, to see that attachment grow over time, to explore it...

But that also might mean that he'd shatter her heart, in the end.

Alice brushed off that thought as Willow walked back over with clean bandages in hand, gently wrapping the cloth around her head wound. There wouldn't be a chance for anything at all if they couldn't figure out what was wrong here. Right now, the Shadow Court couldn't even *remember* Florian.

"There," Willow said, examining her work. "I hate to tell you this, but you'll need to stay up for tonight. Or, at the very least, you'll need to accept the fact that I'll need to wake you up every hour or so to make sure you can regain consciousness."

"You're jokin' me," Alice snorted, but Willow shook her head.

"I am not. It's important." She sighed, taking a seat on the small bed beside Alice. "I'll stay with you as long as I can, but I'll need to take

off at some point. I'm not... Well, I'm not really supposed to be here." Willow winced, crossing her arms over her chest.

"You're not supposed to be... in the sick room?" she asked, brow furrowing.

"In the *palace*. Xavier kicked me out after the wedding!"

"I thought you were his cousin."

"I'm the king's cousin. The *real* one," she protested. "He was—"

"Florian," Alice whispered, grabbing Willow's hands in hers. "You remember him? You remember he exists?"

"I... I knew something was wrong. I knew everything changed so quickly, and I knew that wasn't the person I grew up with, but..."

"You, too?"

Willow nodded sadly. "It just wouldn't come back to me... till I talked to you."

"Why?" Alice shook her head, eyes narrowing.

"I don't know yet. I was working on figuring it out, and then Xavier gave me the boot," she grumbled. "It's significantly harder to investigate while trying to hide your existence."

"How did you get back in after that?" Alice asked. "I tried to leave, and the wards bounced me off like a circus trampoline!"

That was... almost an understatement, actually.

"I never left," Willow said with a mischievous smile. "I walked my shadow form outside while he watched, and hid my physical body in one of the closets."

"Shadow form..." she shook her head, red curls bouncing as she frowned. "You said that before."

"It's a... special shifter form, unique to Shadow Fae," she explained. "We're aligned with shadows because we're meant to keep the balance between darkness and light, to find the middle point between them and stay there. It's how our magic works. The old tales say it helps keep the balance among us, to make sure we know when to use darkness and when to reveal things in light."

"And you... can turn into shadows?"

"Not exactly. My consciousness can move into a form made of pure light— like a projection, if you will. An illusion," she offered. "It's

excellent for scouting, spying, and distractions, but I can't interact with anything physical. We used to play games in Shadow form as kids."

"How do we help him?" Alice asked. "Why can't anybody *remember* him?"

"I... wish I knew," Willow said helplessly. "It's got to have something to do with Xavier, I think. As much as I try, I can't... I don't remember him from our childhood. He wasn't in our lives until recently."

"You're sure?" Alice asked, brow furrowing.

"I'm sure." Willow nodded. "I know my memories are fuzzy, but I'm sure about this."

"They smell the same," Missy said. "I mean, sometimes. Sometimes Florian doesn't smell like anything. Other times they're the exact same."

"Aren't twins usually the same?"

"Not... not like this," Missy chirruped, shuffling around in a little circle on the dusty bed. "I don't know how to explain it, but I can't tell their smells apart. That's not normal, even for twins."

"So much for leaving," Alice said, sighing. "That was a stupid plan."

"I can still get you out, if you want," Willow offered. "But if you stay, you have to be careful. If Xavier finds out you're poking your nose into this, I don't think it will end well." Her eyes narrowed in concern.

"Florian says he needs me to *willingly* finish the blood vows. As long as he thinks I'm stupid and oblivious, I'm in the clear." Alice frowned, resting her head in her hands. "And... honestly, I think he'd probably just come after me if I ran."

It was true enough. He'd just chase her down again, all the way back to Howard's Knob, and there was no telling how much trouble he'd cause in his wake. Ellie's magic was strong, and their little community was a formidable force, but Alice wasn't about to ask them to fight her battles for her. Plus, there was no guarantee she'd even make it all the way back before Xavier caught her again... and then he would just be angry.

It had slowly become clear to her that, somehow, Florian was the key to why all of this was happening. He knew things that only Xavier also knew, but he couldn't speak about them. Alice couldn't leave until she figured out what was happening to Florian.

It might be the only way to shove Xavier out of her life for good.

"Don't push it, Alice," Willow snapped, tone suddenly turning harsh. "I was lucky that I got away with exile. If it wasn't for my family and my position among the Shadow nobles, he would have killed me. He's killed before."

"He... has?" Alice breathed.

"Yes," she confirmed, expression grave. "It hasn't happened often. There aren't enough of us left for it to be too often, really, but... Every now and then, Xavier makes an example of someone, and it has not been pretty."

Alice was almost afraid to ask what she meant by that. There was something cold and dark behind Xavier's beautiful features, and she knew that now, but it was another thing to know exactly how dark his heart might be.

She needed to know that, though, and damn the consequences.

This whole mess had started because she jumped in without enough information, because she hadn't taken the time to examine Xavier, to examine the bargain, to examine *herself* before making a decision. Hartley was right when he'd said she wanted the security of someone to love her, and she was so angry about it that she let it blind her to her own surroundings.

That seemed to be a track record for her, in the end. She lashed out at Ellie as a younger woman because she was angry that Ellie seemed to be the perfect little witch child. She snapped back at her sisters because she was angry that they blamed her for her mother's grief and subsequent personality shift. She helped Ellie with the investigation last year because she was angry that her mother finally broke down and hit her, drawing Alice's blood with her nails in the process. Then, most recently, she'd left her perfectly good home on Howard's Knob because she was angry that the person she'd picked as the best candidate to love her just didn't fall into her plans like he should have.

She felt like an idiot. No wonder Xavier thought she was stupid, with a record of decisions like that in her past.

No more. Never again.

Now she wanted to know everything, and she wanted to base her decisions on something better than raw, visceral anger. For that to happen, though, she needed to know the scary things.

"What happened to them?" Alice finally asked.

Willow took a long, slow breath, hands clenching at the fabric of her robes. She couldn't look Alice in the eye as she spoke, staring off into the middle space like speaking by rote.

"My father used to be second-in-command of the Shadow Court army," she said. "He's now the General. The first in command questioned Xavier's decision to lock down Shadow Court territories from inside and out, and he had him publicly executed for treason."

"Shit," Alice breathed.

"He flayed him alive with a crystal knife," Willow whispered, voice starting to shake. "Right there, on stage, in front of everyone. His blood was on the ground for weeks after, just as a reminder. No one was allowed to clean it up."

"Sweet mother of God," Alice groaned, covering her mouth with her hands to keep back the rising bile.

"That wasn't even the worst of them," Willow said, squeezing her eyes shut for a long moment.

Alice decided that she didn't want to know quite *that* much.

"How many of you are there left?" she asked.

"Ah... in this community, maybe two hundred? Three?" Willow guessed, eyes opening again. "There are many Shadow Fae settlements across your world, but we tend to keep to ourselves. That was part of why it was such a surprise when Xavier insisted on bringing you into our ranks."

"So... Wait, there are branches of the Shadow Court *actually* all over the world?" Alice asked, eyes going wide.

"We do, yes," Willow said proudly. "Our influence is quite vast, though we certainly work in the shadows, if you'll pardon the pun."

"So Xavier is... powerful as shit," she murmured, staring off into space. It wasn't just his formidable magic. It was his influence over the Fae, as well.

"To put it bluntly, yes," Willow said. "Now— I'll find you later, but I need to get back to my hiding spot before the sun rises." She stood from the bed, adjusting her dark robes around her.

"Wait—" Alice said, reaching out for her arm with one hand and into her pocket with the other. "Take this."

She pressed the silver not-watch into Willow's palm, closing her friend's fingers around it.

"The soul trap?" she murmured, eyes wide. "You took it from the table?"

"I took it from Xavier's desk."

"That is... *bad*," Willow whispered, going stock still for a moment.

"What would he use it for?" Maybe there was extra information about the watch that she didn't know or understand just yet.

"Nothing good," she scoffed, shoving the soul trap into an inside pocket of her robes.

"Yeah, okay, I figured that one out," Alice huffed.

"For now, I'll hold onto it. Do you think he'll notice it's gone?"

"I don't know, but I'm more worried about what he's plannin' on doing with it," she admitted. "As long as he thinks I'm dumb as a bunch'a rocks, he won't suspect me."

She gazed down at the floor, tracing her toes through the dust. Missy climbed up onto her lap in a way that signaled she wanted to be comforting if she could, and that felt like a blessing at the moment. Not only did Xavier doubt her intelligence, but Alice was starting to, as well. It seemed like she'd done nothing but make awful decisions since coming here.

"Hey, Alice?" Willow nudged her gently.

"Mm?"

"You're not dumb. Remember that," she said with a smile. "I'll find you soon. Go back to your room after the sun rises."

"Thanks." Alice watched as her new friend carefully slipped out of the room, shutting the door behind her.

Alice left Florian's cloak in the sick room. She could come back for it later, if she was careful and remembered the turns of the hallways, but she didn't want Xavier asking where she got it.

After returning to the bedroom, Xavier welcomed Alice with open arms. He apologized profusely for scaring her, holding her gently against his chest, peppering her face with kisses, and carefully checking the bandage wrapped around her head. He clucked over her like a mother hen, never letting her out of touching range, tucking her into bed with pillows at her back.

To Alice, it was all a bit of a blur. She could feel his hands on her, and though they didn't wander anywhere they shouldn't, she was no longer certain she wanted him close enough to touch at all. That was beside the point now, though.

She had to do this.

She had to stay here if she wanted to find out what was happening to Florian.

Alice said she'd wandered the castle until she found a spare bedroom to tuck herself into after falling down the stairs and hitting her head. He seemed to accept that as reason enough why she had dirt all over her clothes, and why she was still wearing the same dress from the night before.

"Who bandaged you?"

"I d— don't know," Alice stuttered, struggling to come up with an explanation. "I woke up like this."

Xavier raised an eyebrow, but when Alice didn't elaborate, he seemed to simply accept her story.

"Well, I suppose stranger things have happened in these walls," he muttered. "Please, I beg you, do not wander the palace without a guide again. It's very dangerous," he said gently. The honey sweet tone of his voice made Alice nauseous, but she hoped if it showed on her face, he attributed it to the head wound.

"Sorry," she managed, looking away. At the very least, she didn't have to fake the shame on her face. She shouldn't have run away, shouldn't have tried to abandon the palace...

The image of Florian's smile flashed in her mind.

Xavier gently touched the bandage on her head. "I'm glad someone was able to find you in time," he sighed. "Now, get some sleep. You need rest."

"It's morning—" Alice insisted.

"And you are injured. Come here," he said, sliding under the covers on the opposite side of the bed.

Alice's breath hitched as he pulled her towards him, wrapping his arms around her from behind in a way that likely should have felt protective. It might have felt protective only a few days earlier, she realized. With him this close to her, she could feel the slight chill of his too-cold skin, the subtle hint of his slow breath against her scalp, and she could smell—

She could *smell him*, she realized.

Oh, good lord, Missy was right. They *did* smell the same. It was almost eerie, actually. Smell was one of Alice's stronger senses, and the only one besides animal speak with any sort of supernatural enhancement, but she... Well, she simply hadn't thought to check their smells before now.

If she concentrated, she could remember the musk she'd smelled on Florian that day in the library.

Why did they smell like the same person in every way a body should smell? It was right down to the bones, the blood, the sweat— everything. It made her feel on edge in a strange way. She'd never met twins, but this was... Well, Missy was right. This was strange.

She forced herself to breathe deeply, to try to relax as Xavier curled himself around her smaller form. It was tender, she told herself. This was a soft moment. He'd been worried about her, and now that she was back, he could finally get a little sleep. If she told herself that, it might be enough to calm her racing heart and troubled mind.

But she couldn't help but think his arms around her felt more like chains.

It was getting harder and harder to ignore how strange everything felt. The panic at the back of her mind grew louder every day, and she had to fight not to make a break for it sometimes, not to just run into the woods and never look back. She had to stay, though. She couldn't leave

without figuring out the story behind all this. Xavier would just chase her down again.

So, for the time being, she would simply have to fake her affection.

Alice wasn't entirely sure she could pretend to be in love, but... maybe. Maybe if she tried, if she imagined Xavier as someone else, if she swallowed her anxiety enough to make him calm down, enough to make him lower his guard...

That might be the only chance she had.

Very carefully, she urged her tense muscles to relax. She fought the instinct to shrink away from the chill, leaning into his arms instead. For a moment, she even toyed with the idea of imagining someone else holding her... but the sunshine presence she wanted was too far removed from this shadowy chill.

So, instead of sleeping, Alice lay with her eyes closed and *planned*.

She knew a few things. Firstly, she knew that Xavier wasn't telling her the full truth of anything. Florian wasn't either, but at least Florian would admit to it. Secondly, she was fairly certain that Xavier thought she was stupid, and that was certainly something she could use to her advantage. Alice might have a heavy Southern accent and a fondness for the outdoors, but if you were a witch in Appalachia, you grew up understanding that you could live or die on your own cunning. She would have to be careful, but when push came to shove, she thought she could draw on those skills.

Unfortunately, she lacked more information than she had. There were too many gaps in her knowledge to be able to form a solid plan of action. She didn't know how Florian had gotten himself into this situation, didn't understand his relationship to Xavier, and didn't even know what her own abilities were.

She'd jumped into this situation headfirst, and now she was drowning.

Locked in Xavier's chilly embrace, listening to his even breathing behind her, Alice bit her lip so she wouldn't scream. She needed a tangible course of action, not ten thousand questions.

Firstly, she needed to find Willow again... or perhaps wait for Willow to find her. The half-shifter woman was the only sure ally she had in this place.

Secondly, she needed more information on Shadow Fae magic. That could easily be accomplished from a trip to the library, along with finding more information on her own magic. There had to be books in there about seventh daughters of seventh daughters, as massive as the place was. She just had to find them before anyone caught onto the fact that she was looking.

That last part might be tricky, and it certainly limited her time, but it might be the only chance she had.

It was time to stop waiting for someone to come and save her. This time, she was ready to take matters into her own hands.

11 IN WHICH MISSY CAUSES CHAOS

Xavier was not in the bedroom when Alice woke up. It was a relief to find herself only in the company of Missy, who was soundly asleep. Her little chest moved up and down as she breathed, tail slightly twitching now and then.

It had been three days since her escape attempt and resulting head wound, and she hadn't left the bedroom once. Xavier would bring her meals and things to entertain herself with, but she felt very closely watched, even more so than usual.

Even so, Xavier was the only person actively watching her.

She was starting to get a little suspicious that he might be the only person in the castle, after all, but the soft footsteps and occasional noises from castle staff proved otherwise. It was only that Xavier didn't let her interact with many of the other residents. Even etiquette lessons with Lila had come to a screeching halt, and he didn't seem inclined to have her resume them.

Alice put down the sketchbook that she'd already half filled with doodles and drawings. She wasn't an incredible artist, but it passed the time. There were a few books on the side table, as well, but they seemed to be a bit of a random selection. Among the titles were *Little Women, The Wonderful Wizard of Oz, The*

Jungle, and *Heart of Darkness,* along with two volumes of collected short stories.

Of the lot, only *The Wonderful Wizard of Oz* managed to hold her interest. *The Jungle* was too gruesome, *Little Women* too wordy and boring, and she'd made it about ten pages into *Heart of Darkness* before falling asleep with the book in her lap. She found herself picking up Dorothy's tale again, opening it to the bookmarked page. Missy had been enjoying hearing Alice read the tale aloud, but they could always go over the parts she missed when the little possum woke from her nap.

Dorothy and the Scarecrow had just entered a forest with some particularly irritated apple trees when the door to the room opened. Alice jumped to attention, expecting to see Xavier walking inside, though he'd only left her a few minutes ago.

However, it wasn't his crystalline antlers that peeked through the threshold, but another fae.

"Willow!" Alice gasped, dropping the book onto the bed beside her. The jolt from the drop roused Missy, who gave a toothy yawn and stretch before she scrambled up onto Alice's shoulder.

"I told you I'd be back!" she said, smiling. "Sorry it took a minute. I had to be careful."

"It's okay. Found out anything?" Alice asked, beckoning Willow over. Her friend perched on the edge of the bed, shaking her head.

"Nothing. I've looked at what I could in the library, but it's difficult to hide in there, and my Shadow form can't pick up books to read. How about you?"

"I'm under strict watch, if ya couldn't tell," Alice grumbled. "I've been tryin' to poke at him about my magic, but he won't budge. Just says I need to rest."

To be fair, he wasn't entirely wrong about that. Willow's medicine had healed the vast majority of the damage, but three days wasn't enough for the bloody wound to completely close. She had a fresh bandage on, but it still needed regular changing.

"Okay, so... Let's think about this. Besides animal speak, what else do you do?" Willow asked, tilting her head slightly in a way that was

reminiscent of Florian's mannerisms. It made sense that they'd grown up together— they had some of the same quirks.

"Um... kinda nothing," Alice admitted. "I can do basic things, but they're never as strong as my sisters or my ma, even if they do them the exact same way. Why do ya ask?"

As annoying as it was to admit that she didn't have an incredibly specialized or flashy skill set, it was just what they had to work with right now. And, the longer that Alice sat with that information, the more she was starting to realize that it... didn't really matter to her.

She liked being able to speak with animals. She had everything else she needed.

Why did it matter if she couldn't conjure fire from her hands?

"I have a theory," Willow admitted. "Though, it might be far-fetched."

"What... is it?" Alice asked hesitantly.

"I was thinking about how I started to try and remember a few things after I talked to you the first time, just bits and pieces," she said slowly, gesturing vaguely with her hands as she spoke. "I... I wonder if you're a magic eater."

Alice blinked.

"What in the name'a Sam Hill does that mean?"

"I've... heard things here and there," Willow said, biting her lip briefly as she tried to explain. "Sometimes there are people who don't do much magic because their primary ability is to *store* magic."

"... I'm sorry, Willow, I still don't get it," Alice sighed. "You're sayin' I'm a battery that can't power itself?"

"Exactly!" she said, snapping her fingers. "You absorb magic from people just by being near them. It's passive, and it's not enough to hurt, but I bet you've been doing it for years without knowing. You're storing it up in your body, just amassing it for later use."

"What damn use is that if I can't get it out?!" Alice asked. "And why would that help you remember?"

"You absorbed the layer of magic blocking my memories for long enough that I could break through," she said, smiling. "Unfortunately, I... don't know much about how you could go about accessing what you've stored."

That... actually made sense.

Not to mention that if Willow was right, it gave them an explanation for why Xavier kept everyone out of the castle and away from Alice except for the bare minimum staff. If her magic was enough to gnaw away at whatever made them forget Florian, and Xavier claimed he'd never heard of him despite spending hours upon hours in close quarters with Alice...

The only logical explanation was that Xavier was lying. He *did* remember Florian.

He just didn't want anyone *else* to remember him, for some yet unknown reason.

"Great," she muttered, groaning. "Now I gotta figure out how this works."

"You could try the library?"

"Can't do it. Nothin' in there's in English."

"You want me to translate?"

"Nah, that'll take—" but Alice cut off suddenly, standing from the bed. "Actually, yeah. Can ya take a look at this?"

She scrambled around to the back side of Xavier's desk, feeling underneath for the hidden latch. Luckily, he hadn't said a word about her poking around the desk, and he didn't seem to be aware that she'd found the compartment.

Alice slipped the leather-bound book out of the hidden drawer and handed it to Willow. The fae woman blinked at it for a moment, but she didn't question how Alice had managed to find the compartment in the first place.

"It's Xavier's journal," she explained. "Or... I guess I'm assumin' it is. I can't read it."

Willow flipped open the front cover, eyes scanning the text, but after only a moment, she frowned.

"This... isn't fae," she said, squinting at the pages. "*I* can't even read this. It looks like some kind of archaic human language."

"Shit," Alice hissed. There went her idea. She didn't even know anyone who could read ancient languages—

Wait.

Yes, she did.

"You said you know a way outta here?"

"I do. I don't think I'll be able to get past the wards again, though, so if I leave, it better be important."

"It is," Alice said, taking a long breath. "I know a few people who could probably help us out."

Willow immediately brightened at that, eyes going wide. "Why didn't you lead with that?"

"Can you get a message out to Howard's Knob?" Alice asked. "There's a professor that lives near friends'a mine. I think he could probably tell us what's in it."

At the very least, he was the best hope they had.

Hartley was the most intelligent person she knew, not to mention an incredible wealth of knowledge when it came to ancient languages of all kinds, human and Other alike. If anyone would be able to translate it for them, it would be him. She just hoped he wasn't too upset with her for how she acted before running off.

"I can handle journal delivery," Willow said firmly.

"Okay... um..." Alice fumbled, beginning to pace around the room. "Problem: We can't move the journal. He'll know something's wrong."

"Or..." Willow mused, trailing off.

"What?"

"Tell him someone stole it. We'll make the room look like it's been ransacked, like I didn't know where to look." She nodded slowly as she spoke. "He might figure out it was me, but I'll be long gone by then."

"How do I get away with not hearin' any of that?" Alice asked, eyebrows raised. "You wanna lock me in the bathroom or something?"

"No, they still would have heard you scream if someone did come in and lock you away, and I don't want to knock you unconscious..."

"Please do *not* do that," Alice sighed.

"Agreed," Missy squeaked. "There's been enough of that already."

Alice thought she'd had enough of being knocked unconscious to last her a lifetime. It had only been a couple of days since her head wound, and she didn't want another one for a myriad of reasons. Though,

admittedly, her first reason was just... not wanting Xavier to smother her so much.

"Sibella flower," Willow said suddenly. "It's a fae plant. The vines grow down in the garden."

That name sounded familiar... Alice frowned, trying to remember. Florian had said something about them before, tried to warn her away from them.

"Oh!" She snapped her fingers, finally remembering. "You wanna put me to sleep."

"I think it would be best. I'll leave a few of the flowers around the bed. You'd essentially be entirely unconscious until someone came to wake you up."

"*I... don't think I like that,*" Missy said, hissing slightly.

"Then you can be the one to go look for help," Alice said, gently patting Missy's head. "If you act scared and try to bring someone back to help me, that makes us look even more innocent."

"... Okay, I can maybe get behind this after all," the possum conceded.

"Lemme write a letter for ya to give to Ellie," Alice muttered, grabbing a piece of blank paper and a pen from the desk.

"I'll go grab the flowers while you write," Willow said. "How long do you think Xavier will be gone?"

"No tellin'," Alice muttered. "He's usually out most'a the day."

"It'll take me about an hour to brew the sleeping draught from the pollen. It's the safest way for me to control the dose," she explained. "I'll be back as soon as I can."

"You're sure this is safe?" Alice looked up from her writing briefly as Willow turned to leave, but her fae friend only smiled.

"Don't worry. I know what I'm doing," she said confidently. Alice knew that tone. It reminded her of someone she very desperately wanted to see again.

"... So when you go to Howard's Knob, I'm gonna need you to talk to my friend, Ellie," Alice said, twiddling the pen between her fingers. "I think ya'll are gonna get along like a house on fire."

"That's... good?" Willow asked hesitantly.

"Yeah, that's good." Alice couldn't help but laugh.

That Sibella flower was very, very potent.

Even hours after Xavier arrived in a panic to shake her awake, Alice was still groggy and struggling to keep her eyes open. She'd managed to get out of the room by saying she wanted to walk a little, just enough to help herself wake up, and Xavier had agreed to escort her to the castle library so she could wander the stacks.

Willow had done an excellent job absolutely trashing the bedroom. She made it truly look like someone was searching for something, down to leaving the hidden compartment in the desk open, though Alice pretended she didn't see Xavier push the drawer closed when he checked through his desk.

As she rolled her shoulders and stretched for perhaps the thousandth time, Missy scurried back over from where she'd been exploring.

"Handsome prince, incoming at twelve-o-clock," she squeaked.

Alice's heart rate sped up almost instantly, a smile coming to her lips entirely unbidden as a tall, familiar form stepped silently around the corner of the nearest bookshelf.

Florian smiled down at her, dressed simply in a white shirt with the sleeves rolled up, dark pants, and practical boots. His braids were pulled back into a ponytail, and his antlers sparkled in the few rays of sunshine that peeked through the curtained library windows.

They were in the backmost corner of the library's second floor, somewhat shielded from view. Noises certainly echoed in the quiet space, but it would be difficult to pinpoint exact conversations coming from this area. Knowing how delicate the situation was, Alice wasn't completely comfortable with speaking here, but this was as private as they were likely to get.

Time to make the best of it.

"How's the head?" Florian asked quietly, leaning in close to examine the bandage. He absolutely dwarfed her, just like Xavier, but his pale eyes didn't seem lifeless like the king's did. They were expressive, full of life in a way that made her feel almost giddy.

"It's getting better. Willow, uh..." Alice gestured vaguely above her head, and Florian nodded in understanding.

"Good. She's the best— has been since we were kids. I have to thank you, by the way," he said, stepping closer.

"I... didn't do anything?" Alice shrugged helplessly.

"You helped her remember me. That's an incredible gift."

The soft look in his eyes was almost too much to bear, and Alice found herself looking down, a little embarrassed. It didn't feel like she'd done much at all, and she certainly didn't know how she'd done it, but she couldn't deny that just seeing him happy made her feel warm inside.

Was this what it was supposed to feel like, she wondered?

With Hart, she'd wanted him happy, but the thrill had come from when he was pleased with *her*. The gestures he'd made towards her were the ones that made her feel good, not just knowing that he would be happy no matter what. It was so, so calculated, she realized. It was calculated in such a way that it wouldn't break her heart.

Florian, on the other hand, had taken her entirely by surprise.

He didn't have the same mark that Xavier did, she realized as her gaze landed on his bare forearm. He didn't have the scar that marked their blood vows, that was the symbol of their soul bond.

Alice... wasn't sure how she felt about that.

More than anything, she'd been trying not to think about Xavier's claim that they were mirror souls over the last few days. That had proved especially difficult, considering there wasn't much to do but think while she'd been stuck in the bedroom. There was something there, she thought, some kind of pull towards him, but it wasn't... quite... right.

With the half-finished blood vows in the mix, Alice wasn't even sure that she could trust her own feelings anymore. She felt a deep sense of disappointment and dread seep into her bones as she looked at the bare spot on Florian's arm where the scar should be. And then... then she noticed something else.

There might not have been a mark on his forearm, but there was one on his open palm. It wasn't an intricate mark, just a simple slash, but it was there. Alice knew what it was, too. She knew from Ellie and Kaz, from seeing the scars on their palms before and after their case was solved last year.

"Blood bargain..." she mumbled, eyes going wide.

"What was that?" Florian asked, turning towards her.

"Your hand—" she said, reaching out to grab at it, wanting to examine the scar more closely.

"W— *wait*—" he stuttered, trying to pull away, but he wasn't fast enough.

However, instead of grabbing his arm to bring it closer, Alice's hand passed through his.

Through it.

"Y—you're a *ghost*!" she gasped, jumping back on instinct with her hands over her mouth.

Wait.

He couldn't be a ghost. Alice didn't have the Sight like Ellie. She was lucky to pick up on the vague impression of a spirit nearby, much less see one clearly. Alice had never seen a spirit with as much clarity as this in her life.

Not to mention... he'd touched her before. In the library, he held her hand! He couldn't be a spirit. At least... not *all* the time?

Taking a deep breath, Alice forced herself to calm down, taking a hesitant step back towards him.

"... Not a ghost," she amended.

"Not a ghost," he repeated.

"Are ya some kinda haint? Spook?"

"I suppose that depends on what you mean by haint," he mused. "I hear that can have many meanings."

"Then where... where's your *body*?"

Florian's eyes flicked momentarily towards the castle, but the change was so fast that Alice thought she might have imagined it. Instead of responding, he sighed.

"I'm afraid *that* is something I cannot tell you."

Alice huffed, crossing her arms over her chest. She still couldn't quite get the hang of what Florian was allowed to say to her and what he seemed physically prevented from voicing. If she could just pinpoint something, anything, it might be enough to help her guess what was happening, to navigate this strange silence...

And then she remembered something.

"You're in Shadow form, aren't you?" she asked. "Willow mentioned it."

Florian *beamed*. "Clever rabbit," he said, nodding.

"I knew it!" she cried, a triumphant little thrill in her chest. "But... Why hasn't Xavier used it?" Alice shook her head frantically. Maybe he had, though? Maybe she just hadn't *seen* him use it.

"Xavier's... *essence*... does not align well with light magic," Florian said distastefully, nose wrinkling a little. "He can't use this form, not without extreme pain."

"His *essence*?" She raised an eyebrow, blinking at him.

"He is shadow aligned, more so than any Shadow Fae. Truly, I believe it would be more accurate to say he is aligned with darkness, though I would imagine you've suspected that for some time."

So, Xavier *wasn't* a Shadow Fae. Clearly that implication could slip by whatever magic kept him from speaking plainly. Maybe implications were fine, things that allowed her to put the pieces together, but no explicit details unless she'd figured them out already.

That must be it. That was the key— it wasn't about Florian's knowledge of his situation. It was about what Alice already knew and what she didn't understand yet.

"Could you talk to me about it if I already figured out what was goin' on for myself?" she asked quickly.

"*Yes*," he said without hesitation, nodding fervently.

That was progress in itself.

"If I asked if you could show me where books are on something, could you do that?"

"I can do anything not explicitly related to asking for information on my situation," he said carefully.

"Perfect," Alice said, nodding. "I need some information on seventh daughters, and maybe some Shadow Fae history, too."

"I can show you where they are, but..." He trailed off, waving his hands helplessly. "I won't be able to sit with you long enough to read every book to you aloud. Even if I were in physical form, that would be... difficult, to say the least."

Shit. She'd gotten overexcited and forgotten why she hadn't dug into the library stacks in the first place. Maybe it was the head wound getting to her.

The majority of the library was in... not English. The books weren't in the nigh-on-unreadable arcane language of Xavier's journal, but they might as well have been. Alice couldn't read either of them, and Florian was right. They didn't have time to sit and read through everything aloud. It would be faster to skim the text for anything useful.

"Come with me," Florian whispered, motioning for her to follow.

He crept out of the back corner, down the stairs, and around to the back side of some of the bookshelves on the main floor. From here, if they peeked through the shelves, it was possible to see the main library desk and the single librarian, surrounded by books. He seemed to have some kind of eyesight issues, because he very often needed to pick up a magnifying glass sitting close by as he worked.

"What are we doing?" Alice mumbled. Did he plan to ask the librarian for translation help? That seemed like a bad idea, considering that Xavier could simply demand information on anything she brought to him to read.

"See that magnifying glass on the desk?" Florian whispered. "It's a translation glass. The librarian keeps it close by— it's impossible for him to know all the languages in the library, and even he needs it sometimes."

Alice carefully peeked around the edge of the bookshelf,

"How do I get it without him knowing?" she mumbled, ducking back around the bookshelf and out of view.

"I... I'm not sure," he admitted. "I've rarely seen him leave his desk."

"*Leave it to me*," Missy said, sidling up to Alice's leg. "*Possums are excellent schemers.*"

"Okay, then," she said. "Missy says she'll take care of it."

"She will?" Florian asked, looking down at the possum.

"I trust her," she said with a smile.

"I'll distract him. You get the glass while he's gone, then get out before he sees you," she said confidently.

"What about you?" Alice asked, kneeling down closer to Missy's eye level.

"Don't worry, he won't notice me. I'll meet you—"

"Meet us in the gardens after you finish up," Florian offered, unaware Missy had been squeaking about the same thing. "We'll use the hidden compartment I showed you to store the glass and the books."

"*Good plan, pretty man,*" Missy squeaked, giving a very firm nod of her possum head.

"What was that?" Florian asked.

"She... um," Alice stammered. "She said it's a good plan. She also said you're pretty."

"... Pretty?" Florian's brow furrowed as he looked back and forth between Alice and Missy.

Alice's cheeks burned, and she was suddenly quite preoccupied with the library floor. He was very, *very* pretty. Granted, Xavier was pretty, too— they did share the same face, though they were certainly not the same person.

Not even close.

"Okay, let's get cracking. You can flirt later," Missy said.

Alice chose to ignore the second part of that statement, reminding herself that Florian did not possess the gift of animal speech and could not have heard the comment.

"Wait, what are you gonna do?" she hissed.

"*You'll know it when ya hear it,*" Missy said, and then took off into the shadows.

"Could you... um..." Alice trailed off, looking between Florian and the way Missy had gone.

"Keep an eye on her? Certainly," he said, nodding. "I'll make sure nothing happens to her."

Though she wasn't sure how much an incorporeal prince could do, his physical similarities to Xavier would probably be an advantage if any trouble came up, and it made her feel better to know that Missy wasn't alone. Alice and her possum friend were two reckless peas in a pod, and she'd grown attached very quickly.

Once Florian had slipped away, Alice tucked in to wait, carefully watching to see if anyone else entered the library. No one did. No one ever did. The longer she thought about it, the more it made perfect sense

that Xavier might intentionally be keeping the other Shadow Fae away from her to keep their memories from resurfacing.

But... why? And did he just plan to hide her away forever? That wasn't exactly a sustainable plan for the long term.

A bang that made Alice flinch interrupted her train of thought. She could analyze Xavier's motivations and actions later— at the moment, she needed that magnifying glass.

"What was..." the librarian muttered, standing to peek in the direction of the sound.

A much, much louder crashing noise followed.

"What the hell are you doin' over there, Missy?" Alice muttered under her breath, peeking through the rows of books as she watched the librarian step away from the desk and walk towards the clamor.

The desk was out in the open, easily visible from most parts of the library, so Alice chose to wait a moment before she took action, making absolutely certain that the librarian had walked away somewhere entirely out of view. The last thing she needed was a report that she'd taken a translation glass. They couldn't afford any slip-ups.

Thankfully, judging by the awful, continued crashing from a different part of the library than before, it sounded like Missy had things covered. The little possum was probably terrorizing the bookshelves, and having a wonderful time doing it.

Alice bolted for the desk, snatching up the magnifying glass as she passed, and then ducked behind the nearest shelf. The clattering and banging sound continued from the far corner, but she wasn't about to risk running through the room in the open.

Instead, she stuck to the walls and the shadows, only making for the door when she heard a particularly loud crashing sound. Whatever Missy had done, it would certainly be enough to keep the librarian busy while she booked it back to the gardens.

The books tucked under her cloak and magnifying glass stowed safely in her pocket, Alice hurried towards the gardens as quickly as she could. Hopefully, there would be enough time before her expected dinner date with Xavier to dive into reading a little.

12   IN WHICH ALICE READS

Tucked into the farthest corner of the gardens, concealed by the low-hanging branches of a willow tree, Alice poured over the books she'd taken from the library.

She'd only managed to grab two of them, one about Shadow Court history and the other about magical anomalies, but they proved to be interesting, at the least. The Shadow Court history was one volume out of a series, and she'd clearly managed to pick a volume somewhere in the middle rather than at the start or end. It was annoying, but it provided more information than she had. It would just mean another trip to the library later to check the rest of the volumes.

She'd learned a little about Shadow Fae magic, a little more about traditional bargaining tactics, but nothing that might give away exactly what was happening with Florian. Now that she knew he was in Shadow form the times she couldn't touch him, she just had to figure out where his body was.

Unfortunately, her best guess was that Xavier might be the only person who knew that.

Part of her wished that she hadn't given the journal to Willow, but it was possible that the language was so old that the glass wouldn't work on it, anyways.

"So what does this mean for Florian?" Missy asked, sniffing at the book.

"I've got a few ideas," Alice admitted, "but I gotta talk to someone who knows more about wigglin' outta magical trouble than me."

"What do you need?"

"I think, probably, we need to take a little vacation," Alice said, shutting the book. "I need Kaz for this. Maybe Granny, too."

"We already tried running. It didn't work out very well."

"That's why I'm just gonna ask him this time," Alice said firmly.

Missy hissed angrily, letting out a string of possum noises that certainly did not translate into any known language.

"It's... not the worst plan," Florian said.

Alice gasped, hand on her chest. "You have *got* to stop showin' up like that," she mumbled.

"Sorry," Florian said. "Hit a snag on my way here."

"A snag?" Alice asked, raising an eyebrow as she stood from her spot under the tree. Florian extended a hand to help her up, and she took it on instinct. However, he was stronger than she thought, and she must have been lighter than he expected, because he hauled her up so quickly that she wound up standing almost flush against him, her hands on his chest.

Heat flared in her cheeks as her mouth dropped open. She thought about backing away, but then his hands were on her waist to help her keep her balance, and she found she didn't want to.

His humanoid form was... perfect. Wonderful. It calmed some kind of strange ache in her chest to be this close to him, and though he was certainly handsome, the serenity she felt in his presence had very little to do with how he looked. That must have been the snag, then— he shifted forms, and in the meantime had to make his way back from wherever his body had been.

"Are you okay?" Florian asked, checking her over. "I didn't mean to pull you up so roughly."

"I'm fine," Alice squeaked, almost unable to look at him. Her fingers gently traced over the quilted lines on his doublet as she drank in the feeling of standing so close to him, of smelling that familiar musk with the warm skin and warm personality that she adored.

Wait.

Doublet?

"Did... did you change clothes when you changed forms?" she stammered, suddenly looking down.

"I... ah..." Florian took a step back, stumbling. "In a way, yes."

It was annoying that he couldn't give her a straight answer, but at least he *wanted* to. He wanted to tell her the truth, and he tried to tell her at every possible opportunity. Xavier, on the other hand, seemed to purposefully hide things from her. He doted on her at every opportunity, but it felt more like coddling than trusting the longer it went on.

"How long will you be able to stay... like this?" Alice asked hesitantly.

"Physical?" He raised an eyebrow.

She nodded.

"Maybe an hour at most," he admitted, looking away.

"Can you sit with me?" she mumbled, unable to meet his eyes. "Please?"

"O— of course." Florian awkwardly lowered himself to the ground, taking a seat on the soft grass with his back to the same massive tree roots that Alice had been leaning against. She settled herself next to him, close enough that their hips were touching, and awkwardly pulled her knees to her chest.

Maybe this was a bad idea. Alice desperately wanted to be close to him, but she wasn't sure how to ask for that without making her feelings obvious, and she wasn't sure she wanted to talk about them out loud yet. She wasn't ready for the inevitable rejection.

However, as soon as she settled in, Florian wrapped his arm around her waist, drawing her even closer to him. He rested his head against hers almost automatically, like they were meant to be like this, and Alice felt her heart beating like a bass drum in her chest. It was like shaking and falling and flying, but all of them at once.

It was perfect.

"Is this... acceptable?" Florian asked, his breath tickling the top of her ear.

"This is good," Alice said with a smile, letting her eyes flutter closed as she rested her head on his shoulder.

It wasn't permanent, of course, but for now, this was the best comfort that she could have asked for. An hour of sitting together with Florian, she thought, might be worth all the trouble.

<hr>

Florian had known Alice for far longer than she'd been aware he existed.

When Xavier made the bargain with Alice's mother, he'd been there, watching from the trees. He wanted to keep track of everything Xavier did, and he'd watched in Shadow form as Alice's mother traded her daughter for relief from her own grief.

At the time, he thought it was repulsive. Currently, he still thought it was an unthinkable sacrifice, but he also had to admit that without it, he would never have met the woman currently dozing off beside him.

Florian gently played with her bright, red-orange hair as she settled in beside him, snoring softly in a way that he found oddly endearing. As on guard as she was around the palace, he was glad that she felt she could relax in his presence, and he considered it a treat to be able to touch her like this. It wouldn't last long, but it was enough.

He hadn't liked Alice at first.

Xavier kept tabs on her the whole time she grew up in the little witch community outside Boone, checking in every month or so to make sure she was still in place. He never revealed himself, but he wanted to keep track of what was owed to him. Sometimes Florian tagged along, just to make sure that nothing terrible happened, but he'd grown complacent in recent years. For whatever reason, Xavier was biding his time with Alice, and at the time... Well, he couldn't have cared less.

Alice had grown up in a house full of loud women, and she'd learned to be louder if she wanted any attention. She crumbled in the face of her mother, letting the now emotionless woman morph her into a sad shadow of what she could have been, taking every abuse to heart. Alice's tendency towards husband chasing was something he considered incredibly unattractive, and he found her jealous tendencies annoying.

But... then he'd caught a glimpse of her alone in the woods.

Two years ago, he'd decided to tag along in secret when Xavier visited to surreptitiously check on his bargain payment. Florian hadn't expected anything different than usual, just a peek to confirm that she was still where she was meant to be. Instead, they found her out with a basket of berries, feeding them to the local raccoons.

He still remembered her laughing as she talked to them.

"Really? I'm the runt, too, I guess," she said, sighing as she handed the raccoon another berry. He made a chittering sound that Florian couldn't make sense of, but Alice clearly heard more.

"No, don't play tricks! But thanks for tryin' to take up for me, little fella." She gently patted the raccoon on his head, and a few other creatures began poking their way out of the trees.

"Come on, we got enough to share," Alice said, beckoning over two more raccoons and a shy deer.

Seeing her interact with those animals was... an entirely different side of her. It was a bright spot that hadn't been warped or smothered, and it made something in his chest twist to watch. At the time, he'd chosen to ignore it, but that was no longer possible.

He couldn't let her fall into Xavier's clutches.

Florian had a vague idea what his double was planning, and it certainly was not good. At first, he'd only worried about the plan for his own safety, but now he cared less and less for that, and more about making sure that Alice managed to get away from here.

Over the last year on Howard's Knob, she'd *bloomed*. She was brighter, more confident, seemed happier— and more than anything, those wards had kept her hidden for that whole year. Even Xavier couldn't see past them, and it had been a fluke he was out in the woods that day scouting for her.

Terror seized Florian when he realized Alice was in the Shadow Court. He'd only seen her a few times, only seen that softer shadow a little, but he wanted that better life for her. When she arrived, it looked like Xavier was ready to crush her under his heel, but... Florian had been pleasantly surprised by every one of their interactions.

She was sweet and funny. She was also self-conscious and could be snippy. He could never predict what she would say next, and he found himself looking for her more and more, trying to keep watch, trying to

make sure that she stayed safe while she was in the palace walls. With luck, he might still be able to convince her to leave and never return.

Alice wanted to help him, and though it warmed his heart to know that she cared, that the soft and brave side of her had grown and blossomed, he couldn't let her take that risk.

If he was right, Xavier's plans wouldn't just cost him his life, his throne, and his people. They would cost Alice her life, too.

A flashing light roused Ellie from her sleep.

The bedroom she and Kaz shared was on the second floor of their house on Howard's Knob, and there was a flashing light piercing through the mountain darkness. A glass ball on the dresser across the room flashed bright white, on and off. It sat on a delicate iron stand among hairbrushes, papers, and knickknacks, but this one was quite functional.

"What's that?" Ellie groaned, turning her face into the pillow.

"The wards caught something," Kaz muttered, hugging her closer under the blankets.

"Fuck," she said, voice muffled by the pillow.

"We can get it in the morning," he insisted, waving it off.

Ellie, on the other hand, wasn't as convinced. As much as she wanted to turn over and go back to sleep, flashing light or not, she couldn't casually shake off the fact that her wards had trapped something.

In the early days of tweaking the protections, sometimes completely innocent animals wound up caught in the wards. More recently, benign land spirits who happened to be passing through and got a little too close and curious wound up temporarily stuck. The last thing Ellie wanted to do was piss off a land spirit, so it would be best to set them free as soon as possible. It was impossible to program the wards to every spirit, but ones she could talk to were free to wander the land.

... As long as they didn't come in the house. That was a private space, which Ellie felt was reasonable.

"Come on," she grumbled, pushing herself up to a sitting position. "Let's go check."

It would be bad news, in a general sense, to wait till morning. The longer something or someone stayed in the wards, the more irritated it was when you finally let it out. Usually, the wait made benign visitors feel less inclined to stay benign, and malicious visitors were infinitely more annoyed than they otherwise might be.

Not that they had too many malicious visitors, thankfully, but there had been one or two they'd needed to *very firmly* tell to scoot off.

"Fine," he sighed. "Get the lantern. I'll meet you downstairs."

"Wear pants," she said absentmindedly, reaching for a sweater to put on over her nightgown.

Kaz made a noncommittal kind of noise as she slipped on shoes, and Ellie just hoped that meant he would.

Dressed in a nightgown, a baggy sweater, and slip on shoes, Ellie walked downstairs to the kitchen with her long, silver hair flowing loose down her back. The black oil lantern was on the side table at the bottom of the stairs, a careful distance away from the matches used to light it. By the time Ellie shook herself awake and lit the lantern, ready to head out into the mountain night, Kaz had sleepily trudged downstairs.

He *was* wearing pants, at least. No shoes, but at least he had pants.

... This time.

"*I wanna come,*" a little voice cried out, followed by the patter of paws on the stairs.

Rosemary sleepily tottered towards them, the little puppy nearly tripping over her own oversized paws as she worked her way downstairs.

"Go back to sleep, baby girl," Ellie said gently, bending down to gently pet the pup.

"*But I wanna help,*" she insisted, nudging at Ellie's hand. This was a complex sentence for her, as Rosemary was only about two years old. She was in her adorable, fluffy stage, and learning human words quickly, but Ellie would never put her in danger, and there was no telling what might be out there.

"Not this time, honey. Go sleep," she said, bending down to kiss the puppy's forehead.

That seemed to placate her, at least for the time being, and Ellie took off out the door with Kaz behind her. He slung the shotgun over his shoulder by the attached strap, just in case.

"You really think we need that?" she asked. They hadn't needed anything even close to firearms before, mostly dealing with random animals and a few spirits. Yes, there had been one or two belligerent intruders, but a gun would have been useless on them.

"I think it's better safe than sorry, if we run into another one like Xavier," he muttered.

It was a valid point. Firearms definitely would not be useless on a physical Other.

Ellie wasn't entirely sure where the alert had come from, so she scanned the area at the edge of her lamp light, hoping it wouldn't be necessary to walk the entire perimeter to figure out where something had been caught. Sometimes, even incorporeal intruders left physical traces. It wasn't uncommon to see crushed grass, scorched earth, shadows, or a strange shimmer in the air where there shouldn't be, and those indicators typically brought her close enough that her Spirit Sight kicked in, allowing Ellie to clearly see what was at the edge of her protections.

This time, though, it didn't look like a spirit, and the closer Ellie walked to the edge of her wards, the more she could tell there was a shadow cast by something or someone physical. It was an odd shape- certainly not humanoid, or not entirely. She couldn't quite make it out through the gloom.

"What in Sam Hill..." Ellie mumbled, squinting into the shadows beyond her lantern light.

"Who is Sam Hill?" a feminine voice called. "Alice mentioned him, too. Is he a friend of yours?"

Ellie almost dropped the lantern.

"You know Alice?" she asked, surging forward until she was at the very edge of the wards.

Roots and vines sprung from the ground in unnatural volumes, wrapped around and holding in place a... female deer centaur?

She had dark skin with white freckles that almost looked like constellations, crystalline antlers like the man who insisted on taking Alice with him, and a glasslike deer body to match.

"I'm bringing a message from her," she said, very carefully nodding towards the saddlebags slung over her deer body. "It's in my pack. Take it if you don't believe me."

Ellie carefully crept forward to the edge of the wards, only calming a little when the woman didn't try to move or struggle as she approached. She wasn't on the defensive, whoever she was, and wasn't going to try any desperate attacks.

Rather than reach into the pack herself, Ellie directed one of her vines to open the flap, snake inside, and retrieve the letter, pierced through by a large thorn to hold it. The vine brought the letter closer, and Ellie unfolded the paper without trouble.

She wasn't sure what to expect when she unfolded the paper, but she wouldn't have come up with the story on the page in a hundred years.

Dear Ellie,

If you're reading this, Willow delivered the letter.

I'm hoping I'll make it home for a visit soon. I am safe. I counted thirteen crows in the gardens the other day. Hope you enjoy the book I sent you to read.

Love,

Alice

"It's Alice's handwriting," Ellie said as she scanned the text.

"You're sure?" Kaz looked over her shoulder, reading along.

"Positive," she said with a firm nod. Ellie folded the letter and put it in the pocket of her sweater, then waved a hand to dismiss the vines holding their visitor.

"Thanks," the deer woman said with a sigh of relief. She stretched, rolled her shoulders, and shifted her lower body back into two humanoid legs, though they ended in crystal hooves instead of human feet.

It was a little strange to watch the shift. Despite growing up around magic of all kinds, shifter magic wasn't something she was particularly familiar with, and it was a bit disorienting to watch the change from humanoid to animal and back. It was also much easier to see the slump in her posture this way, the human marks of exhaustion. She was practically dead on her feet, and there was no telling how long she'd been running to get here.

On the upside, that probably meant she wasn't dangerous, at least at this moment.

On the downside, no one was getting any real information until this woman got some sleep.

"What's your name?" Ellie asked.

"Willow. I'm a refugee from the Shadow Court. I'm supposed to bring you this to translate, too," she said, reaching into her bag once more.

Good. That was consistent with the letter. Kaz took the book from her, holding it close to the lantern as he flipped through a few pages, frowning.

"That's Hartley's area, for sure," he muttered. "We'll get it to him in the morning. We'll come back and get you then."

"Wha—" Willow started, but she didn't make it any farther.

Kaz turned to leave, already halfway through his first step away when Ellie grabbed his arm, pulling him back towards her.

"I'm not leavin' her outside the wards!" Ellie hissed. "If she's in trouble, she needs that protection."

"And if she's lying, she'll kill us in our sleep," Kaz countered.

"She's got a letter from Alice," she said, putting her free hand on her hip in a way they both knew meant that she wouldn't budge.

"I'm trying to keep you safe, rosebud," Kaz said, sighing as he pulled Ellie into a hug.

"You saw that letter," she muttered, voice muffled against his shoulder.

"I did," he said, "but you come first. You always come first for me."

Ellie relaxed against his chest momentarily, breathing in his familiar scent and basking in the safety of his presence. She loved him so much it was almost overwhelming, but she also knew he could be overprotective. On the other hand, she did have a tendency to trust people a little too easily.

However, if Willow was really a refugee, Ellie didn't want to leave her without any protections. There might be scouts following in the darkness, whether she was aware of it or not.

"I won't hurt you, but I don't think it'll do me much good to say it," Willow said, hanging her head. "I want to help Alice as much as you do."

"You said you're a refugee. Is she in trouble?" Kaz asked, letting Ellie go.

"She will be soon, I think," she said gravely. "It might take a while to explain."

"Then you'll explain in the morning," Ellie said firmly. "Ya need food or water for now?"

"No, I'm alright, but thank you," Willow said politely. "Though, even if I can't come into the house, I would truly appreciate safe passage inside the wards."

Ellie glanced at Kaz, trying to read his posture. His hand was on the shotgun strap, not actively planning to shoot, but ready if he needed it. He certainly didn't trust Willow, but he didn't consider her a strong threat, not at this moment.

Unfortunately, they might be at an impasse. It was possible that they could start a fire and just stay up the rest of the night, but... Willow truly did not look to be in good shape, the longer that Ellie looked at her. Not only was she tired, she appeared to be limping a little.

"We'll keep watch," came a familiar voice in Ellie's mind.

Charlie and Luna, the resident hellhound parents that were close friends with Harper, trotted towards them. They were large for dogs, but not comically oversized as the legends described them, and they were incredibly intelligent. Their pups must have been asleep, because the two parents were alone— after all, Rosemary was back inside.

"Rosemary told us what was happening," Charlie said. "Give her a tent. We'll stand guard."

... Scratch that. Rosemary was clearly not back inside. Squinting through the darkness, Ellie was able to make out a slightly smaller shape standing in the shadows of the two larger hounds. That was probably the pup she was looking for.

"Isn't that dangerous for you?" Kaz asked, brow furrowing.

"I can open a portal into the afterlife at will, and then return anywhere on this plane that I want," Luna said. "I would argue we're the best ones for the job."

"Touche," he conceded.

"Rosemary, come here," Ellie said, sighing.

A smaller shadow peeled away from Charlie and Luna, trotting forward to Ellie. It was a lucky guess that she was out here, as she hadn't seen her so much as... suspected.

"*I helped*," she said proudly. As Ellie knelt down, Rosemary jumped into her arms. This was part of their routine, and Ellie caught her without issue, though she was getting a little big for it.

"You helped," Ellie agreed, assuming she'd brought Charlie and Luna, "but you also didn't *listen*."

Rosemary whined softly as Ellie stood, still holding her hellhound pup. She loved the little hound more than anything, but Rosemary was as reckless as Alice sometimes. Though she'd never been seriously hurt, it was sometimes difficult to keep her out of trouble.

Hugging Rosemary close, Ellie turned towards the newcomer and waved her hand, beckoning her inside. That was all the permission she needed to pass safely through the wards.

"Come on inside the wards, Willow. I'll go grab the camp bed and get ya something for that leg," she said, smiling like a cat who got the cream. Kaz just groaned.

"This is going to be a very long night, isn't it?" he muttered.

"Probably," she said, shrugging, "but it'll be a real excitin' day tomorrow."

"Thank you," Willow sighed, stepping just inside the wards before she collapsed onto the grass, legs practically buckling under her.

"Whoa, there!" Ellie cried, moving a little closer. "Let's get ya a little more inside the wards than that, okay? Stay with me. You can sleep soon."

They finally managed to move Willow to the front porch, where Ellie set up the camp bed with blankets and tended her injured leg. It looked like a sprained ankle, but it was difficult to tell with the combined deer and human bone structure.

Willow was already asleep before Ellie finished wrapping her leg, and the hounds curled in beside her on the porch, promising to meet them in the morning and report anything strange.

"Why do you think she didn't say anything specific in the letter?" Kaz asked as they slowly made their way upstairs. It was a small miracle that they hadn't woken Granny, but... Well, Granny slept like a log. She probably hadn't heard a thing.

"She did," Ellie said plainly. "She used the village distress phrase— thirteen crows."

"Which is?"

"Something we were taught as kids to send if we ever got in serious trouble. It's that old counting crows rhyme— one for sorrow, two for joy?"

"That... sounds vaguely familiar, yes," Kaz said, opening the door to the house. "What's thirteen?"

Ellie laughed humorlessly as she stepped inside. "It's the devil himself," she said. "My best guess is that if Willow got caught, she couldn't risk anyone finding whatever she wrote."

"Damn..." he sighed, rubbing a hand over his face. "So... what does Willow know that was too important to write down plainly?"

"We'll find out tomorrow, after we all get some damn sleep. You know I can't think straight when I don't sleep, and that poor woman looked like she was dead tired."

"You were definitely right about that," Kaz said, sighing as he toed off his shoes. "I don't think she could hurt us if she wanted to, not in that state... but I'm glad Charlie and Luna are outside."

"Me, too," Ellie said, covering a yawn. "We'll do interrogations in the morning. Come here, I'm cold."

She slid back under the blankets and opened her arms for Kaz. Smiling sleepily, he tucked in beside her and wrapped his larger form around hers. It took a while for Ellie to fall back asleep, even resting in Kaz's warm embrace, but eventually she drifted off.

They could find out more when the sun rose.

IN WHICH A BREAKTHROUGH OCCURS

Now that Alice was back to normal after recovering from her head wound— and thank goodness for Willow, because that was her doing— Xavier insisted on spending "bonding" time together each day. It wasn't particularly different than how he'd been doting on her and checking on her while she was injured, but at least she could walk around now.

He didn't take her anywhere special. The library and the gardens were still the main places in the palace she was allowed to explore, though he did concede to taking her to the ballroom one day, just for a change of scenery.

Today, they were in the shadowy library, watching the rays of sunshine peek through dark, sheer curtains as they strolled among the books. Alice held Xavier's arm as he escorted her, keeping herself carefully tucked close to his side. She had something important to ask him, and it wasn't going to go well if he thought she was afraid.

"Xavier?" she said softly, her voice echoing in the quiet space.

"Yes, treasure?" He used that same familiar endearment, but it was starting to really grate on her nerves. At first, it made her feel like something precious. Now, it made her feel like something hoarded away.

"I was just thinkin' that... Well, it might be nice to take a quick trip home?" she asked hesitantly. "Just for a day or two. I could pick up some of my things."

"Are you unhappy here?"

"No!" Alice said quickly. "I just... Well, I've never really been anywhere with totally new people. It gets kinda lonely sometimes."

Xavier went silent, but he continued walking. For a moment, Alice thought he would flat out deny the request. That would be... very, very bad. She didn't exactly have a backup plan besides this, unless she asked Florian to help sneak her out. Still, she wasn't sure she could get away from the castle fast enough to outrun Xavier or any Shadow Fae trackers or—

"I'll take you there myself," he finally said. "It's the fastest way to travel."

Alice beamed, and she didn't have to fake the joy, either.

"Thank you, thank you!!" she practically squealed, grabbing onto his arm in excitement. His expression softened just a little at that, the faintest ghost of a smile twitching at his lips for a moment.

"Only for three days. We have preparations to make for the full moon celebration."

"When do we leave?"

"The day after tomorrow. I'll drop you at the wards, then come back to pick you up," Xavier said.

Perfect.

If Xavier wasn't planning to stay and supervise, that gave her even more wiggle room to ask about everything she'd seen and learned. It was a little surprising that he didn't want to keep a stricter watch, considering she hadn't been let out of his sight this whole time. Then again, her family wasn't a part of the Shadow Court. They had no influence over what was happening here.

Her... family.

Alice had to fight not to show how her mood dropped when the thought crossed her mind. The group on Howard's Knob was family, as assuredly as any blood connection.

And she'd run away from them.

"Though, I warn you... I would hate to have to use force to bring you back," Xavier continued. "Do take care to be ready to return on time. I wouldn't want to make any rash decisions under the assumption that someone tried to keep you away from me."

Ah. There it was. Alice could handle thinly veiled threats— at this point, they made her more determined rather than of a mind to shrink away. She had spent far too long running, hiding, and waiting on others to take action. This time, the battle was in her hands.

"Of course, I'll come back to you," Alice said, shifting her hold on his arm to his hand.

Yes, she would come back, but with any luck... she would come back ready for war.

Alice held up their joined hands for a moment to examine his left arm, taking a good look at the design that matched hers. As hard as she tried, she couldn't find any differences, couldn't see anything in particular that made them different. It was almost eerie what an exact match they were.

Try as she might, Alice couldn't entirely put aside the notion that she and Xavier were mirror souls. It had been gnawing away at the back of her mind as she researched, trying her best to find more information about the blood vows, the matching marks, the idea of mirror souls in general...

But there was precious little information available on mirror souls. Most of it appeared to be legend, something that was highly searched for and coveted, but difficult to confirm. They were said to be souls that reflected each other, not always a romantic match, but a perfect pair in every way. A mirror soul was, apparently, a profound connection that ran through lifetimes, across centuries, bringing you back to each other over and over.

A mirror soul was someone cosmically destined to find you. It wasn't entirely clear how or why the bond worked, but enough people had similar experiences that it couldn't be ignored. Strange dreams, emotional turmoil, a feeling of familiarity upon meeting, and in some cases, even memories of past lives bubbling to the surface— all were commonly reported symptoms of meeting a mirror soul. It was supposed to be something *good*, even if it came with challenges.

So why did she feel so terrible about it?

Despite her attraction to Florian, despite her experiences in the castle, a part of her wondered if Xavier wasn't lying. A part of her wondered if they really were mirror souls, and if so... what if by helping Florian, she pushed away her best chance at love forever?

But... Alice was also no longer sure she wanted a love with Xavier. The thought that they were magically, cosmically, permanently tied together, even beyond this life... It was utterly terrifying. She didn't want to be that close to him, not in a thousand years.

Still. What if she was wrong?

What if he just needed someone to love him into softness, to bring out the soul underneath? What if it just took more time than she was willing to give?

Alice must have been staring and ruminating for longer than she intended, because eventually Xavier spoke up, drawing her out of her thoughts.

"See something interesting?" Xavier asked, smirking as he gently let go of her hand, still holding his arm out so she could see.

That was when she noticed something else. As Xavier let go of her hand, Alice could see a thin scar line across the palm of his left hand. It looked familiar, in that she could recognize what it was, but it was too familiar, too *exact*.

She was absolutely sure that it matched the one on Florian's palm *perfectly*.

"Why do you have a blood bargain scar on your palm?" She asked, turning his hand over to look at the mark.

This one was the same as Florian's scar. Why would he have a matching blood bargain scar on the same palm, but not the matching blood vows? Who had he bargained with? Did they bargain with *each other*?

If so, what was important enough to use blood magic to seal it?

Xavier grabbed her hand again, hiding the scar between their palms.

"Why, indeed..." he muttered, giving her hand a slight squeeze as he laced their fingers together.

That was when she noticed something odd: Xavier's hand was *warm*.

It wasn't hot or sweaty, not unnaturally warm, but it was a far cry from his typical chilly touch. Normally, his skin was lukewarm at best. This felt like the touch of a normal human hand.

"Wha—" she stuttered, eyes wide as she looked up at him.

"Think hard, little rabbit," he said, giving a wink that was very unlike Xavier. Surprised, Alice dropped his hand and stepped away, staring.

He smiled at her softly, the corner of his mouth coming up in a lopsided grin that looked very much like...

But as soon as she had the thought, the moment was over. Eyes closing and groaning in pain, he doubled over, gasping for breath. Xavier shook his head as if to clear it, blinking furiously at her.

"Apologies, my treasure. What were you saying?" he asked breathlessly, straightening. If she wasn't entirely certain what she'd just seen, Alice might have thought she'd been dreaming, hallucinating, or simply imagining things. She might have still thought that, but Xavier's usually unshakeable disposition looked slightly different, slightly off.

Slightly *rattled*.

"What just happened?" she murmured, eyes wide.

"Nothing," he said quickly. "I was simply a little lightheaded."

That was *not* lightheadedness. She knew Xavier had doubts about her intelligence, but even he couldn't deny that something had happened there. It wasn't just a quirk of the light or a flash of dizziness.

"Your hand was *warm*," Alice breathed, panic rising. "It— it was just for a second—"

"Don't worry about it," Xavier said through gritted teeth.

"No, but it *changed*," she insisted. "It was like—"

"It was nothing! Do you understand? *Nothing*!" Xavier reached out in a flash, hands gripping her shoulder so hard that it hurt. "The shadows in this place play tricks with your mind. If you're planning to survive here, you cannot let them get to you!"

His voice echoed through the massive library, reverberating off the stone walls, so loud that Alice felt it in her bones. The grip on her

shoulder was bruising, Xavier's eyes wide and frantic as he bent a little lower to look at her. He looked... almost afraid.

But in that fear, he'd lashed out at her, and Alice had already learned more than enough about people who lashed out like this.

That was it. That was *enough*.

"I'll see you at dinner," Alice said, keeping her tone as even as possible as she gently shook herself out of his grasp.

She wanted to rage and scream and snap at him. She wanted to run away again. Unfortunately, she couldn't do *any* of that if she wanted to keep his trust. The best she could do was stay calm for the moment, act silly and besotted, and hope he thought there wasn't anything bubbling under the surface.

"Alice, wait," he said, grabbing for her hand. "You know I'm only trying to care for you, don't you?"

No, she wasn't convinced of that, however much he wanted her to be. He was trying to do something to her, certainly, but Alice wasn't certain that whatever it was involved *care*.

"I know," she managed. "But it's time for you to go to your meetings," she said, gesturing at the large clock on the library wall.

Xavier cursed under his breath.

"You're right, treasure. Thank you. I'll see you later." He bent a little to kiss her forehead. "Ask the librarian if you need directions back to our rooms."

"Of course," she said, smiling brightly.

As soon as he turned to leave, though, the smile dropped.

Alice was simply grateful that he didn't try to kiss her mouth this time. She was starting to get a little sick of the feeling of his kisses. They left an awful sensation in the pit of her stomach that she couldn't quite figure out how to escape.

Instead of heading back to their rooms, Alice took the side path out to the gardens. They were familiar to her now, and Xavier didn't seem to enjoy being out in the sunlight for long, so outdoor spaces felt like something of a sanctuary. She didn't reach for the hidden compartment with Florian's cloak and her books, though. This time, she just wanted to think.

Something strange happened back there. Alice wasn't entirely sure what she'd seen, but it certainly wasn't normal, and it wasn't lightheadedness. She paced in circles in the garden, going over everything she knew so far.

The most incriminating evidence was the blood bargain scar. That was the connection she couldn't ignore, not with them looking the same on both Florian and Xavier's palms.

Alice turned the corner to make another loop around the gardens, but jumped back as she found herself staring at a familiar figure.

"Alice," Florian said.

He'd been completely silent in his approach, meaning he was likely in Shadow form. She almost wasn't surprised to see him. He had a tendency to show up when she was alone, and especially outside. Omitting a greeting entirely, she launched straight into her theory.

"You made a bargain with Xavier, and it left ya like this. It's *got* to have done," she said firmly. "It explains the scar on your hand *and* why you can't talk about the bargain. It's the magic."

Florian looked surprised for a moment, but then he outright laughed.

"I knew you'd get to it eventually," he said. "How did you put it together?"

"You have the same scar that he does. Exactly the same," she said. "Still working on that part, but I'm gettin' there!"

She still didn't have all the information she needed, and it was incredibly frustrating trying to put pieces together without knowing what it might lead to. The longer she stayed in the Shadow Court, the clearer it became who her real friends and allies were, but she didn't have time to search for many more.

As much as she wanted this to be a perfect marriage, a perfect solution to her problem, she'd gotten trouble instead. Even her husband wasn't someone she could trust. The same husband that claimed he looked for her because they were soulmates.

"And... I think I've got a problem," Alice whispered.

"Mm? What's that?"

"Xavier keeps tellin' me we're soulmates," she said with a sigh. "But I... don't know that I wanna be."

"Why?" Florian asked. "That is, besides the obvious."

Alice couldn't hold back a snort, but she sobered quickly. Florian certainly did not like Xavier, not one bit, and... Well, she was perfectly okay with that.

"I don't... think... he likes me," she said slowly. "That sounds stupid, sayin' it out loud, but I don't think he does. And I can't tell if he loves me."

"What's the difference to you?" he asked curiously, tilting his head a little. He looked like a curious bird gazing down at her, his eyes gentle, but... He did genuinely seem like he wanted to know.

She wasn't even sure if she should be talking to him about this. Who would ever talk to the person that they were infatuated with about their husband, anyways? Though... perhaps this was a bit of a special scenario.

"My ma and sisters— Well, at least my sisters," she amended. "They love me. I know they do. They act like fightin' cats, but I know they'd stick up for me and for each other in a heartbeat if there was trouble. I don't think they always like me, though, and that... still hurts."

"Why not your mother?" Florian prodded gently.

Alice swallowed hard.

"She... I don't think she likes me or loves me," Alice admitted, voice dropping to a whisper. "I don't think she ever did. I'm just a reminder of my sister bein' stillborn and my daddy passin' on before his time."

Florian paused for a moment, taking in the information. He paced in a circle, eyes locked on the ground, opening and closing his mouth. Briefly, Alice wondered if he was trying to find a gentle way to tell her she was whining, that she didn't know what she was talking about, that everything was in her head.

He didn't say that, though.

Instead, he paused, stepped a little closer to her, and spoke very quietly.

"You focused quite a lot on what it feels like not to be liked or loved. What do you think being loved should feel like?"

Alice trembled as she looked up at him. She desperately wanted to touch him, but she couldn't, not when he was in this form. Tears welled

in her eyes, but she pushed them back and shoved them down deep, willing herself to stay calm.

"I think... you should talk about everything you can," she said slowly. "I think it's mutual support. It's knowing you can trust someone."

"Has Xavier ever done anything like that for you?"

Alice looked away, pressing her lips tightly together. She didn't have to speak for him to know exactly what her answer was. A month ago, she might have argued that it would just take time. They were soulmates—they *had* to go together. They had to fit somehow. It just might take a minute to work things out, and then everything should click into place.

But... nothing ever did.

"He claims you're mirror souls, yes?" Florian asked gently. Alice was grateful for the slight subject change, grateful that he hadn't forced her to speak her answer.

"He does," Alice said. "I haven't figured out how to prove or deny it, though."

"Does it matter if it's true if you don't love him?" Florian asked, sliding a little closer to her. In his Shadow form, she couldn't feel his warmth. She couldn't smell that familiar scent. It was still comforting to have him close, though, still just as soothing.

He had a point. The longer she stayed, the more Alice was forced to admit that she didn't love Xavier. She didn't even *want* to love Xavier, not anymore. But how much control did she have over who was her mirror soul, over her destiny, over her emotions?

Looking up at Florian for a long moment, Alice decided that she didn't care if she had no control. She would wrench back into control the wheel that steered her own life, even if it was the last thing she did.

"What do *you* want, Alice?" he whispered.

"I..." she paused, feeling a sudden tightness in her chest.

She wanted Florian. That much was clear to her, though she was afraid to say it out loud. What would she do if he rejected her, too? How would she recover again?

"What if I said I wanted you to touch me?" she asked quietly, unable to meet his gaze.

"I would love nothing more, little rabbit," he whispered, "but I'm afraid that I can't, not in this form."

Alice sat back against the massive tree roots, crossing her arms over her chest as she tried to muddle through the information she had so far. She wished she could compare them side by side, but Xavier and Florian were never in the same room at once—

Wait.

Xavier and Florian were never in the same room at once.

Alice sat up a little straighter, squinting at Florian's Shadow form— the form he said that Xavier couldn't access. She'd felt Xavier's hand go warm before, just briefly, and seen a personality shift that made her think for a moment that she wasn't with Xavier in that room.

Afterwards, he flew into a rage. He wouldn't talk about it, wouldn't let her ask about it, and insisted it hadn't happened. The pieces were slowly, very slowly, starting to click into place. She still couldn't see the full picture, but a few things made much more sense if she plugged in one unlikely, potentially impossible, scenario.

"... You were in Xavier's body earlier, weren't ya?" Alice asked, eyes narrowing. "I felt it. I felt the change."

"Not exactly," Florian said, but he was smiling. She was on the right track. "Think. Think *hard*."

Okay. She could do this. She could figure it out.

It looked like Florian had, very briefly, taken Xavier's place. That... probably shouldn't be possible. Magic made plenty of things possible, though. Ellie had mentioned that spirit possession was something that could happen, but not without some serious dark magic or the willing consent of the physical party, and she wasn't sure how else two people might be able to share a body.

Except... Florian said he wasn't in Xavier's body.

So if the body wasn't Xavier's... then...

"He's in *your* body," she amended, gasping. "He's controlling it. Did— did he... kick you out or something?"

"In a way," Florian said. "When Xavier's consciousness takes over my body, I'm somewhat... forced into my Shadow form as an outlet for my spirit. It's why I'm still able to speak to you even when he's

controlling my physical form— oh, *hell*, that feels good to say." He took a deep breath, letting out a small, slightly panicked laugh.

"Can we get your body back?" Alice asked hesitantly. He looked so real, so corporeal, that she almost couldn't believe that her hand would pass right through him if she tried to reach out.

Florian opened his mouth, but no sound came out. He pursed his lips and nodded slowly. At least she knew, at minimum, there was a way.

"I wanna help," she whispered. "I'm not leavin' you like this."

"Please do not put yourself in danger for me," he hissed, shaking his head. "I don't know what he has planned for you, but focus on saving yourself. *Please.*"

Alice took a deep breath, clenching her hands into fists as she steeled herself.

"I've been waitin' on somebody to save me my whole life. I think it's 'bout time I started doin' it myself," she said firmly. "I'm not leavin' you behind. We're both gonna get out."

"Thank you," he said, looking for a moment like he might cry.

Though Alice had never thought of crying as an attractive quality before, it made her heart melt to see him like that. Florian was like fire— he outwardly expressed so much emotion, had so much life, and it made her want to live, too.

In that moment, she made a decision: Florian was worth it.

It didn't matter if her heart was broken. She could heal from that. She did not, however, think she could heal from losing her chance with him.

"I wish it was you instead," she whispered. "I wish you were my mirror instead."

Florian went stock still, and for a moment, she wondered if his Shadow form might entirely vanish. She wondered if he might run away, might laugh at her, might seem confused.

Instead, he reached out for her with his incorporeal hand, letting his fingers graze her cheek. She couldn't quite feel the touch, as it was something more like a breeze on her skin than a real hand, but Alice didn't take her eyes off him as he stared at her.

"I don't really care if we're mirrors," he said, and Alice's heart dropped.

Maybe this was a bad idea after all.

"I want you anyways," Florian continued, shaking his head. "I want to try."

Alice couldn't stop the tears from overflowing at that. She sniffled, trying to dampen her cries so she wouldn't wail, but the warmth in her chest was too strong. The tears continued flowing, so strong that she couldn't speak, hands over her mouth and slightly shaking.

"Are you—" Florian began, hands flailing. He reached out automatically, but his fingers passed through her shoulder.

"I'm good. Good tears," Alice managed, sniffling loudly.

She wasn't sure what to say anymore, but Florian calmed down a little at that. He moved as close to her as he could, obviously wishing he could touch. It wasn't yet clear what kept him restricted to Shadow form most of the time, but Alice determined right then that if she got another chance to be with his physical form, she planned to hug him and never let go.

"Hey... if ya can't tell me about the bargain, can ya tell me about... you?" she asked, sniffling as she glanced over at him. Florian raised an eyebrow, but he nodded.

"I like fae wine, and I'm incredibly afraid of heights, but I refuse to admit to it in front of anyone," he said, laughing softly. "Is that what you want to know?"

"It's a start," Alice said.

"Let's try this, then," Florian said. "When what you call the Appearances began, when we were trapped on this earth and unable to return to our homes in other worlds, a good portion of my court was here. We were celebrating, taking a special journey to see other lands. My father— the Shadow King, at the time— insisted that it was important to see and interact with humans when we could. The veil between our worlds has always been so thin that he thought it would foster understanding and peace to spend time on earth."

He paused, taking a deep breath.

"What... where is he now?" Alice asked hesitantly.

"Dead," he said flatly, disjointedly, as if distancing himself from all emotion in order to continue speaking at all. "Accidental iron poisoning, long before we realized exactly how prolific the substance is in the human world."

"I would hug you if I could," Alice said. It seemed a little silly, but it was what she wanted to do, and it made Florian smile.

Florian... who wanted her. Who might *actually* love her. If not now, maybe there was a chance for that one day, a chance to build on the trust they were developing that very moment.

"After his death, I desperately did not want to rule. I didn't know what to do or how to be the leader my people needed, so I... made the worst decision I have ever made in my life," Florian said softly. "I had a little too much wine and thought that I might be able to bargain my way out."

"I can't judge," Alice sighed. "I've done stupid things because I was hurting, too."

"You lost your own body, too? What a coincidence!" Florian joked, a bright smile on his face despite the circumstances. She couldn't help but laugh.

"Nah, I just married an evil king and then fell for his lookalike instead," she said, giggling.

"I'm... glad you did," Florian said shyly. "I'm glad to have met you."

"Me, too," Alice agreed.

After everything she'd gone through, and even if this turned out badly... she wouldn't trade it. She was glad for everything that had happened if it meant the chance to meet Florian.

* * *

Where was that damn watch?

Xavier huffed, rubbing his forehead as he took a seat in his desk chair. How did one lose a soul trap, exactly? He'd had *plans* for it. Now those plans would need to be reworked.

No matter. It was a small setback in the grand scheme of things. He'd waited centuries for this, and he could wait a little longer to redo his plans.

The bigger problem was Alice. It was taking far too long for her to accept him, no matter what he did. He took her on walks, they ate their meals together, he flattered and doted on her, but still she shied away from him like a frightened animal.

It was a problem. He needed her *willing* for this magic to take, to be able to use her power as his own. He needed it to break the bargain, to tip the scales in his favor.

He needed to speed the process along, too. She asked far too many questions, and it made him wonder if Alice wasn't as stupid as she appeared to be... but none of that would matter as soon as the marriage had been consummated.

Xavier didn't *want* to force things. He had always been someone who preferred to use coercion, bargains, and mental games to get what he wanted rather than brute strength.

That, and... well, he wasn't entirely certain the blood vows would activate at all if Alice wasn't a *willing* participant.

He would simply need to woo her faster. What did human women like, he wondered? What appealed to their senses? Should he bring flowers? Should he make professions of love written in terrible poetic verse?

Truly, Xavier thought that the best step to take might be to acquiesce to whatever inane requests she made in that entirely infuriating accent of hers. He'd nearly scared her away, and now he needed to do whatever he could to make Alice feel safe here. If she felt safe, her walls would come down in no time.

After all, she was barely more than a child, starved for affection and desperately yearning for a life of her own, yearning for an existence that didn't depend on her abusive mother. All he needed to do was string her along just a little more...

It wouldn't take long now.

14   IN WHICH ALICE DREAMS

Everything was so warm.

The air around her felt hazy and the surroundings indistinct, but Alice knew she was in the gardens. She sat under the same large tree with the roots big enough to cradle her, but instead she was cradled in Florian's arms.

Her back to his chest and his arms gently draped around her waist, Alice felt more relaxed than she ever had in her life. Was this what it was like to have someone near you with no expectations? Was this what it was like to feel the freedom of just being in the presence of another person?

Florian was exquisite. She'd had precious few moments near him and too many nights next to Xavier's icy form, and Florian's warmth was like an addiction that she didn't want to recover from. She turned her head to press her cheek against his collarbone, settling even closer against him.

Sunshine. It was like feeling sunshine on her skin.

Until the cold hit her bones.

"You could stay here forever, you know."

"I... I don't—" she stuttered, trying to pull away, but his grip on her arm was like a vice.

"You'd be happy. I promise."

That was enough to make her fully jerk away from him, scrambling to her feet as she whirled around. His hands were on her again in seconds, pulling her back, back towards the cold, back into his chest.

"Stay," he urged, but something in his voice had changed.

"I— I'd miss my friends—" she tried, still uselessly pulling against the grip. The look in Florian's eyes was uncanny, inhuman, and... utterly unlike Florian.

Xavier. It was Xavier.

"No need to worry. I can bring them here," he said, gripping her hand so tightly that it hurt. "Come and see."

Xavier pulled her along down the garden path, dragging more than guiding Alice through a maze of foliage and flowers, her feet skidding on the too-white cobblestones. They walked for far longer than she felt like they should have, as though they could have circled the palace twice, and when the leaves cleared, Alice found herself in a part of the garden that she had never seen.

She knew every corner of the garden. It was one of the few places she was allowed to explore on her own, and she loved being outside. However... this was entirely unfamiliar.

The white cobblestones that made up the garden path spread out into a circular stone courtyard, surrounded by tall fir trees laden with out of season pinecones. Strange, glowing flowers bloomed both in the grass around the courtyard and between cracks in the sparkling stones, and placed all around the courtyard were... statues.

Sparkling in the sun and beautiful, they appeared to be made from crystal, carved so smoothly that it looked like there hadn't been a chisel at all, and polished to an impossible shine. They were humanoid in shape, and there were seven of them in total.

Alice hesitantly stepped closer, squinting in the bright light to get a better look as her heart pounded in her chest, dread rising as she finally got a clear look at one of the statues.

She almost vomited onto the pristine courtyard stones as she realized that the statue wasn't a statue at all. It was a crystallized, petrified Ellie.

Hands over her mouth, Alice ran from statue to statue, picking out familiar faces and forms. Granny. Hartley. Kaz. Miriam. Sam. Harper.

All her friends frozen in a circle, their faces twisted in fear. All of them placed there by Xavier.

"What did you do?!" she shrieked, whirling to face him.

But he seemed calm, smiling at her from the path they'd just walked, looking like the picture of angelic serenity... and hiding the spirit of what she'd started to think might be the devil himself.

"See? They'll be with you always."

Alice opened her mouth to scream, but no sound came out.

Alice woke suddenly, jolting a little as she realized where she was: in the Shadow Court palace, tucked into bed next to Xavier. His arms around her were heavy and cold, and she had to fight not to thrash out against the embrace.

She shivered uncontrollably, stretching out her arm to reach for a blanket, but the thin wool fabric couldn't stifle the chill that seemed to radiate off the man beside her. It was almost painful to bear after the feeling of warmth and safety from her dream, and when Alice's teeth began to chatter, she finally shifted her position.

Brushing Xavier's arms away, she sat up in bed and tucked her knees against her chest, throwing the blanket around her shoulders. It helped a little to curl into her own body heat, and she rubbed her toes to chase away the numbness as she sat near the foot of the mattress.

In the morning, she'd ride back to Howard's Knob to see her friends— her family. She was surprised that Xavier actually planned to let her go, even for a short time. The anxiety over the idea that something might have happened to her friends while she was gone had taken over in the last twenty-four hours, and coupled with the stress of developing feelings for Florian, trying to hide what she knew from Xavier, and feeling desperately alone...

She was breaking into pieces.

Before she knew what was happening, a strange heat started to run down her face. She was crying, shaking with sobs, and Alice wasn't able to muffle the noise quite enough. While Xavier had slept through the moment she slipped away from him, the muffled cries and sniffles were enough to rouse him from his slumber.

"Alice, my treasure?" Xavier whispered sleepily, pale eyes opening slowly. "Are you well?" He pushed himself into a sitting position with a groan, shuffling a little closer to her.

"Nightmare," she said simply, not bothering to brush away the tears running down her cheeks.

"You're safe," he said, moving to place his arms around her once more. "I promise."

Alice wanted to vomit. Xavier's hold was gentle, but his arms were heavy, and any warmth she'd started to recover almost immediately faded again.

She shuffled slightly, pushing Xavier's arms away as gently as she could, mumbling something about nausea as she slipped out of bed and scurried to the bathroom, the blanket falling away from her shoulders as she moved. Shutting and locking the door behind her, Alice splashed cold water on her face from the sink, forcing herself to breathe slowly and deeply.

It was difficult to recognize the face in the mirror staring back at her. There was the same wild, red-orange hair, the same green eyes, the same pale, freckled skin... but something had changed. The dark circles under her eyes spoke of a kind of haunted resolve that Alice had never seen in herself before, a kind of weariness that even her mother couldn't bring out.

How much longer could she stay in the Shadow Court? A single month had brought her to this state. What might happen in a year?

She brushed away the shiver that ran down her spine at the thought. There was no way she'd still be here in a year, not with Xavier. Either Florian would be free, Alice would run for the hills, or perhaps both.

Steeling herself, Alice unlocked and opened the bathroom door, unsurprised to find Xavier staring right at her, sitting at the foot of the bed, exactly where she'd left him.

"Are you well, my treasure?" he asked, raising an eyebrow.

No. No, she was not well, but it would be disastrous to be entirely honest about why.

"I think I'm just... homesick. Worried about my friends," she stuttered, fumbling for an explanation. "I know I'm goin' to visit

tomorrow, but I'm just... nervous. I'm afraid something happened while I was gone."

Travel anxiety was the best explanation available. She'd packed a small bag the day before, but there wasn't much to take. The bag was mostly a medium for Missy to travel safely.

It wasn't entirely a lie that she was nervous, but it was certainly a risk to tell Xavier that she was afraid something had happened. If he had dared to do anything to them in her absence,

"I assure you, your friends are fine," Xavier said, and there was a hint of genuine confusion on his face that made it truly believable. "There will be no travel problems, either. I'm taking you myself, remember?"

She did remember, and while the speed of riding on Xavier's deer form was an advantage, she was not looking forward to the same exhausting ride that brought her to the Shadow Court in the first place.

At the very least, she thought, there was some comfort in knowing he didn't care enough about her family or friends to use them to force her hand. He might not even have thought of it, considering he seemed to have no family or friends himself. Alice still wasn't sure what kind of creature Xavier might be... but whatever it was, it wasn't *good*.

"I... I need air," Alice stuttered, shaking her head as she walked towards the door, yanking a shawl off the hook on the wall as she went. "I'll be back."

"I'll come with—" Xavier began.

"No," she said sharply, unable to keep the tension from her voice as she wrapped the thick shawl around her shaking shoulders. "No, I gotta do this alone."

Just at this moment, Alice couldn't stand the thought of being near him. She couldn't stand the idea of that body occupied by the wrong inhabitant, of looking at him and knowing that sunshine feeling she so desperately wanted was entirely out of reach.

She forced a shaking smile, glanced back at Xavier, and rushed out the door.

She wasn't sure where she was walking, but not because she was lost. By now, Alice knew the castle hallways and rooms decently well. She hadn't been in and out of all of them, but she knew the layout of the Shadow Court well enough to navigate, even in the dark.

The problem was that she wasn't sure how to find who she was looking for.

As usual, there was an eerie lack of castle staff around the hallways. Granted, it was the middle of the night... this time. No one to see. No one following her. No one to help.

... Except for one person.

"Florian!" Alice hissed, afraid to raise her voice too much. "Come on, you've gotta be around here somewhere..."

Alice's frustrated whispers echoed down the hallway. She simply hoped and prayed they'd catch the attention of the person she needed to see most. That was the downside to looking for someone in an incorporeal form with no dedicated bedroom space: There was no telling where he might be.

Luckily, by the time she turned the third corner, there was a response to her frantic whispering.

"What are you doing?!" A voice from behind her said softly.

Alice jumped, whirling around to face Florian. She hadn't heard footsteps— and there wouldn't have been any, considering that Florian was in Shadow form. She wanted to hug him, to hold him like she had in her dream, but that wasn't possible at the moment.

That was alright. It was enough to see him for now.

"I needed to talk to you," she rasped.

"What could—" Florian began, stopping when his eyes met hers, mouth hanging open.

The prince stared, taking in her red and swollen eyes, the tear stained cheeks, the tension in her posture, the way she wrung her hands anxiously. Then, he closed his mouth, nodded once, and glanced behind them down the hallway.

"What happened?"

"I'm... scared," Alice admitted.

"Took you a while to come to terms with that one, hm?" Florian asked gently.

"Shut up," Alice grumbled, letting out a short laugh despite herself. He was right. She'd pushed back the fear for so long, either out of a desire for love, a desire to understand what was going on in the Shadow Court, or simply a desire to stay alive long enough to see the world outside again.

Now, it seemed like the fear was in her very bones. She couldn't push it back, couldn't get it out if she tried. The only thing left to do was face it head-on.

"I wish I could hug you," Alice sighed. It slipped out before she even thought about it, but it was true. She wanted nothing more than to lose herself in Florian's sunshine warmth, just like in her dream.

Florian seemed to think for a moment, pursing his lips.

"Stay still?" he asked, taking a hesitant step closer. Alice just nodded.

Florian moved to stand right next to her, so close that she would have been able to feel his breathing in his corporeal form. Then, he gently brought his hands up to cup her cheeks, and brought his head down so their foreheads touched gently.

Though she couldn't truly feel him, there was *something* there. A slight tingle, a slight heat where his forehead rested against hers. If his form was made of light, it was like standing in a gentle sunbeam. It was comforting and beautiful and entirely him, and though there was no physical pressure on her skin, it satisfied the itch to hold him in a way she didn't expect.

"It's not much, but it's all I can do," he murmured.

"It's perfect," Alice choked out, tears springing to her eyes.

His fingertips on her cheeks tingled, now that she was paying attention to it. The sensation was subtle, but the intimacy of it made her want to sob in sheer relief. Even in the smallest of ways, she knew he was real. Florian wasn't a figment of her imagination. He was real, and he was here, and he was *good*.

He pulled away far too soon for her liking, but Alice would have stayed there all night if he'd let her.

"Come on. We can't stay out here," Florian said, glancing down the hallway.

He was right. There were very, very few people in the palace, but it was a miracle that no one had caught them together yet. The longer they stayed in the hallway, the more they risked someone spotting them... and subsequently reporting that sight to Xavier.

"I know a place," Alice said, motioning for him to follow.

She remembered the way from the night Willow rescued her from the garden. Quiet steps echoing down the empty hallways, Alice led Florian off to the same abandoned apothecary workshop that she'd slept in that night. The door creaked in a way that seemed louder than a thunderclap to her, but she knew that it was only the oppressive silence in the castle that made it seem that way.

Beckoning Florian inside, Alice shut and locked the door behind them, practically collapsing onto one of the small beds in the room. Clearly once meant for sick patients, it was Alice's second time sleeping on one as a refuge from Xavier's bedroom.

Her bedroom.

She shuddered at the thought, pulling herself up into a sitting position as she looked back at Florian. He stood by the door, staring at her with unconcealed concern.

"Are you...?" He trailed off. She wasn't okay. She obviously wasn't okay.

"I'll be fine. I just need... a minute," Alice said carefully, checking again that the door was bolted. She needed some sense of security right now, of privacy, of anything between her and the man keeping her here. The man that was, unfortunately, her husband.

The thought made her sick to her stomach.

Trying to find anything to distract herself, Alice traced her eyes over Florian's hands. They were calloused in a way that indicated experience with weaponry, though she didn't know enough to guess what kind. She imagined he might be good with a spear or a bow.

Her gaze traced along his fingers, the bones of his hands, and then the veins running up to his forearms... and that was when she noticed something peculiar.

"Your Shadow form doesn't have the same..." Alice gestured to her forearm, pointing to the scar that Xavier said indicated their connection as mirrors. As soulmates. "Your body does, though. Why?"

In truth, it scared her a little. Some part of her wondered, deep down inside, if Xavier could have been lying. Some part of her wondered if that mark really belonged to Florian all along, if it was a fluke or a glitch or something he'd claimed that wasn't rightfully his.

But... Florian's Shadow form didn't have the mark, and if he was really supposed to be her mirror instead of Xavier... that wouldn't make sense. He should have the mark.

Shouldn't he?

"You ask wonderful questions, rabbit," Florian said with a sad sigh.

Alice clenched her teeth so she wouldn't lash out at him. Florian wasn't the reason she was already angry, and it wasn't his fault that he couldn't talk about certain parts of his current condition.

"Fine," she conceded. There was little point in pressing while she was tired and unequipped to dance around answers. "I still don't get where Xavier's real body is. Maybe if we found it, we could... I dunno, force him back into it?"

Florian sighed, looking at her pointedly. He couldn't tell her.

"He did... have a body, right? Before he took yours. It's gotta be somewhere," she said, laughing in a way that most certainly sounded nervous.

Florian's eyebrows raised as he very carefully did not respond. Shit.

Xavier didn't *have* a body. That was the whole reason he'd schemed and bargained to take Florian's in the first place.

"What the hell kinda unholy haint is he?" Alice hissed, brow furrowing.

"That, I'm afraid I do not know. It's not clear if he gained a step closer to the corporeal realm when the Appearances began, as someone from Other planes might have, or if he was always here," Florian said, sighing. "He is... hanging onto consciousness on this earth in some unholy way."

"Is he Other?"

"I... am not sure," Florian admitted, shaking his head. "All I know is that his magic and the bargain combined was enough that he stole my body from me. I was lucky, really. The fact that my consciousness had

somewhere else to go meant that I survived a process that was certainly meant to kill me."

Why *Florian*, specifically? There had to be a specific reason that Xavier chose him. If he was incorporeal and biding his time, he wouldn't have chosen just anyone, and he wouldn't have chosen someone that he knew would cause this much trouble.

It could have been sheer bad luck, of course, but... a body was a serious thing. If she was an incorporeal spirit looking for a physical form, she'd have chosen someone strong. Someone in good health, maybe with powerful magic at their disposal—

Or, she thought, perhaps someone with other types of power at their disposal, too.

"It's a power grab..." Alice murmured, eyes widening.

"What do you mean?"

"Willow says there are Shadow Fae all over the world, working 'in the shadows...' figuratively, I mean. My guess is that they prob'ly got hands in everything on earth. Politics, stocks, trades, industry— you name it."

"That's a damn good guess. How'd you land on that?"

"I read up on Shadow Court history," she said proudly. "That's how the first Shadow Court established their authority, by working underneath everything happening on the surface. They built connections, scouted for information, and didn't move until the time was exactly right."

Her smile abruptly dropped as she continued to speak, a lump of cold dread settling in her stomach.

"If Xavier controls the Shadow Fae, he could control the entire world like puppets on strings."

"It would be an admittedly impressive start towards that end," Florian admitted.

At least that much made sense. There was, however, one piece to the puzzle that still eluded her. No matter how hard she tried, Alice just couldn't seem to make the idea that Xavier needed a Shadow Queen fit into his plans. He was power-obsessed, but he didn't seem to want an heir. He wanted to keep the power for himself.

So... why bother with a queen who could share it?

"I still don't get what he needs me for," Alice grumbled. "Why's it so important to him?"

"Did... Willow tell you her suspicions about your magic?"

"That I'm a big ol' battery that I don't know how to use? Yeah," she said.

"I'm worried that she might be right," Florian said carefully.

Something in his tone made her pause. He spoke slowly, with intention, in the same way that he did when he was trying to get something across to her without saying it directly.

"You know," Alice murmured, realization dawning. "You know what he wants."

"I have an idea," Florian said gravely. "I haven't been able to confirm it yet, but it's a start."

"And you can't tell me." It wasn't a question. By now, she understood that he would have already told her if he could.

"I can't, not exactly," he grumbled. "It's too close to my circumstances. We're going to have to work out a way around it."

"Maybe Ellie and Kaz can help me wiggle around it," she groaned, resting her head in her hands.

"He's actually letting you go, then? I heard some of the staff talking."

"There's staff? Where?" Alice scoffed, gesturing broadly.

"They've been instructed to make themselves scarce, from what I've gathered, and they're explicitly not supposed to talk to you," Florian admitted. "I've been eavesdropping."

Well, at least she'd been right about that theory. The staff wasn't supposed to talk to her, and if they were supposed to make themselves scarce because Alice unintentionally drained the memory magic the longer she was around... Then Willow was right.

She was a battery after all.

That left a few more questions, though. Firstly, how much magic could she store? And how was she supposed to let it out? What could she even *do* with it?

Most importantly, what did *Xavier* want her to do with it?

"I get three days," she huffed. "Hopefully it's long enough to figure somethin' out."

"Three days is better than nothing," Florian muttered, taking a seat beside her on the mattress.

"Can you... stay with me? Just for a little while?" Alice asked. "I don't wanna go back there yet."

"You'll have to be back by morning." Florian bit his lip, wringing his hands. "And I still can't touch you."

"I don't care. I'd still rather be here," she murmured, toeing off her shoes so she could lie down across the small bed. Even in the dusty, disused room with a lumpy mattress and a flat pillow, she'd sleep better than on a plush bed next to Xavier.

Florian turned slightly, still perched on the edge of the bed as he looked down at her, twiddling his fingers in the way he did when he couldn't figure out what to do next. Alice liked that about him. He was easy to read in so many ways, and she didn't have to guess what he was thinking.

"I don't bite," she said, sliding over a little. Alice gently patted the empty space on the mattress beside her.

"You'll go right through me. You don't have to make room," he muttered, but he moved to lie down beside her anyway.

She didn't need to, but she *wanted* to. Even though she couldn't feel Florian's skin against hers, every part of his body movement was so different from Xavier that Alice immediately felt at ease. His posture was more relaxed, his breathing was deeper, and the small smile playing across his lips made her heart flutter.

His face was so close to hers on the shared pillow. Despite the fact that his form was incorporeal, he didn't look any different than a physical man. Alice thought she'd be anxious sharing a bed with someone she cared for like this, but instead she found that she felt incredibly calm. She felt incredibly *safe*.

"What do you want to do?" Florian whispered. "When you get out of here?"

Alice paused, awkwardly looking away from the intensity of his pale eyes, a blush on her cheeks.

"Finish school, prob'ly," she sighed, scratching Missy behind the ears. "I was gonna be a veterinarian before all this."

"That fits," he agreed. "Where's Missy at this hour, anyhow?"

"She's a nocturnal critter, so she wanders at night sometimes. Guess she's out catchin' bugs," Alice sighed. "She's always there in the

mornin' again, though." She shifted uncomfortably, wondering if she'd find herself alone again when the sunlight filtered through the windows of the abandoned room.

"I'm not going anywhere," Florian said. "I'll wake you up when it's time to go back."

How could he do that? How could he read her mind?

Alice had never wanted to be close to anyone as badly as she wanted to be close to Florian. She'd never wanted to hear so much of someone's story, never wanted to imagine a future with anyone else like she did with him. Not even Hartley.

She... loved him.

She loved Florian.

Now... Now she had to save him.

IN WHICH ELLIE MAKES TEA

"Glad to be outta there for sure," Missy squeaked, poking her little nose out of Alice's bag.

"Agreed," Alice sighed.

It hadn't taken long for Xavier to run all the way back to Howard's Knob, but she was just as exhausted from holding onto the back of his ice-cold deer form as she'd been the first time. Luckily, she'd thought to bring a blanket to ride on for this trip. Though her muscles ached from exertion as they shakily stepped up the path towards Ellie and Kaz's house, she didn't feel like passing out from the cold.

She'd managed to force herself to kiss Xavier goodbye, then waited until she was sure he'd left before she walked up the path towards home.

Her *real* home.

The front door opened as she hiked up the path, Missy clambering up on her shoulder to see better. Wide-brimmed leather hat covering his short, black demon horns, Kaz stepped outside the house, pulling on his leather gloves as he went. He turned to walk towards the wood pile, but stopped dead when he saw Alice moving towards him.

"Holy shit," he said. "Holy shit!"

Kaz took off towards her, calling for Ellie over his shoulder.

It only took him moments to cross the distance, and Alice found herself taking off at a run until she practically crashed into him.

Kaz picked her up off the ground in a massive bear hug that had Missy scrambling for purchase on the fabric of her dress, and Alice couldn't help but laugh. Some part of her also wanted to cry, but she held it in for now as he put her back on the ground.

"You are in for a serious talk from Granny. I hope you know that," he said, attempting to let go. Alice wouldn't let him, fisting her hands in the fabric of his flannel shirt and just pulling him in close. It had been far too long since she'd been able to relax in the presence of a friendly, trusted face.

"You have no idea how glad I am to see you," she mumbled against his shoulder.

"Sure seems like it," he said, patting her back a little awkwardly. "You okay there? And who's your... uh... creature?"

"*Missy*," the possum squeaked, but Alice knew that Kaz couldn't understand animal speak.

"This is my friend, Missy," Alice explained without moving away. "And... I think I got married to an evil body snatcher who's trying to kill me," she said, voice still slightly muffled.

There was a long, long pause. Alice didn't bother to let go. Kaz was like a brother to her at this point, and he'd damn well just have to deal with a hug now and then, especially since her legs were still shaking from that ride, and her heart was still pounding from kissing Xavier goodbye. It felt like every bone in her body was screaming, wondering if he'd catch onto the fact that she knew more than she probably should.

He hadn't, thankfully. Not yet. She still had time to figure things out, though it wasn't much.

"The *fuck*...?" he finally muttered, then heaved a sigh. "Let's go inside. Something tells me I'm *really* going to need some of that emergency moonshine for this."

Alice finally let go, nodding slowly. They'd probably *all* need some moonshine for this. Kaz turned around and rushed back towards the house, pulling Alice along behind him by her free hand. She could barely keep up with his long legs, but sheer enthusiasm at arriving home

"What's all the hollerin' about?!" Ellie asked, but then she gasped, immediately pulling Alice into a fierce hug.

Two years ago, Alice never would have dreamed that Ellie could become as close to her as a sister, but this felt more welcoming and concerned than any hugs from her blood relations ever had. It was amazing what someone with a big heart could do for you. It was even more amazing that a moment of pettiness, anger, and sadness had caused her to try to leave this behind.

And then Ellie pulled away, frowned, and smacked her upper arm. It wasn't hard enough to hurt, but it was hard enough to make a point.

"Hey!" Alice cried, pursing her lips.

"*Was that good or bad?*" Missy asked, confused. In truth, it was neither. It was both affection and anger all in one gesture.

"Do you have any idea how bad you scared us?" Ellie snapped.

Alice took a deep breath.

"Y—yeah," she admitted. "I... I'm sorry."

All the wind went out of Ellie at that, shoulders slumping in relief. "Come on inside. We got somebody here who prob'ly wants to see ya."

The living area in the house was large, big enough to hold a crowd around the fireplace or move the furniture for dancing. None of them actually knew how to play the old upright piano in the corner of the room, but they could *try*, if they wanted. There were two sofas and a couple of armchairs, and in one of those chairs sat a woman with crystalline antlers, dark skin, and white freckles that looked like stars.

"Willow!" Alice cried, practically running across the room. "You made it!"

Alice hauled her friend out of the chair, ignoring the book that fell out of her hands in the process, and brought her into a hug. It was an incredible relief to see that she was safe, that her escape had been successful. Willow laughed and leaned into the embrace, teetering a little on her hooved feet from the force of Alice's enthusiastic bear hug.

"How long have you been here?" she asked.

"A few days. The trip wasn't as perilous as I feared, thankfully," Willow said. "How did you get out?"

"Xavier let me go. Well... temporarily," she said, wincing. "I've got three days here."

"Y'all sit down, and she can tell us all about it. I've got tea," Ellie said, bringing over a tray full of mugs as though Alice had just walked down from her upstairs bedroom rather than returned from nearly three weeks of a sudden disappearance on the back of a glass deer.

Ellie put down the tray of mugs on the coffee table, handing them out to Alice and Willow before taking a seat on the sofa opposite them.

"Got your note," she said without preamble, picking up a mug for herself. "You used the emergency code. How bad is it?"

"Bad," Alice admitted, holding her mug of tea with both hands, but not drinking. "It's *real* bad. What did y'all figure out on your own?"

"Willow filled us in on some of it," Kaz said as he plopped down on the sofa. He wrapped his arm around Ellie's shoulders, pulling her in close, and she leaned into the embrace like there was nothing more natural in the world.

"I told them there's an imposter on the throne, and that no one can remember Florian. He's still in the palace somewhere, but I didn't have time to figure out where or how before I had to leave," Willow said. "My guess is the dungeons. It's the only place I couldn't get past the guards to check."

So they understood who Florian was, at least. That was good. There were so many layers to this problem that Alice could barely keep track of them herself, much less explain them to someone else in a coherent manner. She took a long sip of her lavender tea and tried to let it calm her before speaking.

"He's not in the dungeons," she said, shaking her head as Missy climbed up onto her lap. "He's stuck in Shadow form... Most of the time. Sort of. Xavier stole his body."

Willow choked on her sip of tea.

"Wh... I'm sorry, *what*?" she stuttered.

Clearly, Willow hadn't had time to figure out what was happening with Florian's body. She knew he was still around, but... Well, obviously, circumstances required her to leave before she could get much information.

This would take some explaining.

"At some point, Florian made a bargain that ended up in Xavier booting him out of his own body. Then, and I don't know *how*, Xavier used magic to put some kinda block on the Shadow Fae so they can't remember Florian," Alice said slowly, nervously petting Missy's back.

"How the hell is he still alive?" Kaz asked, eyes wide. "That should have killed him. A soul not tethered to a body would be hunted down by psychopomps, at minimum, and there are a *lot* more of those on this plane than there used to be."

"Shadow form," Willow said slowly. "He has an external form that can hold his consciousness, so instead of dying, you're saying he's been stuck *permanently* in... Well..."

"Sorta like a ghost?" Alice offered. "'Cept ya don't need spirit sight to see him. It's a light-based form."

"Lucky duck," Kaz huffed, letting out a low whistle. "I've never even heard of that ability."

"We keep it under wraps as much as possible," Willow said. "It's a rare ability, even among Shadow Fae, not to mention coveted. It's best to take precautions."

"Understandable," Ellie mumbled, taking a sip of her tea.

Alice plunked her empty teacup down on the side table. She didn't think the lavender had actually done anything to help her relax. Or maybe she needed something stronger... Didn't Ellie keep a stock of valerian for this kind of thing?

"Damn," Kaz hissed. "You're in it *deep*."

"Thanks. I know," Alice grumbled, crossing her arms over her chest.

"I'll see what I can do, but you might want to ask Hart. From sheer age, he's the most likely of us to have seen anything like this."

Alice grumbled something unintelligible under her breath.

She didn't *want* to talk to Hart.

"Alice," Ellie said in a warning tone. "You're a grown woman."

"Don't mean I have to like it," she muttered.

Ellie laughed, a funny snorting sound that made Alice's composure break. Kaz, for once, just shook his head.

"What? She's got a point," he said with a shrug. "Anyways, I think you'll wanna talk to him eventually, especially about that journal he's been working on."

"Everybody here is safe, though? Right?" Alice asked, half out of sheer paranoia. Part of her was afraid that she'd return to the same horrifying statues from her dream.

"Peachy keen," Ellie confirmed, nodding.

"Your friends have some very good wards. No wonder Xavier couldn't locate you while you were inside these," Willow agreed.

"Would it... be enough to stop him gettin' inside?" Alice asked tentatively, eyes wide.

"Mmm..." Willow paused, scratching at the starlight freckles on her cheek with one hand. "It's difficult to say for certain. I think it might stop him for a little while, but he'd break through eventually."

"It's a good guess," Ellie said, sighing. "They'll stop a lot, but unless I prep somethin' specifically for him, I can only hold out so much against a magical battering ram. Just kinda depends on how long it takes'im to tire himself out."

"Do the prep," Alice said firmly, a steely undertone in her voice that she hadn't intended.

Her nightmare still haunted her. The last thing that Alice ever wanted was for something to happen to her friends, and that dream made it suddenly, painfully clear exactly how Xavier might manipulate her into doing everything he wanted.

They needed to protect themselves here, or at least make it too much effort to try to get to them.

"What do you know about that I don't?" Ellie asked, eyebrow raised.

"More of a hunch," she admitted. "Prob'ly better to be safe than sorry."

Ellie sighed and shrugged a little helplessly, looking back and forth between Alice and Willow. She flipped her long, silver braid over her shoulder and began to fiddle with her hair in the way she did when she was nervous, thinking, or generally antsy.

"Well, I can redo plans for the day, but I'm gonna need help," she said slowly. "Y'all have more experience with the sparkly bastard than

I do, so you're gonna have to guide me. And we'll need Granny, so somebody needs to go wake her up."

Alice entirely failed to hold back a snort at the idea that Xavier was a sparkly bastard. His antlers did glitter a little in the sunlight, but she'd never thought of him as sparkling, and the idea made her a little less scared.

"I do *not* want to wake her," Willow said, shaking her head.

"Can't blame ya," Alice muttered, shuddering. Granny was a sweet woman, but she did not take kindly to anyone who dared interrupt her sleep. She said she'd been alive long enough to earn some peaceful rest on this side of the grave, and she wasn't afraid to throw things— shoes, pillows, clocks, wooden carvings on her nightstand. Anything within reach of the bed was a possible projectile candidate.

"Then go bite the bullet and get Hartley. He's the only one she won't bother if he wakes her up," Ellie said, making a shooing motion with both hands.

Alice groaned.

"You're gonna have to talk to him eventually. Just go *do it*," Ellie said, eyes narrowed. "The other option is that *you* go wake up Granny."

Alice thought about it for a moment. It was possible that Granny might be excited to see her, and that would override the possibility of any anger at being roused from her slumber. However, she worried that as soon as she revealed they needed her for an actual project rather than a casual greeting, things would go right back to throwing shoes and general grousing.

It was probably better to have Granny in as favorable a mood as possible.

With a sigh, she crossed her arms over her chest and turned towards the front door.

"Fine," she muttered. "I'll go get him."

Xavier was... upset.

It was generally an unpleasant emotion, and he wanted to be rid of it as quickly as possible.

The unfortunate part of acquiring a corporeal form after centuries of living as a disembodied consciousness was that certain feelings and urges came with corporeality, and he was no longer used to them. Hunger was one. He'd managed to figure that out fairly quickly, along with the need to relieve himself and, occasionally, sleep.

Other sensations were stranger than those. The needs of his physical body were one thing, but the chemical reactions causing various emotions were entirely another. At least, he blamed it on the chemical reactions. That's all it really *could* be. Xavier had felt very few true emotions in a long, long time.

This particular emotion, one he could only identify as *worry* or *anxiety*, was possibly the one he liked the least.

Try as he might, Xavier couldn't take his mind off the scene from a dark palace hallway the previous night.

He was afraid that Alice might try to run from the palace entirely, so he'd followed behind her in the shadows, just in case. He couldn't have her running off this close to the full moon, even if he had to use force.

To his surprise, she'd started calling out a name that he hadn't heard in years, a name that he himself had taken great pains to scrub from this palace and the people inside: Florian.

When had she met Florian? How long had she known of his existence? How *much* did she know?

More importantly: Why was she calling out for him?

He'd been right to exile that pesky half-shifter, and especially to send all residents but the most essential staff away from the palace. Alice's magic was stronger than she knew, stronger than Xavier had anticipated. The effects of the memory magic on Willow had severely diminished after only a few minutes of conversation, without any conscious effort from Alice at all.

He managed to correctly anticipate that interactions with the staff might cause something like this, and thankfully, he'd prevented any further complications in that regard. He *should* have thought that Florian

might reach out to her, but he didn't think that the sniveling princeling would ever dare.

Perhaps he'd grown a spine during all those years forced away from his own body.

Worst of all, and the only thing that truly managed to get under his skin: Alice allowed Florian to be close to her in a way that she'd *never* allowed him. Oh, she tolerated his advances. She even bent to them sometimes, allowing herself to let go in a way that was almost endearing. Sweet. Sometimes it was almost like she might *want* to love him...

Maybe it wasn't too late. Maybe her interaction with Florian was more insignificant than it seemed.

And perhaps... perhaps he wouldn't need to kill her after all.

Perhaps her magic was strong enough that he wouldn't need it all to break the bargain.

Xavier blinked.

He wasn't... *no*. He'd lost his heart centuries ago. There was no way that the sight of a stupid, partly *human* woman showing affection to someone else— never mind someone that he currently shared a body with— could make him rethink his decisions. There was no way she could make him want to change his plans.

There was no way he really, truly wanted her to look at him like that. It was just a side effect of having a corporeal form again. Emotions were nothing more than an inconvenience. It didn't matter what he felt or thought any longer. He was committed to his plan.

It didn't matter if she was pretty, or innocent, or a little slow in a way he thought made it quite adorable when she caught onto things...

A human woman might be the *only* thing that could make him regret his choices, though. After all, it was a human woman who started his journey down this path.

When it came down to himself or Alice, Xavier knew who he would choose.

Young and stupid though she might be, Alice was also stubborn, and she'd resisted his attempts to mold her at nearly every turn. At first, he thought she might be useful to him outside of her magic, but she clearly intended to make herself into a thorn in his side. On top of that,

she'd clearly developed some kind of an attachment to Florian, and none of that would work to his advantage. It would be better to dispose of her entirely, from a logical standpoint.

In the end, Alice didn't matter. He didn't want her.

She was a means to an end.

The trip wouldn't last long. Alice would be back in mere days, and that wasn't enough to bother his plan. On the contrary— Xavier hoped his generosity in allowing her to visit home would lull her into a false sense of security.

During the three days she was away, it would leave him free to plan. He couldn't move up the process, unfortunately, since the power of the full moon was essential to his plan. The balance of light and darkness was essential to Shadow Fae, even down to their physical bodies, and he needed it in the mix to take full control.

However... it was clear now that Alice wouldn't consummate their vows willingly. That was a rather difficult problem. To bring his plan to completion, he needed a higher volume of magical power than both parties involved in the initial bargain. That was Alice. Her whole life, she'd been slowly gathering and stocking magical power in her blood and her bones. She was a bomb ready to explode with magic, just waiting for that energy to be directed.

He couldn't do it without her, and he did *not* plan to wait to find another seventh of a seventh. This was his best chance.

Xavier gave a growl that turned into a cry of rage, hurling a dagger from his belt towards a nearby tree.

The dagger hit with such force that it split the thin trunk in two, the tree toppling and the blade flying off into the underbrush. No matter— he could get another one. He could not get another Alice, and he certainly would have a difficult time acquiring another body.

Things had to go his way to maintain his life, his power, his immortality. He had gone far too long searching for the secrets to living forever, to altering the very fabric of souls, to let it end now. There wasn't another option for him.

There had to be a way to force the blood vows without requiring consummation. Surely blood vows were not only used as wedding vows in the past. There had to be another way.

And he had three days to find it.

IN WHICH ALICE APOLOGIZES

Hartley's house was one of three on the property.

Ellie and Kaz had the biggest home, partly because they housed everyone who needed a space to live that did not yet have a home. Harper and Alice had bedrooms there, as well as Granny— though, Granny had notably claimed the attic as her own from day one. It was also because Kaz was responsible for the construction, and he was not known to do things halfway. Their home looked like a scrumbled-together art piece, with patched together colored glass for the windows, walls made of stone, brick, and logs, and it all came together into a structure that seemed chaotically beautiful.

Miriam and her family lived in a standard log cabin style home, which they'd picked for simplicity and reliability. Miriam, Sam, and their two children had plenty of room in that place, and room for visitors, too.

Hartley, on the other hand, was the only resident of his home. The simple siding was painted dark blue at his request, the windows flanked by clean, pale gray shutters. A few wicker chairs sat on the simple, covered porch, the recently painted white railing practically glinting in the sunlight.

As she walked closer, it occurred to Alice that she'd never actually been inside the house since Hartley officially moved in. Of course, she'd seen it as it was built, but she didn't

know what the inside looked like. Hartley was very private, and she'd...
Well, she'd never passed the requirements to enter his home or his heart,
apparently.

Brushing off the bitterness building on her tongue, she forced
herself to look at the other surroundings even as she grew closer to the
dark blue house. In addition to the houses, they had a small barn, a shed
for gardening supplies, and Kaz was working hard on a greenhouse
structure. The familiar surroundings should have been soothing, but Alice
couldn't brush off the thought of the last time she'd seen Hartley.

She shouldn't still feel this bitter. She certainly didn't feel bitter
because she wanted him.

"I think you want to be loved. I do not, for one moment, believe
you really love me as you think you do."

The words still stung, and if she was honest with herself, she knew
why: Hartley was right.

She'd already come to that conclusion when thinking about
Xavier, but being back here made things feel different in a way that she
wasn't expecting. It was amazing how much three weeks away from home
could change you, but perhaps that was also because Alice had never been
away from home. She'd never had the chance to be without people who
saw her grow up, to discover who she was...

And perhaps that was another reason she'd latched onto Hartley.
He hadn't seen her grow up, so she could make herself into what he
wanted in a partner without suspicion or skepticism... but that hadn't
worked. He'd seen right through her.

And now she had Florian, and she was learning who she wanted
to be, just as herself, as Alice... And Florian *liked* it. That thought gave her
enough courage to face up to her past actions.

Hartley was sitting on the porch of his home, just as he had been
the day she'd run away and found Xavier in the woods. He was reading a
book, and though she couldn't see what it was, she was certain he'd
finished the previous one by now. The man read at an incredible pace.

He looked up when he heard footsteps.

It was like Harley to be calm. He was generally unshakeable, no
matter the circumstance, so it wasn't too surprising that he only slightly
flinched when he looked up from his book. Locking eyes with Alice, his

posture stiffened a little, his eyes going almost imperceptibly wider, but that was all.

He was silent as she drew closer to the porch, keeping her steady pace, petting Missy absently to help keep herself calm.

When she came close to the porch, she stopped before walking up the steps, and for the life of her, she could not figure out what to say. Her mouth flapped open and closed as Missy looked back and forth between them, but no help came from her possum companion.

In the end, it was alright, because Hartley spoke first.

"I'm sorry," he said slowly, looking away.

Alice paused, lips parted to speak, but no sound came out. Whatever she was expecting, it wasn't an apology. But... perhaps mutual apologies were in order.

It was time to be an adult about this, just like Ellie said.

"I... I'm sorry, too," she finally said. "And... You were... right."

It was almost painful to admit it out loud, and she couldn't meet his eyes while saying it. Still, it needed to be said. All in all, she'd learned something important from the experience, as painful and embarrassing as it had been.

"I shouldn't have been so harsh on you about it," Hartley said, closing his book. He gestured to the empty chair on the porch. "Sit. Let's talk."

Alice trudged up the steps and plopped down in the second wicker chair, unsurprised when Missy scrambled down from her shoulder to go sniff at Hartley. She probably wanted to get an idea of his scent to see if he was friend or foe, or even to identify him later. Hartley didn't seem bothered by her investigation, holding out a hand so she could smell, and even letting her climb up on his shoulders.

"Who's this?" Hartley asked, chuckling as Missy sniffed at him.

"This is Missy. She's a good friend," Alice said with a smile. "She's been there for me a lot the past few weeks."

"I'm glad. Based on what Willow has told us, it seems like you've needed someone," he said sadly. "I... can't help but feel as though this is partly my fault."

"It's not." Alice shook her head and leaned back in the wicker chair. "It's my fault. I ran off, and I made the choice to follow."

"You wouldn't have run off without my... Well..." he trailed off, frowning.

"Don't worry 'bout it. What's done is done." She sighed, shaking her head. Three weeks ago, she might have pointed fingers and placed blame, but there were bigger things at stake here than that. She'd rather take responsibility and resolve the situation.

"Still, I want to do what I can to help with this," Hartley insisted. "Willow gave me a journal when she arrived—"

"Thank the Lord!" Alice cried, clapping her hands together. Missy squeaked and scuttled back over to her lap, perching in her usual place.

"It's that important?"

"It's Xavier's. Deer man. Or... I think it's his? It came from his desk," she stuttered. "In any case, somebody hid the thing, so it's gotta be important."

"I can certainly agree with that sentiment," he said with a nod.

"So... how's the translating going?" Alice asked hopefully.

Hartley winced.

"I'm working on it," he said, sighing. "The language is something close to Sumerian, but it's a dialect I've never seen. There are words thrown in that aren't in that language at all— it looks closer to something like a bastardized Latin or archaic French, but with the wrong syllabary. The consistency is... Well. It *isn't* consistent."

"But you can read it," she said. He knew the languages, at least. That was already much, much farther than she or Willow had been able to get.

"I can get a basic gist of the content, yes," Hartley said, tilting his head back and forth. "It's far from a specific translation, though, and it feels incredibly jumbled to look through. The sentence structure is baffling."

"I knew you could do it," Alice said, a smile pulling at her mouth.

"Don't speak too soon," Hartley said, letting out a slow breath. "It'll take time to get it into a readable format."

"... How's three days?" she asked, wincing.

Hartley blinked. "I'm sorry— *three days*?"

"It's all I got," she said with a helpless shrug.

"Well," he said, taking a deep breath, "that will have to do, then."

Alice nodded slowly, pausing in petting Missy, eyes locked onto something invisible in the middle space.

Would it be enough? What if they couldn't stop Xavier? She wasn't even entirely certain what Xavier was planning, but Florian didn't deserve to be trapped like he was, and Xavier was... bad news. Very, very bad. The more she thought of his scheming, his violent outbursts, the way the staff was afraid of him, the more she was determined that something needed to be done.

And it made her wonder something about herself, too.

"What are you not saying?" Hartley asked, eyes narrowing. "I know that look on your face."

That was the downside to living in close quarters with people. You got to know their quirks and their habits, and eventually everyone could read each other like a book. And she did have another question, but she was afraid to ask it.

This might be her only shot at a real answer, though.

"If Xavier is my mirror... does that mean I'm that bad, too?" Alice whispered.

It had been on her mind for days. She was too scared to ask Florian, too afraid to confront the question herself, and she wasn't sure why it came out now, in the presence of the man she hadn't even wanted to talk to when she first came here. But... If anyone would know the answer to this, if anyone had any knowledge about it at all... it would be him.

"What?" Hartley asked, blinking furiously. "What are you talking about, Alice?"

"He's my mirror," she said softly, pulling her knees to her chest, skirt pooling over her legs. "An' I don't want him to be."

Hartley stared at her for a long moment, long enough that Alice stopped looking at the ground. Instead, she dared to glance up at him, catching a glimpse of that intelligent, calculating nature peeking through that she'd once found so attractive. Now it just made her feel scrutinized.

Now, it made her long for Florian's gentle smiles.

"Who told you he's your mirror?" Hartley asked carefully. His tone was almost suspiciously neutral.

"I guess nobody needed to, did they?" she sniffed, rolling up her sleeve to show him the scar-like pattern on her forearm. "We got these. They match. That's enough, ain't it?"

Hartley swallowed thickly. He opened his mouth to speak, and then closed it again. Finally, he took a slow, controlled breath, and looked her right in the eyes, his expression grave.

"Mirrors don't *have* marks, Alice," Hartley said softly. "I can confirm that for you myself."

But... That made no sense.

"So what's... what's this, then?" she asked, pointing at the mark.

"It's a bargain mark, I believe," he said confidently. "I can only assume it's from when you were promised to Xavier at birth. Fae, in particular, like to leave visible evidence of a bargain on skin. Though... I admit I'm not entirely certain how *you* wound up with a mark when your mother made the bargain."

"I was part of the deal. I thought that was enough."

"Not usually, no," he muttered, shaking his head. "You'd need to be a major party involved in the bargain, the one who made the deal. Not a bargaining chip."

But she... was a bargaining chip, wasn't she? Her mother promised her to Xavier, and that was it. The only other thing that tied them together was—

The blood vows.

They were just another type of bargain, weren't they? At the end of the day, it was a special set of promises to be magically fulfilled by both parties involved. It wouldn't be unreasonable to think that they resulted in a mark.

It wasn't the first bargain that caused the mark on her skin. It was a second one made on top of it.

Xavier told her that the design was a manifestation of their bond on skin. That could be true. It would certainly be easy to goad a baby into drinking the mere drops of blood required for the vows, and easy to twist the wording to imply consent from an unsuspecting child.

It also wouldn't be unreasonable to assume that someone like Xavier would want to mark her. He wouldn't want to be tricked away from the exact girl he bargained for, and this was a way to do it. He'd even

said that the first part of the three-part marriage vows had already taken place... presumably when she was a baby. Her mother must have taken the vows on her behalf.

The scar was a remnant of their marriage contract, etched into her skin her whole life. It was the first of the promises she'd made, knowingly or unknowingly— promises that Alice now desperately wanted to run from.

"... Have you heard'a blood marriage vows?" Alice asked.

Hartley paled.

"You didn't."

"I... *technically* haven't," she muttered, looking away. "Not completely."

Hartley sighed in relief, rubbing a hand across his eyes. "Good. Blood vows were outlawed in my home world a long, long time ago. They're dangerous."

"It's not a marriage thing?"

"It's to bind two souls together so that they become one," he explained. "Or, at least, as close as possible to one. It's often used by people who want to simulate the bond of a mirror soul, but from everything I've heard and read, it's... nothing like it at all."

"I thought a mirror was like... looking at yourself. Why wouldn't that be the same if you merge?"

"You're still independent beings as mirror souls. You have your own thoughts, free will, and independent magic. Blood vows... they take that away."

She opened her mouth to respond, but the look on Hartley's face stopped her.

He was... sad. Not *just* sad, either– he looked *anguished*. He looked like a crucial part of himself had been ripped away from him, like he'd been to hell and back, like there were shadows behind those eyes she'd never even begun to guess at before.

"How do you know so much about mirrors?" she asked carefully, eyes narrowing.

It could be his age. Hartley knew a lot because of his sheer age, which he generally refused to reveal to most people. However, something

in his unflappable façade seemed to crack a little at that question, seemed to shake a little under the scrutiny in a way she hadn't seen before.

Hartley crossed his arms over his chest, looking away. He didn't speak for a long moment, but the tension in his posture was almost like nothing she'd ever seen in him. Instead of looking calm and collected, he seemed agitated and nervous. It was almost like he wanted to run away from the room, his hands curling into fists and uncurling over and over again as he tapped his foot impatiently.

"I found mine," he finally said.

Alice let out a breath she hadn't realized she'd been holding.

Something clicked into place in her thoughts, in her memories. It made sense that he was avoiding romantic connections. It didn't matter how long ago it happened. With a connection as strong as that, losing them would be incredibly scarring, and... Well, it seemed like he hadn't taken it well.

"It was a long time ago," he confirmed.

"What... happened?" she hazarded, almost afraid to ask.

"She died," he said flatly. "And I decided it was time to work on myself." It sounded detached, distant, like a wound that hadn't yet healed over. It didn't matter how long it had been. Things hadn't settled for Hartley, not yet.

That would, at the very least, explain the haunted look in his eyes.

"I'm sorry," she said. It felt hollow and superficial, but they were the only words that she had.

"I am, too." Hartley took a deep breath before he continued. "I know some sources have... conflicting information about mirror souls, to say the least. I'm not sure how some of those rumors came about, but I can tell you what I know."

"What..." Alice sighed, frustrated. "Okay, not to sound stupid, but what even *is* a mirror? I keep hearing that it's this profound connection, but I'm not seein' how it happens and I'm not *feelin'* it happen, either."

Hartley nodded slowly. He didn't speak for a moment, like he was trying to think of how to describe it in the clearest way possible.

He didn't call her stupid, either, though. He never would, and she knew that. At one time, she assumed that was because he might have

some kind of romantic love for her, but now she was starting to understand that was just part of how Hartley treated his friends with respect.

"You know how you pick up habits from people you live with?" Hartley asked.

Alice nodded.

"Imagine picking up habits across centuries. Across lifetimes," Harley said slowly. "Imagine someone whose soul has become so well tangled with yours that it's no longer certain if the reflected pieces originate from one side or the other."

"Your other half," she said dreamily, but Hartley shook his head.

"A mirror isn't half your soul, Alice. You exist as a whole person all on your own," Hartley said softly. "They're not your only hope for love, either, even if you do meet them. They can even be platonic."

"Then... then what's the *point* of havin'em?!" Alice huffed. "If a soulmate is such a big damn deal, you shouldn't have to work for it, too."

"A soulmate isn't there to suddenly be everything you've ever needed, they are there so you can grow *together*," he snapped. "It's a mutual responsibility, not an instant solution to your problems."

"How can you ever tell, then?" Alice asked, throwing up her hands. This all seemed too complicated and painful for her to worry about.

"I think you know for sure when you stop asking yourself if it's important that they're your mirror or not," he admitted. "When it doesn't matter anymore. You just want to be with them, come hell or high water."

"I..." Alice sighed. "That seems annoying."

"I know," Hartley said with a small laugh. "Trust me, I know."

Well, that...

That certainly, absolutely, without a single doubt... did not apply to Xavier.

Despite the heaviness of the moment, Alice felt a sense of relief. It was like a weight off her chest knowing that she really, truly was not permanently tied to Xavier. He wasn't her cosmic perfect match across lifetimes. He wasn't even her match in this lifetime!

She'd been right all along not to trust him.

However... there were still questions unanswered. There were still too many variables, too many missing pieces to make out the full picture.

"So what was Florian trying to tell me about the mark...?" Alice mumbled. Or, rather, what *couldn't* he tell her about the mark?

"Florian?" Hartley asked, suddenly perking up. "You met the Shadow Fae prince?"

"It's compl—" Alice cut off, eyes narrowed. "Wait. How do *you* know about him? Did Willow tell you, too?"

"Willow mentioned him, but a friend of a friend had some information about the Shadow Court. We did a little research after you left," he explained.

A friend of a friend? Willow giving information was one thing, but if someone outside the Shadow Court could remember Florian's existence, that meant he hadn't been entirely erased. That was good. That meant Xavier's magic had a limit.

"The memory lock must only work inside the walls..." Alice mumbled.

She wasn't sure how the memory block or his claim to the throne affected the communities of Shadow Fae around the world, but if he could establish his authority over one, he could likely branch out to the rest of them in time. He wouldn't *need* to make them forget Florian, eventually.

However, if there was a limit to his magic... That meant Alice could do something about it.

That meant she might be able to eat away at it with her own magic. If she could figure out *how*, that was.

"Memory lock?" Hartley asked hesitantly, jarring her out of her thoughts.

"I... think I have a lot to explain," Alice said with a sigh. "Sit. This is gonna take a while."

17

IN WHICH XAVIER READS

The library was massive and cloaked in shadows, but it was still too bright for him, and he preferred to spend as little time there as possible. He'd rather spend his hours in the darker recesses of his bedroom, or even in a closed off, disused office in the corner of the palace where there was no light at all. This trip was highly necessary, though, as the head librarian was the one staff member that Xavier instructed to stay at his post.

Of course, he was also instructed not to speak to Alice. That was too risky, considering he couldn't guarantee the librarian's reaction to learning the truth of his situation. However, Xavier needed someone with eyes on his wife, just in case trouble ever arose.

Trouble was here.

Xavier approached the desk without hesitation, inwardly satisfied as the man rose to greet him, giving a deep bow.

"Ah, good morning, my king!" he said cheerfully. "You haven't borrowed my translation glass, by chance, have you? It seems to be missing."

"I have not. You must have misplaced it," Xavier said, fighting not to roll his eyes. The man was scatterbrained, yes, but surely he could keep track of a valuable item like a translation glass. It was necessary for his job,

considering the massive number of languages in the different library volumes.

"How may I assist you, then?" The librarian's plastered-on smile became a little tense, but it did not falter. Xavier had the fleeting thought that he did not remember the man's name.

His next thought was that he did not care.

"Rise," Xavier said as he waved his hand dismissively. "I need to know what books my wife has been reading."

"Looking to share interests, then?" he asked with a small smile.

Xavier just frowned. He didn't quite understand the point of sharing interests. It seemed like such a faraway concept, and he hadn't even worried about it in years. Either people had similar goals to his, or they did not. They agreed, or they did not. That was the end.

He did wonder what she was thinking, but not quite in the way that he wanted to share those thoughts. It was more like he wanted to study her, to know how her mind worked.

The librarian chuckled awkwardly and continued without waiting for a response, which was probably for the best.

"She's mostly been wandering the Shadow Fae history section, though I'm not sure which books she's been reading. She's quite careful to place them back."

Xavier practically growled. That wouldn't be helpful at all, considering how large the historical section was. He needed something else, something more specific.

The librarian flinched, eyes widening as he took a step back, putting distance between them. "O—of course, there was a book or two she left on a table. I b— believe they involved Shadow forms, as well as the earlier history of our people."

"Where can I find them?" he snapped.

"The early historical volumes are shelved on aisle eighteen," he said. "Of course, I doubt you'll be needing the Shadow form volume, considering that you possess one yourself—"

"Where?" Xavier interrupted.

That was the downfall to the memory magic. The easiest way to rig the situation in his favor was to change the memory of Florian's name to his name, and to erase most of the prince's childhood. Unfortunately, a

few things still slipped through the cracks here and there, including several crossover memories of Florian that people now clearly thought were of *him*.

He *didn't* have a Shadow form. He couldn't stomach a form made of pure light— and how stupid was it to call a form made of light a Shadow form, anyhow? Ridiculous.

"Aisle twenty," the man squeaked, shrinking a little.

Idiot. Xavier would be more than happy to replace the entire castle staff once he...

Once... he...

What was the plan again?

His thoughts had been entirely scrambled since the theft of his journal, and he still wasn't sure who had taken it. His recent memory was one thing, but the details of his past felt fuzzy, distant, more impressions and colors than true memories at this point.

The bargain needed to break, firstly, and he needed Alice to do that. Once the bargain was broken, he planned to use the power of the Shadow Court to his advantage, drawing on their research, their resources, their magic, their darkness. It would be so easy not only to take control of this entire, pathetic human world, but to extend his own lifespan into infinity. There would be an endless source of bodies with an endless source of inhabitants ready to sacrifice themselves to him.

He would be their new god.

And... there was something else. There was something in there about not only his own infinity, but someone else's, too. There was something about a body, something about a soul, something about bringing someone back from... a mist?

He wasn't quite sure how that thought occurred to him in the first place, though. There was something... something about a woman, but he couldn't remember her face or her name any longer, not without his journal to help him dredge up those thoughts from a mire of painful, wasted years.

Xavier sighed as he pulled the book the librarian had referenced from the shelf. To his surprise, there was only one reference book written on Shadow forms. He knew they were a well-guarded secret, known only

to the Shadow Fae, but he hadn't considered the scarcity of information available on them.

Opening the volume to the table of contents, he mentally wracked his brain to remember how to translate the ridiculous fae language the book was written in. How had Alice managed—

Ah.

She'd stolen the translation glass. Perhaps she was smarter than he'd given her credit for... but it didn't matter at the moment, as Xavier *could* read fae. It had simply been a while.

Once he managed to remind himself of the language structure, he flipped past the section describing the history of Shadow forms and straight to the header that intrigued him most. It was a chapter labeled "Care and Warnings," and Xavier truly did not understand why a Shadow form might need those. Was it possible to become stuck in it? Could you even hurt yourself in a form made of light alone? Did you need to eat?

As he skimmed through the text, he realized that the answer was even more peculiar than he expected.

"Interesting..." he murmured, a slow smile stretching across his features.

Very, very interesting.

◆

Alice felt like scratching her eyes out.

After spending the night in her familiar bedroom, she'd woken up at the crack of dawn and almost immediately started pacing around the living area, a piece of paper in hand. After scratching out about the tenth idea of what Florian could have possibly bargained for, Alice found herself running headfirst into the wall.

The resulting collision left her with a bruise on her forehead and an irate Granny stumbling sleepily down the stairs. Granny immediately put her to work cooking breakfast for the still-sleeping residents of Howard's Knob, which was at least enough to keep her distracted for the next couple of hours.

Once they filled the table with fry bread, bacon, eggs, fruit, and juice, her thoughts strayed from cooking and went straight back to Florian. She barely managed to keep calm until Hartley walked through the front door, looking slightly more rumpled than usual and stifling a yawn with one hand.

"Late night translating?" Alice asked, practically jumping up from her chair and trying to keep the hopeful tone out of her voice.

"Indeed," he mumbled, apparently too sleepy to notice her enthusiasm.

"How's it going?" She wove her fingers together and forced herself to act calmer than she felt. It wouldn't help to needle him to get on with the project. He was doing his best, and she knew enough to trust that he would work as quickly as possible.

"I've got part of it, at least," Hartley said as he put a few pages down on the table in front of them. "It's a little choppy, but it's legible, and it's better than nothing."

"Thank you," Alice said, heaving a sigh of relief as she picked up the pages. Even a little insight into the mind of whoever wrote this journal was enough to help them.

The pages were messy, littered with Hartley's translation notes and crossed out, scattered translations replaced with more coherent sentences. It took her a moment to get a handle on the format, but after a moment, she understood how to read the notes.

I am old now, and I will be older (ancient?). These pages help me remember why. (Note: Why what? Why how? No specification.) I do not want to forget my work.

I do not remember child life (childhood?). It was old time/long ago. I remember Falina (name? no known translation equivalent), I remember love, I remember hurt, but it is far away. My human life is finished now, and I live (lived?) as a spirit.

The body I (have/took/acquired) will take me far on my journey. I am close to my goal, but I need more first.

"More what?" Alice asked, brow furrowing.

"Not sure," Hartley sighed. "The book seems to reference something about extending life, and it isn't just once. It's like he's... trying to remind himself of something?"

"How old would he need to be to have to do something like that?" Ellie asked, raising an eyebrow as she glanced at Hartley.

"And *why* are you looking at *me*?" He crossed his arms over his chest, glancing at her pointedly.

"You know why," Ellie said, mirroring his expression.

Hartley huffed and rolled his eyes. "For an Other, it might take thousands of years for memories to deplete to that level. I have trouble remembering my childhood, yes, but that was... a while ago," he said, tapping his foot as he thought. "For someone born human— and it seems he *was* human, at least at some point— it's difficult to say. Even if he became a spirit of some sort, he isn't a true Other. He's a human with an incorporeal existence, somehow hiding from the psychopomps, somehow with access to bargain magic... but still human."

"If he's a spirit, I might could force him outta that body," Ellie mused.

Ellie was, primarily, a spirit worker. She had strong green magic, a deep connection with the plants of the area, but her spirit magic was even stronger.

"Bad plan," Kaz deadpanned, cutting his eyes towards Ellie.

"I could always try," she grumbled.

"As happy as I am that you're more confident in your abilities, love, I'd rather you didn't attempt to oust a clearly powerful evil spirit of unknown origins without considering other options first," Kaz said, gently patting her shoulder.

"Well, it can't hurt to give it a shot—" Ellie began, but cut off suddenly, looking towards something on the other side of the room. "Dammit. That's the wards again."

Ellie went to the front door to peek outside, pointedly scanning the edge of the property. If there was something physical or spiritual out there, she'd be able to see it. Alice followed her towards the door, fear gripping at her throat. What if it was Xavier? What if he came back early?

Peeking outside, her nightmares were confirmed when she saw a tall, dark-skinned form with crystal antlers standing just outside the wards. However, she could also see a familiar, small, gray body running through the grass towards him.

Missy?

Missy had probably been out all night, which was why she was outside, but Missy wouldn't run towards Xavier. She couldn't stand him any more than Alice could. However, Missy *would* run towards someone else.

"Florian?" Alice murmured, squinting.

And then Missy jumped up, and her little body went *right through the figure*.

"Florian!" she screeched, hiking her skirt up to her knees and taking off at a full sprint.

"Hey, wait up!" Ellie called, following behind. "Don't go by yourself!"

Alice was streaking across the mountain before Ellie finished her sentence, and she wasn't going to stop... Until she hit a groundhog hole near the edge of the property.

She cried out as she flew forward, tumbling over the edge of the wards and rolling until she rested in a heap next to Florian, dizzy and disoriented. Missy squeaked something in her face, but she couldn't quite make it out.

"Are you alright?!" Florian asked, eyes wide and hands flailing as he hovered over Alice. She was fine— her ankle was a little sore, but her pride was really the injured party.

Luckily, it only took Ellie a moment to catch up. Her long legs and pants meant that she could run faster than Alice. Skidding to a stop right beside where Missy squeaked and fretted, Ellie took a knee and checked her friend over, ignoring Florian for a moment in favor of Alice's safety.

"So you're the guy?" Ellie asked, panting as she pulled Alice to her feet.

"Hi," he said sheepishly, giving a little wave. "Sorry to intrude."

"Smart man," Ellie said approvingly. "Knew enough to stop before he tripped the trap wards and wait 'till we got here."

Alice felt a little burst of pride at that, a slight warmth in her chest. She wanted her friends— her chosen *family*— to like Florian. She wanted him to fit in here, and she could see him settling here in the future, maybe with a house of their own and...

And she needed to stop that line of thought *right now*, before the blush on her cheeks became any more pronounced.

"What are you doing here?" Alice's eyes narrowed, hands on her hips. "I know you. You came all this way for a reason."

"Can I...?" he asked, glancing at Ellie.

The silver-haired witch nodded, gesturing with one hand towards the edge of the invisible, magical barrier that kept their home safe. She nudged Alice back towards the house, back towards their area of safety, and Alice followed without complaint. Florian took another few steps forward, his Shadow form crossing the protections just like he belonged there.

As far as Alice was concerned, he already did belong there, but she knew Ellie's permission was what allowed him to cross through.

"I can leave any time I want," he said firmly, his eyes locked on hers. "You can't, though, which is why you should take advantage of this. You're outside. Don't come back in."

"I *am* taking advantage of it," Alice groaned, bending down to scoop up Missy. "I'm using the time to come up with a plan where I know I can trust people."

She thought that was a perfectly good use of her time, and quite frankly, she couldn't imagine a better solution given the circumstances.

At that moment, Kaz and Hart also managed to make it to the edge of the property, Kaz with the same shotgun as before slung over his shoulder. Thankfully, this time he wouldn't need it.

"What's happening?" Kaz asked, looking half ready to shoot at any moment, but he dropped the firearm when he realized they were all safely inside the wards, letting it hang from his shoulder by the strap instead.

"I... Don't think that's Xavier," Hart said, placing a hand on Kaz's shoulder, holding him back just in case he was ready to charge forward. It wasn't as though he could do anything to Florian's Shadow form, truly, but Alice was glad someone held him back. She wouldn't want Kaz getting hurt in an attempt to attack a being made of pure light.

"I'm trying to tell you to *stay here*," Florian said firmly, his tone tense and clipped. "Stay where it's safe, and never come back!"

"Definitely Florian," Kaz said, shoulders slumping.

"And I'm tellin' you that I'm not gonna leave you like this!" Alice snapped. "You're stuck with me."

The corner of Hartley's mouth twitched upwards in a small smile.

"I hear you're stuck outside your own body," Kaz said, looking on sympathetically. "That's a hell of a bargain gone wrong."

"If I had to guess, it's not complete," Hartley muttered as he paced in a circle around Florian.

"I agree." Kaz stepped a little closer, squinting at Florian's Shadow form. "What was the exact wording?"

"He can't tell us," Alice grumbled.

"Fuck," Kaz said, swiping a hand across his eyes.

"We can wiggle around it, sort of. If we ask the right questions." Alice knew that it was sometimes difficult to *find* the right questions, but it wasn't impossible.

"I'm gonna make tea..." Ellie sighed, shaking her head. "Y'all meet me inside later. I think we'll all need it."

"Thank you, sweetheart," Kaz murmured, catching her hand for a moment before she left. He pulled her in to kiss her cheek

Rather than let herself be distracted by the admittedly adorable display of affection, Alice ran through all the facts she had so far. Even in all her theories this morning, she still had questions. What could Florian have wanted so badly that he would risk bargaining for it?

Was it love? Money? No, not money. He was a prince. Revenge, perhaps? No, that was equally unlikely. Florian didn't seem like a vengeful person.

Power, then?

Florian didn't want power.. In fact, he'd tried to get out of having power. He said it was a terrible decision, but he did admit to giving up the throne entirely because he hadn't wanted it in the first place.

Alice gasped. *That was it.* That was the key!

"You said you gave up the throne," Alice said slowly. "Did it have something to do with the bargain?"

Florian smiled, but stayed silent.

"How did you feel when your father passed on?" Hartley asked.

"Empty. Broken," he said, sighing. "I didn't think I could ever be what he was. I was... a little wild as a younger man. I liked hunting and

training with the guards more than studying politics, and that meant I was massively underprepared for a situation like this. I thought I'd have time. I thought maybe the Shadow Court needed a different ruler, but the advisory council said that since we were starting over in a new world, they needed the stability of a familiar face on the throne. They needed me."

"You didn't think you could do it?" Kaz pressed. "That's a hell of a job."

"I didn't. I wanted to ask for help, but I didn't know where to go to get it. I thought it would make me look... weak." A frown crossed Florian's face that looked a little closer than a scowl. "I should have known better than to take a risk like..." He trailed off, shrugging, glancing at Alice in a way that begged her to finish his sentence. He was coming closer to the point of the bargain.

"Xavier," Alice said, nodding. "You found Xavier."

It was the only thing that made sense.

"And asked him for *what*?" Scratching at the stubble on his jaw, Kaz looked more than a little tense. He wasn't particularly fond of indirectness or dancing around something on the best of days, preferring blunt honesty over subtle strategies. Unfortunately, blunt honesty wasn't on the table at the moment.

"To turn you into a king worthy of that role," Hartley said slowly. "That's what you wanted, wasn't it?"

Florian's shoulders slumped as he nodded.

"That's it," he said, a small laugh slipping out. "I was afraid no one would be able to figure it out." The relief faded in only a moment, replaced by tension as Kaz began to mutter under his breath.

"Shit," Kaz groaned. "Now that is vague enough that something stupi—" he cut off, pausing in his scratching, mouth hanging open.

"What?" Alice asked, brow furrowing.

"That's vague enough that Xavier could have, essentially, put his own spirit in Florian's body and mentally twisted the idea to fit the bargain terms. If he's convinced enough that he's the leader they need, and Florian's body is still involved..." Kaz cursed a blue streak under his breath.

"Is that even possible?" Her mouth dropped open, eyes wide and staring.

"Yes, and it's genius!" Kaz said with a huff. "I'm almost annoyed I didn't think of it myself. Not that I'd steal a body, but I don't really enjoy being out-bargained by anyone."

"The good news is that it looks like you're locked in stasis until someone tips the scales their way, so you're not in danger at the moment. I think," Kaz sighed. "The bad news is that it might be tricky to untangle. It involves a lot of perspective and opinion, not concrete wording."

"Exactly. Who decides what makes a worthy king?" Hartley offered, frowning. "Clearly, in Xavier's mind, he's the leader they deserve, and his place in the court is king."

"I would guess he intended on killing you by forcing you out of your own body, but he probably didn't know you had a secondary form," Kaz said.

"Killing Florian would render the bargain null and void, so it would make sense as a tactic to steal the body... but yes, it appears he hit a snag he wasn't expecting," Hart agreed.

"I'm certainly glad not to be dead, for the record," Florian sighed. "I just wish I'd been smart enough not to bargain with him at all."

"I understand," Alice said softly. "But... it's done, and we're here now, so let's fix it."

If she'd learned anything from this whole ordeal, it was that blame wasn't as important as solutions. In a case like this, the outcome mattered more right now than who was responsible, at least in this moment.

"If we get Xavier out of Florian's body, would that be enough that he could just kinda... go back to it?" Alice asked, waving her hands vaguely as she spoke.

"It might, but what would stop Xavier from just going right back to the body? He's still got the bargain on his side."

"So we need to finish the bargain," Alice muttered. "Somehow."

Not that she had any real idea how to do that. She felt smarter and stronger every day, but not smart enough to figure this out. Even knowing the wording, it was difficult to figure out how it might be possible to wiggle around a deadlock like this one. Florian was in his body sometimes, but... Well, apparently Xavier was capable of existing without a corporeal form. He could just steal the body back, eventually.

Xavier had to be dealt with *permanently* in order to ensure Florian's safety, and Alice had no idea if there was even a way to do that.

"We could figure out a loophole in the wording, but I suppose the simplest way is through sheer, dumb force. If we can manage it, that is," Hartley muttered.

"What are you talking about?" Alice blinked, turning away from Florian for a moment.

"If we had enough raw magical power, it's possible it could override the bargain," Hart explained, waving his hands absently as he spoke. "It's how more powerful beings can undo the workings of those with less magic. They barrel through it like a rhino in a china shop. Less finesse, more... battering ram."

Battering...

Battery.

"I'm a magic battery..." Alice muttered.

The ghost of a plan started to form in her mind. If she was lucky, if she was very, very lucky, there might be something she could do with her magic to help out. It could be a long shot, but it seemed possible in theory.

"*Alice—*" Florian warned, but he didn't get a chance to finish.

"You think I might be able to force it with my magic, just make it go your way instead of how Xavier wanted it?" Alice asked quickly, excitement building in her chest.

"*No!*" Florian cried, hands raised and eyes wide. "Absolutely not."

"I'm the seventh of a seventh," she snapped, standing up a little straighter. "If there's a witch out there with enough magic bottled away to make this work, it's gotta be me."

She had logic on her side. This was the most obvious solution to their problem, and probably the quickest. Yes, it might take a little experimenting, but if she'd been passively gathering magic power for twenty-five years, that should be more than enough to crack their problem wide open. The memory magic likely wasn't the only time she'd drained power off other people, and all that had to go *somewhere*.

The only question was how to access it.

"Kaz? Hart?" Alice asked, looking back and forth between them.

IN WHICH

"The theory is solid, but I can't say I'm fond of gambling on this," Hartley muttered.

"Twenty-odd years of gathering magical power seems like it would be enough to me," Kaz said with a shrug. "If you really soaked up that much magic for that long, there's probably a lot you could do through force... but do you even know how to do that?"

"I—" Alice paused, fighting the urge to pout. "I'll figure it out," she muttered.

"See? It's dangerous," Florian pressed. "It's too experimental."

"All I need to do is smack the bargain bond with magic until it snaps, right?" Alice asked, shrugging. The concept didn't seem over-complicated to her.

"It's not that simple—" he tried again, pale eyes locking with hers.

"It sounds pretty simple to me," she countered. "Give the magic a nudge, and it should ram through the bargain so hard that it breaks."

... To be fair, that was simplifying it a little too much. There was still the matter of directing the magic, monitoring how much went through, figuring out what type of magic was inside her once it was stored for so long... but she could figure that out in time.

"Alice, if you force an equal exchange, *it will kill you in the process*," Florian insisted. "Please. Please do not do that."

Alice blinked.

She swallowed hard, the world going cold and blurry around her as she did her best to process that statement, to gather her scrambled wits into a coherent thought.

"*What*?" she breathed. It was all she could manage.

"As I understand it, all the magic inside you is raw, unshaped power, and there's a *lot* of it," he said hesitantly, unable to meet her eyes. "Losing that magic so quickly would throw your body off balance at best, and without careful monitoring, it could drain you of all the magic in your body... so much that it drains you of your life as well."

Something clicked in her mind at that exact moment.

"That's what Xavier wants me for," she whispered.

"I... think so, yes," Florian admitted. "That's why you can't go back. He's trying to use you to force the bargain to completion by using

your power like a battering ram. It's the only thing that makes sense. Like Hartley said, it's about sheer, dumb force at this point."

"I— I don't know how to do that, though," she rasped.

True, she could figure it out for Florian's sake, but she didn't arrive with that knowledge. How did Xavier plan to use her for something she didn't understand how to manage?

"He does. That's all that matters, really." Florian squeezed his eyes shut for a moment, then took a deep breath before he spoke. "I was afraid of something like this."

"Why?"

"The blood vows. They bind you in body, soul, and magic— shared magic. Once completed, Xavier will have access to the full spectrum of your power, and he can direct it and use it for himself."

"So why don't we beat him to the punch and swing things our way first?"

"Because I'm not certain I can do that without killing you, and I won't take that risk!" he snapped. "I won't sacrifice you for that. I won't even come close. You deserve a better life than being used as a spell component— yes, you have the power, but be *smart* about this."

Florian stared Alice down, but she didn't back away, matching his gaze with a fire of her own. She understood that he was concerned for her, and that was sweet of him, but nobody got to underestimate her. Nobody.

She refused to even underestimate *herself* any longer. She deserved better.

There was a pause in which Kaz and Hart exchanged glances, having some kind of silent conversation that only lasted moments.

"I like him. He passes," Kaz said, nodding.

Hartley nodded back in agreement, but Alice wasn't entirely sure what invisible test Florian had passed. For the moment, she decided that it was best to move on. And, frankly, she wasn't about to leave anyone under the illusion that she planned on running and hiding.

"Oh, I'm goin' back," Alice said firmly, standing up a little straighter. "I'm goin' back to kick his ass."

Xavier was done for. She would make sure of it. He'd meddled in her life for far too long, and she was done with passively letting people take control of decisions that should belong to her and her alone.

Her magic did not belong to him, and it never would.

"Not without a plan," Hartley snapped. "Florian is right. If you don't take precautions, you'll get yourself killed."

Out of habit, Alice huffed and shoved her hands in her pockets. She was almost surprised when her fingers brushed across something cold and metal, realizing she'd left an old pocket watch in one of her skirts.

And that... That gave her an idea.

Hopefully, Willow still had what she needed.

"You translate," Alice finally said. "We'll start planning."

18 IN WHICH ALICE RETURNS TO COURT

Alice paced circles around the living area on the morning that Xavier was due to pick her up. It was just past sunrise, and she didn't know when he planned to arrive.

Hartley was still working on the journal, and she was still working on her plan. To be fair, she had a decent idea of what needed to happen when they arrived at the Shadow Court. However, she had to wait until they arrived at the palace to enact her plan... and then troubleshoot a few more potential problems that she couldn't quite get off her mind.

Yes, they had a vague idea of how to possibly break the bargain. It involved trying their best to get the Shadow Court to remember Florian.

However, Alice wasn't entirely convinced that it would work. Thus, she still wanted to figure out how to use her newly discovered— and very, very locked away— well of magic to force it to break. If she needed to force it, she wanted to be able to do so.

For now, she'd humor Florian and try something that was a little less risky. Rash decisions got her into this mess. It was unlikely that rash decisions would get her out of it.

It was only when Hartley's silhouette appeared at the window that she stopped scrambling around

the room. At least she wouldn't have to worry about Xavier's arrival before she got the translation.

"You're awa—" Alice began, turning towards the door, but then she got a solid look at him.

Hartley looked like he'd been hit by a truck. There were dark circles under his bleary green eyes, and he moved a little slower than she was accustomed to. If Alice was feeling particularly brave, she might have said he looked his age, but she wasn't *that* brave. *No one* was that brave.

"What happened to you?" It slipped out before she really thought about it.

Hartley just glared.

"I finished translating," he said, rubbing his eyes.

In his hand was what appeared to be a thick journal with a red cover, the paperback spine cracked in several places from being pressed open roughly while writing. If she didn't know better, Alice would have said it was old, but it had simply taken quite a bit of abuse in the last several days.

"Were ya up all night?" Alice asked as she gingerly took the book from him.

"Yes," he grumbled, stifling a yawn. "I haven't slept since our conversation with Florian, but it was more than worth it for the information. You don't have time to go through it here, so keep this hidden. It would be best to read it and burn it."

"*Burn it?* You just said you were up all night writing it down!" Alice protested.

"You think this is my only copy?" Hartley raised an eyebrow. "I made another one, and we've got the original. I would tell you to replace it, but based on what Willow told me of how she acquired it, that might cause more suspicion."

Smart. She should have guessed— Hartley was practical to a fault. Of course he would have made a second copy.

"Yeah, that's prob'ly a good plan," Alice admitted, nose wrinkling as she frowned.

"Alice," he said urgently. "Be careful with him. Xavier might have been human once, but there's no telling what he is now. There's no telling what he's made himself into."

"What do *you* think he is?"

She'd trust his opinion more than just about anyone else. It annoyed her a little, but she couldn't deny that he knew his stuff.

"I'm not sure, truly." Hartley sighed, mouth opening and closing for a moment. "I do know, however, based on that book..."

Alice motioned for him to get on with it. She'd waited far too long to hear the truth about Xavier, even a small sliver of it.

"I think he traded his soul to be able to exist as a spirit indefinitely," Hart said quickly, wincing.

"You can *do* that?"

"I've heard of it once or twice, or some variation of it. It never works out well— having a soul is part of why we're able to process emotions, memories, the things that make us ourselves. It's not the source of it all, of course. Our souls go on to live other lives, and they change and grow, but—"

"Hart. Point, please," Alice deadpanned.

"Right," he stuttered, blinking quickly. "He's stopped his ability to reincarnate and grow, and he's also stopped his ability to process any emotions. It's like that human expression of information going in one ear and out another. The loss of a physical body mutes that processing twofold."

"Meaning he... can't feel things at all in spirit form and can kinda-sorta feel them in Florian's body?"

"Put simply, yes."

What did that mean for Florian, she wondered? Did he retain his emotions and soul without a corporeal form?

But wait— Florian was born with his Shadow form. That probably meant that things weren't the same for him as they were for Xavier, who had forced himself into a spirit form in order to elongate his own life.

Alice thought back on the interactions she'd had with Xavier. Was that why he was so physically cold all the time? And why had he been so affectionate with her? Was he simply mirroring what he thought he should do because he wanted to win her over?

Probably, yes. And Alice had gone along with it, because he'd mirrored everything that, for a time, she'd thought was supposed to

happen in relationships. This wasn't working out like the fairy tales from her childhood, though. This was much, much worse.

The glass ball on the side table started to flash with bright white light, roughly jolting her out of her thoughts like a strike of lightning rather than a silent glow.

"That's the wards. He's here," Ellie said, scowling.

That sour expression was more comforting than it might have been in the past. At one time, Alice might have seen it as impertinence, as Ellie wanting more than she should. Now, it was the look of a protective older sister figure, and it made her feel safe.

"I better go." Alice stuffed the book into her knapsack and beckoned to Missy from where she was sniffing at the remains of breakfast across the room. The possum skittered over and jumped into her arms, taking her usual place on Alice's shoulder.

"Before ya leave," Ellie said softly, pulling a bottle off one of the kitchen shelves, "take this."

She pressed the tightly corked flask into Alice's hand. It didn't feel like anything special, so it took her a moment to realize exactly what it was. Ellie and Granny kept it around for cleaning and cleansing, and just in case anything particularly nasty managed to make it inside the wards.

"Holy water?" She blinked and squinted at the bottle. It wasn't too big, maybe enough to hold a single cup of liquid.

"Can't hurt," Ellie said with a shrug. "It's good for more'n just cleaning and exorcisms. It'll burn anything with unholy intentions."

"Might be helpful, then, yeah..." Alice muttered, slipping the bottle into her skirt pocket. Better safe than sorry. There really was no telling what kind of abomination Xavier had become after centuries of plotting, planning, and exposing himself to the darkest kinds of magic.

"You better let us know if you need help. We'll come running," Ellie said firmly.

Alice couldn't help but smile. She should have been able to tell who her family was all along. She shouldn't have let one moment of sadness and rage guide a decision that could shape the rest of her life.

It might still shape the rest of her life, if she wasn't careful.

"I will. We can't risk it right now, though." She sighed and reached out to hug Ellie, then Kaz, and even Hart—

She did hug Hart from the side, a little awkwardly, but she hugged him.

It was time to face her fears in the best way she knew how.

The ride back to the Shadow Court was exactly as exhausting as she remembered. The blanket helped, but this time she was aware enough to realize that the ride also came with rising altitude, making the air thinner and colder as they traveled.

By the time they made it to the empty courtyard, Alice was ready to go to sleep and continue planning in the morning. Unsurprisingly, there were no staff members present for their return, and she let Xavier guide her up the empty hallways, around corners, and back to their bedroom without complaint.

"How are you doing, darling?" Xavier asked as he opened the door.

Darling?

That was new. Usually he called her "treasure," and... to be entirely fair, now she knew why. That pet name was really and truly how he thought of her.

She was an object to be used, something of power, something of good fortune. She wasn't a real person to him.

"Tired," she moaned, flopping onto the mattress, and at least this much wasn't an act. The ride back was exhausting. Even Missy seemed a little listless, immediately crawling over to rest beside her.

Xavier perched on the bed beside her and started... to... untangle her hair?

Odd. He was usually a little doting, but not this openly affectionate or considerate. Either way, Alice didn't really mind. That wild ride through the woods had done a number on her curls, and they were knotted beyond belief. It felt good to have someone fuss over her a little.

Though, she admitted that part of her imagined that it was Florian helping to fix her hair. That certainly helped with any jitters she felt from being so close to Xavier after a few days of freedom. It was possible she

should have taken her freedom and run away... but that was a plan they'd gone over many times, and it always ended badly.

Xavier crashing through their wards, Xavier kidnapping her, Xavier generally making things much worse than they already were... All of those were possible results. It was better to be slow and sneaky, if they could.

"Make sure you're well-rested for the full moon ball, treasure. That's all I ask," he said gently.

Ball?

He hadn't mentioned anything about a ball.

"A ball? Like with other people?" Her voice was muffled from the pillow, but he seemed to get the hint, chuckling as he continued to untangle her hair.

"Yes. What else would a ball entail?"

That was it.

Alice could have screamed from the jolt that went through her.

That was when she had to make her move. It would have to be the full moon ball— that was the only time she was guaranteed to be able to contact the maximum number of court members at once. She couldn't do this one person at a time. Not only would it take too long, but there was always a chance that the memory magic would take over again, and then she'd be forced to start over from scratch.

"When is it?" she asked quickly, trying not to show her excitement.

"Two days."

"Okay. I'll be ready," she confirmed, pulling the blankets over her body.

"I'll leave you to sleep, then," Xavier said, bending down to place a cold kiss on her forehead. "I'll bring food later."

Alice mumbled something noncommittal. Though her body felt ready to drag her into the sweet embrace of sleep, her mind was wide awake and whirling.

She would certainly be ready for the ball. There wasn't much time to prepare, but she had all she needed now. With luck, everything might come together exactly as planned. She'd just need to find Florian

tomorrow and update him on everything they'd decided and discovered at Howard's Knob.

Forcing her heavy muscles to move, Alice pushed herself into a sitting position and walked to the chair where she'd put her knapsack. It was careless of her to leave it lying around like this, especially knowing what was inside. The holy water and the soul trap watch were small enough to live permanently in her pockets, but not the journal.

Unfortunately, there weren't many hiding places in the bedroom. She couldn't go off wandering now, either— leaving the room after she told Xavier that she planned to sleep would only arouse suspicion.

For the time being, Alice lifted up the corner of the mattress on her side of the bed and tucked the journal underneath. After a short sleep to help settle her thoughts, she could start reading.

19

IN WHICH FLORIAN REMEMBERS

Xavier only left her alone when he was called away for a meeting about the upcoming ball. Unfortunately, that meant that Alice hadn't had too much time to read the journal, but she'd had enough to skim the important parts.

Cloak around her shoulders to conceal the book, now she made her way out to the gardens. The air was a little chilly, the last bits of summer finally giving way to a crisp mountain fall. Soon, the leaves would start to change, painting the woods with beautiful reds and oranges all across the Appalachians.

Alice aimed to see those leaves from Howard's Knob, tucked safe and warm in her own bed, the Shadow Court far behind her.

Florian was already waiting by the large oak tree that had become their meeting spot. Alice tucked herself in between the roots on the far side of the trunk, concealed from the view of anyone who might be watching from the palace windows, and pulled out the book.

"What did you find?" Florian asked excitedly.

"A few things. Seems like he kept the book to help him remember stuff, which..." she paused, tilting her head.

"What?" He sat down on the grass beside her, just close enough to make her think that he was really there in corporeal form.

It was nice. If she didn't think about it too hard, it felt a bit more like a picnic than a serious meeting.

"I don't know. It feels weird. I still don't get why he has so much trouble remembering," Alice said with a sigh. "Even Hart doesn't have *that* much trouble, and he's way older than Xavier."

"How... how old is he?" Florian asked, eyebrows raised.

"Uh... *old*," Alice said vaguely. "Thousands. Double digit thousands."

"Shit," Florian whispered, blinking.

She couldn't help but giggle. That might have been the first time she'd ever heard him curse, and the sheer surprise on his face was a rare look. It melted into a smile when he heard her laughing, and it made her heart feel warm.

Soon they were both smiling, the grim atmosphere lifting from their shoulders like removing a heavy cloak. That small moment of light was enough to give her the courage to face the next few days, to breathe easy for an hour or two, to keep going and keep planning for the future.

"Alright, alright," Florian sighed, still laughing. "Tell me what you found. I know you're limited on time."

Slowly, Alice went through the details of Xavier's history based on what she'd read.

Xavier started his journey as a human. By the time he'd written the journal, he wasn't sure where in the world he'd been born, but he knew that, at one time, he was a human man. His family passed away in a plague that ravaged his home when he was still very young, and watching their slow deaths led to a lifelong obsession with never experiencing the same thing himself. Ever.

At first, he'd simply searched for means to keep himself healthy, to keep himself young. Then, eventually, he stumbled upon magic— real magic, true magic, Other magic.

Alice wasn't sure how one found Other magic before the Appearances. She'd have to ask Granny, as her bloodline stretched farther back than Alice's did. Xavier had clearly found some form of

Other magic well before the Appearances, too, and he seemed to have learned about it through a woman named Falina.

She was his mentor, and eventually his lover. Alice was unable to tell from the tone if his relationship with her was really love, though. There was sex involved, of course, but that wasn't love. It reeked of a mutual obsession, of wanting someone to be with you when the rest of the world fell away, of wanting someone else willing to do absolutely anything to get there.

"... That's about it," Alice finished, absently riffling the pages of the little book as she spoke.

That was the point where she'd stopped reading. There was more information, but she hadn't finished yet in the limited time she'd had without Xavier in the room.

Florian didn't exactly seem reassured by the extra knowledge, tapping his foot impatiently as Alice communicated the contents of the book.

"I still think you should leave," Florian said, shaking his head. "You should get out of here. You still have a chance to live a better life than this."

"But I... I want a better life with *you*." Alice's voice cracked slightly as she spoke.

The look on his face nearly broke her heart. She thought that it might be easier if she could hug him, but that wasn't possible, either. Xavier's magic appeared to be stronger now than it was a few weeks ago, when Florian had control over his own body for short spurts.

"You don't need to do anything to endanger yourself," he murmured. Florian reached out momentarily, like he planned to touch her, but then remembered that his spirit body would only slide through her solid form. "I may not have had control of my body the entire time, but I've seen you from this form. I know who you are. You deserve more than this."

"And I'm gonna get it... but not without you," she said, crossing her arms over her chest.

Florian stared at her for a long moment. He didn't speak, just analyzed her face, checking over her posture, looking for any weaknesses. Alice knew he wouldn't find any. She'd already made her decision.

Even if whatever was between them never went anywhere at all, she wouldn't leave Florian behind. She'd never forgive herself if she ran without trying.

"You're really sure." It wasn't a question. It didn't need to be.

"I am." Alice nodded once.

Sighing, Florian ran his hand through his long braids. For a moment, he reminded Alice of Ellie, who also played with her hair when she was thinking or upset. The thought occurred to her that she wanted to learn all of his other ticks and quirks, but she couldn't bring herself to voice it.

"Alice..." he said slowly. "I know I couldn't tell you about my bargain, but I *can* tell you about yours. If you want."

Alice blinked.

"What do you mean?" she asked slowly.

"I was there when Xavier made the bargain with your mother. I was watching, though he wasn't aware of my presence." He sighed, shuffling his weight a little. "And... I think that if you want to know, you deserve to know?"

"Why now?"

"If something goes wrong, I don't want to have any secrets from you," he whispered. "If it all goes right, then I *really* don't want to have any secrets from you."

She was almost afraid to ask what he meant by that. If things went right, they'd be out of here and... Well... maybe... together? That would be nice.

It would be nice not to have any secrets if that were the case, too.

"Tell me," she said softly, ignoring the rising heat in her cheeks.

"I saw him meet your mother by a creek in the woods. I couldn't hear everything they said, but I did hear part of it," he said carefully. "He bargained to take away her pain in exchange for her daughter, once the child came of age."

Unfortunately, she knew that much already.

"Anything else?" Alice asked, biting her lip.

"I remember... I remember she stood up, and she looked around," Florian said, eyes fixed on some invisible point in the middle distance. "I remember that she asked if he took anything else."

Anything else? What else could he have taken that the bargain would have allowed?

"He didn't respond," Florian continued. "But he did hold you for a minute, and then he pricked your finger. And he pricked his finger—"

Fuck.

"Did he make me drink a drop of his blood?" Alice asked quickly, leaning forward.

Florian nodded.

That was the answer she'd been looking for, one of the missing pieces to the puzzle of Xavier's mirror lie. Now she knew exactly where the mark on her arm had come from. It was a bargain mark— one she'd been coerced into as an unknowing baby, before she even understood what was happening around her.

"I was right, then," Alice said softly. "He started the blood vows when I was just a baby."

"How does that work?" Florian asked, shaking his head. "I thought you needed consent for those."

"I don't know what he whispered, but it was enough to get through a loophole," she muttered. Xavier liked those stupid loopholes, and he liked pure lies, too.

Lies like telling her she was his mirror, that they were soulmates, that they had a profound connection that went beyond space and time, that they were meant to be together...

She wished more than anything that those words came from Florian's mouth instead. She did feel the draw to him, just like Xavier said she should with a mirror. But she had felt that same draw when Xavier said he wanted her before, and that hadn't worked out at all.

Perhaps what she thought was a profound, universal connection was just attraction. And, while that was embarrassing and said quite a bit about her romantic experiences, that wasn't necessarily the worst thing to ever happen. At least she figured it out before it was too late.

But... There was still a small possibility. At this point, she wasn't sure if she even *wanted* a mirror. She wasn't sure she cared any more. She did want to *know*, though. Some part of her wanted that closure.

"Hey... Do you... think we're really mirrors?" Alice asked hesitantly. "Not Xavier, but... you. Normal you."

"I... truly can't say. I wouldn't know how to begin confirming something like that, either," he admitted, sighing. "Why do you ask?"

"Thought it would be ironic," she sighed. "Honestly, it doesn't really matter."

"It... doesn't?" He raised an eyebrow.

"I think I'm done with fate an' destiny. We're goin' our own way," she sighed.

"I like that idea." Florian smiled, and it was enough to make her heart pound.

Destiny, as far as Alice was concerned, was a highly overrated concept. Too many people had too many hands in her future, and she was sick of it. None of them had to live her life, so none of them should ever get the chance to control it. She didn't care about fate or the universe.

She cared about Florian, though. She was starting to learn to really care about herself, too. Alice was important simply because she was Alice. It had taken too much for her to develop a sense of her own self-worth. This was no time to give up early.

"So... what if it does all go right?" she asked tentatively. "What happens to us?"

Florian shot her a lopsided smile, but it only lasted a moment before he became serious again. "Tell me the plan first."

Okay. She could do that.

"Everybody's comin' to the full moon ball. I think I can probably use that as a chance to get rid of the memory magic and swing the whole thing our way," she said proudly.

"How do you plan to do that?"

Alice opened her mouth... and almost immediately closed it again. That was where the plan admittedly fell short. She did have another trick up her sleeve, but she wasn't sure it would work without taking away the memory magic.

The working theory they'd come up with at Howard's Knob was that Xaiver wouldn't have put so much effort into placing and maintaining the memory magic if it wasn't important to the bargain to do so. It wasn't quite clear how, but the Shadow Court's faith in him had to do something

with maintaining control over Florian's body. Thus, Xavier needed as little persuasive power on his side as possible when they made their move.

The ball was clearly the best opportunity to make that happen in one fell swoop, but unfortunately, there wasn't a clear way to help everyone remember all at once without immediately being shut down by Xaiver.

"Uh... does 'make a scene' count as a plan?" Alice asked, wincing.

Florian groaned and leaned back against the wide oak tree, momentarily covering his face with his hands.

"I'll take that as a no," Alice grumbled.

"The worst part is that I can't say I have any better options to suggest," he admitted. "I'm worried. It's too... out of character."

"What do you mean?"

"Do we have any idea why he's calling this ball? He's kept the Shadow Fae as far away from here as possible except for your wedding night—"

"Don't remind me," she muttered, grimacing.

"— and they needed to see you there. A wedding is an official, formal Court event. Even if he'd planned to kill you, marrying you in secret wouldn't go over well."

"So you're sayin' that this is probably official Shadow Court business, too?"

"No," Florian said, brow furrowing. "It's *not*. That's what's so odd about it."

"Full moons aren't, like... a thing you celebrate?"

"Not normally, no. Not in a formal manner, and not with a large gathering like this," he explained, starting to fidget a little. "If it's not formal Court business, then I'm afraid of what he might be planning. Did he say anything about it in the journal?"

Alice glanced down.

"I haven't gotten too far into it yet."

"*What*?!" Florian's eyes went wide, shoulders hiking up as he openly stared at her.

"I just got the translation yesterday!" she protested. "What you know is as far as I got. I can't read at the speed'a light, ya know. Plus, he's

obedient to Xavier, and she was just as power-hungry as he was. In the end, that search for power killed her in a magical experiment. Xavier did not record the details of that day, but he did say that her loss was devastating. He felt he'd lost the one person who truly knew him, who understood what he'd gone through.

He also said that the same experiment that failed for Falina, killing her, succeeded for him.

It turned him into a spirit in exchange for his soul, protected from psychopomps, able to move freely in incorporeal form, never aging or dying.

He was still left with a mortal mind, though, and that was why he needed his journal. He'd found a way to slowly keep his memories moving forward, but what was lost could not be restored through any means so far available to him.

However, if he had more power, he might have the means to restore his memory, to become a person truly at his prime once more.

Xavier wanted to live forever, yes, but... he wanted to *control* that forever. He wanted to oversee not only his future, but the lives of everyone around him. Xavier wanted to build a world for himself, and in essence, he wanted to become the new god of that world.

The idea of a human elevating themselves to the status of a god only made Alice more convinced of what she needed to do. Anyone with that level of hubris and greed, anyone with that lack of emotion and empathy, couldn't be trusted to fight for anyone except themselves.

He needed to be gone. Permanently. Trapped, caged, or dead—she cared less and less as time went on. Granted, Alice wasn't sure she had the stomach to kill someone. If anyone had earned it though, if anyone had plotted and planned and murdered their way to where they were, and if anyone planned to keep going, it was Xavier.

That didn't make her feel much better about her chosen solution to this situation. Yes, he was horrible. Yes, he was a murderer. Even knowing all that, Alice still had to be the one to deliver justice, in the end, and it made her feel a little sick.

She shoved her hand into her dress pocket, feeling for the now familiar, cool metal of the pocket watch. In her other pocket, she felt for

the bottle of holy water— she didn't have a plan for it at the moment like she did for the watch, but it made her feel safer.

"Come on, Missy," she said firmly. "I've got a job for you."

"Reporting for duty," Missy said cheerfully, scrambling up from her position curled on the pillow.

"Let's go. *Quick,*" Alice said, beckoning her forward.

She didn't know how much time they had before Xavier returned, but it probably wasn't much. Alice picked up Missy and practically sprinted down the hallway, tracing the now familiar paths down to the apothecary room.

Luckily, it didn't seem like anything had been disturbed since their last visit. That made her feel a little more confident. At least there was one place inside the palace that Xavier wasn't aware she'd been.

Missy hopped down on the counter, little feet making pawprints in some of the dust that hadn't yet been swept away in their previous trips to this room. While she investigated some of the mysterious books and jars on the shelves, Alice got to work.

Alice was not a master herbalist. However, she knew a few things from Ellie. She knew more things from the animals in the woods. Combined, she knew one very important thing: smelling like the stinky, wet ground in the fall woods made you invisible in the fall woods.

As she started pulling bottles from the dusty shelves, Missy sniffed at them and hissed.

"What are you doing? I thought you didn't know how to make herbal brews," she squeaked, skittering a little farther down the counter.

"I don't," she said flatly, starting to open various bottles and dump them into a bowl. "I need you to get a message back to Ellie. Ya think you can do that for me?"

"I'd tell ya I could if the creek don't rise, but I'm a good swimmer, too," she said proudly.

"You be *careful*. I can't lose you."

"Oh, you're stuck with me for a long time, trust me. You're too much fun."

"I mean it, Missy," Alice said firmly. "You better come back."

"I'm comin' back with help behind me," she squeaked. "Now, get me the message."

watchin' me like a hawk. I gotta make sure I'm really alone when I'm reading."

"Then *go read*," Florian said pointedly. "I'll see what information I can sniff out about the ball."

"Missy's on that, too," Alice said, though Missy was sniffing out information more in a literal than a figurative sense.

"Good. That's even more reason for you to go back and keep reading. I'll talk to you again before the ball." He made a shooing motion with both his hands that irritated Alice beyond belief, but she couldn't blame him. It was out of concern for her safety, at the root of it all, and that was kind.

"Fine," she said, sighing. She managed not to roll her eyes from sheer willpower. It was a grave situation, but she couldn't deny that it still felt a little like homework.

Sneaky homework.

Sneaky homework with very limited time before it was due.

"Alice," Florian said seriously. "This could be life or death. We need that information."

"I know," she sighed, shoulders slumping. "I'm just... tryin' not to think so hard about it that I get scared. I never make good choices when I'm scared."

She would simply have to do her best to change that.

◆

Xavier paced around the palace courtyard, trying his best to be patient. He'd seen Alice go out to the gardens, and he assumed she was speaking to Florian. That was the only explanation that made any sense. It accounted for both her frequent absences and where she'd found shelter on the rare nights she left their room.

There was a fire in his chest that he wasn't quite familiar with. It wasn't the same as anger. Instead, it was the awful, nauseating feeling of jealousy rooted deep into his bones.

Having a corporeal form was incredibly, horribly inconvenient. He hated the building emotions that came with the slow integration of his

spirit self into his new body, and those emotions were only growing stronger the closer they came to the full moon.

If Alice wouldn't obey, then he'd simply have to make her obey. She would be his obedient little wife, and perhaps he wouldn't have to kill her. It wasn't about affection any longer— this was a battle of wills. As long as she submitted, he would show her all the care, all the affection, all the love that she wanted.

Now he understood this strange rising possessiveness. It wasn't just about studying Alice. It wasn't about learning what made her tick for the sake of knowing someone.

It was about *conquering* Alice.

Now, if only he could get his journal back... but, based on what he'd seen tucked under the mattress while Alice slept, that might be a more attainable goal than he feared.

There was... someone in the back of his mind. It wasn't just Alice. There was someone else, someone latched onto his very soul, impressed upon his heart like a brand. He couldn't remember the name, but he could remember the feeling of her. He could remember the suggestion of her skin, remember the timbre of her voice.

He could remember that he was supposed to bring her back... but without more information, he felt torn.

Alice was here. She was now. She was...

She wasn't going to love him, was she?

She wouldn't submit to him. She wouldn't do as she was told. She was too stubborn and stupid to be a good queen to him if he let her live. It didn't matter how strangely endearing he found her in some ways. They were incompatible, and this body had betrayed him with the odd attraction towards her.

Perhaps it was coming from Florian, he thought. That would be incredibly ironic. There was no way the Shadow Prince felt anything for that ridiculous woman, and it likely wouldn't bleed back into this body even if he did.

... Probably. This was uncharted magical territory.

Well, then. Back to square one.

20 IN WHICH ALICE AND FLORIAN PLAN

Alice spent most of the next day reading the journal. The ball was in less than twenty-four hours, and she was running out of time to garner useful information.

She managed to work her way through the rest of the writing, and she figured out a few things in the process. Unfortunately, Xavier never wrote anything about his plans for the upcoming ball. Instead, he detailed the rest of his time with Falina, as if he needed to remind himself that she existed.

But... it wasn't quite love, or at least it wasn't love as Alice understood it. This seemed more like an obsession, like someone he needed to have nearby because it kept him in check. She had turned into more of an object than a person over time, a treasure lost to time, someone Xavier desperately reached for through the ever-thickening fog of his memories.

Why, though? Why focus on her like that? He didn't seem to have any future plans involving her, and she was long dead.

If he was incapable of loving her... then what was the point of this obsession?

Then again, maybe that was all love could be to him in his current state: obsession.

By the time Falina passed away, she was no longer the mentor. She was absolutely, entirely

"Gimmie a minute," she mumbled, tossing her bright orange curls over her shoulder as she pounded the herbs and water into a pulp. The whole mixture quickly turned brown and slimy, looking particularly unpleasant in the low lighting. It also smelled unpleasant, though Alice resisted the urge to pinch her nose.

It was perfect.

"Stay still for me a minute, okay?" Alice scooped up some of the slimy slop on her hand as she spoke, rubbing it between her fingers to check for texture.

Missy hissed a little, but she didn't run when Alice practically ground the mixture into her fur, working it into the hairs like it was shampoo.

"*Ewwwwww, it smells*!" the possum whined, shuddering and fidgeting.

"This'll help hide ya from anything tryin' to sniff ya out on your way there. It should last about eight hours, I think," Alice mumbled, picking up another handful of the foul-smelling rub.

"*You owe me for this*," Missy grumbled, hissing something in pure possum tongue that Alice couldn't quite translate.

"For the message?" She kept rubbing in the goo, trying to stay as calm as possible. No point in alarming Missy.

"No, for making me smell like this! I know I live in the woods, but I bathe," she groaned.

"Okay. I'll get you a treat if this all works out, I promise," Alice said.

Missy seemed perfectly happy with that solution.

Alice, on the other hand, just prayed that they'd all make it out of this alive. Every new piece of information seemed to make it clear how dire their situation really could be, and she couldn't risk anything going wrong. It wasn't just her life on the line now. She didn't even want to think about what Xavier could accomplish, given enough time to plan for it.

They had to stop him here.

Missy headed out immediately after Alice tied a note around her neck. There shouldn't be a problem with finding the path— the little possum had a good sense of direction. She just hoped that Missy could deliver the note in time.

On the way back from the apothecary room, Alice made a brief stop in the gardens, calling out for Florian by the oak tree. She didn't have much time. With any luck, he'd be there, considering it was one of his usual haunts, but she wouldn't be able to wait long if—

"You called?" Florian asked, eyebrows raised as he stepped out from behind the tree.

She could have cried with relief. There was one more piece of information she needed, and he was the only person who had it.

"You had to exchange true names to complete the bargain, right? What's his?" Alice asked, jumping straight to the point.

"Xavier Havelock was the name he gave me. Why?" He sounded hesitant, shoulders tensing. On some level, it was hard to blame him. The entire situation was tense, and they were running incredibly short on time with only a vague idea of a plan.

"I've got an idea. Need his full name for it, and it's not in the journal," she mumbled, fidgeting with her skirts. It wasn't her *favorite* idea, certainly, but it was the best one she'd had so far, and the most likely to work.

"Why do I think I'm not going to enjoy this idea?" Florian sighed, shuffling his weight from foot to foot, hands shoved in his pockets.

Her ideas weren't historically that bad, were they? Risky, yes. That was something she was working on, though! And this wasn't risky so much as... rash.

Rash, and also one of the only options available.

"I think I'm gonna have to use my emergency out," Alice said, resting her hand on the outside of her skirt pocket.

Florian's eyes went wide as he realized what was in her pocket.

"You think it'll work?" he asked, cutting his eyes back up towards her face.

"I think it's worth a shot." Not to mention that it was the only thing they had left to try that stood any consistent chance of working. Reliability was the best they could hope for at the moment.

"Fair point. I haven't been able to think of anything else that would have as much of a chance to work as this, and... I can't say I'd be upset to see him gone," he admitted. Though Florian couldn't meet her eyes and his posture was slumped, she couldn't blame him for feeling that way. Xavier had stolen his body and his life, but not only that, he'd stolen the memory of Florian's existence.

"I've been turning things over in my head, and this is it, yeah. At first I thought maybe I could turn the ritual around on him and steal his magic instead," Alice said, crossing her arms over her chest. "But I... don't know how. Also, I'd still have to sleep with him, and I really don't wanna do that."

"Thank all that is holy," Florian said with a sigh, leaning back against the tree.

A smile tugged at Alice's mouth, and she couldn't quite force it back down.

"Oh?" she asked innocently. "Why's that?"

Florian floundered, suddenly very fascinated by the grass under his feet.

"Well... it's... it's just that I don't want you to do anything you'll regret."

"Nothin' at all to do with the fact that it's your body?"

"If I'm honest..." Florian trailed off with a sigh.

"What?" Alice pressed, laughing, but her laughter stopped when she saw the look on his face.

He seemed almost shy. His pale eyes settled on the grass, the tree roots, and then her face, but quickly back to the flowers in the distance.

"You said he seemed like he had the capacity to care," he said slowly. "I think it's bleeding into my body... from... me." His voice grew softer with every word.

It was adorable.

"Well that... makes sense why he suddenly developed... something," Alice stammered, absolutely floundering. She felt like a little girl with a crush, but the situation was already much more serious than that, and what she felt for Florian was far more than a casual crush.

"I don't think he's ever cared about anything, at least in the fifty years that I've known him," Florian grumbled, blushing as he tried to change the subject.

"He did at one point, I think," Alice said, frowning as she thought of the way he wrote in his journal, "but that's gone now."

"What are you talking about?"

"I think he did love Falina— from the journal. Once. Maybe," she said hesitantly. "Not now, though. Now it's like... she's a fixation or something, based on the way he writes about her."

"What... happened?" Florian asked, blinking.

"He forgot her, I guess. At least partly," she said with a shrug. "At least... he forgot how he felt, I think. I don't know. He might have just forgotten that he knew her, too."

"She's a fixation that he *forgot*? That's a very poor fixation, if you ask me," Florian grumbled.

"I don't get how it works, either, but I think we snatched something more important than we realized when Willow took the journal," Alice said, pursing her lips. "He says over and over in the writing that it's there to help him remember. I think... something happened when Willow and I removed it. He didn't have it to remind him, so he started changing."

"Changing... how?"

"He seemed a little softer when I came back," Alice admitted. "It was almost like he... had the capacity to care, but it was really, really fleeting."

She still didn't quite understand where that had come from. It did make sense that he'd gotten those emotions from Florian somehow, considering that they were effectively sharing a body. However, it didn't make sense that it had taken this long for them to show up, though.

Florian showed her kindness from the beginning. He'd been genuinely caring from the very start. Logically, shouldn't that have somehow taken root in Xavier during the past decades, before Alice even arrived at the Shadow Court?

"What if the journal isn't just to help him remember?" Florian asked slowly. "What if it's more?"

Alice blinked.

"I... don't follow," she said.

Though a part of her was happy she felt comfortable enough to admit not knowing something, and without feeling stupid at all in front of Florian, a bigger part of her was simply confused. What was *more* than memory?

"What if it's an anchor for his entire personality?" he explained, clapping his hands together. "Without it, he's lost his memories, and he's more susceptible to changing into someone else. He'd be a different person without fixating on who he was and what he wanted."

"And he can't stand the idea of losing the future he worked so hard to plan for," Alice said slowly nodding along. "That makes sense."

"Can we use that to our advantage?"

"I don't know," Alice admitted. "It might take too long."

"That, and..." Florian muttered something under his breath, looking annoyed.

"Eh? What's that? Speak up."

"I don't like him drawing off my emotions," Florian said, sighing. "It feels invasive, not to mention unfair to you. He's not even really feeling what he's feeling... as strange as that sounds."

In any other case, that sentence wouldn't have made any sense at all. However, there weren't exactly many cases of body stealing that it would apply to. Alice certainly *hoped* there weren't any more cases out there. This one was difficult enough to deal with on its own.

"It's okay," Alice mumbled, forcing a small smile. "I've seen enough of him to know what's really hidin' under there."

Florian slid a little closer to her, so near that if he were corporeal, she might have been able to feel his breath on her skin. He reached out and traced his ghostly hand across the curve of her cheek, but Alice didn't feel a thing.

"You have no idea how badly I want to touch you," he admitted, pale eyes fixed on hers.

"You could. The times you're in your real body." She ignored the heat in her cheeks and tried to maintain eye contact, but it was incredibly difficult to do so.

"I won't," he said, shaking his head. "I won't until my body is mine again."

"You don't... feel the same, ya know," Alice mumbled.

"What do you mean?" he asked, brow furrowing.

"He feels cold to me. It's like there's no blood in your veins when he's in control, but you..."

"What do I feel like?" Florian asked, a small, mischievous smile on his face.

There was only one word she could think of.

"Sunshine."

21

IN WHICH PLANS GO WRONG

It was not often that Granny screamed.

Thus, when Ellie heard a very identifiable shriek ring through the house, she dropped the book she was reading upstairs and clambered down to the kitchen as quickly as possible. Granny had the itch to cook today, and when Granny wanted to do something, it was best to just let her do it.

Granny also kept things particularly spick and span around the house, insisting on cleanliness and a sanitary brewing environment wherever possible— and that extended to potions of a witchy nature, perfectly mundane medicinal brews, and any food cooking on the stove.

That was why it was particularly surprising to see a mud-covered ball of fur squeaking and hissing insistently at Granny, tracking dirt all over the floorboards with its little paws as it paced in circles.

"*Why* is there a possum in my kitchen?!" Granny shrieked. "Y'all know what happened with the damn raccoon, and we are *not* havin' a repeat of that day!"

No one on God's green earth would want a repeat of that day.

Luckily, Ellie was fairly certain
"Missy, calm down," she said.

The possum stopped chittering and sat still. Granny just stared.

"You speak animal? When'd ya learn that?" She looked back and forth between Ellie and the possum, squinting. It would have been comical if Ellie wasn't a little worried about why the animal was here in the first place.

"It's *Alice's* possum, Granny," Ellie said pointedly, picking up the furry little creature... and holding it as far away from her as she could. "*Whooo,* and you need a bath, don't ya?"

Missy was absolutely *covered* in sludge. Leaves and twigs stuck to the top of the sticky, foul-smelling layer, making her look a little more like a bush than an animal It almost seemed like the mud had been ground into her furry coat, as though she'd purposefully—

Ah.

Alice must have done it, Ellie realized. It would help disguise Missy's natural scent as she traveled through the woods on the way here. That was good thinking, but... it also made her wonder who or what could have followed along behind. It could be nothing, of course, but why send Missy without anyone else, especially when Alice knew none of them possessed animal speak?

As Ellie sat the little creature down in the sink, she noticed a chunk of something rolled up and tied to Missy's neck on a now stained length of ribbon. It was in one piece, though, and it looked readable.

"You read the note. I'll wash the critter," Ellie said, handing the paper to Granny. The older woman held the equally sludge-covered paper with two fingers, nose wrinkling unpleasantly, but she didn't complain.

Missy the possum was surprisingly well-behaved during her bath. In fact, it seemed as if she *liked* being scrubbed down clean, which was almost a little comical. The sludge came off easily with a little soap, but Ellie was more concerned about the contents of the note Missy brought with her, checking over her shoulder as she worked to watch Granny's facial expressions as she read.

Her face was, unfortunately, almost unreadable. The old woman had a poker face when she wanted to, and this was absolutely one of those times. It only made Ellie more anxious to watch Granny read without any expression, and she fought not to fidget.

"Shit," Granny hissed, sighing.

"What? How bad is it?" Ellie briefly turned away from Missy to look over her shoulder. The grave expression on Granny's face did not fill her with warm and fuzzy feelings.

Harper and Willow burst through the front door before Granny could answer, both looking around in a panic.

"What's happening? I heard a scream," Willow said, blinking furiously.

"Possum scare. Note from Alice," Ellie said curtly as she rinsed Missy. Granny waved the note from her position at the kitchen table.

"May I?" Willow asked, holding out her hand. Granny passed the note without comment, which did not make anyone in the room more comfortable. No comment meant "difficult to explain," which often went hand in hand with trouble.

Harper leaned over her shoulder

"Shit," Harper said.

Well, *that* wasn't good.

"Gimmie that," Ellie said. She wrapped the newly scrubbed and rinsed Missy in a kitchen towel to dry her, then sat her on the floor and snatched the note.

The writing was messy, but it was clearly Alice's penmanship. The scariest part, though, was that it was only two lines.

I need help.

Come ASAP.

"Shit," Ellie said, pinching the bridge of her nose.

Alice was long-winded. She liked to explain things. If she hadn't taken the time to say everything that was happening, it meant she was both afraid of someone intercepting the note on the way *and* in a big hurry.

That was bad. Big hurries were *always* bad in crucial situations.

Ellie had almost agreed with Florian while he was here. Almost. She thought it would be a good idea for Alice to stay where it was safe, if she was completely honest. However, she also knew that none of them would ever forgive themselves for leaving Florian behind.

Alice especially wouldn't forgive herself.

More than anything, Ellie knew what it was like to be in love, and she knew that if it had been Ben or Kaz in that situation... Well, she'd have gone back, too. No one could fault Alice for that decision.

"We need to move, and *fast*," Willow said. "You did a great job, Missy, but there are only hours left before the full moon."

"Where we goin'?" Ellie asked, spreading a map out in front of Willow. The fae woman pointed towards a spot past the Virginia border, deep in some of the roughest parts of the mountains.

"Here. That's where the Shadow Court is."

"There's no way we can get there in a day," Kaz sighed, tapping his foot. "I could travel almost instantly if she summoned me. We could send a message to her?"

"That spell takes time to set up, and I'm not sure we've got that time," Ellie muttered.

"Then we'll run there," Willow said, nodding.

"*Run*?" Harper spluttered. "I mean, *I* could, sure. I don't know how everybody else is gonna keep up."

"I'm fast, and I can carry one with me on my back when I'm in half shift," she explained.

"Take Ellie," Harper said immediately. "She's got the strongest magic."

A hissing sound came from the corner, where Missy was already trying to crawl her way up Willow's leg. Luckily, Willow didn't seem bothered by it.

"I'll carry Missy," Harper said, reaching out to pick up the possum. "Can Rosemary ride with y'all? She's not gonna leave Ellie."

"You'll... carry her?" Willow's brow furrowed.

"I can keep up," Harper said, smiling so her fangs showed. "Vampire speed and stamina."

Missy immediately stopped attempting to climb up Willow's body and jumped into Harper's arms, seeming perfectly content now that she was included in the plan. She settled onto the vampire's shoulders like she belonged there, little claws grabbing at Harper's sweater.

"I think I can manage one person and a dog, then," Willow said, nodding, "but we need to leave *now*."

"I'll get my shoes. Granny, grab the emergency bag, will ya?" Ellie called, already shuffling towards where her boots sat by the front door.

"I'll let the boys know what's happening and meet you at the door," Harper said, Missy still settled on her shoulder.

She was off before it was even possible to blink, leaving the front door open in her wake. Vampire speed was something Ellie still couldn't get used to. Harper didn't use it often, as it took quite a bit of magical energy, and she said she liked to enjoy the scenery, but in times like this, it was useful.

"Perfect. That's three of us." Willow nodded, but she still seemed a little uneasy.

"Better than nothing," Ellie conceded.

The odds were not incredible, of course. It would be better to have as many people as possible on their side, but this was the option available, and Alice needed help. They'd just have to take their chances.

✦

The afternoon before the ball, Alice was still waiting on Missy. Time was running short, and that made her nervous. She still wasn't entirely sure what to do or how this plan might work, but it was the only chance she had.

She needed to get dressed, and then she planned to excuse herself for a brief walk to the gardens to meet with Florian before the ball. In preparation for the event, she'd swapped from keeping the watch in her pocket to around her neck, and she wore it at all times. The bottle of holy water was already in the pocket of her dress for the evening... just in case.

She felt like crying and wondered if she was shaking, but the reflection in the mirror showed that she wasn't. She simply looked tired.

Standing in her nightgown in the bedroom, Alice was surprised when Xavier came up behind her, wrapping his arms around her waist. It was surprisingly gentle for him, though he pulled her back towards his body firmly, placing one hand on her hip as he bent to kiss her neck.

Alice knew what was coming next. It was the same thing that had happened for the last three days.

He still wanted to sleep with her.

Each time it happened, it was a little more gentle but a little less subtle all at once, like he planned to coax her out of her shell. With any luck, this would be the last time she'd need to deny him. She wasn't sure how much longer she could keep it up.

"Won't you let me touch you?" he asked gently, tracing his cold hand up her jaw. It gave her the shivers, and not in a good way.

She could fake calm and affection, she could even go along with playing stupid and acting as though she knew nothing about Xavier's plans or history... but not this.

Not after knowing what it felt like to touch Florian.

Not knowing that Xavier didn't care if she lived or died.

Not knowing that consummation would complete the bargain he planned to use to take over her magic entirely.

"No," Alice said, taking a step back. "I'm not ready. I'm sorry."

She kept her tone as gentle as she could. She tried to look sorrowful, shy, hesitant— anything to make him think that this was still a case of a young woman with nerves.

However, somewhere deep in her bones, Alice knew something was wrong.

Xavier pursed his lips. For a moment, he looked almost sad. It was a little strange to see an expression so full of regret on that face, knowing that Xavier inhabited the body and not Florian.

"Then you've made your decision."

And then he smacked her across the face.

It was a hard slap, and it sent her reeling across the room. For a moment, she was too dizzy and disoriented to do anything but watch the scenery spin, but when the fog cleared, Xavier was walking towards her.

This was a familiar dance now. He raged, she ran. They knew the steps, and now would be no different.

Alice tried to bolt on instinct, but Xaiver was too fast. He grabbed her arm and hauled her backwards with one hand, ripping one of the curtains from the bed with the other. She pulled against him, but running was useless. His grip was too strong.

Clearly, this was a dance that Xavier had chosen to let her lead in the past. He could have stopped her if he wanted to, but he *chose* to let her go, to put on the performance of a weak man who wouldn't force

anyone into submission. Now, the tables had turned, and Alice was not prepared.

"Be a good girl and stay still," he grunted, hauling the fabric around her waist.

She didn't. She bit his arm instead, teeth not quite managing to tear through like they would human skin, but it was painful enough that he hissed and lost his grip. Alice tumbled to the floor and rolled across the room, tangled in the black fabric. As she struggled to her feet, she was pleased to see a line of turquoise blue blood welling up in a half-circle mark on his forearm.

Good.

She took off for the door without looking back again—

And promptly fell to the ground, feet caught on the stupid bed curtains wrapped around her like a cocoon.

This time, Xavier gagged her first, tying a separate strip of fabric around her mouth before he bothered to try and get her off the floor.

"That should muzzle you," he muttered distastefully, rubbing at his arm, but he didn't try to heal it.

Interesting... That meant he didn't know about the power contained in the very antlers he'd chosen to borrow. Alice was fairly certain that healing wasn't all it could do, but it was too late to test anything now.

"I'm sorry it's come to this, for the record," he murmured, reaching out to brush a lock of hair out of her face. "I thought we might be able to live a life together... but the only way to end things is to proceed with my original plan."

She would have bitten him if she wasn't gagged.

He wrapped the fabric even tighter around her torso and roughly tossed her into the single armchair in the bedroom, wrapping the rest of the curtain length around the back. She pulled against the black silk, but to no avail. It withstood every attempt, and slipped away from even scratching with her nails.

"You know, I really, really wanted to *try* letting you live," Xavier growled, continuing like she wasn't tied to a chair. "I think that offer is off the table now, though."

He reached under the bed to pull out a coil of rope, and Alice's eyes went wide. How long had he been planning for this exact scenario?

Xavier hummed a soft tune as he wound the rope around her body, tying Alice to the chair. Her arms were locked to her sides from the silk curtains, but he finished by tying her ankles together, rendering her entirely immobile in a way that made her feel claustrophobic.

"Comfy?" he asked sarcastically, raising a single eyebrow.

Alice tried to curse at him, but her voice was muffled through the gag. It was a little difficult to breathe with it on, actually.

"What? More to say?" he deadpanned, crossing his arms. Sighing in exasperation, Xavier pulled away the cloth, apparently satisfied now that she was unable to move her limbs.

"Are you—" Alice coughed, gasping as she took in air. "Are you telling me you actually thought you loved me?"

"I could have, if you'd simply done as you were told."

"That's definitely not how that works," she scoffed. "You don't get to tell me you'd love me if I was a good little doll. My momma tried that once already."

All it had left her was bitter.

Bitter, and with a better understanding of real love.

"It doesn't have to go this way—" Alice tried, still struggling against the ropes, though it was a futile effort. She might have been able to tear her way through the fabric or the ropes alone, but not both. She was stuck.

This was... bad. Very, very bad.

She was supposed to meet Florian before the ball to go over the last bits of the plan. If she wasn't there, he'd know something was wrong... but who could he call for help? Missy was already on her way to Ellie, assuming she'd even made it all the way to Howard's Knob.

"It does. I need it to go this way," he said noncommittally. "If your magic is strong enough to turn the bargain my way, it's surely strong enough to complete the rest of my plan. Once I take it from you, that is."

"What?" Alice gasped. "What else do you *want*?"

"Finishing the bargain is only half the story, stupid girl. Thought you knew everything, hmm?" Xavier scoffed. "Why? Because you found my journal? Thank you for returning that copy, by the way. It was rather helpful, even if I'm not certain how you managed to translate it. It certainly wasn't with the translation glass you stole from our poor librarian," he said, a smug smile crossing his lips.

"H—how did you—"

"You really need better hiding spots, treasure." He rolled his eyes and shrugged, adjusting his robes.

"You're all washed up, anyhow," Alice muttered. "No sex, no complete bargain, no usin' my magic. I know how this goes."

Just as Florian had said, she was safe as long as she didn't consummate the marriage. It had to be a willing consummation, too, which meant that Xavier was entirely stuck without her consent. She might be slightly less safe now, of course, but she was still a walking well of some kind of power.

He still needed whatever lay at the bottom of that well. Seventh daughters of seventh daughters were rare, as well as seventh of seventh *sons*. He wouldn't come across another one of those easily. It would be better to make use of what he had... which both gave Alice hope and scared her.

Xavier outright laughed at her, dashing that hope to pieces almost immediately..

"Luckily for you, I can complete the vows with or without consummation," he said. "It's more complicated, but it's worth it for the payoff. If you hadn't been such a stubborn ass about it, we wouldn't have to do things the difficult way.."

... Shit.

That was new.

"The library is wonderful for finding unorthodox solutions, don't you think? I heard you've been doing lots of research," Xaiver said, that same smug smile taking over once more. "Perhaps we could go there together sometime."

Alice wanted to scream. How long had he been onto her? How long had he known that she was suspicious? She should have been more careful, should have taken more precautionary measures—

But it didn't matter now. She was in this situation, and there was no getting out of it.

"Ain't no '*we*' in this deal, you shit-eatin' hellspawn!" Alice spat, resuming her struggle against her ties, but all she managed to do was tip her chair over with a painful *thunk* that reverberated through her entire body.

Xavier did not look happy about that, but he didn't respond to the insult. He also didn't bother to put the chair upright.

More importantly, he'd learned how to complete the blood vows without consummation. Alice wracked her brain, wondering if she'd come across the information in her own searching, but she couldn't remember anything of the kind. She'd also wanted to know more about the purpose and function of blood bargains than the making and breaking, so it was possible she could have skipped it. What a time to wish she'd paid more attention to a book!

Shit. That must be why Hart was always on her about reading carefully and completely. She'd never tell him that, though... assuming she made it out of here.

For now, she needed Xavier to talk. There was the possibility of gathering information if she could keep asking questions, if he thought that she was at such a disadvantage that revealing information wouldn't hurt. It didn't matter what innocuous or inane question Alice asked— she just needed him to *talk*.

"So this is it, huh?" she grumbled. "Killing a random person to fix your stupid bargain that you fucked up in the first place?"

Okay, making him angry wasn't part of the plan, but it certainly made Alice happier about the whole situation.

"You're hardly random, seventh daughter of a seventh daughter," Xavier sighed. "Still stupid, I see."

She chose to ignore that, quite literally biting her tongue to stop from lashing out. Alice knew better now. She wasn't stupid. She was smart and capable and even kind some days. It just took a while for her to be able to see it in herself

Xavier continued, ignoring Alice's glare.

"Besides, breaking a bargain likely won't kill you in the process. Probably. That's not my main concern, at least. It's raising the dead that's the real issue." He practically yawned as he said it, but the impact was like a strike of lightning.

Raising the dead was nothing to be taken lightly. It was magic considered to be against the natural order. Not to mention, it was easy enough to raise a body from the dead, but to bring back a soul?

Horrifying.

It was like someone coming over after you'd moved away to drag you out of your new house and back into the old one, completely against your will and after you'd become used to life in a new place. It might not even be possible to find the address of the new home, in which case the person casting the spell would be left with a soulless husk of a body... which was even worse.

Then there was everything around healing the body and restoring the flesh to working order on a level as small as every organ and piece of tissue and cell—

Needless to say, it was complicated, messy, and dangerous. There was very little reason that anyone would want to do it unless it happened to be tied with a healing spell *immediately* after death. Fatal gunshot wounds and the like? Sure. If a person was gone for thirty seconds, it was very different than if they'd been gone thirty years, or even thirty days.

She'd already come to the conclusion that Xavier was some kind of psychopath, but this absolutely confirmed it.

"Raisin' the—" Alice cut off with a gasp, thoughts whirling as she desperately tried to put together the pieces. She understood exactly what he wanted now.

All that time that his journal was missing, he'd been trying to remember the rest of his plans. Breaking the bargain was one thing. It was right in front of him, and it was clearly causing problems.

Now, though? Now Xavier effectively had his history back, and there was one person in particular that stayed throughout his entire existence... until she died.

"Falina. You wanna bring back Falina," she said slowly.

"I don't '*wanna*,'" Xavier said mockingly, hauling Alice's chair back to an upright position with one hand as though it weighed nothing. "I *will* bring her back."

Gritting her teeth against the impact of the chair legs on the hard floor, Alice decided this was not the time to fight him about her accent.

Though, when this was over, she certainly would never be made to feel ashamed of it again.

"Why? You didn't love her." Alice's nose wrinkled in confusion. The thought popped out of her mouth almost before it entered her conscious mind. Falina showed up in the journal, of course, but she was a twisted obsession, not a true love.

Apparently, that was the wrong thing to say.

"I did! I lost the other half of my soul when she died!"

"Well, ya damn well didn't sound like it in your stupid book!" she spat, stomping her tied-together feet from sheer anger. "Sounds like you lost your fuckin' soul when ya traded it for some stupid long life! You don't even want her, you just want somebody to make you feel like you're not all alone in your godforsaken power quest—"

Alice cried out as he slapped her, his large hand leaving behind a warm stinging sensation. It felt hard enough to bruise, but she didn't even care. They were clearly done playing games and dancing around the truth.

He couldn't make her shut her mouth anymore. No one could.

"Her body waits for me to restore her spirit," Xavier hissed, breath coming in ragged, enraged gasps. "I will siphon the magic off you, and then I will go to her."

"Oh, so you remember where she's buried?"

Xavier practically snarled as he opened his mouth, clearly set on correcting her...

But he paused, mouth open, hand halfway reaching out, face frozen as his expression transformed to something like shock, or maybe even sorrow.

He didn't remember where she was buried. He'd lost that, too. It was yet another piece of his memory only preserved in that journal. How much of him had wasted away over the years? How many opportunities had he rejected that might have led to a transformation into a better man?

Instead, he chose to hold on to who he was, to keep his claws firmly latched onto his past self, past motivations, and past fears. Xavier could have stepped onto the path to a better existence many times.

He chose to become what he was, though. He chose this path at every turn. There was no coming back from this, not now.

"You're lucky that I need to wait till moonrise to kill you," he snarled.

Anger boiled in her chest, and rather than frightening her, those words gave her confidence. As long as the moon wasn't up yet, she was safe. She had time.

She could needle him for information.

"Bringin' back Falina won't help you," Alice spat. "I don't know what you think you're planning, but I'm willing to bet her spirit's already moved on—"

"She has not!" Xavier roared. "Her spirit will wait for mine, and then we will shape the world in the image we want. It will be ours, and it will be that way into infinity."

He was truly furious now, and that was good. Furious might keep him talking. It might be enough to get him to slip, to stumble, to feel overconfident. Even if Missy managed to carry that message back, she might be on her own for this one, and she needed Xavier at his weakest.

"Oh, it'll be that way without ever really being able to love her again? Without being able to love *anyone* again?" Alice pressed, struggling against the ropes. "How do you plan to do that without your *soul*, Xavier?!"

"I don't need a soul to rule the world, and I don't need your pathetic, mortal opinion about it!"

"Well, you're definitely not gonna get me to do as I'm told, so ya better get used to it!" she snapped back immediately, anger taking over rather than fear.

"Oh, don't you worry about that. Once you see what's waiting for us in the ballroom, I think you'll do *exactly* as you're told," Xavier said slowly, a cold smile spreading across his face.

That was not a statement that gave her much confidence or hope. Whatever he had planned, it wouldn't be good.

Alice kept glaring at him from sheer spite, determined not to flinch or show weakness. She wouldn't give him the satisfaction of seeing any chip in her defenses, no matter what.

She would not let the fear creeping up her spine like a horrible, icy shadow win this battle.

Alice let Xavier guide her into the ballroom several hours later, dressed in a delicately embroidered silver dress. She was glad she'd managed to pack a couple of items in the pockets before the encounter with him earlier, because Xaiver watched like a hawk as she dressed to make sure nothing strange happened.

"Couldn't you just do what you needed to do before and not make a spectacle of it?" she snapped, pulling against his arm, but the tugging was mostly to annoy him.

"We need to take advantage of the peak of the full moon for this. Not to mention, the Shadow Fae need to swear their fealty to their new king," he said. "Preferably with blood."

With... blood...?

Blood vows.

"It's not just mine. You're planning to take their magic too, aren't you?" she hissed. "How's that going to work? Are you lacing their wine with your blood or something?"

Xavier scoffed. "Smarter than you look, apparently. Don't worry, treasure. We'll take care of you first. They're just a convenient second course."

"Then why go to all the trouble of the memory magic?"

"I wanted a court of willing comrades, but this is truly just too

much *work*," he said with a sigh. "Better to start fresh, and better to use the power of the moon to help me do it."

Start fresh? As in... kill the entire Shadow Court to build his own group of followers from scratch? The more Alice heard, the worse things seemed.

He pulled her through the doors of the ballroom to thunderous applause. Xavier smiled and waved, but Alice didn't bother hiding her anger. She stepped up to the dais, the same platform they'd stood on for their marriage vows, and wondered how everything had become so tangled in such a short period of time.

Then again, it was really all tangled from the start. She simply hadn't seen it.

"I wouldn't cause a scene if I were you. Could get dangerous for the former prince," Xavier murmured in her ear, putting his arm around her waist to pull her close.

"He ain't *here*." Alice just glared.

He might be able to convince her to be quiet, but he couldn't do anything about a grumpy face.

"I *know* he's here," Xavier insisted. "He's here because *you're* here."

"You don't know a damn thing," she hissed.

In reality, Alice was fairly certain that Florian was here somewhere. She'd missed their meeting time before the ball. More likely than not, he'd be snooping around for information

"I know he wouldn't let you go to something like this without watching from nearby, meaning it's only a matter of time until he comes out of hiding... but it doesn't actually matter if he's hiding or not, so long as he's nearby."

Unfortunately correct on Xavier's part. Alice wasn't entirely sure what he'd seen or how he'd come to this conclusion, but it was accurate enough that it made her wonder exactly when he'd caught them together.

"Did you know that shadow forms can be killed?" Xavier whispered. "All you have to do is put them in a place where there are no shadows."

She absolutely refused to give him the satisfaction of asking what that meant.

There were very few places on earth that had no shadows. The darkest caves technically had no shadows by virtue of being shrouded in shadow. Some places, if very carefully lit, could also have no shadows, but that would be difficult to reproduce.

Alice refused to let him see the tiny prickle of anxiety in the back of her throat.

"Now, normally that would just force a Shadow Fae back to their body, but... hmm. I wonder what happens when there is no body to return to? Could be an interesting experiment."

"He does have a body," Alice said through gritted teeth.

"But not the will to force me away from it," Xavier countered. "Now, you have choices. If you move to alert him, if you scream, if you take one wrong step— I will douse this room in a darkness so thick that not a single ray of moonlight will permeate it," he hissed.

That... sounded more logical than she wanted to admit. In fact, it sounded incredibly logical, and if he'd been digging in the library, it wasn't impossible that he'd come across that little tidbit of information in one of the books. It wasn't impossible that his threat was very, very real.

"What do you want me to do?" Alice spoke slowly, carefully, fighting not to snarl.

If there was one thing that most people understood about mountain folk, it was that messing with one of their own was trouble waiting to happen. Florian was one of her own, as far as she was concerned. No one got to threaten people she cared about and get away with it.

For now, she'd need to play along, but Alice desperately wanted to sink her claws into him in any way that she could.

"Finish the blood vows," Xavier said firmly.

"How?" she spat, trying not to raise her voice.

"We are about to host a ceremonial toast to begin the ball. You will put a drop of blood into your goblet, I will put a drop in mine, and then we will exchange glasses before drinking."

He gestured towards a small, round table that she hadn't noticed before. It sat at the corner of the dais, covered by a floor-length black cloth. A pewter pitcher sat by two empty cups, a sharp knife between them.

"That can't be enough—" Alice began, and she hated the way her voice shook.

"It's enough for my purposes," Xavier snapped. "I only need the bond to last for a few minutes before I suck the life from your chest."

So it was a temporary blood vow, then? Was that even possible? Was that strong enough? Was there even enough time to worry about that?

No, probably not.

"Go to the table. Pour the wine. Prick your finger," he said curtly. "You know what happens if you don't."

The threat was enough to make her move, at least. On shaking legs, Alice approached the table. As she walked, Xavier said something to the crowd gathered for the ball, but he may as well have been speaking underwater. She wasn't paying attention.

She had to *think*. Florian always said she was smarter than she knew, but she didn't feel that way at the moment. All prior planning went up in smoke in thirty seconds when he'd trapped her in that bedroom, and there was very little she could do with the supplies on hand.

The soul trap was tucked down her bodice, but there was no guarantee it would work fast enough to stop Xavier casting a darkness spell. She couldn't risk Florian's life.

If she could compromise him just for a few seconds, it would probably be long enough to get the trap to work.

"Pour the wine," he growled, beckoning towards her.

Alice poured his cup first. If she could get just a moment of distraction, then it might be enough time to do something, but she needed a moment when no one was looking at her, and that would be difficult from the stage.

Xavier took his goblet from her and turned back towards the audience, raising it high.

As slowly as she could manage, Alice picked up the second goblet. Her hands were shaking, and if she wasn't careful she thought she might drop it, potentially spilling the wine everywhere...

And that gave her an idea.

Alice exaggerated the shaking, letting her hand go a little limp as she tried to hold the second goblet so she could fill it from the pitcher.

She was a little afraid of what might happen if she spilled the whole pitcher of wine, but she let the empty cup clatter to the floor with a jarring clank of metal on stone.

Thankfully, it went right where she'd hoped it would, and rolled under the cloth-covered table where the wine sat. Alice turned over her shoulder and waved awkwardly at the crowd, trying to make light of it.

Mortified, Xavier swiped his hand across his eyes and made some sort of joke to brush the moment off. Uneasy laughter floated through the room, but Alice didn't hear what he'd said. She was concentrating, and he'd taken the bait.

With her back turned to Xavier, she bent to the ground to retrieve the cup from under the table. As quickly as possible, Alice shoved her hand into her skirts, removing the corked glass bottle tucked into her side pocket. She shoved the cork off with her thumb, letting it roll under the cloth covered table, and emptied the clear contents into the pewter goblet.

Before he had a chance to turn back, she stood and poured her wine into the goblet, using the sharp tip of the knife on the table to prick her thumb. Purposefully standing so Xavier could see, she let a small trickle of blood drip into the goblet, and then walked back towards him.

Standing close together, Xavier glanced at the cup, nodded his approval, and bit his own thumb with his sharp canines. A trickle of blood poured into his own goblet.

Alice wasn't entirely sure what the group of onlookers thought of this display, or perhaps strange rituals were common at full moon, but she had higher priorities. Her entire focus was on the man in front of her, and she couldn't afford to waiver.

"I give myself to the bind," Xavier said.

He made a motion that clearly meant Alice should repeat him, but she stayed silent. In reality, she hoped he might drink before

"Say it," he grunted, eyes locked on hers.

"I give myself to the *stupid fucking bind*," she muttered, shoving her goblet towards him.

Xavier glared as he took the cup, putting his goblet into her free hand, but apparently it was good enough.

"Now, we drink," he said, raising his goblet briefly.

The rest of the room seemed to take that as their cue to drink as well. The court members lifted their glasses to drink. Alice could see them out of the corner of her eye, but that was the least of her concerns at the moment.

Alice kept her lips closed as she raised the goblet of wine and blood to her mouth, taking a swallow that was nothing more than air. She wouldn't complete the bargain unless this didn't work, but she would certainly make a show of it for now.

Xavier seemed satisfied for the moment, raising his own cup to his lips. He downed it in one swoop, swallowing a mixture of wine, blood... and holy water.

And then he started to scream.

One thing that was for certain was that, regardless of his origins, Xavier had become something unholy. He had turned himself into something against the natural order, into someone that actively worked against the natural order. On that basis alone, Alice had hoped for a reaction to the water, but wasn't expecting one quite this *severe*.

It looked like Xavier had swallowed acid instead of wine. White smoke poured from his open mouth, face twisted in agony as burns and blisters appeared on his lips and tongue. Alice scrambled away, letting her goblet of wine spill over the floor.

Xavier tried to reach towards her as his screams turned from pain to rage, but it almost looked like his limbs wouldn't obey his command. As his legs gave way and he fell prone, one of his crystalline antlers hit the hard stone floor and snapped, breaking off a large chunk that skidded across the floor towards Alice. Even as he tried to crawl forward with his arms, the strength drained from him.

Xavier was still in the body. He hadn't left.

It was a good thing that wasn't her real plan.

"Allergic to holy water, ain't ya?" Alice snapped as she fished in her pocket.

Xavier just screamed, the smoke still billowing out from his mouth.

"Get her! She tried to kill the king!" someone from the crowd shouted.

That... was bad.

Alice couldn't identify the voice that cried out, but she knew it wasn't a good idea to have a mob after you. A few people tried to run for the exits, a few started to rush the stage, but Alice did the only thing she could think of as a few of the noble guests began to mount the steps to the stage.

"This man isn't your king!" she shouted as loud as she could. "Would a real Shadow Fae have *that* reaction to holy water?!"

Apparently, that was enough to give them pause. It was, at the least, enough that they didn't try to attack her.

"I know y'all haven't known me long, but please!" Alice begged. "You've gotta try to remember! And— an' if you just can't remember Florian, remember everything Xavier did to you!"

"*What*?!" Xavier bellowed, barely able to enunciate.

"You told me yourselves: anyone who stood up to him got booted outta here like an old shoe," she continued. "*You* have power over this! Don't give him your trust— he doesn't belong here, and you know it!"

Unfortunately, while the Shadow Court members did, in fact, seem to agree that Xaiver couldn't be trusted, they also didn't seem to think that Alice could be trusted. She couldn't blame them— for all they knew, she'd willingly married the man and had been living blissfully with him since.

That was probably why the court members started to make a beeline for the gigantic double doors at the back of the ballroom.

Running away was, in theory, the worst possible thing that they could do at the moment. Yes, it would probably help their own sense of self-preservation, but the problem was that Alice needed them to be present if she was going to do anything about the memory magic. Her power wasn't enough to sweep the world for Shadow Court members. They were right here, right now, and she couldn't risk them leaving... but she also didn't know how to stop it.

As the doors swung open, her heart sank, but only for a moment.

The doors very quickly slammed shut again, and Alice realized that it wasn't the Shadow Courtiers that had opened them at all. The crowd hadn't even made it to the exit. Instead, the doors had been

opened from the outside, and two familiar silhouettes stood at the back of the room.

"*No one* leaves!"

Willow's voice echoed through the ballroom.

"You stay down, you son of a bitch," Ellie said, hand extended towards Xavier.

Vines grew from the stone, lashing him to the floor. While Xavier was already on his knees, the plants pulled him fully prone. He broke a few of the smaller vines, but it wasn't enough to stop the plants from fully covering him, taking advantage of the weakness induced by the holy water to grapple him.

"Never been happier to see you!" Alice said, fighting not to drop to her knees in sheer relief.

"Sorry we cut it kinda close! We came as fast as we could," Ellie said, moving towards the dais as she called more vines to wrap around Xavier. "Holy water helped, huh?"

"Yeah, it did!" Alice cheered, unable to keep the absolutely relieved smile off her face.

The courtiers, on the other hand, seemed absolutely panicked.

Understandable, but not what she wanted, and Alice didn't have the skills she needed to calm them. Instead, Willow kept her position in front of the doors, arms spread wide, speaking directly to the people she'd known from birth.

"If you won't hear Alice, then hear *me*!" she called. "You know something is wrong here. We need you to fix it, and we need you to stay. You've known me since I was a child! *Please!*"

Alice couldn't understand all the shouting responses.

A few people did step back from the doors, hesitantly looking towards Ellie, Xavier, and Alice. Those must have been the few who truly were willing to put their trust in Willow.

The majority of them, however, only paused for a moment before beginning the scramble towards the back door with new vigor. Dodging and weaving, Willow barely managed to squeeze her way through the crowd without being crushed. She managed to make her way to the front of the room, gathering a small crowd of onlookers in the process.

"Ellie, we need an intervention— preferably soon!" Willow said, eyes wide. "Harper can't hold it by herself, and a possum and a dog aren't going to be enough help."

Harper?

Of course— her vampire strength was likely enough to hold the doors closed from outside! She must have followed along. Alice had never been more relieved to know another ally was outside, but even vampire strength couldn't hold the doors closed forever against a whole horde of Shadow Fae courtiers.

"I can only do so much at a time, ya know," Ellie muttered, but she moved one hand towards the back door.

A wall of sturdy, woody brambles grew in front of the doors, supernaturally large and covered in thorns longer than Alice's forearm. It wasn't the only exit, but it was the main exit, and the others could be secured quickly... after dealing with Xavier.

There was no guarantee that the crowd wouldn't turn on them all and attack them, but at the very least, Shadow Fae weren't known for their offensive magic. This would likely be enough to keep them in place, which was good, because Alice wasn't sure she could finish what she needed to do without the Court.

"Hurry it up, Alice!" Willow cried. "Whatever you're doing, do it now."

Right.

Alice fished the pocket watch out of her bodice, pulling it out by the chain, and held it up in front of her. She was careful to turn the face towards where Xavier lay covered in vines. He visibly twitched when he saw it, increasing his futile efforts of struggling against the plants.

"*Xavier Havelock,*" Alice said pointedly. "You *will* have a place in this court— sittin' on a pedestal in the dungeon, lookin' out from this watch."

And she pushed the button to open the watch face.

... And nothing happened.

It wasn't working. Xavier still writhed on the ground under the pile of Ellie's vines, and it didn't seem like he'd been deterred even slightly by the watch opening. Granted, Alice wasn't sure what was supposed to happen. She only knew what Willow had told her, but she was fairly certain this wasn't what was meant to occur.

Was he so strong that even a soul trap couldn't pull him in? Was it something about the disconnect between Xavier's soul and body?

Or...

Oh, shit.

Xavier didn't have a soul. Not really, not anymore. He'd traded it away.

23 IN WHICH FLORIAN GAINS A BODY

Alice thought her throat was going to close. She felt like her chest was burning, like she couldn't breathe.

The pocket watch in her hand meant to trap Xavier's soul was doing nothing at all, and it was all her own fault. She forgot the one key thing about Xaiver— he'd traded his soul for the form and power he possessed now. He never had a soul for it to trap.

Maybe she was stupid after all.

"What's the problem?" Ellie asked, still focused on her vines even though Xaiver was firmly lashed in place by now. Instead, she moved her hands from door to door, window to window, creating plants that sealed the group of panicked courtiers inside the room.

It was for their own good, in the end, but they certainly didn't see it that way at the moment. The clamor only grew louder as they tried in vain to leave, as a few of the people who chose to listen to Willow tried to calm the rest of them.

However, Alice had her own problems to deal with.

"He doesn't have a soul anymore! The trap won't work—" Alice shouted, backing away.

"It'll work, just give it a minute! Hold it steady!" Ellie nodded, and that was enough encouragement for Alice to steady her shaking hands.

It would work. It had to work. It would, it just needed another minute. It just needed enough time to find him, to lock on. Alice's focus narrowed entirely to the watch and Xavier, to the distance between them, to the warmth of the metal as it heated in her hands.

She would never be able to forget the sight of what happened next.

There was no way that anyone could have prepared her for what it looked like to watch a spirit as it was forced to leave a body. She wondered if this was something that Ellie had ever seen before, but it couldn't have been. Black smoke poured from the mouth of Xavier's stolen body, and it almost looked like tar began to leak out of every opening of the body. Eyes, ears, mouth, nose— all of it poured a horrible, dark substance that seemed to move towards the watch in her hand as if drawn in by a magnet.

Alice forced herself to keep hold of the soul trap, no matter how badly she wanted to drop it. She forced herself not to look at the myriad of screaming faces that the dark sludge twisted itself into as it flowed towards her. She tried not to listen to the terrible sounds of broken screaming and sickening squelching as the murky tar-fog entered the face of the watch, impossibly sucked inside until it was no more.

The face of the watch closed on its own as the last vestiges of the smoke and sludge slithered inside.

Xavier's screams of anger turned, slowly, into groans of pain.

Except that it was no longer Xavier.

"Let him go!" Willow cried, though the vines were already retreating into the patches of bare earth showing through the cracked tile flooring. "Let him go now!"

"Don't worry, I'm doin' it, just gimmie a second, will ya?" Ellie sighed.

As the vines pulled away, it was clear that the burns from the holy water were still in place. Though the spirit inhabiting the body had caused the reaction, the physical damage was still there. That was something Alice hadn't anticipated, and Florian was clearly still in pain. If she knew how to heal him, she would, but Alice wasn't a healer, even with the supposed well of magic inside her.

Willow was, though, and thanks to Xavier's fall earlier, they had exactly what they needed for her to work her healing magic.

It took a moment to find it, because she wasn't entirely sure where it had fallen, but it wasn't hard to locate the piece of crystal on the ground, shining in the moonlight. Alice snatched the stray piece of broken antler from the ground, then ran to the table and grabbed the knife she'd used to prick her thumb.

She ran back to where Willow knelt beside her cousin, pressing the knife and the antler chunk into her hands.

"Can you heal him?" Alice asked.

Willow's eyes went wide for a moment, but then she nodded, setting her jaw. "I've got him. Do what you need to do."

Now that Xavier was trapped, there was only one piece of her plan left. It was time to undo the memory magic... and also to let the people out of the ballroom, as the Shadow Court members looked understandably terrified. They had moved as far away as possible from the commotion, gathering at the back of the room, and they were dead silent.

"Sorry, y'all. Desperate times," Alice called, waving awkwardly with one hand while she scratched the back of her neck with the other.

Ellie snorted, walking up to stand beside where Willow was shaving off pieces of antler like salt from a block.

"How did you know the watch would still work?" Alice asked, looking up at her silver-haired friend. "I never told you I was gonna use it."

"Soul traps and spirit traps ain't all that different," Ellie said with a shrug. "It takes it a minute to grab onto the target without a soul, yeah, but it'll get there eventually."

Made sense. Alice sighed, letting out a manic giggle that could only come from surviving a near-death situation.

And then something began to clatter.

It was a jittering, metal sound, and it only took a moment to realize that it was coming from where Alice had placed the soul trap watch on the crystal table. It was vibrating, shaking, and a strange, black smoke had started to leak out of the object in eerie, dark tendrils.

"Shit," Alice whispered, staring at the jittering watch.

Ellie surged forward as if by instinct, grabbing the watch in both her hands. A bright, blue-tinted light grew around where she held it closed, pushing back the dark smoke as it tried to seep from the cracks between the lid and the face of the watch.

"What's happening?" Alice asked, still pulling at the last of the vines around a dizzy and disoriented Florian.

"It's not enough," Willow breathed. "He's fighting back— the bargain isn't done!"

"Well, how do we *finish* it?" Alice cried, eyes wide as she instinctively started to move towards Ellie.

"Stay back!" Ellie warned, speaking through gritted teeth. "I can hold him in here for a lil' bit, but y'all better think fast. He's a strong sucker, even as a spirit! Willow, get Florian up *now*!"

"Doing my best," Willow grunted, still working with the knife.

Pieces of antler dust floated down onto Florian's face and into his open mouth, but for a moment, there was no change. His breathing was raspy and labored, and Alice couldn't help but blame herself. She didn't know what else she could have done in the moment, but she also didn't know what she would do if Florian died.

Losing him would be disastrous. She didn't do all this to save him only to come up short, and certainly not now, certainly not from a little holy water that shouldn't have even hurt him in his typical state.

"Will he...?" Alice began, looking at Willow.

"He'll be okay. In theory, as soon as the spirit transferred, the holy water stopped being a bane to him and started to work in reverse. We just need to treat the burns," she muttered, still gently patting the ground antler against his skin.

"Alice, I need you to try to break that magic," Ellie said, clearly struggling to keep her tone even.

"I don't know how!" she insisted, biting her lip, looking for any way she might be able to access her supposed well of magic, or maybe any way she could drain the magic off things a little faster... but there obviously was no answer in front of her. There was no sign in the stars, no perfect moment

"I know, but we're outta options. I need you to *try*," Ellie urged.

Try?

It had never been enough when she'd tried in the past. It had never worked out, it had never gone well, and it certainly wasn't something she wanted to do now, without any guidance or instruction. Ellie was right, though. They were out of options.

She forced herself to take a breath, to close her eyes, to try and sense the flow of magic in the room. She could feel the hum of it in her bones if she tried— every witch could. There was a certain nuance to sensing a spell or the effects of a spell, and there was certainly one at work here.

Alice took a moment to concentrate, and within her whirling thoughts, within the chaos of the room, strung between almost everyone there, she found a sticky web. It wasn't pleasant to touch when she reached out with her senses, but the air felt numb and foggy around it, and that was the only major working in the room. It had to be the memory magic. There was no other option.

So Alice reached out with her own magic, and she *pulled*.

It wasn't exactly a comfortable sensation. It felt like trying to swallow a gulp of water that was a little too big, like something was stuck in her throat that made it difficult to breathe. There was a *lot* of magic in the room, and it was hard to pull only on the foggy threads of power blocking the memories of the Shadow Fae, but she kept at it until her head was pounding, until her hands shook and her heart raced far too quickly in her chest.

And then it all snapped back.

Alice gulped in gasping breaths of air as she shook her head.

"I can't— I can't do it!" she said, tears leaking from the corners of her eyes.

She wasn't strong enough. She wasn't powerful enough, didn't know enough, didn't actually understand anything about magic at all. It didn't matter if she could sense the web if she couldn't do anything with it.

"Alice?"

It was only one word, but it was enough to snap her out of her spiral. It was soft and kind, gentle and soothing, such a sharp contrast to every word Xavier had ever spoken.

"... Florian?" she croaked, ready to cry.

"It's me," he rasped, pushing himself into a sitting position.

He leaned on a tired-looking Willow, and for the first time, she could really see the similarities in their features. They were certainly related, and their family bond made Alice's heart swell in the best way.

Alice threw her arms around both Florian and Willow as a sob broke free from her throat. Her entire body was shaking, and for a moment, everything else around her seemed to fade away.

He was so, so warm.

There was no time for celebrating, though.

"Hate to break this up, but could ya hurry it up over there?!" Ellie called. Her hands were firmly clasped around the watch, but sweat ran down her forehead as she struggled to keep up with Xavier's attempts to break free.

Ellie was strong, but they were running on borrowed time. She only had one idea left.

"I need you," Alice said frantically, grabbing Florian's hands in hers. "I need you to finish the blood vows with me."

"*What?*" Florian cried, trying to pull away, but Alice wouldn't let him.

"I need you to help me drain off the memory magic," Alice explained. "I can't do it myself— I don't know *how*."

"What the hell are you talking about?"

"They don't trust Xavier, we know that. They don't remember *you* yet, though. If they do, I think we can complete the bargain, but it's gotta be fast, and it's gotta be *now*!" she insisted. "You know how this magic works better'n I do, so *help me use it*!"

Florian opened his mouth, but no sound came out.

It was the only way. They needed to do this— she *trusted* him to do this. Everything would be okay if it was Florian on the other end of the blood vows. They'd make it work. They'd find a way.

"... No," he finally said.

"What?"

"You can do this yourself. I *know* you can do this yourself."

"I just tried," she insisted. "I'm not strong enough. I can't do it."

"Yes, you can," Florian whispered, moving to take her hand in his, "but let me try to help."

"Okay," Alice agreed. She sniffled loudly, wiping her runny nose, and was surprised when her sleeve came away bloody. Whatever she'd done, her body didn't like it. She was pushing her limits... and she didn't know if that was a good or bad thing.

Luckily, Florian didn't see. He kept her hand in his, but he was already urging her towards the edge of the dais, pulling her to stand beside him as he spoke to his people.

Something in them felt the change. Alice could see it— the crowd moved from panic to curiosity, still with an edge of fear, but there was something there that made them want to listen to them. The memory magic couldn't be forever, and it wasn't unbreakable. She just needed to give it the last little nudge.

"I made a mistake!" Florian cried, voice echoing off the stone walls. "I left you all. I never meant to, but I did. I wanted to be a better leader, but I chose to try to shortcut that instead of working and learning as I should have."

This time, Alice reached out. However, instead of trying to pull the magic towards her when the sticky web didn't want to move, she decided to *push*.

If her power could work like a battering ram, then so be it. She'd batter the magic to shreds and then take it as her own. As she tried to sense the threads of power, tried to understand how to throw her own meager supply of magic at it to break it, Florian's voice kept her grounded.

"If you'll give me that chance, I want to rebuild what we've lost," he continued. "If there's anything I've learned from all this, it's that you deserve better than someone who tries to shortcut things."

She'd always been told she was small. Useless. She'd been told she didn't have much magic at all, that there wasn't any point in trying.

Alice shoved all that away and *kept pushing*. She kept digging and draining and looking for more until her vision blurred with black spots and the world spun around her.

"Alice. You have to stop— you're reaching your limit!" Willow cautioned, but the words sounded far away.

She really was at the bottom of her well of power, but Alice wouldn't stop. There wasn't any more magic, there wasn't any left in her, it was dry and useless and terrible, and not enough to break one single bargain, much less undo a complex web of power—

"Please," Florian whispered, and it was enough to get through the whirl of thoughts and sensations speeding through Alice faster than lightning. "Help me help us all."

And then the bottom of the well cracked open.

Alice gasped as her senses flooded, eyes wide open. It felt almost like a shot of adrenaline to her entire system, but it felt like relief, too.

Like water in a desert.

She fell into the reservoir of her own power, and in that place, she found peace.

In that place, she also found a sense of herself. That raw magic could be anything that she wanted it to be, do anything that she wanted it to do. She just had to will it, to ask it, to make sure it knew its task.

At the moment, its task was to batter Xavier's memory magic to smithereens.

It took a flick of her hand, a single thought, and a rush of power came from deep in her bones, or maybe past her bones. Maybe it came from somewhere she couldn't name. It tore through the threads and the fog like a tornado through a field, throwing strands of magic everywhere in the process. It wasn't delicate or subtle, but it did the job.

A wind whipped through the room, seemingly from nowhere, but Alice understood what was happening. It was the physical part of her magic, swirling through and picking up every last bit of rogue memory magic, barreling through it just like she'd asked... and then it took all that gathered magic and turned back to her.

The tornado returned with full force, enough that she barely managed to stay on her feet, but she felt herself swallow that power, felt it become enveloped by her own reserves of magic until it was no longer memory magic. It was no longer a fog. It had been transformed inside of her, and she'd added it to that well of power saved for future use, ready to be molded into whatever she needed.

Alice took a slow, deep breath through her nose, and she opened her eyes. She hadn't even realized they'd been closed.

The ballroom was silent for the first time that evening. The moon shone high overhead, and Alice looked out over a group of calm courtiers. They, admittedly, looked incredibly confused, but they were calm.

"Your... highness?" a small voice asked, echoing throughout the crystal ballroom. Ah. It... was the librarian, and he stared up at Florian with a kind of awe and reverence she'd never seen on his face before.

"What happened to us?" asked another, and Alice was able to identify the voice as one of the palace maids.

"Prince Florian?" came another voice. And then another, and another, all shouting Florian's name, all wondering where he'd gone and how they'd managed to forget him for so long, all wondering where Xavier had come from in the first place.

Was it possible to feel dizzy with sheer relief?

"Thank the Lord," Ellie muttered, the blue light fading from around her hands. "Not sure how much longer I could'a held him in there."

Ellie dropped to the ground, sitting cross-legged with the watch in her lap, slumped over and clearly trying to catch her breath. Whatever it took to keep Xavier in there, it drained her like nothing Alice had ever seen before. It was a good thing that Ellie was as strong as she was— there probably wasn't another spirit worker below the Mason-Dixon line that could have contained him like that.

"Thank you," Alice said, reaching over to put her hand on Ellie's arm.

"It's what we do for our own," Ellie mumbled, grabbing Alice's hand in hers. "Though... you got a little..." She squinted, gesturing vaguely to her upper lip with her free hand.

Alice turned away, letting go of Ellie's hand to feel her face, but she found herself immediately face to face with Florian, who was looking at her with concern. He pulled her into a strong hug that didn't last near as long as she wanted before he pulled away again, looking her over for injuries.

"Are you well?" Florian asked, taking her face in his hands.

"All good," Alice rasped, taking a slow, deep breath.

"Your nose is bleeding." He dabbed at her face with his sleeve. It appeared that the bleed became even worse, but that was alright.

"Nothin' an antler can't fix," she muttered, using her own sleeve to wipe away the rest of the blood.

In reality, she felt... decent. The stress of depleting her initial well of power hadn't been good for her body, and she was tired, but the rush of tapping into that hidden reservoir was more than enough to make up for most of it. She still wasn't sure what she wanted to do with all that newfound magic at her fingertips, but learning how to shape it could happen another day.

Florian snorted in that way that she adored, and he shook his head. "You'll need to be more careful. I can't take this kind of thing often, you know."

"Having your body stolen? Me either. Can't say I'd recommend it," she shot back, unable to stop a smile from spreading across her face. Willow joined them from where she'd been trying to calm the court members, finally coming up to hug her cousin.

"You know the worst part? He *did* make you the leader your people deserve," she said softly, her white freckles practically glowing in the dim ballroom lighting. "Not in the way he wanted, though."

"I suppose it's true that I wouldn't be where I am without him," Florian said, groaning as he glanced at the pocket watch in Ellie's hand. "I learned what kind of leader we needed by... having my position stolen. The irony."

Ironic, indeed. Strangely... Alice was glad for it.

Mirror or not, she wanted to stay with Florian. She wanted to see where this would go. He was worth it, and it was a journey she didn't regret.

Well... she could have done without almost dying, but at the end of the day, she'd learned too much about herself to regret it entirely. The good outweighed the bad, and moving forward, she just hoped to keep tipping the balance in that direction.

"Y'all better teach your kids not to make bargains with dangerous spirits," Ellie grumbled, brushing stray strands of hair from her face and wiping sweat off her forehead as she finally stood. She pressed the pocket

watch into Florian's hand, closing the prince's fingers over it and patting it firmly. "I ain't doin' that shit again. No way."

Alice's mouth hung open as she tried to figure out exactly what to say about the idea that she might have children with Florian one day, but she never really came up with a response.

"Really? Because that was incredibly impressive," Florian said, giving a small bow.

Ellie saluted him back, but she shook her head. "Outta my pay grade, bud. I'm gonna need a nap. A long one."

Alice thought that sounded like a good idea for everyone involved.

Ellie declared that she was going to sleep for the next twenty-four hours, and that no one should bother to disturb her unless they had food. She and Rosemary went up to one of the many, many spare rooms in the palace, and presumably curled up for a long rest. Alice hadn't seen her since, but she'd told Kaz where to go looking when he arrived at the Shadow Court.

The court members who showed up to attend the full moon ball were, understandably, not in the best of moods about their temporary detainment in the ballroom, but the majority of them were more than willing to look past that in the wake of having their memories restored. Florian decided that, considering there were more than enough rooms for everyone, they all needed a good rest before the council convened the next morning.

Harper and Willow were doing their best to answer questions, organize rooms for everyone, and generally trying to keep the crowd calm. Ellie had only taken the vines down around one single exit, so they wrote down names as the courtiers left the space, taking inventory of everyone involved in the incident. Most of them were quite cooperative with the process, and those that weren't... Well, Harper's fangs were quite convincing, even if she wouldn't dare bite someone without consent.

Missy very happily jumped into Alice's arms as soon as the back doors were open... and Alice's legs almost immediately gave out from under her. She had reserves of magic like she'd never known, yes, but the toll of working with that magic on a massive scale when she'd never done it before was *massive*. It took a good twenty minutes— and sniffing some horrible antler dust— for her nose to stop bleeding, and even then she still had trouble standing.

Florian, who insisted he was perfectly fine, if a little tired, picked her up and walked them both back to the same bedroom Alice had been sharing her whole stay at the Shadow Court. She didn't know what time they finally made it back— probably somewhere in the wee hours of the morning— but she didn't care. It was time to take a well-deserved rest.

When Florian put her down on the mattress, he threw open the curtains to let in the bright moonlight. As though that wasn't enough to chase away any darkness that Xavier left behind, he also turned on the magical fae lights in the room, making it as bright as possible.

"Is it really over?" Alice asked, blinking in the warm light.

"For now," Florian said. He removed the silver watch from his pocket, placing it on the nightstand.

Alice didn't want to even think about that thing, but she could understand why he wanted to keep it close for now. It would probably be the best way to ensure that no one opened it, and to make sure none of that awful clattering happened again. No one wanted Xavier to get out.

"At least he's gone," she muttered, almost to herself. Gone, and hopefully never to return.

"That isn't the only thing we have to deal with, unfortunately," Florian said quietly. He flexed his hands in front of his face for a moment, as though he wanted to make sure they were still physical.

Alice raised her eyebrows, waiting for him to continue.

"My decision to bargain with Xavier had consequences, some of which are yet to be seen," he said with a sigh, yanking at the white cravat around his neck like it was choking him. "I paid my personal price, but I still have to own up to the Court. They deserve to know what really went on."

"Yeah... I guess that's fair," she said with a sigh.

It wasn't like the Court saw any of what happened behind closed doors, and they certainly didn't know about Florian's bargain. To them, an imposter swooped in, stole their memories, and stole the authority of the Court for fifty years. Not to mention, they still probably didn't understand exactly what Xavier had tried to do to them at the full moon ball.

All that considered, Alice could admit that they really did deserve a debriefing. In their situation, she would be highly confused, too. It just felt unfair that Florian would have to jump back into all that so soon, and she couldn't deny that public speaking was a personal fear of hers.

Dangerous spirits? Doable. Big speeches to a crowd? No.

"They need to know about you, too. You saved me." Florian took her hand, and though she let him interlace their fingers, Alice wasn't about to let herself be named the sole heroine of the hour.

"I didn't. I don't get all the credit for that," Alice said, shaking her head. "We did it together. And with some friends."

As determined as she'd been to do things on her own since the very day she was born, Alice had to admit that she couldn't have made it through the last month without her friends— her chosen family.

She liked it that way, too. She was glad to have the support. Instead of making her feel tied down, it made her feel safe.

"Friends... I like the sound of that. I used to have quite a few of them, but it's a bit difficult to find real friendship when you grow up royal," Florian sighed. "Now it's mostly Willow."

"Well, I hope you're okay with being adopted by a few of them, 'cause I don't think you're gonna get rid of us all that easy," Alice said with a laugh.

"Have I mentioned how much I love your accent?" He practically sighed it out, and the genuine affection in his voice made her clam up a little. She'd never heard someone say that to her before.

It was beautiful. He was beautiful. He was everything she'd wanted in a man, and she desperately hoped this worked out, desperately wanted to try to make this last. It seemed like it had potential to work in a way that nothing else she'd wanted before did.

That did bring up a crucial question. Something had been on Alice's mind for a while, but she wasn't quite sure how to voice it, and she

wasn't quite sure if she should say anything until it was all worked out with Xavier.

Things were settled now, though, so it was time to ask.

"A— are we..." Alice began, wringing her hands together. "Are we married?"

"I..." Florian stiffened, eyes wide. "I hadn't thought about... Ah... If you want to formally annul the marriage—"

"No!" Alice said suddenly, but then flushed pink and backtracked. "I— I mean, I don't really mind, it's just that it seems... it's a little *weird*," she admitted, her voice growing softer every moment.

"We could go slow?" Florian suggested. "I certainly don't mind being legally married to the woman who saved my life."

"... Legally," Alice muttered.

"Come here, little rabbit," he said with a soft laugh, wrapping his arms around her waist. Alice was comforted by how his chest moved when he breathed, by the softness of him against her skin, and by the sound of his heart beating in his chest. She found herself hugging him back, and she never, never wanted to let go.

She'd found something precious in Florian.

"I love you. I won't be shy about that," he said quietly. "I don't want to scare you away, but I don't want this to be all we have together."

"What... does that mean?" she asked, frowning.

"It means that I would like our love to grow." Florian smiled down at her and lowered his head, planting a kiss on her brow. "We haven't known each other all that long. I want to know you more every day, and I don't want this to be our ending. It's a *beginning*."

"I like that plan," Alice said, nodding. "Go... slow, yeah?"

"Slow is good," he agreed.

Alice took a deep breath, fisting her hands in her skirt as she finally voiced something that had been on her mind the last several days.

"I... don't think I can be a queen for you, though," she said quietly. "I don't really *want* to be a queen."

It surprised her to hear those words out of her own mouth, but they were true. If anything, she'd learned in the last month that she never, *ever* wanted to be a ruler. The idea of luxury and respect was wonderful,

and the fantasies of balls and parties were beautiful in her mind, but the reality was all stressful legal jargon and making decisions that could affect many, many people.

Alice... didn't want that. She'd rather live a simple life on Howard's Knob, finish up her schooling, and help make the lives of various animals in the area a little bit easier. Where she'd previously wanted to be a pampered princess with a husband to take care of her, now she found there was a kind of indescribable comfort in the anonymity of quiet living that she'd never seen before.

She was afraid to admit that she no longer wanted the throne. On some level, Alice wondered if this might lock her out of Florian's life forever, but... she couldn't do it. She wouldn't be happy, and the last thing she wanted was for the pressure of any role to turn her against someone that she wanted to learn to really, truly love.

Florian just smiled down at her

"I've decided to do what I should have done from the start: I'm turning my position at court over to Willow," he said, and she could almost hear the relief in his voice.

"You're sure? After all that stress to be a better leader?" Alice's eyebrows were sky high, mouth hanging slightly open. It almost seemed like he was giving up something he'd finally managed to put in the work for.

Florian looked at peace with his decision, though, and that was all that mattered.

"Sometimes the best way to be a wise leader is to simply step aside for someone better. All that time, I was so concerned about becoming the leader my people needed... and the leader they truly needed was right in front of me," he said with a shrug. "She will be a much, much better ruler than I ever could be. I, on the other hand, will be taking over as an advisor and trainer for the Shadow Knights," he explained, looking almost more relaxed than she'd ever seen him.

"You really want this, huh?" Alice smiled. It was more of a statement than a question.

Willow would be an excellent queen. Alice hadn't known her for long, but it was clear that her friend had a disposition suited to the job, and that the Court trusted her. She understood the ins and out of Shadow urt politics, and she was genuinely interested in the wellbeing of her people.

It was a good decision.

"I think I'll be much, much happier as a general for Willow's knights than a king." He paused, suddenly looking sheepish. "But... if you think I should reconsider—"

"No!" Alice cried, but then slapped her hands over her mouth. Her cheeks went fiery red as she glanced at the floor, the ceiling, the window drapes— anything but Florian's face.

"Well, that was enthusiastic," Florian muttered, but he was laughing. "Someone *really* doesn't want to be queen."

Alice elbowed him in the ribs, rolling her eyes, and he just laughed harder. She might have been annoyed under other circumstances, but she was so happy to be able to hear his laugh that she didn't even mind.

"It's your life. You should make your choices, not me," she scolded, wagging her finger at him. "Ain't that what got you into this in the first place? Lettin' other people tell you to be king when you didn't want to?"

Florian stopped laughing, face scrunching into a boyish pout.

"... Fine," he admitted.

Well, at least she'd managed to call his bluff there. It gave her at least a little satisfaction to know that this massive, fearsome-looking, and highly magical prince would pout for her without feeling strange about it. She was happy to see this side of him, happy to know he was just as much a normal man as anyone.

"Besides, I didn't really like bein' a queen, if I'm tellin' the truth," Alice said with a shrug. "Too much stress."

"That part is incredibly true," Florian said, sighing as he sat down on the mattress.

Slowly, Alice moved to join him, taking a seat on top of the comforter and learning against his side. Some part of her wondered if she should feel strange being around him like this, if she should fear being close to him, but... she didn't. The warmth, the manner of speech, the gestures— it all made it clear exactly who inhabited the body in front of her.

"This means I get to spend more time with you, too, right?" she asked carefully, reaching out to place her hand over his.

"It does." Florian laced their fingers together as he spoke.

"Then I'm happy."

And she was. She was happier than she'd ever been.

"Change into something more comfortable, and then we can sleep off the day," Florian said, leaning over to briefly press his forehead against hers. "... Assuming you're comfortable if I stay?"

He pulled away slightly, waiting for her answer.

Alice swallowed hard, but she nodded. Where Xavier had pushed and pushed for a physical relationship, she trusted Florian not to do that until she felt ready. That, and... she just wanted to be close to him.

Shoulders slumping with relief, Florian stood from the bed and unbuttoned the stiff, embroidered, silver-and-black jacket that Xavier had picked for the ball, tossing it into the side in a heap. His nose scrunched in distaste as he looked at it, one hand coming up to his broken antler. Perhaps it was something that Xavier had picked. She couldn't imagine what it felt like for him to finally have his body back.

Alice undid the front laces of her outer gown, glad that fae clothing was easier to take on and off alone. She tried very hard not to look over at Florian, who didn't seem uncomfortable at all with changing in front of her. Perhaps fae weren't typically shy about their bodies? But she felt shy around him in a way she hadn't in front of Xavier.

Rather than putting on a real nightgown, Alice just curled up on the bed in her soft underdress, pushing her bare feet under the blankets. On the other side of the room, Florian had pulled on a real nightshirt, and looked ready to sleep away the chaos of the evening.

"If... if we ever... um..." Alice trailed off, gaze suddenly very fixated on the far wall. "It's just... what about the blood vows?"

Florian rolled up the sleeve of his shirt to show her his forearm— his *bare* forearm.

Alice blinked, immediately yanking her sleeve out of the way to look down at her own left arm. She hadn't even taken the time to peek at it, what with all the chaos, but to her surprise, it was also blank. It looked like the mark was never even there at all, only freckles and smooth skin.

"The combination of body and soul that you started the bond with no longer exists," he explained. "I would wager this means that Xavier is well on his way to oblivion already, but regardless— you're free of it."

It was like a weight she didn't even know she was carrying dissolved into nothing. Alice flopped back against the pillows, letting the last bits of fear slough off as exhaustion truly set in.

"Oh, thank Jesus," she sighed, rolling onto her side to face him. "N— not that I've got a problem with you, but it's..."

"I wouldn't want blood vows for either of us. Don't worry," Florian said gently. "That's part of why I refused to take part when you asked."

She was grateful for that, in hindsight, even if it had been frustrating in the moment. It didn't change the trust she felt, in the end. In fact, it only made her want to trust him more.

"Sorry about that," she mumbled. "I couldn't think of another way."

"It's alright," Florian said softly.

He moved to pull aside the comforter, and Alice wanted to cry with relief as he moved to lie down next to her. She reached out to him on instinct, settling herself against his chest without even asking, and for a moment she wondered if it was the wrong thing to do.

However, only a breath later, his arm came around to hold her close, tracing down her hip, urging her to drape her leg over his body. His shoulders relaxed, his breathing slowed, and he rested his head on hers so his nose was almost in her fiery hair.

"I've wanted this," he murmured.

"Me, too," Alice admitted.

All that time, she'd wondered if how Xavier treated her was how marriage was supposed to feel, if that was how relationships were meant to go. It was all performance and show, nothing beneath the surface, nothing she could really grab on to in times of trouble. This, though... this was different.

This felt like what she'd really been looking for.

"You know, in most fae cultures, there's a complex gift-giving system for engagements," Florian said. "Is there anything like that for humans?"

"I mean, I won't say no to a gift, but there's nothin' specific," Alice said, laughing quietly. "It's sweet, but I really don't need anything."

She had everything she could ever want. Her family and friends were safe. She had a wonderful man who she wanted to stay with. She had food and shelter and so, so much joy. There was nothing more she needed in the world.

"Anything you want," Florian said, the sound reverberating through his chest.

Alice tilted her head to look up at him, surprised to find that he wasn't laughing. He seemed... almost expectant?

Oh. He was... he was *serious*.

Alice paused. Really and truly, there was only one thing she would like, if she had to name something.

"Well... How would you feel about askin' Ellie if we could maybe set up a house on Howard's Knob?" Alice asked. "I know you couldn't be there all the time, but maybe as somewhere to go when we need to get away from all this?"

Florian paused, eyes fixed somewhere on the middle space, and for a moment she was afraid he might say no. However, after a moment, he started to nod.

"Truthfully, I could travel back and forth between here and there if you want to stay with your family. I'm not opposed to getting away a little myself, or finding new family members," he said.

Alice loved that he knew exactly what she was getting at.

"I like it," he continued. "As long as you think they'll let me move in after everything that's happened."

"Eh, I don't think they'll hold it against ya too much," Alice said, waving her hand vaguely. "Kaz might tease ya about bein' a shitty bargainer, though."

"I think I can live with that," Florian said, chuckling as he pressed a kiss to Alice's forehead.

The last thought Alice had before she fell asleep on his chest was that it would be a wonderful way to live.

EPILOGUE

Time absolutely flew.

It was, in part, because everyone was so busy, but Alice was mostly just... happy. She was happy with her life, her circumstances, and her husband. Six months after the day she met Xavier in deer form, Alice could say that she didn't regret the decision to take his hand.

Not that her happiness had anything to do with Xavier at all.

Their house went up in record time, adding a fourth residential building to the community very quickly turning into a small village. Florian took over as the resident hunter and trapper, freeing Kaz to work on his true passion— writing novels and articles. His written work was very quickly taking off, too, and it was a good source of income.

Ellie continued her apothecary work, and Alice was learning alongside her. Missy stuck around, too, and was a willing participant in testing some of the herbal remedies designed to help animals with their scrapes and scratches. The little possum often got into trouble and needed a bandage or two, and she'd even approved one of the stinkier brews as almost immediately helping with the pain.

Alice was well on her way to finishing her veterinary studies, and she hoped to set up a clinic in town at some point, but that would have to be in the future. For now, her

favorite days were ones like today, when she and Florian were able to sit in peace together.

Ellie and Alice had just finalized a new herbal tonic recipe, and Ellie was testing it out in the kitchen of her home. The smell of dried plants filled the air, and Florian held her around the waist from behind, unwilling to let go. Touch had become very, very important to them after the initial circumstances of their meeting. It was a way for them to make sure that all of this was, indeed, real.

"So did y'all ever figure out if you're sayin' you're married?" Ellie asked, eyebrow raised as she worked on pounding the life out of a few herbs with a mortar and pestle.

"We are," Alice said, smiling brightly as Florian pulled her in for a kiss.

The silver-haired witch sighed, pouring the herbal concoction into a pot of boiling water.

"Well, dammit," Ellie huffed. "I was gonna ask if you'd be my maid of honor, but I guess you're gonna be the matron of honor now."

Alice absolutely screeched, barely managing to wait until Ellie finished pouring the herbs into the pot before she bear-hugged her friend, practically knocking her into the kitchen counter.

"*Oof*— we can talk details later!" Ellie grunted, patting Alice's back. "I just wanted to check—"

But a knock at the door cut her off.

That was... strange. Beyond strange, really. Whoever got this close would have needed to get past the wards, so they likely weren't dangerous. There were simply very few visitors that made their way this far from Boone, especially after word got around that witches resided on Howard's Knob.

Alice and Florian exchanged glances as Ellie went to answer the door. She opened it, but rather than conversing through the crack, she stepped out onto the porch... and then was gone for long enough that Alice became nervous.

"Who do you think it is?" Alice whispered, walking towards the door. Florian shrugged, following along as he looked over her shoulder.

It took until they were only a few steps from the door to see the silhouette outside. At first, Alice didn't recognize it, but she could hear the

frustration in Ellie's garbled voice, and decided it was time to intervene. Maybe she'd be able to help out or shoo them away.

When she stepped onto the porch, mouth already half open to greet their visitor, Alice almost turned around and went right back into the house.

Out of all the people she thought might have been outside, Alice never would have guessed that her mother was waiting outside the house.

Olive Little stood in front of the porch steps, not quite ready to step close to the house, but certainly present. She had the same wild hair as her daughter, though it was graying a little, and she wrung her hands anxiously, shifting her weight from foot to foot as she waited.

"You don't have to see her if you don't wanna," Ellie said, keeping her voice low so that only Alice could hear.

"Nah," Alice said, setting her jaw. "Let her talk."

Florian caught her eye, silently asking if he should stay or go. As an answer, she grabbed his hand. She might be able to handle talking to her mother, but she didn't want to do it alone.

"Momma," she said by way of greeting, her tone flat. "How'd you find me?"

"Asked in town," she said, brushing a curl out of her face. "It broke, didn't it?"

Alice swallowed, pushing down the flare of anger and sadness and panic in her chest.

"What broke?" she rasped, deciding that playing dumb was best for her sanity.

"You know," Olive insisted, nodding towards Florian. "He looks just like him."

"He's *not* him," Alice snapped, stepping in front of her husband protectively. "You leave him be."

"I don't plan to hurt anyone, honey," the older woman said sadly. "I did more damage already than I could ever dream."

Well, at least she was lucid enough to realize that.

The longer she stood there, the more Alice realized that her mother looked legitimately different. She seemed tired, as always, but less *angry* than normal. Instead, it was like the anger had been replaced by

sadness and anxiety, almost like someone else had taken over like Xavier did with Florian, but... no. That was her mother.

Perhaps that was the scariest part of all. The change was so severe that it made her wonder if this was even the woman who raised her at all.

"He took my pain from me," her mother admitted. "The grief over your daddy, the grief over your sister. I thought I was gonna die every day from feelin' that pain. I couldn't take care'a you— your sisters were doin' it all. And... I thought a life with him might not be bad for you."

The bargain that Xavier made must have broken with his death. Olive Little was free now, but all her pain had returned to her as well... and none of it had ever truly been processed. Her mother was holding a twenty year old hurt, plus more, and that seemed unfathomable even to Alice.

But her mother had also done this to herself, and she'd willingly traded her child for that relief.

Some part of her wanted to forgive. She couldn't, though. She just wasn't ready, didn't want to put her trust in her mother again, and couldn't see how this could end in any way but with pain.

Yes, her mother was hurting, but Alice was hurt, too.

"Okay," Alice said, squeezing Florian's hand a little more tightly.

"It don't make it right, the way I treated you," Olive said carefully. "That's what happened, though."

"I can forgive you," Alice said softly, "but I'm not ready to forget."

"Do you... want me to come back?" Olive asked carefully. There was hope in her voice, but Alice couldn't find it in her to respond to it.

"Not now," she said, but she couldn't bring herself to say more.

It was the most positive thing she could bring herself to say. She didn't want her mother to move in with them, certainly. She liked her independence, and she wasn't ready for the paranoia of having a parent around, especially a parent with... Well, with the history they had.

"Letters?" her mother asked.

Alice paused for a moment.

"Letters are good. I think I can do that," she said, nodding. That much did feel alright. It settled in her chest in a way that felt normal, not

painful or afraid, and she thought that maybe it could be a good step forward for the two of them.

"So he's...?" Olive asked, looking once again towards Florian.

"My husband. Maybe you'll hear the whole story one day," Alice said calmly.

She hoped to be able to tell it, but she couldn't. Not now. They needed more time.

"Okay." Her mother nodded, seeming satisfied enough with that. "If you feel like it, this is my address. Your sisters are there, too. We... we miss you."

Olive Little held out a folded piece of paper towards her daughter. Alice took it, but she couldn't bring herself to say anything back. It was nice that they missed her, she supposed, but too many bridges were burned and broken between them for her to want to come back. Yet... a part of her did want to go back, at least for a little while. She wanted to see if they could be the family she wanted.

And if not, she had all the family she needed right here.

"Have a good day, momma," she said softly.

Alice forced herself to breathe. She forced herself not to crumple the paper in her hand, but to tuck it safely into the pocket of her dress, and she forced herself to watch as her mother walked away and disappeared over the hilltop.

A strange sense of nostalgia, numbness, and a deep sadness washed over her all at once, and she was very glad Florian was there to be her rock in that moment. They kept each other grounded, anchored to reality. When he woke from sleep with nightmares of being trapped in Shadow form, Alice was there. When she flashed back to years of her childhood that instilled a sense of self-loathing, Florian was there to snap her out of it.

Now, it was no different. He kept her safe and sane as she watched over the hill, still staring after the silhouette of Olive Little had disappeared.

"How do you feel?" Florian asked, placing a gentle hand on her shoulder.

"I... don't know," she admitted. "I don't know what to feel."

She didn't want to lose her mother forever, if she could avoid it. Then again, it might already be too late. Only time would tell. In any case, letters were an olive branch she felt she could actually accept. It would allow contact without too much closeness, and maybe with some work... maybe they could be okay one day.

And, speaking of forgiveness, there was someone else she had to see.

"I'm goin' on a walk. Want to meet up in a bit?" Alice asked, turning to her husband. "I could... maybe talk about it a little. Maybe."

She was starting to learn that talking was good, even when it felt hard.

"By the creek to the north?" Florian asked. "I finished making a new bow, and I'd like to try it out."

"I'll see you there, sweetie." Alice pulled him down to her height, kissed his cheek, and leaned against the porch railing for a minute.

Her hands were shaking, and she hated it. She wanted to be stronger than that, but she also had to admit that facing her mother was its own kind of strength. Unfortunately, there was no easy answer to the problem. There was no quick solution, no way to simplify everything they'd both been through. All she could do was try.

Taking a deep breath to settle herself, Alice marched on towards Hartley's house.

In the time since her return from the Shadow Court, they had very much patched up their relationship. She considered Hartley a friend now, and could somewhat sheepishly admit that her previous attachment to him resulted from... Well, he was largely the only eligible man she'd interacted much with since relocating to Howard's Knob.

However, Alice was happily married now, and she liked their relationship much better as friends than she ever would have as romantic partners.

Hartley sat on his porch, a glass of wine in hand. He wasn't typically one to drink, but every now and then he appreciated a good glass of something-or-other. Prohibition was still in full effect, of course, but that didn't stop mountain folk with the right tools. He also insisted that he'd been alive long enough that the government couldn't deny him a glass of alcohol once a month.

Clearly, it was his day to indulge just a little.

He looked content. Not inebriated, but at peace, perhaps pondering something as he scribbled in an old notebook that sat in his lap. When he noticed Alice, he stopped scribbling and looked up.

"You look like you're doing well," Hart said, smiling as he took a sip from his glass.

"I am," Alice said quietly.

And she was, really and truly. A small smile played across her face as she thought of everything that had happened to her in such a short amount of time. She felt more like herself than ever, and after spending two months at Howard's Knob with Florian, she felt even better about their potential future together.

He was a good man. Florian wasn't just kind, he was also a hard worker. He loved to laugh, and he loved the outdoors just as much as Alice did. He even asked if it was possible to learn animal speak if you weren't born with it, but Alice was still working on a solution to that one.

"Are *you* gonna be okay, though?" Alice asked.

"What..." Hartley trailed off, looking a little lost for a moment.

Alice gestured to the place where the mark on her arm had once been. It was no longer there, of course, with the blood vows dissolved and Xavier trapped as the watch slowly unraveled his spirit thread by thread.

She shuddered to think about it, and generally tried to avoid wondering what it felt like inside that thing. Whatever was happening now, Xavier had done more than that over the centuries.

Hartley got the point though. He took another sip of wine before he answered, like he needed it to steel his nerves, numb his emotions, or both.

"I'm working on myself," he said with a sad smile. "It's all I can do at the moment."

"You really think she's gonna come back?"

"I don't know," Hartley admitted. "I buried her a long time ago."

A chill ran down Alice's spine as she watched him.

Alice wondered how it was even possible to meet someone again after death, but she was a little afraid to ask. Hartley was old. He'd seen many things. It was even possible he'd seen many people in different

lives— literally. However, this point was clearly a sensitive topic. She didn't want to cross any lines, but... Well, she wanted to know.

"How does that... work?" she asked carefully.

"Not well," he deadpanned. "But it makes room to process the things I need to process on my own. It makes room for the work that needs to be done... until I meet her again."

Alice was silent. She couldn't imagine what it would be like to know someone and not know them all at once, to wonder what could have been and what would be. It seemed like too much to carry, especially when... Would Kalia even know who she was?

"What if she's not the same?" Alice ventured.

"She won't be," Hartley said firmly, his gaze firmly fixed on some distant mountaintop. "That's not the point."

"Then what is?"

"The point is that I want to do everything in my power to give her the peaceful life that she wasn't granted the last time around," he said slowly. "It's my fault she didn't get a chance for that before. It's the least I can do to make sure that she gets it now."

"Atonement," Alice said softly.

"Atonement," he agreed. "Among other things."

"Hart..." she said tentatively. "Are you doin' that for her, or for you?"

He didn't speak for a long moment. Alice leaned against the porch railing, not quite feeling like she wanted to sit down, but she did desperately want to know the answer to this. She wondered if he'd even really thought about it.

In the end, Hart downed the rest of his wine before he spoke.

"I'm not sure I know anymore," he rasped, gaze sliding back into focus. "I can't separate my soul from Kalia any more than I can separate the right half of my body from my left."

That sounded... nightmarish, in a way.

Alice couldn't imagine being separated from Florian, but there was something different in the way that Hartley spoke about his lost love. It wasn't just the separation. It was raw, terrible, unresolved pain.

She just hoped that he had a chance to smooth it all over somehow.

"The college is finally getting that Other Studies program off the ground," Hartley finally said, straightening his vest. "They've asked me to join."

"You think you'll do it?" she asked. It would probably be good for him to have something else to do. Though he worked as a professor, she often wondered if his heart was in it. He loved teaching, but he might be happier working with a group of young Others to help straighten out their lives in a new world. Maybe it would give him a sense of purpose.

"I think it would be a service to my community, and perhaps an opportunity to atone for other things. Things unrelated to Kalia."

Alice's eyes narrowed as she looked him up and down. "You think you'll ever tell anybody what those things are?"

Though their friendship had grown, there were still many things that Hartley wouldn't talk about, not to anyone. He huffed a little, staring off into the mountains spreading out far beyond their home.

"Maybe. For now, that's between me and the Creator."

Hart closed his eyes and leaned back in his chair, clearly finished with the conversation.

As she turned to leave, Alice saw the needle on the compass around his neck begin to turn. That was strange. Perhaps the magnet was off?

A question for another day.

ACKNOWLEDGEMENTS

Thank you all so much for joining me on this journey through Alice's story. When I first created her character, I never intended for her to have her own arc, but I decided that I liked her, and that she deserved the development.

If you're reading this and liked the book, I also ask that you please take a moment to consider contributing to 2024 Hurricane Helene relief efforts happening in the Appalachian mountains. Many people were left homeless from the storm, and in some cases, whole towns have been washed off the mountain. The people there need all the help that they can get, and the relief effort will continue for years to come.

It's been such a journey between the first and second edition releases of this book. I bought by ISBNs, learned some typesetting tricks, and also decided that I was going to embrace the idea of a whimsical book interior. I love graphic design and writing, and I'm so happy with the way that indie publishing has allowed me to make my books aesthetically how I want them.

Thanks to every single person involved in this process, especially to Briit, who helped me edit this book, and to my mom, who listened to every single complaint and crying session I had about learning to typeset. Thanks to my coworkers who let me bounce ideas off them, and to all my friends who cheered me on. I love you all, and I am so grateful that the good Lord allowed me the chance to meet you.

CONNECT WITH ME AT
CAMELLIACARROLL.COM